"AMBITION AND BETRAYAL . . . A VILLAINOUS IMAGINATION!"

—*Kirkus Reviews*

"Blanchard and Barsocchini deliver a facile tale about the ugly business of beautiful women."

—*Publishers Weekly*

"Blanchard definitely knows the secrets and scandals in the real world of the modeling business."

—*Affaire de Coeur*

"A fast-paced novel."

—*Abilene Reporter News*

"THE AVARICE AND EVIL OF THE FASHION WORLD . . . A HIGHLY ENTERTAINING AND SATISFYING NOVEL."
—*Washington Post Book World*

"Scandal, drugs, sexual abuse, blackmail, and betrayal are the norm in the ruthless world of high-fashion modeling portrayed in this first novel. . . . Spicy scenes will attract readers looking for escape into the troubles of the rich and famous."
—*Library Journal*

"A novel about the industry that markets pretty women, viewed from the inside out."
—*Atlanta Journal & Constitution*

the
LOOK

Nina Blanchard
and Peter Barsocchini

A SIGNET BOOK

SIGNET
Published by the Penguin Group
Penguin Books USA Inc., 375 Hudson Street, New York, New York 10014, U.S.A.
Penguin Books Ltd, 27 Wrights Lane, London W8 5TZ, England
Penguin Books Australia Ltd, Ringwood, Victoria, Australia
Penguin Books Canada Ltd, 10 Alcorn Avenue, Toronto, Ontario, Canada M4V 3B2
Penguin Books (N.Z.) Ltd, 182-190 Wairau Road, Auckland 10, New Zealand

Penguin Books Ltd, Registered Offices:
Harmondsworth, Middlesex, England

Published by Signet, an imprint of Dutton Signet,
a division of Penguin Books USA Inc.
Previously appeared in a Dutton edition.

First Signet Printing, October, 1996
10 9 8 7 6 5 4 3 2 1

 REGISTERED TRADEMARK—MARCA REGISTRADA

Printed in the United States of America

PUBLISHER'S NOTE
This is a work of fiction. Names, characters, places, and incidents either are the product of the author's imagination or are used fictitiously, and any resemblance to actual
persons, living or dead, events, or locales is entirely coincidental.

To Eileen and Jerry Ford
for their encouragement and advice over the years.
To Merv Griffin
for my many appearances on his show.
And, of course, to all the models and actors
who have been my clients and friends.

ACKNOWLEDGMENTS

Thanks to Virginia Barber and Elaine Koster.
And special thanks to Audrey LaFehr for creative input
and wonderful attention to detail.

PROLOGUE

1979

They crossed the Mexican border early in the morning, but already the desert whined from the pounding sun. The boy driving the patched-up Pontiac Trans Am was in his early twenties, with a Texas Rangers baseball cap pulled down over his stringy black hair; he sucked a longneck Lone Star and mumbled to himself, one hand on the wheel, the other on the fast-forward button of the cassette deck. *Merle Haggard's Greatest Hits* blasted from the scratchy speakers. The boy looked angry and scared, but mostly angry.

Next to him sat a thirteen-year-old girl. Despite disheveled blond hair, pale complexion, overly made-up eyes, and ill-fitting clothes, this girl was pretty, and anyone could see that she'd grow up to be beautiful, the kind of beauty nature stumbles upon once every few million tries.

Slumped down in the seat, she sipped a Slurpee and read a Captain Planet comic book.

The boy glanced over at her.

"How can you read that comic book?"

"I'm just looking at the pictures." The girl knew he hated her comic books, but he had been ignoring her for most of the drive, so she flipped the pages loudly to get his attention.

"It's stupid," he said.

"No it's not."

"Besides, it makes you sick to read in the car."

"I'm already sick," she said.

"No you're not."

"I feel sick," the girl insisted.

"You feel jittery is all," he said, and reached over to tickle the back of her neck. He didn't want to hear about her being sick; in fact, he preferred that she didn't talk. And it wasn't that he hated comic books, it was just that it disturbed him to be with a girl who liked him.

As soon as the boy took his hand away, the girl lit a Salem and sucked in a huge drag. The boy snatched it from her mouth and threw it out the window.

"You look silly smoking that thing," he said.

She smiled at him, enjoying the attention.

"Take these," he said, pulling out two pills from his shirt pocket.

"What are they?"

"They'll make it so you won't be nervous and you won't be sick."

"Are they aspirin?"

"They're like aspirin, only better."

The girl didn't like pills, but took them because he wanted her to. Besides, he knew things, this boy. She liked the way he disdained the locals back home. He said they were all idiots, especially her father. He hated their small-town lives, and told her that nobody from around there would be anything in life because they didn't know how to plan. All they knew was boats and fish, and beers at the end of the day.

She swallowed the pills; one was Valium, the other Percodan.

"I don't like this music," she said after a while.

"You don't have to like it, you just have to listen to it."

"Why can't we listen to Aerosmith?"

"Because they're a bunch of faggots and I hate their music." He lifted his hand as if he were going to strike her, but didn't; he didn't want to have her crying on top of everything else. He scrabbled around in the glove compartment, found a foil-wrapped towelette, and tossed it on her lap.

"Wipe that makeup off your face. You look like a whore."

Reluctantly, she wiped away the eye makeup. He hated it when she tried to look grown-up by smearing makeup on her face. She was a real pain, this girl, he had decided long ago, but she had something . . . he couldn't pinpoint what it was. Just something. She looked good even when she didn't know anyone was watching her. Everyone noticed it. Something about her face and eyes. No one walked past her without turning his head.

"Well, I don't want to listen to Merle Haggard all day," she said.

"Too damn bad."

"He's an old man."

"He's been to jail and now he's a millionaire. So don't talk about Merle Haggard." He pumped the volume.

She covered her ears and glared at him. All the boys her age would do anything she wanted. Everyone told her she was the most beautiful girl in Texas, and because of that she always got her way. Except with this boy. He was older, in his twenties, and she let him do things with her that she'd never let anyone else do. She was afraid not to, because she was afraid of losing him. The others tripped over themselves to do things for her. But not him. He did what he wanted. She liked that. She was scared of him, and she liked that, too.

They drove south two hours toward Piedras Negras, until the boy saw a sign, checked directions he'd scribbled on the back of a newspaper, and turned down a dirt road.

The girl awakened from a nap and looked around, uncomfortable because the sun was up now and she was sweating. The air blowing through the open windows was hot and dusty.

"I don't feel good," she said, her words slurred from the drugs.

"A few hours we'll be back in Texas and have some beers and forget about it," he assured her.

"Let's forget about it now. Maybe it'll just go away."

"It's not going away, goddammit."

"If my father finds out, he'll—"

"He's not going to find out anything, because you're not going to say anything and I'm sure as hell not. Got that?" The boy didn't like the mention of the girl's father, because he knew him to be a slack-skinned mean drunk who carried a .38 that he liked to handle when he was drinking.

The boy drove past a few houses, then saw one with a red cross painted on the gate. He pulled into the dirt driveway.

Chickens had the run of the yard, and the smell of animals rose from the hot earth. An elderly man slept on the porch, covered with a blanket despite the searing sun.

The boy stuffed a Percodan and Valium into her mouth, then dragged her inside. The living room of the house had been converted to a waiting room, with a pair of old couches and three chairs. A Mexican woman, short and fat, wearing Levi's and a red University of Texas sweatshirt that fit her so tight it looked like the skin of a tomato, entered the room holding a beer in one hand and a stubby pipe in the other. The pipe tobacco was soaked in rum.

The woman spoke broken English. "Closed."

"She needs your help."

"Come tomorrow," the Mexican woman said.

"We're here now."

"Not today."

"Today, goddammit. We've got the money."

"No."

The boy dug into his pocket and pulled out a wad of cash. He peeled off two hundred dollars in twenties.

"Tomorrow," she said.

He felt like hitting her in the face, but he blew out some air and lit a cigarette instead. The girl on the couch grew paler by the second.

"Today," the boy insisted.

The woman left the room and returned with an old rifle.

"Leave."

He reached into his pocket and counted out another two hundred dollars.

"No," she said, letting the money sit on the small table.

"How much do you want?" he asked.

She stood there smoking the pipe and holding the rifle, then finished off the beer. The Mexican woman was in no hurry.

He went into his pocket and put everything on the table but twenty dollars.

"I have to keep twenty," he said. "For gasoline."

She didn't respond.

He stormed out to his car and returned with a paper

bag, from which he took a black .45 automatic to lay on the table with the money.

"That, too," he said. "You can have that gun. It's worth a lot. Can't be traced. Know what that means?"

She stood, impassive.

Then he emptied the rest of the bag on the table. Plastic cassettes tumbled out. The woman eyed the tapes. Country-western mostly, and a few of Elvis Presley.

The woman looked at the girl.

"She's sick."

"She's carsick from driving down here."

The woman set the rifle down and scooped up the money, took the Elvis tapes and the gun, then disappeared from the room.

When she returned she told the boy to wait outside.

He went to the porch, where the old man sat and stared at the desert.

"You want a smoke?" the boy said to the old man.

"*Sí.*"

He handed him a cigarette but the old man made no effort to put it in his mouth.

"Light?" the boy said.

"*Sí.*"

He held up a match for the man, but the man still didn't put the cigarette in his mouth.

"Are you just gonna sit there and hold the goddam thing?"

The man stared blankly.

"What are you staring at, mister? There's nothing out there, absolutely nothing." But whatever it was the man stared at, it was enough for him.

An hour later the woman emerged from the house and motioned for the boy. She brought him into a room that had a single bed and a sink. The girl was sleeping, paler than ever.

"She stay. Come tomorrow."

"No fucking way, señora. We're leaving."

"She stay."

"Look, we have to get the hell back. Is it done?"

"Yes."

"Then we're leaving."

"No," the woman said again.

But he picked up the girl and carried her out to the car, put her in, and drove out. He backed up so quickly that he ran over a screeching chicken, which spun around in a pool of its own blood. The Trans Am blew down the road, leaving behind a haze of dust and exhaust.

It was an hour before he noticed the blood. First, he saw dried flecks on an ankle, then fresh blood on her leg. He pushed her skirt up, and what he saw caused him to lean out the window and vomit. There was blood everywhere, draining from her crotch. He shook her, but she did not wake up. Her forehead felt cool, and there was no color in her face. He had seen people die before and they looked like this.

"For shit's sake," he said. "Do I fucking need this?"

He edged to the shoulder of the road, thought for a minute, then ripped two Percodans from his pocket and stuffed them into his mouth. Seeing no traffic, he jerked the Trans Am into the desert. It bounced and slid across the parched ground. He drove a mile into the desert until he reached a rock formation, where he dragged the bleeding girl out of the car. He wrapped her in the blanket and laid her down behind some rocks.

The boy tossed the girl's overnight bag and jacket out of the car, and everything else that belonged to her. He then opened two of her comic books and spread them across her face to block the sun.

"You've got a better chance of making it than I do," he said to her.

The boy jumped back into the car, slammed another Merle Haggard tape into the deck, turned the volume full-bore, and drove back to the road, Then he headed south, deeper into Mexico.

part
ONE

chapter
1

1990

The large newsstand at the corner of 29th and Fifth Avenue in Manhattan served as a quick stop-off for business people on their way into or out of the office buildings nearby. Newspapers were stacked for easy access, and behind them wooden racks displayed hundreds of magazines, everything from *Vogue* to *Byte, The Economist* to *Guns & Ammo*. Passing pedestrians scanned the glossy buffet of print media, and in split seconds a magazine's cover either seduced a potential buyer into a closer look or was passed over, to remain on the rack like an unopened invitation.

Jessica Cartwright spent a few minutes of each morning watching the public work the newsstand. She noticed which magazine covers captured the public's attention, which models possessed the magic to pop off the page and entice passersby into a second look. Jessica carried these observations with her to the converted townhouse offices just around the corner, the location of her company, the Cartwright Agency.

On this particular June morning, instead of staking

out the newsstand from her usual position next to the
coffee vendor, Jessica watched from a limousine. She
looked at the faces on *Mirabella, Elle, Harper's
Bazaar, Allure,* and *Cosmopolitan;* she knew each of
the cover girls personally, and the Cartwright Agency
represented many of them. During the years Jessica
had worked in the model agency business, she had
never lost the thrill of seeing one of her discoveries
splashed across the cover of a magazine like *Vogue,*
a magazine so important that it turned unknowns
into stars overnight. The professional photographers,
agents, stylists, editors, and advertising executives used
their instincts to select cover girls. But the public made
the final choice by buying the magazines or walking
past them.

At 7:55 A.M. a delivery truck pulled up to the newsstand and dumped several bundles of magazines. The
clerk, Gage, a sawed-off block of a man, unwrapped
the new issue of *Time* magazine and stacked it for sale,
then hung several copies from the newsstand's awning.
And it wasn't long before the passing public took the
bait, just as Jessica anticipated they would. After all,
this issue of *Time* featured the hottest model in the
world, Caddie Dean. Her blue eyes, blond hair, and fair
skin radiated health and warmth. Caddie appeared ac-
cessible, unimpressed with her own beauty. Yet there
was seduction in the face, an undercurrent of sexuality
that leaped through the lens. Caddie posed in an oversized white T-shirt and a pair of blue jeans, her hair
slicked straight back. A slight rip in the T-shirt revealed taut skin of a worked-out torso, and suggested
heat behind the cool gaze. Somehow, the girl looked
both intensely sexy and wholesome. Women admired
her, men gawked. She was approachable, but unattain-
able. The magazine sold.

Gage plucked one of the copies from the pile and
brought it to Jessica's limo.

"Going in style this morning, Miss Cartwright," Gage said, eyeing the shiny limo; he was used to seeing her arrive for work in a cab, or on foot.

"I thought I'd treat myself," Jessica answered. "I'm flying out to Los Angeles to see Caddie and celebrate."

"I can see why," Gage said, handing the magazine to Jessica. "Tell her I said hello."

That Gage would send a personal greeting Jessica considered an interesting measure of Caddie's appeal. In the early days of her career, Caddie had always stopped at Gage's stand to buy copies of magazines that featured her covers, and as one cover became more popular than the last, buying the first copy from Gage became Caddie's good-luck ritual. In recent years, her globe-trotting schedule hadn't permitted Caddie many visits to the 29th Street newsstand.

As the limo fought its way through Manhattan's midtown morning traffic, Jessica scanned the article. The cover line read "Caddie Dean—Billion-Dollar Beauty." Being on the cover of a magazine was old news to Caddie; she'd been on hundreds since the age of seventeen. But being the cover story of *Time* meant a different sort of recognition. The article focused on the fact that modeling was not only a glamorous occupation for a lucky few, but also big business; Caddie Dean was credited with selling over a billion dollars' worth of merchandise in one year. Most of it for Aaron Adam, America's premier designer; Caddie was the Aaron Adam jeans and swimwear girl. Modeling, the story declared, once thought of as a path for a pretty girl to make a nice living before marriage, had changed; thanks to Caddie Dean and powerhouse agents like Jessica Cartwright, a model's income could now climb into the stratosphere—one million, three million, as much as ten million dollars a year.

The article acknowledged Jessica's growing role in the explosion of the model business. This recognition and worldwide exposure, Jessica told herself, should mark this as the proudest day of her professional life. But as she boarded the American Airlines flight to Los Angeles, she felt uneasy, and tried to understand why.

"You're Miss Cartwright, aren't you?" one of the female flight attendants said to Jessica as the plane leveled out.

Jessica looked up from her magazine. The flight attendant was a slender, sandy blonde in her late twenties, fit and cheery-looking. Quite attractive.

"For years I've tried to work up the nerve to come to your office and see you. I've thought about being a model for a long time," she said to Jessica, and then planted herself, waiting for Jessica's response.

"Why would you ever leave a good job like this?" Jessica said, hoping that would be enough of an answer, knowing from experience that it would not.

As Caddie's fame had increased over the years, so too had Jessica's. People recognized her name if not her face. Mothers pushed their daughters in front of her. Girls approached her in Bloomingdale's. It was never easy telling them they weren't model material, that they weren't quite right. Anyway, what was right? Jessica couldn't say for sure, but she damn well knew right when she saw it. And wrong was also easy to spot. But just lately, telling women and girls they didn't have the look had become increasingly difficult for Jessica.

Perhaps, she thought, it had to do with a birthday she'd had a couple of weeks ago, her fortieth. Lately she'd been thinking more and more about the compulsive need of women to be recognized for their looks. It wasn't enough for a husband or boyfriend to tell them they were beautiful. There seemed to be another standard that women felt compelled to measure up to. Models were everywhere, in magazines and newspapers, on billboards, on television, in stores, and on product packaging. Jessica was in the business of feeding that standard of perfection, and for the first time in her life, when she looked in the bathroom mirror each morning and saw small lines at the corners of her eyes, she questioned the very ground upon which she'd built her business. Instead of getting easier, it had become more difficult for her to look at someone, like this flight attendant, without instantly focusing on wrinkles that come from years of smiling, faint facial lines that might be called "character" but to the camera look like canyons.

With this new issue of *Time* on the stands, Jessica realized, she would be called upon more frequently to be the arbiter of beauty, to decide what look women should have. That was her business, so why should it make her feel uncomfortable? Perhaps, she realized, that this flight attendant looked like a younger version of herself had something to do with Jessica's uneasiness. She saw the faint lines in the girl's face, and wondered how much more prominent those in her own face must be.

And while those thoughts flashed through Jessica's mind, the flight attendant took the hint. Disappointment flickered in her eyes.

"The least you could do is answer me," she said to Jessica.

"I'm sorry," Jessica replied.

"You know," the flight attendant said, leaning down so as not to be heard by other passengers, "you're not so young yourself."

Jon Ross paced the hallway outside the dressing rooms used by guests of *The Tonight Show* at NBC's Burbank studios. There were monitors all over the place, and in between puffs of his Marlboro, Jon watched his wife, Caddie Dean, being interviewed by host Jay Leno. A security guard approached Jon and told him that smoking was not allowed in the hallway.

"That's my wife on the show," Jon said to the guard. "What are you going to do, have me arrested?"

One of the show's talent coordinators interceded, and Jon continued to puff away. He was tall, with the stocky and slightly slack build of an athlete who no longer worked out. His curly black hair fell down to his shoulders in the back but was trimmed away from his forehead and ears, setting off a face that was boyishly handsome.

Leno wrapped up the interview with Caddie Dean, closing with another look at the cover of *Time*. Moments later, Caddie appeared in the hallway. As the talent coordinator and producer thanked her for the appearance, Jon took her arm and swept her toward the exit.

But the exit was blocked by a couple of dozen people, most of them holding copies of *Time* for Caddie to sign. These were stagehands and office workers, all of whom knew they were not supposed to bother the show's guests, but Caddie was irresistible to them.

Jon went outside, unnoticed by the crowd, and started the Mercedes 560SL and pulled it up to the door. He was used to attention flowing his wife's way, but this was something new. More like movie-star attention, the kind that renders invisible anyone around the star. For a few minutes he was fascinated watching this new crush of fame surrounding his wife, but as the wait dragged on he hit his horn to signal Caddie. Finally, security guards cut off the replenishing crowd of autograph seekers and escorted Caddie to the car.

He swerved onto Barham Boulevard and fought his way across town, narrowly avoiding parked cars and oncoming traffic.

"Jessica won't mind if we're a little late for dinner, honey," Caddie said to her husband, wincing at a near collision. "Maybe we can take it easy. It's been such a rush all day. I just need a little breather."

Caddie's day had started at four in the morning with a live hookup to *Good Morning America* in New York, then continued with a wardrobe fitting for an upcoming shoot, a print interview, an appearance at an advertising executives' luncheon, a photo shoot for a charity event, an hour workout with her trainer, then hair and makeup for *The Tonight Show*.

"If you need a breather so bad, why did you hang around to sign autographs? You weren't in any hurry to get away from that studio."

"What could I do?"

"Leave."

"Those people had been waiting a long time."

"So was I. You knew I was waiting."

"I'm sorry, honey. We'll have a nice dinner with Jessica and Phil and then get to bed early."

"Let's skip dinner."

"I can't do that to Jessica."

"She works for *you*. You can do what you want," Jon said.

"She flew out here just to have dinner with us, Jon," Caddie replied.

"You thanked her enough times on *Good Morning America* and Leno. That ought to keep her happy."

"She's not out here to be thanked," Caddie said, leaning her head back and closing her eyes. "This is supposed to be a celebration."

As Jon ripped through traffic, he stewed over Caddie's television interviews. Both shows had run montages of Caddie Dean photos, most taken by the famous photographer Anton Cellini, the man responsible for creating Caddie's Aaron Adam blue jeans ads. Jon Ross, also a photographer, though of minor note when compared to Cellini, actually had worked as an assistant to Cellini during a two-week shoot in Jamaica six years ago. It was during that shoot that Jon had met Caddie; he had married her a year later.

"You thanked Jessica," Jon said, following a long silence, "you thanked Cellini, you had plenty to say about Aaron Adam. I'm surprised you left out the girl that does your nails."

She looked at him. Her voice became quiet, apologetic. "Those people made my career, Jon. That's what I get asked about."

"*We* have worked together, Caddie. I've only taken about ten thousand pictures of you."

"I love you. You're more important to me than those other people, Jon, and you know it."

"You could have asked the shows to use some of my pictures."

"I didn't have anything to do with it. I just turned up and there they were."

"Goddam Leno asked you about the future—"

"And I said someday I wanted to have a child with my husband. Was that the wrong thing to say?"

"You might have mentioned that your husband was working on becoming a film director. Everybody in Hollywood watches that show. I would have had a hundred calls tomorrow."

"I didn't write the damn questions. It was all I could do to get sound to come out of my mouth. It's scary out there." Caddie leaned over and kissed her husband on the cheek. "Next time I'll mention you. I'm used to having my picture taken, honey, not giving interviews. I'll get better at it."

Jon cut a hard right off Melrose onto La Cienega and then swung left into the driveway of L'Orangerie, the elegant French restaurant. Pulling in, Jon nearly bowled down a dozen photographers, who scrambled out of the car's path. Their eyes first checked the car's driver, then, in unison, like heads following a tennis match, turned toward Caddie. Instant recognition.

Cameras raised and flashed. From inside the car, all Caddie and Jon saw was a wall of strobing light. The valets fought through the paparazzi and opened the passenger door, assisting Caddie out of the car. Jon pushed his own door open. Traffic on La Cienega slowed to watch the spectacle. The photographers clustered around Caddie and saturated her with light. Jon brusquely elbowed his way to his wife, took her by the arm, and pushed toward the restaurant's door.

"Caddie, here!" photographers called.

"Give us the smile . . . come on . . . there it is!"

The gaggle of photographers had caught both Jon and Caddie off guard. This was not a restaurant that tipped off reporters about their reservation list for the night. This was an old-money, quiet establishment frequented by people who owned the companies and businesses that owned the celebrities.

Until now, Caddie had avoided the attention of tabloids and gossip columns. She lived a quiet life off-camera and stayed out of the Hollywood and Manhattan social scene. But the cover of *Time* attracted other media, from CNN right down to the bottom-feeders like the *Enquirer* and the *Globe*. They'd want pictures of her arriving and departing places . . . they would no longer just want pictures of Caddie Dean, they would now want pictures of her *being* Caddie Dean. After all, she might trip on the way into the restaurant, and then the pictures would really be worth something, because the scandal sheets could say she was drunk, or fighting, or whatever a clever headline writer invented.

Already waiting inside the restaurant, Jessica saw the flurry of flashes and caught a glimpse of Caddie's shiny, thick blond hair. She rushed to the entry just as Jon pulled Caddie out of the crowd and through the open door. Caddie, jostled by the photographers, looked to Jessica for reassurance.

"It makes me nervous seeing all those people taking

your picture for free," Jessica said to Caddie, hugging her.

She shook Jon's hand and motioned them toward the table.

"Did you set up those interviews?" Jon asked brusquely, as he followed Jessica.

"Pardon me?"

"*Good Morning America* and Leno."

"No."

"Your office handled the arrangements, though," Jon persisted.

"We passed on the messages, if that's what you mean."

A maître d' pulled out a chair for Caddie, who sat down, then one for Jon, who remained standing close to Jessica, speaking quietly but insistently.

"Then who set the interviews?" he asked again.

"A publicist for *Time*."

"I want a name."

"Was something wrong? I watched this morning, and thought Caddie was terrific."

"I just want to talk to the person."

"Give Sascha a call," Jessica said, referring to her agency's top booker. "I'm sure she can help you. Now," she continued. "I want you both to meet Phil Stein, the agency's new lawyer. He's in town on business, so I invited him to join us."

Phil Stein stood awkwardly waiting for the introductions, then quickly extended his hand to Caddie, pumping it with the zealousness of someone unaccustomed to meeting the famous.

"You look too young to be a lawyer," Caddie said to Phil.

"Well," he replied, "being a lawyer ages you quickly."

In fact, he was only thirty years old, a junior partner at the staid New York firm of Litwack, Carter & Roole.

Privately, the firm considered representation of a model agency a minor curiosity, and it had assigned the account to the relatively new Mr. Stein. However, when the older partners reviewed the size of certain contracts submitted to top models they were more than a little impressed.

For her part, Jessica was comfortable from the start with being assigned the young lawyer. During the twelve years since the inception of her agency, Jessica had learned that a young woman launching and running a business was rarely met with great enthusiasm from bankers, lawyers, or other established sources of assistance; younger people, like Phil Stein, were more likely to be helpful.

Phil had a slender, fit build and wore a dark double-breasted suit; his neatly combed and stylishly cut brown hair contrasted with his typical Manhattan pallor, but the smooth contours of his face and the strength of his handshake evidenced time spent in the gym. The most striking feature of his face was his jade-green eyes. Their intensity was almost unsettling; clearly, nothing that passed in front of those eyes went unnoticed. Especially Caddie Dean.

As soon as Jessica took her seat, a waiter popped a bottle of Cristal and began filling the glasses

Before Jessica could raise a toast, Caddie did.

"It's a long way from Houston Street," Caddie said.

"Amen," Jessica said, then turned to Phil. "That's where my first office was."

"More of a closet," Caddie said.

"Okay, closet," Jessica agreed.

"And I was one of its first mops," Caddie continued. "But when I showed up there the first time, the mops looked a lot better than me."

"Not entirely," Jessica said.

"Yes, entirely." Caddie looked at Jessica in the cocoon of knowledge shared between them.

Jon Ross was bored with the exchange of pleasantries and history. He quickly downed his glass of
champagne and didn't wait for a waiter to refill it. But
Caddie seemed to be savoring the moment, and certainly had Phil's rapt attention. "I really did look awful
when Jessica signed me," she continued. "I was seventeen and it was my first trip to New York. It's hard to
believe she let me through the door."

Phil responded with polite laughter; looking at this
twenty-eight-year-old paradigm of American beauty,
he found it hard to believe there was ever a time when
she wasn't sensational-looking.

"It must be nice to come home here to Los Angeles,
then," he said, "sitting right on top of the world. Your
parents must be very proud."

Caddie gave a practiced smile but said nothing. Nor
did Jessica. Phil wondered why Caddie's parents, who
according to the *Time* article lived locally, weren't
joining them for this celebratory dinner, but he was too
polite to ask about it.

Another bottle of champagne, compliments of L'Orangerie's owner, arrived at the table in honor of
Caddie. The chef had prepared for them a special
five-course meal, which was served by a phalanx of
waiters and busboys who hovered near the table waiting for an opportunity to refill Caddie's water glass or
replenish her bread plate.

Phil watched the display of overzealous attention
with quiet amazement. Mostly, his clients were small
medical corporations and family businesses, none of
which generated the kind of intense public focus he
saw being lavished upon Caddie Dean. He looked at
Jon Ross and wondered exactly what kind of man
would command the attention of a beauty like Caddie.
Jon offered Phil little clue, as he sat silently downing
glass after glass of champagne while Jessica and Caddie reminisced about their years together and a steady

stream of well-wishers approached the table to meet Caddie.

Finally, Jessica called for the check.

When Caddie emerged from the restaurant the paparazzi again leaped into action. Jessica stayed out of camera range; she knew the photographers didn't want her cluttering the background of their shots. But Phil, disoriented by the sudden wall of flashing light, walked toward it like a child seduced by something shiny. The paparazzi shouted at him to move, but Phil didn't know what they wanted. Finally, one of them yanked him out of the shot. Phil jerked his arm away from the offending photographer, then found himself swept into the pack of paparazzi as they shifted to keep up with Caddie and Jon. And just as suddenly, Phil was spit out of the pack, like a canoe dumped from the rapids. He was stunned, then angry about being treated as an insignificant blip in the face of fame. He felt another tug on his arm and whirled around.

"They're crazy," Jessica said, indicating the photographers. "Best just to stay out of the way."

But Phil looked back at the halo of light hovering above Caddie and seemed transfixed.

Jessica watched Jon and Caddie. A valet pulled the car up, and Jon, instead of opening Caddie's door, left her standing while the paparazzi pressed in on her. Clearly, Caddie had had enough of the cameras and wanted to leave. But Jon let her stand, pinned to the car, while he walked casually around to the other side, tipped the valet, and slid inside.

Finally, he popped the passenger door and the valet assisted Caddie into the car. Jon gunned the car into traffic.

Jessica felt a sudden wave of concern as she watched Caddie's blond hair, radiant even from a distance, disappear into the taillights and darkness.

chapter
2

"Caddie's husband certainly didn't have much to say," Phil Stein said to Jessica, settling into the backseat of the limousine.

"I noticed," she replied, a hint of concern in her voice. "Usually he has quite a bit to say."

"Not tonight. I guess he figured it was Caddie's night."

"Maybe," Jessica said. "But it's still not like him."

"I think we should have another glass of champagne," Phil said, opening a small refrigerator in the back of the limousine and pulling out a bottle of Cristal and two glasses.

"I've already had plenty."

"You can have another glass," Phil said. "After all, this is your night, too. How often does a client appear on the cover of *Time*? It must mean something to you—you flew all the way out here for one dinner."

"I wanted to do it for Caddie," Jessica said.

"Oh, come on, Jessica," Phil chided her. "You have to be a little proud. I am. I'm very proud of you."

Jessica looked at him and said, "You seemed pretty thrilled to meet Caddie."

Though Phil was the agency's lawyer and attended various social functions where the models also appeared, he had never actually met Caddie Dean; her schedule was such that if she was in New York it was to work, and then she was usually on a plane to Europe, the Caribbean, or whatever exotic location her next shoot called for. When Phil did meet the other models, he demonstrated a reserve that Jessica took notice of and admired. Usually, thirty-year-old men like Phil stumbled all over themselves in the presence of top models. But he displayed a cool that suited his position as the agency's lawyer, and suited Jessica. In fact, their business relationship had grown into something more, starting out with a few long Saturday-afternoon lunches and blossoming from there.

"I did enjoy meeting Caddie," Phil admitted, pushing the button that rolled up the opaque window between the driver and the passenger compartment of the limousine. "Seeing her name and all those large numbers on contracts does create a certain amount of curiosity, I'll admit."

Jessica noticed the driver turn north off Sunset onto Beverly Drive, and head up Coldwater Canyon into the hills.

"I thought we were going to the hotel? Where is he going?"

"He has his instructions," Phil said, smiling.

He opened the champagne and carefully poured out two glasses.

Caddie and Jon's Los Angeles home—they also had an apartment on Park Avenue in Manhattan and a beach house in Amagansett—was located above the Sunset Plaza area of Sunset Boulevard, a few steps from the famed Sunset Strip.

Jon Ross drove up La Cienega to Sunset, but instead

of turning west toward the Plaza area, he turned east on Sunset, then north on Laurel Canyon.

Caddie had closed her eyes to rest, but sat up when she sensed the car heading the wrong way.

"Where are you going?"

"I feel like driving," Jon said.

"Oh, Jon, honey," Caddie groaned. "I've got a six-o'clock shoot in Malibu in the morning."

"I don't."

"If I don't sleep, I'm going to look like a hag in the morning."

"No you won't."

He wound the car up the curving Laurel Canyon drive, then turned west on Mulholland, the road at the top of the Hollywood Hills.

"Please, we've both been drinking. We shouldn't be driving."

"I'm fine."

"Let's go home, take a hot bath, and get into bed."

Jon screeched the small Mercedes around a curve, cut across the oncoming lane, then cut back into his own. He laughed.

Caddie winced. "For God's sake, Jon."

"We used to drive here all the time."

He pulled the car to a lookout thirty yards off the main road, with a view that carried all the way to Playa del Rey to the south and across the San Fernando Valley to the north. He killed the engine and turned off the lights.

"I'm sure you remember this spot," Jon said.

On one of their first dates, Jon had taken Caddie to this secluded spot on Mulholland Drive for a summer-evening picnic and a candlelight gin game that lasted until dawn. At that point in her life, Caddie had been so used to men's attempts to get her into the sack that Jon's taking her to Mulholland, a road famous for its romantic trysts, first disappointed her; but the picnic and gin game surprised and delighted her and launched the relationship.

"Of course I remember this spot," Caddie said, looking out the window at the city lights below. "But I've been up since four this morning, and since you care about me I thought you'd want me to get some rest."

"I listened to you and to Jessica and that lawyer for two hours. So maybe now we can do something I want to do for a while."

"I'm sorry," she said. "I know I've been going full-speed all day. They just had me overbooked."

"Do you think Jessica might have talked about something other than your damn career all night?"

"She's happy for us. She's proud."

"I might as well have stayed home rather than listen to that same crap."

Caddie pointed to the copy of *Time* that sat on the dashboard. "Not every agent would fly all the way across country to do that, to bring me my good-luck copy of a magazine from my favorite newsstand."

"She ought to shine your fucking shoes if you want her to."

Caddie leaned over and kissed him. Then she whispered. "Let's go home."

But he leaned over and started unbuttoning her blouse.

"We haven't done it here in a long time," Jon said.

"Let's go home, Jon," Caddie said quietly.

He stopped kissing her and pulled his hand away from her blouse. He looked at her a moment, then he hit her. A hard slap across the face that sounded loud and mean in the quiet night. The red mark left by his hand was visible even in darkness.

At first she was too stunned to move. Caddie had never been hit by Jon. It came as a surprise, so much so that for a couple of seconds following the blow she didn't even know what had happened. Then she felt the sting.

"If I say I want to fuck, we'll fuck," Jon whispered in a tone that she'd never heard, a voice so measured that it frightened Caddie more than the slap.

Tears filled her eyes as she looked at her husband and saw a tight, strained expression that made him seem like another person. She jumped out of the car and walked to the edge of the promontory, holding herself, crying, frightened and exhausted.

Jon's footsteps crunched on the gravelly earth. Caddie did not turn around. Then Jon's strong hands wrapped around her shoulders, and she went rigid. He squeezed. Then harder. But his touch lightened up, and he began massaging her back and neck. He leaned forward and kissed her neck and ears and pulled her gently into him. Caddie let out another sob, one of relief. She turned to face him. A car passed around the curve, washing them in light. Then darkness again. She felt embarrassed and tired, and wanted to forget what happened, attribute it to alcohol and a long day. But then Jon's hands started squeezing again. Hard. He held her hips and squeezed, then his fingers crawled heavily up her back, pressing so hard that she felt the fabric of her blouse tear. He pushed his hands on her breasts. Caddie tried pulling away, but he held on.

"Fuck me," he said.

She broke free and started for the car. But he caught her from behind.

"Jon!" she yelled. "That's enough!"

A guttural rumbling escaped from his mouth, and he tore at her blouse, ripping it clean off her back, grabbed her breasts with one hand, then pushed her facedown on the hood of the car. Caddie felt the heat from the engine through the hood against her stomach and face and breasts. Holding her down with one arm, he ripped her skirt with the other, dropping it to the ground, then he tore her white thong panties away from her hips. She gasped for breath. Using his knees, Jon wedged Caddie's legs apart and pushed himself into her from the rear. She choked out sound but could barely breathe, much less speak, as she felt an animal-like pounding of flesh inside her and on her hips and the back of her legs. Jon's knees dug into her, holding her in place, as he pumped himself deeper inside. Another car made the turn, washing them for a split second in white light. But the light and the sound of the car instantly disappeared. The distraction didn't stop Jon. He grunted and pushed and held her face against the hood, squeezing her head so hard that his hand felt like a vise closing around her skull. At the last moment, he pulled himself out and ejaculated on her back. He staggered back. Caddie heard his dark, heavy breathing.

When she opened her eyes, still lying on the hood, she saw her own picture on the cover of *Time*, wedged between the dashboard and the inside of the windshield.

"Get in the car," Jon said, tossing her skirt and blouse on the hood. "We're going home now."

The limousine carrying Phil and Jessica rolled along Mulholland, taking the winding curves slowly. Inside, Phil slid up next to Jessica and kissed her softly on the mouth, the warmth of their lips burning through the cool taste of the champagne. He put his glass in the cradle of the console, then took Jessica's glass and kissed her again.

"Phil, I don't want the driver talking," Jessica said, pulling back.

"I booked the car under the name Henry James," he said, "so who cares if a limo driver goes around L.A. saying that Jessica Cartwright was in the back of a car making love to Henry James?"

They both laughed, and kissed again.

Jessica did not want her clients or anyone else to know she'd been seeing her agency's lawyer for the past four months, and Phil knew that if the firm found out he was having an affair with a client he'd be on the street so fast he wouldn't have time to clear out his desk. It wasn't a good idea for either of them, which of course made the relationship more interesting. Phil liked Jessica's quick mind and professional confidence, and for Jessica, Phil's sudden romantic interest was a tonic for the difficult years that had followed the breakup of her marriage, and for twelve years of working six-day weeks, looking after her models, and trying to build a business that had finally taken off. The fact that Phil spent the night of Jessica's fortieth birthday making love to her in the cushy bed of a Vermont inn went over particularly well with her. She was embarrassed to tell her friends that she was seeing a thirty-year-old lawyer; it seemed too obvious to her, the forty-year-old woman looking for a younger man. But then her demanding work schedule prevented her from having many friends to confide in anyway.

"I don't think I'm really a backseat kind of girl," Jessica whispered to Phil as he kissed her neck and brushed his lips against the outline of her breasts.

The car lurched around a curve and threw Phil right on top of Jessica. He felt the heat of her body, and it excited him. He kissed circles around her neck and the base of her throat. Above all, she thought, feeling his lips travel lower, he knows how to kiss. Phil kissed with a passion and fervor he kept hidden during the cool deliberations of his professional life. Jessica sparked in him a feeling of freedom, a feeling that she really wanted nothing from him other than affection and friendship. Most of the women of his own age he met were more concerned about what Manhattan nightclub was the latest spot, or what his intentions were be-

fore he even felt he knew them—Phil realized he was
considered something of a catch among young Manhat-
tanites, but he was too busy thinking about his career to
want to be caught. Jessica loved the closeness and
companionship, but was too wrapped up in her business to seem overly concerned about his intentions.

As the limo took a series of tight turns, Phil and Jessica rolled in each other's arms. He unbuttoned her
blouse and pressed his face to the warm flesh of her
stomach; he loved the fresh and faintly sweet scent of
her skin. Phil kissed her stomach, lifted her skirt, and
ran his tongue along the outline of her panties. To Jessica, it felt like a hot match being pulled along her
skin. Her breathing deepened and she gripped the firm
muscles of his shoulders. He dropped to the floor of the
car and pressed his face between her legs.

"You're too young to be this good at anything," she
said, gasping for air.

"I'm a good lawyer, aren't I?" he asked playfully.

"Right now I wouldn't care if you were a chimney
sweep," she said, pulling him toward her.

After they'd made love, Jessica groped around for
her blouse and skirt. She couldn't at first find them and
in a panic wondered if Phil had thrown everything out
the moon roof of the limousine. But he handed over her
clothes and pulled on his own.

They laughed and dressed as best they could.

Phil found another bottle of champagne in the refrigerator and uncorked it.

The limo rounded a turn on the stretch of Mulholland
between Coldwater and Laurel Canyon, and through
the dark tinted glass Jessica caught a glimpse of a man
and a woman parked thirty yards off the road, leaning
against their car. The limo's headlights illuminated the
couple for just a brief flash and then darkness returned
as the car sped on.

Jessica reflected on the image of the woman against the car, and then asked Phil if he'd seen them.

"Seen who?"

"That car and those two people."

"I didn't see anybody. I'm still recovering."

"I'd swear it was Caddie."

"Oh, please."

"I'm not kidding."

"Caddie and her husband parked on the side of the cliff?"

"The color of her hair—"

"I must not have been any good. You're still thinking about your clients."

"You, my dear, give the word 'good' a good name."

"Then forget about work for five minutes. It wasn't Caddie. You're hallucinating."

She realized he was probably right. Caddie and Jon lived back at Sunset Plaza. And Caddie had an early call in the morning. She would definitely have gone straight to bed.

But the image stayed in Jessica's head.

"What if it was Caddie?" she said to Phil.

"What if it was? She's allowed to be up this late."

"There was something wrong . . . I could see it in the woman's face. Whoever she was. I mean, it was only a second, but I just have a bad feeling about it."

"So, call her at home."

"I'm sure she's asleep."

"Jessica, you're not making sense."

"I guess *I* need some sleep," she said. "Let's get back to the hotel."

"Right. Quit worrying about your client and start guessing what I'm going to do to you when we get to the hotel."

He grinned in that way that made her take a deep breath, and as his arm came around her and pulled her close, she tried to relax and not think about Caddie.

chapter
3

Jessica felt the dull ache of a champagne hangover in her head as she turned over in bed and saw sunlight streaming through a gap in the curtains. Something was wrong. Then she realized it was the quiet—no incessant blaring of car horns on the streets below. Of course not, she told herself, sitting up, this was Los Angeles.

She walked unsurely over to the window, feeling that last bottle of champagne drag the steadiness right out from under her. Being a New Yorker, she was unsettled by quiet. And she was used to the telephone ringing, usually before her alarm clock went off, and continuing to ring right until she walked out the door. With models shooting on location all over the world, she expected calls to come in from various time zones at all hours of day and night. The quiet of Phil's hotel room felt artificial to Jessica. She dressed and left the room without awakening him.

Jessica's room in the Beverly Hills Peninsula Hotel was just down the hall. The message light pulsated on the telephone unit in her room. She punched into the voice-mail system and heard three messages from Edie, her secretary in New York. The first had come at

6:00 A.M. West Coast time, followed by another fifteen minutes later, and a third that had just been left at 8:00 A.M. Jessica had told Edie she would call her from the airport lounge prior to her 10:00 A.M. flight, so these messages were a surprise, and not a good one.

"What?" Jessica said, as soon as Edie picked up the private line in Jessica's New York office.

"You want the good news or the bad news?" Edie said.

"Just tell me what's wrong."

"You should call Caddie Dean," Edie said.

Jessica looked at the clock-radio: 8:20 A.M. "Have you got a number on the set?" Caddie was shooting a cosmetics advertisement on the beach at the Malibu Colony this morning. Her makeup call was 5:30 A.M., so Jessica calculated they would be well into the shoot by now.

"You can't call her on the set," Edie said, "because she's not there. She called in sick."

"What?"

Caddie Dean had not missed a shoot in seven years, and she certainly didn't call in on the morning of the shoot, when an entire crew was already assembled, and cancel at the last minute.

"There was a message from Caddie on the service when I got in this morning," Edie told Jessica.

"Caddie's got my pager number, and she knows where I'm staying. She wouldn't leave a message on the service. She's never done that."

"What can I tell you? I've already heard from the ad agency. They're all standing on the beach in Malibu waiting for Caddie. And before you tell me to connect you with Caddie, I've already called her four times this morning. Her service picks up."

"What does Sascha say?"

Sascha Benning was the Cartwright Agency's top

booker, the person who dealt directly with the models and clients on a daily basis.

"I'll put her on."

"I called Caddie's neighbor, who told me Jon came out to pick up the paper this morning," Sascha said. "I even called my contact at the LAPD to see if Jon or Caddie had been pulled over on a 502 or something last night. Nothing. It's weird."

"Then I'm going over there," Jessica said.

Jessica showered and quickly dressed, then went down the hall and knocked on the door to Phil's room. He answered with his face half covered in shaving cream.

"The flight's not until ten," he said, noting the look of urgency on Jessica's face.

"There's a problem with Caddie," she said. "I'm going over to her house. If I can make the plane, I'll see you there. If not, I'll come in later."

"I've got to be on that plane," Phil said. "I'm having dinner with Litwack tonight."

"I know, don't worry about it."

"What's the problem with Caddie?"

"I don't know."

"Maybe I should stay and help."

"I don't think this is your area, Phil."

Whenever Jessica told him about the myriad problems she faced with her top models—from bad-hair days to lunatic boyfriends—he had always just shaken his head and rolled his eyes; it struck her momentarily as odd that he thought he could help with this one. Phil's duties were contract law, not schmoozing the models. She knew she was overreacting to his offer of help, but it was hard not to, since most men who dated her at some point realized that her access to models was like a map to the motherlode. It made for constant, annoying anxiety in nearly all women who worked in the business.

She kissed the already shaven half of Phil's face. "I had a great time last night, and I'd better not see it on my bill." She smiled at his look of mock hurt, and turned to face the first crisis of the day.

When Jon and Caddie returned home the night before, Caddie had gone to the guest quarters, showered, and climbed into bed. Jon was repentant and apologetic, but Caddie insisted on being alone. Jon set his alarm for quarter of five, fifteen minutes before he knew Caddie's alarm would go off.

When his alarm sounded, Jon leaped out of bed, padded silently into the guest room, where Caddie lay in a deep sleep, and turned off her alarm. He then left the cancellation message with the Cartwright Agency answering service, instructing the service to report the call as being from Caddie. Next, he got busy in the kitchen.

Minutes later he ascended the stairs, carrying a lavish breakfast. Jon knew that the professional clock inside Caddie's head would sound its own alarm at six, the time she was due on the set. It was a point of pride with Caddie that she arrived on time and ready to work, without star attitude and unusual demands (unlike the famous model Platonia, who habitually arrived two hours late and demanded no one speak to her unless she spoke first, having read in a *People* magazine that England's royal family were treated that way).

Caddie opened her eyes just as Jon walked into the room. She looked at the clock and jumped out of bed.

"I've got breakfast for you," Jon said, making no attempt to stop Caddie as she raced to the bathroom.

"I'm late, I've got to call the set," she said.

He didn't respond. He waited for her to get to the bathroom and look in the mirror.

"Oh, God," she said, staring at her face. "Oh, no."

The right side of her face was red and swollen under

her eye. She knew immediately that the marks were too prominent to be covered by makeup. And Jon knew that even if the marks were less severe, Caddie would be too embarrassed to have a makeup person know that she'd been struck. Makeup artists heard every excuse in the world from models and actresses with marks on their faces, from "I fell" to "It's a rash" to "The garage door closed on me." But they knew what facial skin looked like when struck, and no matter what blood oath of silence was sworn in the makeup room, by the end of the day half the town knew who was getting hit and how hard. All of this flashed through Caddie's mind in a matter of seconds. And then she began to cry.

Caddie turned and saw her husband standing in the doorway.

"I'm sorry, baby," he whispered. "I'm so, so sorry."

She turned away, but when he approached her, she let him hold her. She wanted reassurance, even if it came from the man who had caused her this pain.

"I had too much to drink," he said in a soothing, hypnotic voice, stroking her golden hair and gently massaging the small of her back. "I was way out of line. You know I love you more than anything."

"I can't go to work like this," Caddie said coolly, continuing to look at herself in the mirror.

"I know, baby. I called them. I took care of it. And now I'm going to take care of you. All day. I'm going to make it all go away."

That's what she wanted, for it all to go away. Yesterday, with all the interviews and adulation, she'd had one big overdose of herself. Everybody wanted a piece of the Caddie Dean that appeared on the *Time* cover, which to Caddie, after a day full of autographs and publicity, felt like an entity that floated up around her, a glowing form of blond hair and white teeth that wasn't her at all. Jon was usually the person to bring her back to earth, to joke with her, make her laugh, tease her, talk to her like a friend, separate her from the flashing lights and the phoniness and the glossy paper. What had frightened her last night was that his eyes seemed to belong to someone else, and for those awful moments she did not know him and he did not know her. The experience dragged her to a dark place where she did not want to go, a place she could not tell Jon about, truly did not want to think about at all.

Jon saw the brooding in Caddie's eyes and thought it was about what he'd done the night before. And she knew exactly what he was thinking, and did not want to correct him.

After she had eaten her breakfast of fruit, eggs, yogurt, tea, and fresh orange juice, Jon put Caddie in a warm bath, slipped a Chopin CD in the machine, and massaged her temples while she lay in the soapy water, drifting off to the music. It surprised Caddie that the phone wasn't ringing off the hook with calls from Sascha and Jessica; she was unaware that Jon had turned off all the telephones.

"I want our marriage to be okay, Jon," she said finally. "I want it to work."

"It works, Caddie, it works. Last night . . . "

"Let's not talk about that," she said.

He looked at her, his thoughts racing.

"I'll be honest," he said. "I was a little jealous. I felt bad about things during dinner."

"You hardly said a word."

"I'm a photographer, but it's the movie stuff I really want. It's so hard to get it going, though. And there you are on the damn cover of *Time*. How do you think I feel?"

"I'm a model, Jon. People take my picture. When I get old, they'll stop taking my picture. You're working to make movies. That takes time—it's a career."

"Movies are about the contacts, getting the right stuff to the right people. That's all that matters. But no one's going to send me a good script to direct. If only I could get the rights to something big, a great script or a book, develop my own material. That's the way to get in the door. But that's money, baby. That takes big money."

"We've got money, Jon."

"It's your money."

"Our money. We're married. If it takes money to get film projects off the ground, then that's what we've got to do. I don't want our marriage on the rocks because we won't spend the money we've got."

"It doesn't feel right," Jon said carefully, slowly massaging her shoulders.

"You heard Jessica last night. That cover is going to generate things for us. We'll have money."

Jon thought a few moments, then said, "I'm worried about that, about all the things that are going to be happening because of that story. The offers, the opportunities—"

"Jessica handles that. It's not our worry."

"That's my point. I think maybe we *should* worry."

"I don't understand."

"I wonder if she's enough for you," Jon said.

"Jon, she's been my agent since I was seventeen years old. Look what she's done for me."

"But you're in a different league now. She has you, and a hundred other clients. She makes you feel like she does nothing but think about you twenty-four hours a day, but she makes all her clients feel that way. This *Time* story is going to bring her more business than she'll know what to do with."

"She's already got a lot of business and handles it all fine."

"That's why I think you'll need more personal attention, guidance with the business things. Caddie, I've always stayed out of your career. I'm wondering if maybe I should get more involved. I think that's really part of what was making me crazy last night, the feeling that with all the things going on, business will just push us apart. I don't want that to happen. Maybe I should be looking after things for you. Maybe a way for us to stay close is if I acted as your manager. We could be more of a team."

Jon massaged Caddie's scalp and allowed his words to settle in. He watched her face carefully for her reaction.

"Jessica will be offended by that idea," Caddie said.

"Because we want to help? She shouldn't be. She'll probably be relieved."

"I can ask her about it," Caddie said uncertainly. After a moment she added, "I've never not shown up for a booking, Jon. Do you understand that? Never."

"Other models cancel all the time."

"But I don't. I don't know what to say to Jessica."

"I'll talk to her, honey. I'll tell her you were overbooked yesterday and you got sick. Simple. You don't have to do a thing but relax today. I'll give her a call for you. Hey, that's a manager's job, right?"

Caddie nodded, staring at the dwindling bubbles in the tub. Her mind kept flashing back to last night, with her face pressed against the hot hood of the car. She felt her breath getting short, as if all of the air had been sucked out of the room. Her mind tried to go back further, but she fought to stay in the present moment, to shut out the past.

Jon, watching his wife closely, saw a look on her face he had never seen before, a distant, haunted expression that chilled him.

With the swiftness of a cat, one of Caddie's hands exploded out of the water and snatched Jon by the shirt. Her blue eyes seemed to darken and drill into his.

"Don't ever touch me like you did last night," she said.

"I—I told you I was sorry, baby."

"No," she said. "That's not what I want to hear. I want you to say you'll never touch me like that again."

She held his collar so tightly that he could feel the fabric digging into his skin.

"I won't," he said, trying to pull away, but afraid of angering her further. This wasn't the Caddie he knew, and he didn't like it.

Jon Ross had just set Caddie's breakfast dishes in the sink when the security system indicated a car had pulled up to the gate. He looked out the window and went cold when he saw Jessica Cartwright stepping out of a cab.

Jon bolted up the stairs and into the bedroom, where Caddie had gone back to sleep. He shook her awake.

The front buzzer sounded.

"Did you call Jessica?" Jon yelled.

"What?"

The gate buzzer sounded again.

"I didn't call anybody," she said. "I don't want her to see me like this."

Neither did Jon.

He stopped Caddie's hand on the way to the speaker button.

"I'll take care of it," he said.

He went flying down the stairs, pulled open the front door, and charged down the driveway.

"Jon, we've been worried about you two," Jessica said brightly just on the other side of the security gate.

"We left a message that Caddie was canceling today. What the hell else do you need?" Jon didn't open the gate.

"Caddie has my private numbers. It isn't like her not to call me or Sascha if there's a change in her schedule. Is she all right?"

"Something she ate last night made her sick, and she

was overbooked yesterday. Whatever . . . she wants the day off, and I told her to take it," Jon said.

"I see."

"We left a very specific message on your service. In the future that should be sufficient."

"It's just that she's never done it, Jon. You can understand my concern for the both of you."

"Concern for the both of us my ass."

"What's wrong, Jon?" Jessica said, her voice losing its professional pleasantness.

"I told you Caddie doesn't feel well."

"Caddie has not felt well in the past and she has gone to work. Is there some reason you don't want me to talk to her?"

"She's sleeping."

"You listen to me, Jon," Jessica said, putting a hand on the gate as if she were going to rip it open. "I haven't worked my butt off for the last eleven years to take crap from you about Caddie Dean. I knew Caddie a long time before you, and I intend to know her for a long time in the future. Caddie is my client, not you. And if I want to speak to my client, I expect you not to get in the way."

"There's something I need to inform you of," Jon said.

"What's that?" Jessica said.

"Caddie and I have made a decision as a couple," he said. "Caddie's career is expanding to the point where it needs the kind of one-on-one focus a manager provides. She's just too busy to be making all the decisions herself, and so are you. So we've decided that I should act as Caddie's manager. Of course, you will remain her agent and continue to act in that capacity as long as we all see eye to eye. But from now on, Jessica, you'll present all of Caddie's business to me first."

Jessica drew a breath and held it. Then she slowly exhaled. "Jon, this sort of thing . . . it might have been useful for us to discuss this at dinner last night. I don't see the point of—"

"It doesn't require a meeting, Jessica, or even a discussion. This is what Caddie wants and what I want. Caddie's on the cover of *Time* magazine, and that requires more attention than an agent can provide."

Jon turned and began walking up the path to the house. Then he stopped and turned around.

"And don't ever come to one of our homes again without being invited."

He went inside and closed the door.

c h a p t e r
4

Jessica Cartwright arrived five minutes early for her breakfast with Aaron Adam at the Regency Hotel in New York. He had not yet arrived, but Jessica knew he would not be late, and that to keep him waiting would be a mistake. Jessica waited for the maître d' to seat her, though she already knew which table was reserved for A.A., as he was known in the business, since on many occasions she had seen him taking breakfast meetings at the Regency. Aaron Adam always said hello to Jessica, but an invitation to join him for a private breakfast came only when her client Caddie Dean made the cover of *Time*. This was a definite sign of her ascension in the ranks of model agents, and Jessica assumed it also meant that Aaron Adam wanted an early negotiation to extend Caddie's contract to sell A.A.'s MaliBlues Jeans.

Aaron designed and marketed everything from couture to men's underwear, tableware to sunglasses. His SunCoast Swimwear line sold more bathing suits than any other company in the world, made famous by Caddie Dean, first in the annual *Sports Illustrated* bathing suit issue, then as SunCoast's feature model for the past seven years. The annual SunCoast Swimwear catalog had become a collector's item, to the point that Aaron and Caddie, via Jessica, now marketed a calendar that sold in the millions each season. The high-fashion ball gowns and bathing suits received most of the publicity, but blue jeans had made Aaron Adam a multimillionaire.

Like many fashion industry moguls, Aaron Adam was his own creation. He arrived at his Madison Avenue offices every morning riding a Harley-Davidson motorcycle, wearing blue jeans, leather jacket, and a T-shirt, then changed into a business suit. At least two nights a week he could be seen in the hottest nightclubs in town, always with an entourage of employees, clients, and models. To be part of his group was considered validation within the business. He never granted interviews to the press, other than the occasional conversation with Liz Smith, whom he considered trustworthy. But he did frequently appear in Aaron Adam advertisements in *Vanity Fair, Vogue,* and *Elle,* always looking fierce and fashionable.

What the general public, and many in the fashion industry, did not know about Aaron Adam was the extent to which he had designed his own image. Yes, his company owned a converted warehouse in SoHo where he gave the hippest parties in town; yes, he could be seen roaring on his Harley through Central Park on the way to lunch at the Café des Artistes; yes, his limousine was instantly recognized by doormen at every major hotel and restaurant and nightclub in town. But that part of his life took place between Monday morning and Thursday cocktail hour. Thursday evening a helicopter picked him up at the 39th Street heliport and transported him to his private estate in Connecticut, where he lived with his wife of twenty years and their three children. There his mail arrived addressed to Arnold Behrstock, his real name.

His three-day weekends were spent helping his kids with homework, manning the ring-toss booth at their school's fund-raisers, playing golf with his wife at an ultraconservative and exclusive country club. On weekends he dressed like a Connecticut Yankee on leave in Ralph Lauren land. His cutting-edge New York lifestyle was a show for the media, industry, and public, the creation of an image to sell product. On Saturdays he preferred to play Scrabble with his wife and children, and the only work he performed on weekends involved voracious reading of the world's popular magazines and newspapers and viewing of tapes prepared for him by staff that kept him abreast of world events and fashion trends. He wanted to create and anticipate trends, not follow them, and his homework in this area was extensive. The Aaron Adam displayed in a twenty-page *Vanity Fair* spread was unrecognizable to those who knew Arnold Behrstock on the golf course. That was the way he wanted it, so that was how he designed his life.

Jessica took a hit of black coffee, feeling the lack of sleep after taking the red-eye flight in from L.A., but the subterranean current of energy and power that permeated Manhattan gave her the necessary jolt of alertness. And she didn't mind at all that every eye in the restaurant focused on her when Aaron Adam joined her at the table.

"Caddie was charming on Leno the other night," Aaron said.

Aaron was tall and slender, and he was one of those rare people who could emerge from a tornado without mussed hair or wrinkled clothes.

"I thought so, too," Jessica said.

"You had dinner with her."

"How did you know?"

"I have spies follow you everywhere, Jessica, you know that."

They laughed. She assumed Aaron Adam had a minimal tolerance for small talk and waited now for the point of the breakfast to become clear. Despite basking in the importance of having a private breakfast with A.A., she knew better than to let her guard down.

The waiter set half a grapefruit, coffee, and dry toast in front of Aaron.

"The *Time* cover story concerns me," he said, scooping out a section of fruit.

Of all the things he might have said, this caught Jessica by surprise.

"I assumed you'd be thrilled," she replied cautiously. "It'll probably sell another million pair of jeans for you."

"That's short-term," he answered.

"What else is there in this business?"

"Caddie is going to be swamped with offers."

"That won't be anything new for her," Jessica replied.

"Very large offers," he persisted. "Bigger than she gets now."

"I guess I've been doing my job then, Aaron."

"You've done a superb job with Caddie. And she's done a superb job for us," he continued, "and I'm sure she will continue to do so."

Jessica struggled to sense where this conversation was leading, and assumed it had to be about money. "Aaron, if you think I'm going to suddenly demand a renegotiation of her contract with you just because she's on the cover of *Time,* then you've misjudged me."

"No, that is not your style. My concern is that the kind of offers that will be coming in for her will prove rather irresistible. We'll be seeing an awful lot of Caddie Dean over the next couple of years. Even more than we're used to."

"I'll control the quality of what she does. I won't overexpose her, Aaron. I never have."

"My major concern is for my blue jeans. We've sold

them on the California look, and it has worked well. But *Time* magazine institutionalizes a person, don't you think? The next generation of buyers will want to feel that they're doing something dangerous and new when buying my jeans. Caddie is going to be invited to a state dinner at the White House next month for prominent Americans, I happen to know." Jessica barely managed to conceal her surprise at this news. Aaron went on, "She will be in every magazine on the social pages. It is troubling when the model becomes more famous than the product, at least when you're talking about blue jeans. Should the Aaron Adam jeans girl be dining at the White House?"

"Aaron—"

"Hear me out. If I decide to make a change, Caddie will remain with SunCoast Swimwear, of course, and the amount and term of her contract will remain in force, whether or not I ask her to do only swimsuits. I will, in fact, give her a lifetime contract at this very moment if you ask for it. I will back my loyalty to her with money. I've made no decisions about the jeans. But I wanted you to know my thinking, and I naturally expect your discretion, since I have not shared these thoughts with even my closest associates."

Jessica wanted to say, *If you haven't decided about replacing her as the jeans girl, might not do it, and haven't told another soul, why tell me?* But she knew better than to verbalize her doubts. Aaron Adam had reasons for every move he made, and if the reason was not immediately clear to others, then that was their problem.

Aaron thanked Jessica for meeting him, then excused himself. Jessica checked her watch. Breakfast had lasted exactly nineteen minutes.

When the cab turned from Fifth onto 29th, Jessica saw the usual chaos unfolding in front of her offices and directed the driver to the rear delivery entrance. Thursdays the agency held open call, meaning that anybody who ever thought of herself or himself as model material had the opportunity to walk into the doors of the agency and have the staff take a look. The staff dreaded Thursdays. It meant the hallways filled with kids hoping to be the next Caddie Dean, Claudia Schiffer, or Cindy Crawford. Ambition, hope, and anxiety emanated from the would-be models in palpable waves. Yet, 99 percent of the time, these kids were not model material. Not even close. Of the fifteen to twenty thousand kids who submitted themselves to the agency annually, less than ten ended up working as a model. But one of those ten just might have the look to launch an entirely new fashion trend, and with it a major career. For that slim chance, Jessica kept the open call intact as a company policy.

A hopeful girl would walk into the agency's lobby on open-call day having recently arrived in New York from a small town where she was considered the best-looking person within hundreds of miles. This kid, used to being gawked at, smiled at, and treated with the deference that society bestows on the fair, would suddenly find herself among a hundred other girls who were as good looking as she, and frequently better-looking. Jessica knew it was disorienting for these kids to be, for the first time in their lives, nothing special. A busy agency booker needed only seconds to look at a girl's test shots and know whether she had a prayer of making it as a model, but the kids often required months, or years, to recover from the news.

Jessica had a difficult time explaining to anyone outside the business that she didn't look for girls who were simply pretty or even beautiful; someone could be quite beautiful to the naked eye, but the camera would find flaws. Jessica saw the shock on people's faces when they met certain of the world's famous models and realized that much of the model's beauty emerged only when photographed. No one mistook these girls for homely, but the mysterious, alchemical process that occurred when light fell upon certain faces and a camera captured them in two dimensions was something that eluded understanding. Two beautiful girls could stand side by side, but only one would look beautiful to the camera. Jessica had seen this happen a thousand times. She didn't know the why of it, but her practiced eye instantly knew which girls had a model's look and which didn't. That was what open-call day was all about.

Jessica instructed her staff to be kind when meeting the hopefuls, to tell the kids that they were very, very pretty, but being a model had genetic requirements other than pretty. A five-foot-two-inch girl couldn't learn to become six feet tall. A girl with thin hair couldn't suddenly grow fifty thousand new strands. A man with a weak chin or gigantic ears or close-set eyes—these were things that couldn't be changed. But as sensitive as Jessica hoped to be, she often found her professional opinion interpreted as an insult, as though telling someone she was not suited to be a model were a personal rejection. She explained to the hopefuls that modeling was not like acting—it could not be taught. Acting required talent and skill and craft. And though certain skills were useful when modeling—knowing how to move in front of a camera, knowing one's best angles and how to cover certain flaws—basically modeling was a genetic gift.

Rejected models constantly begged Jessica for a second chance. It was difficult to explain that in the model business, second chances meant nothing. What about plastic surgery? they constantly asked her. Jessica cautioned against it, though privately she admitted that models with breast enlargements worked more often than flat-chested girls, and collagen injections to make

lips appear voluptuous, if done by an expert, sometimes improved a look. But eyes and noses and cheekbones . . . they belonged to nature. Yet, hopefuls still
spent thousands on plastic surgery, convinced that a
surgeon could do what nature had not. Jessica remembered one girl who returned to the open call five times
over the course of a few years, each time after another
round of cosmetic surgery. Cheeks, nose, eyes, breasts,
lips. All of it. And none of it made her into a model
when photographed.

Then there were the legends that kept the lobby of
the Cartwright Agency filled on Thursdays. Like René
Russo, who walked into an agent's office in Los Angeles shortly after the agent had spoken with renowned
photographer Richard Avedon, who was desperate to
find a new girl for *Vogue*. The agent looked at René
and immediately sent her picture to Avedon. Within
three weeks René Russo was on the way to New York
to be photographed for the cover of *Vogue*, and within
months she was the hottest model in America. Or there
was Tani Shyler, who first came to Jessica's office to
solicit funds for a high school marching band and
walked out of the office with a contract. Tani earned
six hundred thousand dollars during her first eight
months as a model. But for every René Russo and Tani
Shyler there were a million girls who failed. And Jessica felt as if every one of them had been through her
office on one Thursday or another.

This Thursday was the worst in memory. The line
waiting outside the Cartwright Agency stretched
around the corner and down Fifth Avenue. At least
three hundred kids, and undoubtedly more to come.
Half of them clutched copies of *Time* with Caddie on
its cover.

This promised to be a long, long day, made longer by
Aaron Adam's stunning revelation regarding Caddie's
future.

Jessica greeted the office receptionist, then nearly collided with Sascha Benning. Sascha was pacing the office floor, speaking into the microphone of her telephone headset that trailed a thirty-foot cord to its wall jack.

"So is Aaron Adam going to throw buckets more money at Caddie?" Sascha asked Jessica.

"He offered a lifetime contract for the swimwear," Jessica said.

"Then why aren't you smiling?" Sascha replied.

"Still jet-lagged, I guess," she answered.

As much as she trusted Sascha, Jessica knew better than to reveal the details of her meeting with Aaron Adam. The fashion industry was the most gossip-ridden business in Manhattan, and one slip about Caddie and her jeans contract and suddenly the industry would be buzzing about Caddie Dean's imminent collapse.

Sascha clicked a button on the phone's portable control panel and plowed into another call. At twenty-eight years old, having spent her entire professional life at the Cartwright agency, Sascha had dealt with hundreds and hundreds of models and their innumerable problems, ranging from abusive boyfriends to bad-hair days, from drug habits to the inability of some girls to remember a call time even with it tattooed on their palms. When it came to the whims and mishaps of models, nothing surprised her.

Starting out as a receptionist, Sascha then worked as Jessica's assistant, next as a junior booker, and was now the senior booker of the firm. And Jessica paid the top salary with pleasure, because Sascha operated at the epicenter of the agency business. She spent her days married to a telephone, deciding which models' books—portfolios of tearsheets—were appropriate to send out for each job, scheduling the interviews, negotiating payment, coordinating travel, tracking model conflicts to make certain models weren't auditioning for jobs that might have competing products. She handled client complaints about models' work habits, and dealt with rock stars who made a second career out of spotting girls in ads, then trying to ferret out their home phone numbers.

Sascha oversaw the two other bookers, Alan and Kale, and two additional junior bookers, and she made the decisions about which new girls to bring to Jessica for signing. She read every relevant magazine published, knew which models were thinking about leaving other agencies, and stayed on top of the trends that could foreshadow a change in model styles. It was a frenetic job with a high burnout rate, but Sascha thrived on it.

No one mistook Sascha for one of the Cartwright models. She was five feet two inches tall, and plump, and had a voice that could slice hard cheese. Until recently, she had smoked three packs of cigarettes a day. Jessica had finally convinced her to quit, so Sascha had switched to chewing celery sticks and gum and bumming the occasional butt. Because she spent the day making and receiving up to three hundred phone calls, she sometimes staggered out of the office at nine in the evening with the telephone headset still dangling around her neck.

She finished her call and followed Jessica into her office.

"That was Caddie Dean's . . . *manager,*" Sascha said, with a sardonic smile on her face.

"Now what does he want?"

"He says he's not happy with the photographer on the Cover Girl shoot."

"Danson Furst has been shooting Caddie for Cover Girl for, what?—six years now?"

"Yes."

"Tell Jon Ross to stuff the damn phone right up his—"

"Caddie's getting two hundred thousand for the day's work."

Jessica sat back in her chair. It crossed her mind that the agency had not grossed that much money in its entire first year.

"What exactly is it that Jon wants?" Jessica asked.

"Approval on the final photos from the shoot."

"Oh, God . . . just stall him. I'll talk to the Cover Girl people. I really don't want to spend my day worrying about Jon Ross. How's it going with open call?"

"Did you see the line?"

Jessica nodded.

"I've already seen two hundred kids this morning," Sascha said.

"And?"

"Nothing," Sascha said, then paused dramatically. "Nothing except for one."

Jessica knew Sascha well enough to sense there was more to the story. She waited.

"You're not going to like her, I'll tell you that up front," Sascha said.

"Then why look at her?"

"Because I want you to see her, and I'm telling you that there is a problem so you won't freak out when she walks in. But I want you to meet her."

Sascha had discovered at least ten girls who had gone on to big careers, and Jessica trusted her judgment, but couldn't understand the caveat.

"Just wait here and I'll get her. Have an open mind. Drink your coffee."

Sascha returned minutes later, followed by an attractive woman in her thirties. Dumbfounded, Jessica tried to comprehend what Sascha had in mind. This woman might have been a beauty ten or fifteen years ago, but by model standards she was now on the wrong end of the rainbow. Then another face appeared from around the corner.

An extraordinary face.

The kind of face that causes people to stop in the street and stare. A once-in-a-lifetime stunner. Jessica stared at the girl, awestruck.

The girl's thick blond hair cascaded past her shoulders, shimmering with body and health. Her pale green eyes were large and clear, with an untainted luminosity that meant to Jessica that this girl had never seen anything bad. The mouth was a perfect kiss, with lush, soft lips that didn't fully close. The features were classic, but the girl had a look all her own, a signature. One glance at her and Jessica knew she would never forget this girl's face, or want to.

But the problem was instantly apparent to Jessica.

The girl couldn't be more than twelve years old.

She had the height necessary for a model, and she wore no makeup, so the slight red blush in her cheeks was either natural coloring or simple shyness.

"Jessica," Sascha said, "I want you to meet Nona Fischer and her daughter, Ginny. They're visiting from Wisconsin."

A copy of *Time* protruded from Mrs. Fischer's purse.

"Lovely to meet you," Jessica said, shaking hands with both of them. She gave Mrs. Fischer a careful look, then asked her, "Did you used to be a model?"

"Just locally, back in Wisconsin," Mrs. Fischer replied, embarrassed. "Fashion shows, that kind of thing." Jessica noticed Nona Fischer's eyes soak in the photographs on the office walls: superstars like Caddie Dean, Cheryl Tiegs, René Russo, Sharon Stone, Naomi Campbell, and Cindy Crawford.

"You never went to New York or Los Angeles?" Jessica asked.

"Oh, no," she answered, reflecting on the thought. "No, I didn't think . . ." Her voice trailed off.

"Both you and your daughter are absolutely beautiful," Jessica continued, then looked at Ginny. "Do you want to be a model, Ginny?"

Ginny nodded, blushing. "I guess so. I think so," she answered, looking at her mom.

"How old are you, dear?"

"Twelve."

Jessica nodded. "Do you like where you live?"

"Yes."

"You're in junior high school?"

"Yes."

"Do you like it? Do you have nice friends there?"

"Oh, yes," Ginny answered, brightening at the mention of her friends.

"What about sports?"

"I play basketball on the school team."

Nona Fischer shuddered. "I'm always afraid they're going to break her nose."

"Mom . . ."

"Sascha," Jessica said, turning to her booker, "why don't you show Ginny around the office so I can talk with Mrs. Fischer."

Sascha escorted Ginny out of the office.

"We didn't plan to come to your office, Miss Cartwright," Nona Fischer said apologetically, as soon as her daughter disappeared with Sascha. "I brought Ginny to New York as a birthday present. We saw the Caddie Dean story in *Time* and thought, what the heck."

"Your daughter is exquisite, Mrs. Fischer, and she is going to become more spectacular-looking as she grows up. There is no question that Ginny has a future as a model. I don't make guarantees to people about that, but I might break my rule in her case."

"Well, this is very exciting." Nona took another look around the room at the famous faces, and Jessica could see her mind racing.

"Mrs. Fischer," Jessica said, "I want you to come back to New York with Ginny . . . in three years."

Nona Fischer's face fell. "Three years?"

"She's too young."

"They don't allow girls to model at her age?"

"Oh, there's no law against it. It's just that in my experience I've found it to be not a very good idea."

"But Ginny is actually very mature."

"I'm sure she is. But we don't sign girls until they're sixteen. Once in a while we'll take a fifteen-year-old, if she lives here with her family. I must tell you, it is a very, very difficult business for a young girl. Emotional maturity is just part of it. The demands on these girls are tough, from the discipline of showing up places at dawn to putting in fourteen-, eighteen-hour days. They've got to deal with crazy photographers, stressed-out advertising executives, and men who make a sport of sleeping with as many young models as possible. Plus, the girls, particularly the new ones, have to learn to deal with rejection that is often harsh. They go out on interviews, and most of the time they don't get the job. For one reason or another, the answer they hear most of the time is no. And sometimes it means wearing a skimpy bathing suit, walking into an office that's filled with men who look the model up and down then say, 'No, you're totally wrong.' That's hard on anybody, but particularly on a child. There are a lot of reasons I don't think this is a business for a twelve-year-old."

"There's nothing in the world I would do that would hurt Ginny, but I've seen young girls in some ads . . ."

"Yes, and there are agents who will sign them. But there isn't much work in the sub-teen category, and it doesn't pay well. Your daughter is far too glamorous for those *Sixteen* pimple ads. Ginny is going to be high-fashion, top-of-the-line. And I'm telling you right now there'll be smaller agents who'll sign your daughter, if she's willing to move here. But I've been at this a long time, Mrs. Fischer, and I haven't seen any girls who started that young grow up to be happy people. Brooke Shields is the exception, but I can name dozens of girls who started at Brooke's age who went the opposite direction. I don't like to see kids like Ginny lose those years of their life, because they can't get them back. This business forces them to grow up very quickly. Of course, in a few years I'll be begging you for a chance to represent her. That's my best advice."

"I appreciate it, and I don't want to do anything that might be bad for Ginny," Nona Fischer said. "I just think she has this opportunity to . . ."

Mrs. Fischer's voice trailed off. And Jessica observed the confusion in her eyes.

Jessica had seen that look before, and followed a hunch. "May I ask you something personal, Mrs. Fischer?"

"Yes."

"Obviously, you're very young. So you must have been married quite young."

"Well, yes."

"And Ginny was born shortly thereafter?"

"Yes, I was only twenty when Ginny was born."

"Before you knew it, you were raising a daughter and looking after a husband, and in the back of your mind you wondered about that little dream you had, which you probably didn't share with your husband, about going to New York and being a model."

Nona Fischer blushed and looked away from Jessica.

"I don't mean that critically, Mrs. Fischer. I wanted to be an actress when I was younger, and I got sidetracked by a husband who was more than I could handle."

"I sort of always thought," Nona said, "that I wouldn't spend my whole life in Genoa City." Then she rushed to add, "I love my husband and my daughter and where I live, but sometimes I wonder what my life would have been like if . . ."

"I understand," Jessica said.

"I used to really like having my picture taken for ads, and people recognized me at the county fair and things like that."

"It can be fun. I wanted to be on Broadway and have my picture taken walking into Sardi's on opening night. One day I had a casting director take a quick look at me and say I'd better have talent, because I sure wasn't going to make it just on my looks. So I married a talented actor who would do anything to avoid work. One of us needed to earn a living, so here I am."

"But you've become famous."

"My models are famous," Jessica said. "My job is simply to represent them."

Jessica saw the unmistakable swirl of unrealized dreams wash across Nona Fischer's face. "My guess," Jessica said to her, "is what will make you happiest right now is to see that your daughter enjoys being a teenager, gets her education. There's time for her to grow up and come here, and I know you'll be very proud of her, whatever she does. I can see that she's not just lovely to look at."

"Thank you."

Jessica put an arm around Nona Fischer and walked her out of the office. "Let's find your daughter. *Elle* magazine is giving a fashion show and cocktail party this evening. How about if I arrange an invitation for you and Ginny?"

"We'd love that, but you don't have to . . ."

"You'll be my guests."

Nona turned and caught a last look at the "wall of fame" in Jessica's office.

They found Ginny thumbing through model portfolios.

Jessica said her goodbyes, then Sascha walked the mother and daughter back to the lobby.

Sascha came roaring back to Jessica and pleaded with her to reconsider Ginny Fischer.

"Let's break our rules this time. That kid is a major star."

"She's a child."

"Not for long."

"She's twelve, Sascha."

Sascha groaned, "I know, I know, but look." She pointed at the hallway jammed with would-be models lined up for the open call. None was remotely as stunning as Ginny Fischer. "And kids grow up a lot faster today, Jessica. If we want to stay on the cutting edge of this business, we can't stick our heads in the sand. Who says we have to take the high ground?"

"She's twelve," Jessica repeated.

"This isn't about principles. We're talking about money and business. That girl is a walking gold mine. You see it and I see it."

"I don't see it."

"Ginny and her mom probably haven't even reached the lobby yet. I can go get them and we can talk this out."

Jessica shook her head and walked down the hallway toward her office.

Sascha stood there, pained at the thought of letting Ginny slip away; she felt like an art dealer who had stumbled upon a Van Gogh selling for a hundred bucks in an antique shop . . . but her partner refused to buy it because it wouldn't be ethical to fleece the shop owner.

Sascha waited for Jessica to leave the room, then flipped over two Polaroids she'd taken of Ginny. The girl was every bit as photogenic as Sascha had expected her to be. Sascha placed the Polaroids in an envelope and slipped it into her desk. It took all her strength not to tell Jessica that if she weren't so busy being glorified by *Time* magazine for discovering models, maybe they could find a few new ones. When Sascha had read the article, she did a slow burn over the fact that her name was not even mentioned. The writer had interviewed her for an hour, and used the information but not her name.

Sascha locked the drawer where she had stashed Ginny's pictures and turned her attention to the hopeful throng of waiting girls.

chapter
5

If you do not know the nature of business transacted in the open-air market in Tangier, Morocco, on your first visit you might think, listening to the tenor and intensity of the voices, that you have fallen into a teeming pit of anarchy. Vendors plead like parents about to lose their children, while buyers express outrage or indifference over the fluxing prices. There are stalls, tents, shops, carts, even overcoats that serve as display racks for almost any kind of merchandise one might require. At first you can't get over the din of voices, animals, cars, trucks, and music; after a while, the sounds blend together into a rolling hum.

Walking amid the dusty chaos, Garret Stowe looked calm, observant. His eyes flicked left and right, observing vendors and buyers, recording gestures and facial expressions the way a predatory animal studies the strengths and flaws of potential victims. Garret never stopped moving. Even when he paused to look at produce or merchandise, he moved, edging slowly forward, keeping the legs loose and poised for a quick pivot, keeping the hands open and free to deflect or grab. Garret's path through the bazaar was consciously

unpredictable, and with practiced casualness he peri-
odically checked his flanks and rear, his narrow green
eyes sorting through the crowd to note if any one face
reappeared in his wake.

He wore rumpled muslin drawstring pants, a T-shirt,
running shoes, a long blue-and-gold-striped caftan that
opened like an overcoat, and an orange-and-blue Miami Dolphins cap. A splotchy several-day beard pro-
tected his skin from the intense morning sunlight.
Garret looked to be in his mid-thirties, nearly six feet
tall, with a wiry build. Submerged in his seedy appearance existed a good-looking man. Not conventionally
handsome: sharp angular features, wide mouth, set in a
face that seemed too big for the body. But it was a face
everyone looked at twice, drawn by the fierceness of
the eyes and an unmistakable sexual confidence that
propelled his movements.

"American! Fresh American!" a vendor called out to
the crowd, pointing to a tableful of merchandise. "Airplane this morning. U.S.A.!"

Garret glanced at the merchandise, then moved in for
a closer look. There were CDs of popular bands,
dozens of T-shirts with photographs of Madonna, a few
Levi's jackets, different brands of American cigarettes,
and several magazines.

The vendor spotted Garret eyeing the merchandise.

"Fresh American! All new today from airport, brand-
new!"

Garret poked around in the magazines and stopped
when he came to a couple of copies of *Time*. Staring
back at him was Caddie Dean's golden smile.

The vendor gave a broad grin, and wished he had a
few more teeth in his mouth.

"You miss your American wife, mister?" the vendor
cackled, pointing to the picture of Caddie Dean. "Take
her with you." He snatched the other copy of *Time* and
held it up to passersby. "American girl just for you!"

Several men stopped to leer at Caddie's provocative T-shirt pose.

Garret studied the cover line: "Billion-Dollar Beauty."

He opened to the article, saw the picture of Jessica Cartwright, with the subheading "The Woman Behind the Girls." Suddenly, the magazine was snatched out of his hands.

"Buy, buy, buy!" the vendor croaked.

"How much?"

"Ten American."

"One dollar," Garret said.

The vendor reacted as if he'd been shot in the chest; his shoulders sank, his face fell. He looked up at Garret, wounded.

"Ten dollar American," he repeated.

"One dollar," Garret said.

"Fresh from airport this morning. Only mine. Two copies." He snapped his fingers. "I sell like that, you'll see."

Garret shrugged and started to walk away.

"Five dollar," the vendor said.

Garret turned and walked back to the table, leaned into the man. "You stole all of this from a truck at the airport. I know the man at the airport who owns the shop, and he will be happy to know who stole it. One dollar."

"Five dollar best price."

"One."

The vendor waved his hands, then folded his arms. "No."

Garret walked away again, and this time the vendor did not call after him. At least, not until the man looked down at this table and saw that one of the copies of *Time* was missing. He cursed and looked into the crowd. He yelled when he spotted the orange-and-blue cap. The vendor chased after him, pushing through the

throng and cursing loudly, shouting, "Thief, thief!" As
he closed in on the hat, the vendor dropped a hand inside his jacket and drew forth a bone-handled ice pick.
Shoving people aside, he reached toward the hat and
grabbed it. But when the man turned around, it was not
Garret. It was a startled-looking Moroccan who was
showing off the new American hat given him moments
ago by a stranger.

A few blocks away, Garret walked up the steps to his
apartment. He pushed open the door, and a girl spun
around to look at him.

"Rani, I want breakfast," Garret said, emptying the
pockets of his caftan. He had fruit, eggs, and bread, all
stolen from the bazaar and stashed inside the caftan.

It was a small three-room flat in a part of the city in-
habited by poor working people. The view from the
kitchen window was of another building, and the thin
walls did little to repel the constant street noise. Rani
was listening to Moroccan music, the sound of which
annoyed Garret more than the traffic. He slapped off
the radio without a word to the girl. Rani served tea, as
Garret sat down at the tiny wooden table and opened
the magazine. She set the cup down in front of him,
measured out two spoons of sugar, and stirred it into
the steaming tea. The Moroccan girl was well groomed
and pretty, with smooth skin and long dark hair tied in
the back. Her face was strangely devoid of expression.
She was silent, but nodded whenever Garret spoke to
her. As Rani stirred the tea, testing the temperature
with a fingertip, Garret kept his eyes on the magazine,
but he ran a hand from the back of her leg up to her ass
and patted her.

"I'll have a bath after breakfast," he said, not looking up.

She nodded.

What was disquieting about the exchange with this
girl was her age. She was young. Disturbingly so.

Maybe thirteen years old. Maybe. She had a woman's body, but she was a child.

While Rani busied herself with breakfast, Garret studied the magazine. He opened straight to the article about Caddie Dean and the world of big-time models. As he read, Garret ran a finger down the columns of text, mouthing the words. He finished the article and read it again.

As soon as Rani set the food in front of him, Garret shoved it quickly into his mouth, taking huge bites, stuffing more in while he was still chewing. He never took his eyes off the text.

"Is the bath ready?"

She nodded.

He walked to the bathroom, dropped his clothes, and climbed into the small tub. Garret sat back and reread the article. Rani knelt on the floor by the tub and scrubbed him with a cloth and soap. He finished the article again, then closed his eyes and enjoyed the massage. When Rani had finished cleansing him, Garret rinsed off from the shower head, while Rani waited patiently with a towel. Before taking the towel, he walked over to the mirror and looked at himself, pleased with what he saw, but not completely. He decided to shave.

When he had finished, Garret again looked at his naked body and now clean-shaven face in the mirror, then looked at Rani, who waited silently in the doorway. From Garret's eyes, she knew what was next, and she obediently walked to the bedroom, dropped her dress, and lay down on the sheets. Garret paused in the doorway and stared at her naked form. It was a firm, beautiful body. Garret walked over to the window, pulled the thin curtain, then knelt on the bed next to Rani. He nodded, and she, still with an impassive expression, began to lick him with the steadiness of a cat.

* * *

When the telephone rang, Giselle Rochas contemplated not answering it. She knew it was Garret Stowe. No one else would call her at this hour on this line. Rain pounded against the large dining-room window, where she stood listening to the storm's thunder and watching the lightning briefly illuminate the rooftops of Paris. Not the kind of night Giselle felt much like going out into; yet she would not have Garret over to her home.

The dining-room table, polished mahogany with a place setting for one, was of museum quality, as were the rest of the home's furnishings; some single pieces, if sold at auction, would fund most people for a lifetime. A fire burned silently in the marble-manteled fireplace, behind a brass-and-glass screen. In her late forties, with a cool patrician beauty to her face, Giselle Rochas had silver-blond hair, cut short and set off by a charcoal-gray Chanel suit and black silk blouse. Sipping coffee from bone china, she gazed at the storm outside.

Finally, she picked up the phone.

"Good evening," Garret Stowe said, knowing that only Giselle would pick up this private line. "I'm in Paris."

"I thought you'd gone to Johannesburg," she replied.

"I was there briefly. Since then I've been in Morocco."

"And how did things work out for you?"

"Fine," he said impatiently. "I've got something very, very good to talk to you about. We need to talk in person."

"Things are busy just now," she said, "at least for the next couple of weeks."

"I want to talk tonight. Right now."

"What is so pressing, Garret?"

"Business."

She sipped her coffee.

"If you are short of funds," she said, "I'll send something to tide you over. It's not necessary that we discuss it."

"I want your advice on a business matter. And I want to see you now."

She wandered away from the window and paused near the mantel, on which were displayed a dozen silver-framed photographs. Several were of Giselle Rochas, younger, with her husband and daughter. Happy, family photographs. There were also photographs of Giselle with European leaders, British and French prime ministers, and one of her with Jacqueline Onassis in the courtyard at Château Rochas, the famous second-growth Bordeaux vineyard that she had inherited.

Giselle looked at the photographs with curiosity and detachment, as if viewing an exhibit rather than pictures from her past. When looking at these photographs, which she did not do often, she felt moments of disbelief, wondering if the people in them were real or images preserved from a dream. Was it possible to have imagined one's past? she wondered. Was it nature's protection that caused memories to fade, slowly but surely, as the images of her parents, husband, and daughter would in time fade from the photographs? Giselle made a conscious effort to stop her thoughts; she did not like to think about anything as irrevocable as the past.

"If you don't want to come out in this weather," Garret Stowe said, "I can be at your—"

"Meet me at Chat in half an hour," Giselle said abruptly, hanging up the phone.

Giselle walked the mile and a half to the Café Chat. Few people were on the streets in this storm, and she enjoyed the privacy. The driving rain and rolling thunder were like a medium through which she passed into the secret part of her life that included Garret.

Chat was filled with students and a post-cinema crowd. It was not a place where Giselle would run into people she knew. She took a table in the corner and ordered a cognac.

"Garret," Giselle said when he sat down.

"I'm here about a business opportunity I know I will do very well at," he said, skipping social pleasantries. "And I want to know what you think."

"What is the business?"

From the pocket of his rain-soaked overcoat he pulled out a rolled-up copy of *Time* with Caddie Dean on the cover and held it in front of Giselle.

"Do you know what these women earn?" he asked.

"No."

"This one earned over two million dollars last year."

"I've seen her. She's quite famous, I suppose."

Garret opened to a dog-eared page and pointed to the photograph of Jessica Cartwright. "And," he said, waving away the waiter who had approached to take his order, "this woman made forty percent of the two million dollars earned by the model."

"She is the representative?" Giselle said, looking at the caption.

"Yes," Garret said. "The agent. And to make that forty percent of this girl's earnings, all the agent had to do was find the girl. She walked into her office off the street. And now this—"

"I'm certain it's not that simple," Giselle interrupted.

"What interests me," Garret continued, "is that it *is* that simple. One star and the agency is made. They are quite clear in the article about that. It is not a business that requires much capital. Telephones. A small office. And there is something else," he said, leaning forward to gather in her attention. "The big money is made in America, of course, and there are only a handful of top agencies there. They charge the same commissions, the same fees. Surely there is room for competition."

"That business has been around since Coco Chanel. It's hard to imagine someone is going to reinvent it."

"Why not? You reinvented your winery . . . or, I guess you call it, your château. I've heard you on the phone undercutting prices to gain market share. I'm sure your fellow château owners were not pleased."

"Wine is a very competitive market in today's world. We were rebuilding our business for many years. We were willing to forgo profit for some time in order to reestablish ourselves."

"Yes," Garret said. "Competition."

"What is it that you want?"

"I want to start an agency."

"Just like that. Open the doors and turn on the phone."

"Yes, like that," he said.

This was another in a series of Garret's ideas to make easy, sudden money, she thought. Just like that. Open the doors and turn on the cash register. She had backed him on a commodities deal he was certain would make a million dollars in a month. It had failed, of course. And then there was a jewelry-exporting plan he had. It also had failed. She had lost several thousand dollars on that. And it wasn't the money that bothered her as much as knowing that he never put in the effort necessary to make the venture plausible, let alone a success. She decided not to play that game anymore.

"Garret . . ." she began.

"I want to open an agency," he interrupted, "but not right now."

She looked at him.

"First, I want to learn about the business. See how it is run. Where the money goes, how it is spent."

This surprised her. And he saw that he had regained her attention.

"The success will be in America. But not now. Not yet."

He pulled out three pages torn from a telephone directory and dropped them on the table.

"There are over a hundred model agencies here in Paris alone. Most of them very small, I'm sure. Someone will have me, and I will learn."

"If you're interested in this business," Giselle said, "then that's what you should do. Go work for one of them."

"I won't be working for them for long," he replied.

"I wish you well. What is it that you need from me?"

"Nothing."

"You didn't fly here today from Morocco simply to tell me about this magazine article and this idea of yours."

"But I did. I wanted you to know."

Garret had not made this trip to share his enthusiasm, Giselle knew. Yet he was not asking for anything, which she found unusual. She thought she knew him well. But perhaps not. He, like her, had his secrets.

"Then I will drink a toast to your venture," Giselle said.

"And to your own," he replied, clinking glasses.

"What venture are you speaking of?" she asked.

"When it is time for me to start my agency, I want you to be my partner."

"I'm not looking for a new business, Garret."

"And I'm not actually looking for a partner. What I'll need is an investor. Someone who is looking to make a good return on their money."

"If that day comes, I will listen to your proposal."

"That is what I came to Paris to hear. Have you missed me?"

"No," she said, honestly.

"Not at all?"

"When I don't see you, I don't miss you. I don't know why, but I don't question it."

"There is something else I want," he said. "On the plane I read in the paper about the hundredth anniversary of Château Rochas. The dinner you're having here in Paris."

"That's my business," she said dismissively.

"You should include me."

"It's business," she repeated.

"It's quite a guest list. I want to be there."

"No."

"But I want to."

"We have an agreement."

"I won't embarrass you, if that's what you're worried about. I can carry on a conversation with any of those people. I probably read more than most of them . . . don't you remember, you taught me? I'll use the right fork and drink from the right glass, won't I?"

"We won't talk about it any more, Garret. The answer is no."

The dining-room ceiling in Giselle Rochas's fourteen-room apartment on the Ile St. Louis soared twenty feet from the polished parquet floor, gently illuminated by a massive Waterford crystal chandelier. The flames from the fireplace, in front of which Giselle warmed herself upon her return from meeting Garret, shimmered in a sterling-silver candelabra atop the table. During the past few years, Giselle had often studied this fiery reflection. She thanked the butler who brought her dinner, though she never took her eyes from the flames. In the years since she had lost her family, Giselle had learned to enjoy the experience of sitting alone in her dining room with a fire, a well-prepared meal, and a bottle of Château Rochas. And she particularly enjoyed such an evening when it was raining. Giselle had discovered that studying patterns of raindrops on the dining room's leaded-glass bay windows could be therapeutic.

In the Rochas household of Giselle's youth, meals had been formal affairs; attendance was mandatory and specific dress and behavior were required. Her family had owned a large estate outside Paris. Giselle was an infant during the occupation of France by the Nazis, and for years her only memories of that time were auditory: trucks rolling through the night, airplanes, soldiers shouting; there must have been gunfire, too, but she had blocked out that sound.

Giselle's parents had been members of the French resistance, but were exposed by Nazi collaborators and executed in front of the family home. After the war, a childless aunt and uncle took over the family estate and business in Bordeaux, and raised Giselle. She grew up at the Château, befriending the winemakers and field workers. Private tutors saw to her education, and each evening she was required to dress up and dine formally with her aunt and uncle, who frequently entertained the most important people in Europe. In that household, Giselle learned the finest manners, and was raised to be a member of European society.

At age twenty she married the Parisian banker René de Sonneville, a powerful figure in French business and politics. Giselle devoted herself to their marriage, and she managed to remain active with Château Rochas, since at age twenty-one she had inherited a major portion of its ownership. When her daughter, Catya, was born, Giselle plunged into motherhood with characteristic passion. Rather than being overwhelmed by the additional responsibility, Giselle found that motherhood provided yet more opportunity to find joy in a life she already loved.

In prior years, Giselle hit a mental wall when she tried to remember her parents—she had been only three and half years old when they died. Pictures of them

only brought on a dark shudder within Giselle, a sense
of deprivation that she had been frightened to pursue.
But this seeming lack of memory of her parents had
only deepened Giselle's devotion to Catya and René,
motivating her to create warm memories of her own
family.

When her husband and daughter were killed in the
crash of a small airplane five years ago, Giselle Rochas
had withdrawn from the life she knew, because that life
suddenly did not exist.

Friends were kind and respectful to Giselle in the
wake of the tragedy, but often the collapse of a family,
by either death or divorce, proves to be as disorienting
for friends as it is for those directly involved. Giselle's
social life and daily routine had been structured around
René and Catya. Without them, the usual routines felt
uncomfortable. Dinner parties, once a social constant
in her and René's life together, became painful; to sit
alone at a table with three couples felt like swords
plunged into Giselle's heart.

René and Catya's deaths unleashed a demon within
Giselle. The wall between herself and memories of her
parents finally broke down, and when it did she wished
that it had not.

That her parents had died when she was three and a
half years old was all Giselle believed she knew about
them. But one night after René and Catya's deaths,
while dining alone, Giselle suddenly saw the image of
her father crumpling against a wall, blood spurting
from his neck in the place where the first bullet struck
him. Then she remembered her mother falling on top of
him, embracing him and trying to stop the bleeding by
pressing her dress against the wound. The Nazi guards
allowed her a minute to tend to the gushing wound.
Then they shot him in both legs. Then the stomach.
Blood drained from everywhere. Mrs. Rochas frantically tried to cover the wounds, then realized the futili-

ty of it; drenched in her husband's blood, she looked up at the Nazi soldiers, screaming with shock, horror, and hatred. It was sport to these men, watching the woman unravel. Finally, bored with the spectacle, a soldier killed Giselle's mother with a single shot to the back of the head. Giselle recalled that the Nazi guard who held her and forced her to watch the slaughter laughed when he set her down, saying something in a derisive tone about the dead bodies on the ground.

These images returned to Giselle with sudden ferocity; the memories had been buried so deeply that only losing the two great loves of her life, her husband and daughter, triggered their reemergence. Whatever narrow channel to the world had still remained open within Giselle following René and Catya's deaths closed at the precise moment of that recollection.

For a year following René and Catya's accident, Giselle stayed home. And when she emerged from seclusion, friends found her to be a different person. She managed her business, and gradually participated in certain social events, but she was fundamentally changed. Giselle simply felt devoid of any emotion. Nothing moved her, nothing reached her. When someone touched her she felt nothing, as if the nerve endings in her body had died. The polite grace of her aristocratic world carried no emotional resonance, and visits inward summoned devastating images of her parents, and her husband and daughter. If asked to recall what she thought or felt during that time of her life, she could not, nor did she express interest in reopening the doors that had sealed shut within her.

It was during this lost period of her life that Giselle Rochas stumbled upon a strange, secretive Parisian underworld that was to be for her a river of discovery, a journey that in years past she would never have pursued.

c h a p t e r
6

Unable to sleep one night, Giselle dressed and went walking to feel the pulse of street life. Of course, she knew it was foolish and dangerous for a woman of her age, for anyone, to be walking the streets of Paris alone late at night, but lack of feeling bred lack of fear.

She found a café, took a corner table, and ordered a cognac. She drank it quickly, then ordered another. The waiter understood that Giselle didn't want her glass to remain empty; he didn't ask if she was all right, or if she should be drinking so much. He simply served her. The café was filled mostly with students and middle-class couples out for a nightcap. It was painful for Giselle to look at the couples, to see them talk and touch and be so comfortable with each other.

She noticed a woman of her own age sitting alone at a table. The woman had fine features and nervous hands, wore a purple beret pulled low on her forehead, and remained in a Burberry overcoat, even though the café was quite warm. Giselle immediately recognized the quality of the coat, and of the beautiful gray-and-black silk scarf tied at a fashionable angle around the woman's neck; one would not expect a woman who could afford such clothes to be sitting alone in an out-of-the-way café. Giselle believed that the woman carried secrets. Why she felt this, she couldn't pinpoint . . . something in the woman's furtive manner, the way she methodically rotated her cup of espresso with long, pale fingers, or perhaps it was the way the woman sucked in quick bursts of smoke from her Gauloise, then blew small clouds and seemed to search the smoke for messages. The woman avoided looking at the café's patrons, but glanced continually in the direction of the doorway.

When it seemed to Giselle that the woman's anxiety had reached a point that would cause her to combust spontaneously or simply leave the café, another woman arrived, a girl actually. Late teens, perhaps, though it was hard to tell, because the girl wore a flannel poncho that covered her tall frame. A fashionable bicyclist's hat was pulled down almost to her eyes, and a hint of blond hair peeked from beneath the rear of the hat. The girl's complexion was sallow, as if she was strung out on drugs, and her movements were awkward and uncertain. She had deep blue eyes that seemed dulled by whatever substance was affecting her demeanor; yet, despite the girl's disheveled, unbalanced state, Giselle could see a native beauty in her mostly hidden face. She arrived at the bar with an audible whoosh, the tails of the poncho trailing behind her. Instant recognition and excitement ignited within the older woman, who quickly stuffed out her cigarette, left a large tip for the waiter, then joined the other at the bar. Giselle stared and strained to listen as the women exchanged a few hushed words; she caught their names, Annick for the older and Dani for the younger. Dani downed an espresso while Annick spoke rapidly into her ear. Dani seemed reluctant about something, but finally she put down a second espresso and the women hurried out the

door. Watching them round the corner, Giselle grabbed
her handbag and impulsively followed.

In pursuit of Annick and Dani, Giselle at last felt her
heart beating, felt an urgency of purpose, as uncertain
as that purpose might be. She watched as the women
pulled their scarves over their heads, angling their
faces down and away from anyone they passed on the
street. The older woman put her arm around the taller,
younger Dani as they walked in silence, passing a cigarette between them, moving at such a pace that Giselle
had almost to run to keep them in sight. They turned
off the Boulevard St. Germain and stopped at a corner
kiosk covered with fliers, posters, ads, and notices. Annick scoured the kiosk as if searching for a winning
lottery ticket. Finally she located a piece of paper that
she studied carefully. Giselle stepped into the shadows
of a storefront and watched as the woman read the
flier, then led Dani down a dark side street.

When the women were halfway down the block,
Giselle raced to the kiosk and found the flier. It was a
handwritten note the size of a large postcard. There
were numerals and a few words written in a circle. The
words did not form a sentence, and Giselle assumed it
to be a code. She looked down the street. The women
were not in sight, and Giselle felt jolted by disappointment. She ran down the street in the direction the
women had taken. At the next intersection, she spotted
Dani and Annick turning another corner, a block away.
Then the women stopped at a second kiosk. It took Annick several minutes to find another message. Waiting
in the shadows, Giselle was grateful for the respite.

This time, once Annick found the message, she led
Dani back up to a busy street and hailed a cab. Giselle
hailed a cab of her own and followed the other to an in-
dustrial area near Montparnasse. Dani and Annick continued on foot into a warehouse district; not a place for

women to be alone, day or night, Giselle knew, but she remained in pursuit.

Annick and Dani reached a run-down warehouse where a large man leaned in the doorway, smoking and seeming to stand guard.

"Fracasser!" Annick barked at the man blocking their way. He nodded politely and stepped aside. Giselle saw the women descend a staircase and heard the sound of a door opening and quickly closing. Giselle stared, mystified. *Fracasser.* "Crash." Did the women mean it as a command, or a password? The man at the door had acted with deference, though Giselle noticed that the guard had never directly looked at the two women.

Giselle circled to the rear of the warehouse and searched for a window. It was dark back there, and the night sky grew cold from a steady drizzle; Giselle felt animal fear as her muscles tensed and her mouth suddenly had a metallic taste. She found a grimy window facing a back alley, but as she walked toward it, a *clochard,* a vagrant, suddenly loomed growling out of the alley. Her heart exploded and she froze in fear, but the man passed by, talking to the night. Giselle struggled to draw breath. The window was filthy on the outside and blacked out from the inside, but through scratches in the paint and grime she saw stacks of steel and other construction materials, illuminated by portable lights; the lights faced different angles, spilling dim pools of color in the otherwise darkened warehouse. Music pulsed inside. Then Giselle caught sight of hooded figures moving in and out of the colored light, dark forms that followed no predictable pattern.

Giselle felt drunk enough, curious enough, and empty enough to want to know more, to know what secrets Annick and Dani pursued with such tenacity. She walked to the guard in front of the warehouse and barked, *"Fracasser."* The man made no eye contact;

he simply stepped aside, looked at his watch, and said, "Last one." Giselle cautiously descended the steps, opened the door, and entered the building, then heard the guard lock the door behind her.

A hooded woman sat at a table in the warehouse anteroom. The hoods were actually monk's robes, the hood large enough to hide a woman's face in its folds. The woman at the table looked at Giselle, who could only make out the outline of the woman's mouth and the tip of her nose.

"Who told you?" the woman asked.

"Annick," Giselle said reflexively, hoping she'd overheard the name correctly.

"Tonight is five hundred."

Giselle scavenged her purse for the cash and turned it over to the woman, who then motioned her toward the main room, handing Giselle a hooded robe.

Just inside the anteroom was a small lobby, with open cardboard boxes lined up across the floor; the boxes were filled with women's clothes, right down to underclothes. Giselle checked for any boxes with men's clothes, but saw none. Again, Giselle thought about turning and running out of the building, but the woman from the entry closed and locked the anteroom, leaving the guard in the outer room. The sound of the door closing and the lock clicking was in a way a relief to Giselle; her heart pounded, but now she could not run. Here she stood, deep into the night, in a dark warehouse full of strange sounds; it felt to her like a dream, stepping into an unknown world, but a force pushed her forward.

The desk woman walked past Giselle and whispered, "Don't resist," then was gone before Giselle could ask anything. Adrenaline pumped through her veins, and for the first time in her life, fear felt enlivening to Giselle. She pulled off her clothes as quickly as possible, leaving no time for reflection, and dropped the robe over her head. The coarse cloth scratched her skin, and the sensation startled her; she realized how long it had been since she'd even been aware of her own skin.

Giselle stepped tentatively into the main room, where music hit her like hot wind, electronic techno-pop rock and roll, loud and relentless, filling the cavernous warehouse, bouncing off the stacks of steel and echoing back from an unseen ceiling. Columns of light and darkness marked the dimensions of the vast space. Boxes of dry ice sent pillars of cold vapor floating through the lights. Bottles of Cristal champagne and Hine cognac were strewn about. No glasses. The participants grabbed a bottle, took a pull, then left it for someone else.

Giselle counted maybe twenty women in the warehouse, all wearing the same type of robe. Some wandered, others danced, alone or in groups. Others kept to themselves, singing, shouting, or drinking. The volume of music did not permit conversation. The focal point of the room was a platform that had been pushed between two stacks of steel girders. One of the girders had been pulled across the top of the two stacks, bridging them. Four purple lights were trained on the platform and girder, creating a kind of stage.

Giselle felt a hand grab her shoulder; she whirled, but the hand and its owner were gone. Then another woman, laughing and holding a bottle of champagne, danced out of the darkness, took one of Giselle's hands, and whirled her around. She, too, disappeared into darkness. Giselle saw no pattern or requirement or pace to the activity. Everyone acted as she wished, and whatever boundaries of rules existed within the room were not evident to Giselle. It was unsettling to be in a world without rules of behavior; she had been raised with so many codes of conduct, and here she was, a woman of nearly fifty years in this unknown warehouse, stripped of the knowledge of what to do next.

Until her husband and daughter died, Giselle had always felt she knew what was expected of her and what she expected of the world.

Suddenly, she heard herself emit a sound, a sort of bark or wail that originated deep behind her stomach and shot from her mouth of its own power. When the sound leaped out of her mouth, she tried to bite it, hold it back like a sudden sneeze. But the sound flew out as if yanked by an unseen force. Her body shuddered. She then found herself swaying to the music, or, more accurately, being swayed by the music. She had no sense of trying to move her legs; her body moved of its own accord, a spasm of release rather than a dance. Giselle closed her eyes as other sounds were ripped from her throat, sounds that were foreign to her, guttural wailing; she believed she felt the marrow in her bones boil as her body vibrated.

Warm tears fell down her face as her body shook and the strange sounds forced themselves from her. For a moment, she thought she was having a seizure, and wrapped her arms around herself, literally to hold herself together. Her ribs expanded with sobs, then she heard herself laughing hysterically, loudly, uncontrollably. Giselle felt the music pound into her body, breaking up stratified layers of pain that crumbled and exploded from her throat. She didn't know what was happening, where these sounds were coming from; they seemed to travel up through channels in her body she'd never felt before. It was useless to resist, so Giselle surrendered to the volcanic sensations.

Women in robes moved around and past her, but none of them found Giselle's behavior remarkable. The hoods hid most of the face, but Giselle caught glimpses of mouths and eyes and cheeks. Many of the women seemed to be around Giselle's age. There were a few as young as Dani. And though the older women, as best as Giselle could tell, were what she might call average-looking, the young ones were all stunningly beautiful. Like models.

She felt expectation permeating the atmosphere within the warehouse and sensed an increasingly frenzied undertow. One woman lifted her robe, revealing her naked body, and danced across the platform. This seemed to be a signal of sorts, because the other women shouted in unison.

Then the music changed. Rock and roll gave way to a taut synthesized pulse. Women grabbed bottles of champagne and cognac and migrated toward the platform. They repeated a word that at first Giselle could not understand. Then the word became a chant.

"Balle! Balle! Balle!" The word meant "bullet."

The women chanted, danced, and reveled in the sound of their collective voice. Instead of feeling drained, Giselle felt light. She positioned herself at the back edge of the group. When she realized that her wailing and strange movements had caused no alarm or concern in the room, she felt a wave of freedom, and shook her robe to again feel the sensation of the coarse cloth on her skin.

From a darkened area of the warehouse a robed woman appeared, leading a young man by the hand. Giselle could see he was in his late twenties, wearing jeans, black T-shirt, leather jacket, and motorcycle boots. He had a rugged, weathered, but fiercely handsome face, and eyes that flicked around the room with cool menace. This was the kind of young man Giselle might have seen on a street corner as she passed by in her chauffeur-driven car, just the kind of boy she would have dreaded her daughter being attracted to. The woman yelled *"Balle!"* at him, and he peered into the darkness with a predatory intensity as he was led to the platform and allowed the woman to remove his jacket.

Now the women stopped their group chant, but

individuals intermittently yelled *"Balle!"* at the man
and at each other. He did not try to focus on faces, nor
did he resist when the lead woman threw a chain
around the cross girder, handcuffed him, secured his
hands through the chain, and stretched it lengthwise.
From the women surrounding her, Giselle sensed a
mood of power, anger, and excitement. She saw them
looking at the *balle,* their eyes privately reflecting personal journeys of pain, pleasure, sorrow, sin, remorse,
and joy. His presence summoned intense emotions in
the group. He was a lightning rod for whatever secrets
Giselle had first sensed in Annick.

Once the *balle* was secured to the metal beam, the
woman who'd led him in pulled her hood back, looked
at the assembled women, and screamed wildly, *"Fracasser!"* Giselle jumped back, startled; it was the first
time she'd seen any of them make eye contact. They all
turned, eyes wide and wild, screaming *"Fracasser!"*
The word meant nothing to Giselle, but it rose above
the music like a battle cry. The music intensified, and
most of the women pushed back their hoods and flew
into motion. Some kissed, others danced, a few just ran
around the room yelling. Robes swirled and skin
flashed all around Giselle.

Two women ran to the platform and ripped off the
balle's shirt. They doused him in champagne and cognac, while other women pulled off his boots and
pants. Then women took turns using their hands and
mouths on the *balle*'s rigid penis, and it soon became a
touchstone for everyone in the room. Giselle tried to
stay in the shadows but several times was swept by
other women into dancing groups. She danced awkwardly and felt her face burn with embarrassment until
she realized no one cared, nothing mattered in this
room, there was no judgment. She released her body to
the music, sobbing and laughing, feeling as if she were

dancing on a tightrope stretched over a deep chasm, and the fear of falling was exhilarating.

Women took turns, singly and in groups, taunting, teasing, and molesting the *balle*. Some licked the champagne that dripped down his body, others spanked him. One redheaded woman slapped him hard on the face, then licked his ears. Annick lashed at him with the rope sash from her robe.

Giselle looked at the faces. Most were well-groomed, prosperous-looking women. She recognized one of them as the wife of a French cabinet minister, an elegant woman who Giselle prayed would not recognize her; but from the wild look in the women's eyes, Giselle understood that this was not a place one came to identify or judge others. She caught sight of Dani, who kept her robe and hood on and continued to drain a bottle of champagne; Dani seemed disoriented rather than excited like the other women. Dani danced to the beat, watched the frenzy of activity around the *balle,* but seemed unwilling to release whatever demons clouded her eyes.

The *balle* was surrounded by women pleasuring him, ritualistically torturing him, lashing him with belts, running ice cubes up and down his legs, nipping him, scratching him, massaging him, doing anything and everything that did not draw blood. Some of the women began having sex with each other. One, a slender brunette who looked barely twenty, with wide-set eyes, close-cropped black hair, and a face that changed from striking to strange to classically beautifully as she moved in and out of the pools of light, dropped her robe, and three women descended on her with their mouths. Others continued dancing to the music.

Two women ran their hands up Giselle's robe from behind, across her thighs and stomach and up to her breasts. Giselle froze, wanted to scream and run. But didn't. She soundlessly released herself to the hands, which were gentle and firm and eager. She had never been touched with such blind passion. Tears continued to fall from Giselle's eyes, a release of pain and emotion that caused her body to tremble. Unseen lips kissed Giselle's face; she didn't know who or how many; she felt warm, tender sensation and let the tears fall without trying to stop them, and now the tears seemed to fall not just from her eyes but from every pore in her body.

The music changed and the cry of *"Balle!"* again rose in the warehouse. The women surrounding the man backed away. His penis was hard and bathed in purple light. His body was marked and wet, and it was impossible to know if his flushed face was painted by rage or pleasure or both. The lead women produced a syringe from a black bag and injected something directly into the man's penis.

They unlocked the cuffs. Immediately, the *balle* grabbed the lead woman, spun her around, and thrust himself inside. He pumped her hard, and the woman gasped but made no effort to get away. Giselle watched as another woman slapped his back, and he pulled out, turned and pushed that one down on the platform, and thrust himself inside her, while a second woman knelt and kissed the other woman's face. Annick straddled the *balle*'s face, and he pushed his tongue between her legs while she watched the still-robed Dani, who stood in the shadows a few feet away, with obvious passion.

To Giselle, the *balle* did not seem real, was more of a force of male energy unleashed like a funnel cloud inside the warehouse; she felt his energy, a dark, tightly wound power; it frightened her to see him loose, yet for all his uncontrolled fury, the female energy in the room surrounded and buffeted him, as if he were a boat trying to manage turbulent waters; the women sensed their collective power, and were able to move it about the room like an invisible orb.

The *fracasser* continued for two more hours, becoming for Giselle a tumbling, frightening, erotic, liberating dream. Much of the time she kept her eyes closed, allowing her body to guide her. The only words she heard spoken were *balle* and *fracasser*. At one point she found herself lying in a nest of robes, with one woman methodically kissing her breasts and stomach and another massaging her scalp, then she felt a pair of strong hands, male hands, spread her legs; she resisted, but his strength overwhelmed her, and she let go. She felt him push inside of her. Giselle had not been with a man since the death of her husband nearly a year ago, and this man did not care about being gentle. She opened her eyes and saw his face; he stared at her with malevolent pleasure as he thrust in and out of her. He had an animal roughness she found repulsive and yet, inexplicably to her, exciting. She wanted him dead and wanted him to continue. And then he was gone, pulled away by another woman.

Giselle retreated to a corner and stared for a long while into the portable colored lights suspended from metal beams. At one point she looked back at the frenzy of activity around the *balle* and saw him pushing into Dani from behind; Dani was supported in front by Annick, who kissed her hair, rubbed her back, and watched the *balle* perform on the girl. Dani's eyes were glazed, presumably from drugs and cognac, and Giselle thought the girl probably didn't even know what was happening. Still later, Giselle saw Dani, her robe pulled back on, watching the *balle* drape himself over two of the other young women, lying on top of them in a tableau of flesh. The thin red scar that ran from the *balle*'s right armpit nearly down to his hip almost seemed to glow against the pale white skin of the girls. Dani stared at the scene with an expression that indicated to Giselle that she was slowly coming out of her stupor.

Suddenly, the pounding rock and roll gave way to classical music, signaling an end to the evening. Giselle pulled herself up from the floor and saw the women, some robed, others naked, walk toward a back room. It turned out to be a workers' locker room, with four stall showers. Women showered off in the dim light of a single bulb. Giselle walked with them, feeling bound and buoyed by this group of women. A pile of thick bath towels had been neatly stacked in a corner, and the women dried off in silence. Then they went to the room with the boxes and changed into their clothes, each returning her robe and towel. Still in silence, they fixed each other's hair and checked their garments. Evidently, the *balle* had left by another route, as he was nowhere to be seen. Giselle desperately wanted to ask what this was all about, who these women were, how this group had started and when they met. But she sensed it would be an unforgivable breach of protocol to ask anything.

The women did not say goodbye. They walked up the steps and dispersed. There were many cars parked along the street just around the corner, and another man waited there, standing guard. A few of the women walked to the main boulevard, where limousines waited for them, engines running.

Recklessly, Giselle walked home, clutching her coat around herself. Her body vibrated with a primal hum. She didn't think or question, she just walked. At home, she bathed again, then fell into a deep sleep and did not awaken until noon the next day.

In the weeks that followed the *fracasser,* Giselle realized that her nightmares of the death of her parents and the loss of husband and daughter had ceased. She still felt the ache of loss in her soul, but the ugly dreams had stopped. Whatever deep-flowing channel the *fracasser* had tapped, it released a clenched pain that Giselle had carried for most of her life. It stunned her to think she had participated in such a scene, but the sense of emancipation she'd experienced following the *fracasser* was undeniable. She wanted more.

She returned to the café where she had first spotted Annick and the young Dani, hoping to see them again, approach them, and ask questions. But Annick and Dani did not return to the café, though Giselle went there every night for two weeks. She retraced her steps to the kiosks, but found nothing, and a visit to the warehouse revealed only a shuttered building with a lease sign on its door.

Finally, one afternoon while walking in the Tuileries, she spotted the man, the *balle*. His face was indelible to her. He spoke to a pale, angry young woman. She did most of the talking, her frustration clearly growing as he appeared impassive in the face of her fury. Suddenly, the girl stalked away, and the man sat on a bench and lit a cigarette.

When Giselle approached, he eyed her steadily. She could see his eyes processing a friend-or-foe calculation, and sensed that this young man was not used to being approached by anyone for reasons other than trouble. The sense of urgency emanating from Giselle only increased his caution.

"I need to speak with you," she said haltingly, in French.

"I don't speak French," he replied.

She repeated herself in English. He was American, with a slight accent she didn't recognize. She realized he had not uttered one word at the *fracasser*.

"What do you want to talk about?" he asked.

"It's rather private. Can we walk a moment?"

"No. Tell me what you want."

She gathered her breath, then went on. "In the warehouse that night," she said, "six or seven weeks ago . . ."

Giselle waited for a sign of recognition, but none came; his eyes remained stony cold.

"I don't know what you're talking about," he said.

"The *fracasser* . . . the *balle,* the bullet . . . that was you, was it not?"

"I don't know one goddamn thing you're talking about."

"The warehouse, the women in the robes . . ." He stared back at her, and she realized that if she was to learn anything, it would not be for free.

It cost her two hundred American, and then he agreed to go with her to a small café. There he ordered a great quantity of food and ate until his stomach would take no more. While he ate, he acted as though Giselle were not at the table. He concentrated on the food and the several beers he guzzled. Then he ordered a double espresso, and he talked.

It had been the guard at the warehouse who had recruited him for the *fracasser.* The man had approached him in a student café on the Boulevard St. Germain. A two-month screening process ensued, during which the man spent time ascertaining temperament, assessing the danger factor. Would he hurt the women? Would he ever recognize them? During this period, he was paid a thousand dollars for cooperating.

Then the guard introduced him to a woman calling herself Pilar, though he was certain that was not the woman's real name. He was taken twice to doctors for examinations and blood tests. All he was told about the night was that the women would not injure him and he must not injure them, at least not intentionally. Plus, he must agree to be injected with a blend of papaverine, phentolamine, and prostaglandin E1, a compound used to maintain an erection for several hours. For the night itself he was paid ten thousand dollars, to include his services and his silence.

Afterward, he had learned more about the *fracasser*

from another woman in the sexual underground of Paris. He learned that it had been started by three wealthy Parisian women. Most people thought it to be only a myth, but of course he knew better. There was no official club or group or contact. The *fracasser* centered around finding an appropriate *balle,* or bullet, who had to be a young man, not French, who did not speak French or plan to stay in Paris. The founding women took turns screening various candidates, procured for them by the guard, who was in the employ of one of the women. When a man passed all the necessary criteria, the woman "posted" by placing the announcement on a selected kiosk in Montmartre. Then a proper venue was located, one providing anonymity, access, security, electrical power, showers, and a suitable atmosphere. These preparations might take as little as two days or as long as a month, he'd learned.

The *fracasser* participants communicated via codes and the kiosks. Most of these women were wealthy, and none of them discussed or acknowledged their activities outside their tight circle; his information was gleaned from a few of the young girls, mostly models and party girls, who had floated in and out of the scene.

How Giselle would attend another *fracasser* he could not tell her, because he didn't know which kiosk in Montmartre they used to start the chain, nor did he know how to interpret the code. He had heard that sometimes the women had nights that did not involve men at all, when the younger girls were recruited as playthings for the older women, but those were just rumors, and the Paris sexual underground was always full of rumors.

Then she asked him why he had participated in the *fracasser.* It was the money, of course. He said he'd come from Chicago, traveling through Europe to forget a bad marriage and to think about a new life. She assumed all of this to be lies, but it didn't really matter.

When he asked Giselle about herself, she lied, too. But she couldn't shake the feeling that the part of her that responded to the *fracasser* was attracted to something in this young man, something dark and unformed; of course, she quickly realized that what she was responding to was not about him, but inside of herself. It frightened her, but when he stood to leave the café she walked outside with him, and told him she wanted to see him again. She would pay.

Of course, he knew that she too had lied about her background. A housewife from outside Paris who had stumbled into the *fracasser*? He knew better, looking at her clothes and jewelry and the way she wore them.

He asked for a telephone number. She thought quickly, then gave the number of a guest apartment she kept in the city, one she used for visiting family and friends.

He wrote down the number, then wrote his own name on another scrap of paper, which he handed to her.

"I'll think about calling you," Garret Stowe said, then left.

A week later, he called and they arranged to meet on a Friday afternoon. She drove him to a house outside Paris that she'd rented for a weekend. Giselle owned an estate in the country, but of course did not want Garret to know its location or her true identity. Leaving the city on her own with this stranger, Giselle realized, was dangerous and foolish, but she decided she would rather feel fear than nothing at all.

At the house, Giselle told Garret she wanted to explore more of what had gone on the night of the *fracasser,* to travel as far as her shadow side would take her. To her, it would be a process of liberation; for him, she acknowledged, it would be a job. For his services she offered him a considerable sum of money meant to guarantee his availability, confidentiality, and exclusivity.

During the week that had passed since they met at the Tuileries, Garret had also done some thinking. He suspected, correctly, what she would ask of him, and he had considered what compensation to seek.

His request surprised Giselle.

He did not want money. Or, at least, not nearly as much as she was offering. Just enough to pay for rent and food. What he did want from her was the kind of education she could provide. He had sensed from the first moment that Giselle was an aristocrat and an educated woman, part of a world as distant from him as the service he agreed to provide was distant from her. Garret admitted to Giselle that he could barely read. He wanted her to hire an English tutor, and then a French one. He wanted her to teach him the manners of her class, and how to present himself in a way that would be acceptable in the circles she traveled.

Giselle agreed to Garret's terms, and using a false name she leased another apartment in Paris that she told no one about, not even her business managers. It was at that apartment that she and Garret met regularly to continue Giselle's sexual journey. And this was an area Garret seemed to know everything about.

Living up to the contract, she hired language tutors for Garret. He was relentless and disciplined about his education. With Giselle he spoke only French, and within six months forged a working command of the language. He insisted upon reading aloud to her English stories from the *Herald Tribune* and French stories from *Le Monde*. Everything, every story, no matter how trivial. Then he asked questions about politics and business, and she found that he learned very fast.

Inevitably, he saw Giselle's photograph in a magazine and learned her identity. Her response was ferocious. She told Garret that if he ever tried to cross over into her "real" life, she would see that his time in Paris ended quickly. Her fierceness surprised him, but he respected it, knew he wanted her for an ally.

After the first year of their liaison, Garret's linguistic abilities increased dramatically, and he began disappearing for weeks at a time, pursuing one scheme or another, trying to build his own stash of money. But when an opportunity detonated, as in his case they all seemed to do, Giselle would receive a message from the code name they had selected, Mr. Fredricks, and they would rendezvous again and continue their mutual education.

When Garret called Giselle this evening, it had been two months since she'd spoken with him. That he wanted to see her so urgently meant that he had one of his business ideas to unfold. She had heard many of them over the years. Most of them had been ill-conceived. But she had a vein of admiration for his tenacity, for his desire to lift himself from whatever abyss he, or fate, had dropped him in. In these years following the death of her family, Giselle had gradually reentered the life she had once known. She again went to dinner parties and formal functions. She ran Château Rochas and her other enterprises with skill and vision. People now commented on the remarkable resilience of Giselle Rochas. She had not remarried, nor did she plan to. In fact, she never wanted to become as close to anyone again as she had been to her daughter and husband.

And though her friends now thought of her as healed, there were still those nights, like this one, when she sat in the empty dining room, transfixed by the changing patterns of raindrops forming on the large window, feeling nothing.

chapter
7

Garret Stowe took twenty thousand dollars of seed money given him by Giselle Rochas and went shopping. First, he spent an afternoon combing through *Gentleman's Quarterly* and *Homme*, studying the latest fashions. He clipped several photographs and brought them to the boutiques on the Rue St. Honoré, befriended a few salesgirls, and assembled a wardrobe mostly of Armani and Versace. Two nights spent cruising the model bars, like Sol and Bon-Bon, listening to the models discuss which agencies booked the bulk of the work, and he was able to narrow his list of target Paris agencies down to a dozen.

His first approach was to walk in and announce his interest in obtaining a booker's job. He was told to leave his résumé, which of course did not exist. At one agency he at least was allowed to speak to the head booker, who suggested he seek a position as a messenger. As the agencies were crossed off his list, he found himself in offices of increasingly modest dimension and decor.

On the fourth day of trying he walked into the Zola Agency, located in an unfashionable area on Rue St.

Berg. The offices needed cleaning. Their phones, unlike the constant buzzing and ringing phones at the large agencies, were quiet. The photographs of girls on the wall, blowups of magazine covers, featured looks from the seventies and middle eighties. Garret noticed one receptionist, another assistant, and two bookers, who shared a desk, all joking with each other. As he turned to leave, he was confronted by Marie Zola, a short, wide woman in her late fifties, who had auburn hair tied in a bun and wore oversized black glasses that magnified her eyes to a strange proportion.

"You are kidding, aren't you?" Zola said to Garret, sizing him up with the jaundiced stare of a veteran agent.

"Kidding?"

"You are about twenty years too old to think about being a model."

"I'm not here to become a model."

"Then what do you want?"

"I'm here to save your business," Garret said on a sudden inspiration.

"I've owned this agency for thirty-four years. I don't see how it needs saving."

"With all respect, Miss Zola, take a look around."

She did. The bookers were tossing paper wads at each other. The phones weren't ringing any more than they had been a few minutes ago. Members of the staff kept an uncomfortable eye on Garret, which he took note of.

"They think I'm your banker, don't they?" he said to Marie Zola, who suddenly seemed to be trying to pull herself together.

Now she looked carefully at Garret. How could he know that Zola's bankers had been calling? The business had gradually deteriorated, and cash flow was a third of what it had been ten years ago. How could he know she had just come from the offices of her attorney, where she had been discussing her financial situation?

"Who are you?" she asked.

"Garret Stowe."

"What business are you in?"

"This one."

"I've never heard of you."

"Then it is fortunate I happened to come in today."

Now everybody stared, sensing this was a serious business conversation.

"Perhaps we should go for a walk," Marie Zola said.

Marie had been carrying a heavy shoulder bag full of papers and agency records for review by the attorney. Garret politely took it from her and carried it as they walked. He told her that he was an investor and gave her his card—no address, and the telephone number was an answering service. He explained that he was considering a move into the model agency business, but before investing his funds he wanted to learn the business.

"I don't know who you are and I don't have the inclination to investigate," she told him, "but I promise you that I did not walk into Paris this morning from a lifetime in the country. What can you offer me? Nothing."

"What do you need?"

"Mr. Stowe, if there is anything I have learned in my thirty-five years in this business it is that there is one thing and one thing only that matters, and that is the models."

"You had famous models at one time," Garret observed.

"Yes, and General De Gaulle was once president of France. The model business does not care about what once was, about yesterday, or even tomorrow. The model business cares about today. This hour, this minute. I no longer go to the nightclubs and student cafés and parties looking for models. I am too old. That is the job of my bookers. And they do not do it particularly well."

"Then fire them."

"And hire who?" she asked. "Top bookers are not easy to come by. I have to either buy them at a great price with money I do not have, or they have to come to me with a model. Someone we can build on. But the models here in Paris, they think I'm an old lady, and so do the clients. I am not dancing until dawn with my picture in the paper, so they are not as interested in me as they once were."

"What does it take to turn it around?"

"A girl. One girl. The right girl."

"Hire me and I will find her for you."

Marie Zola looked at him with her large insect eyes. He could see that behind her somewhat daffy exterior there was at least curiosity about what he was saying, an interest in his presence. And he took this as a gauge of her desperation.

"You have been to the other agencies," she said. "You would not have spent so much money on these clothes you are wearing and then come to Zola first. You have been to Paris Models, Bon Bon, Slick, and the rest of them. And perhaps they offered you a job as a messenger, but they would not consider hiring you in any other capacity. So you have found me. And I will not hire you either, because I am a businesswoman and I don't hire people without experience or references."

"My reference will be the model I bring you. When we are partners you will consider today the moment when your company was reborn."

She smirked at his dramatics.

He held the shoulder bag of papers out before her.

"Are these funny, as well?" he asked her.

"In truth, nothing is very funny to me these days, Mr. Stowe."

* * *

Garret felt a pulse of excitement in his body as he walked away from the Zola offices. The situation, it seemed to him, had enormous potential. Here was an agency that had a name, a faded and tattered one to be sure, but a name known from over thirty years in the business. It was like a once-grand hotel that had gone to seed; tourists knew the name but no one stayed there anymore, unless he was using a very old guidebook.

He headed to the Mistral Café, frequented by models and agency people. The outdoor café was dotted with the large portfolio books the models carried to their interviews.

During his tour of the various agencies, Garret had befriended a booker named Delph Groleau, a gay man in his early fifties, always elegantly dressed, with his white hair slicked back, and small wire-rimmed glasses that gave him a bookish air. He was English, but spoke several languages. In his youth he had been a male model, and now made a comfortable living running the men's division of Paris Models. Delph had recognized Garret from certain of the wilder clubs in town, places Garret had frequented before his association with Giselle Rochas. Garret knew that Delph was most interested in a liaison, and he used the attraction to glean information from the experienced booker. Now, seeing Delph having coffee at the Mistral, Garret joined him and turned the discussion to the Zola Agency.

"A dinosaur," Delph said dismissively. "Nice enough old bird, but a bit daft at this stage, I'm afraid."

"Does anybody still know who she is?"

"Of course. The name is known in New York and Milan, but she no longer represents any girls that call attention to her."

"What if she did?"

"Then anything's possible."

Delph watched these thoughts flood Garret's dark

eyes, took a sip of espresso, and put a hand on Garret's forearm. Garret made no effort to remove the hand; he waited to hear what Delph had to say.

"A suggestion for you, Garret," he said. "I wouldn't waste your time walking the streets of Paris looking for a young girl to revive Marie Zola's agency. That is quite unlikely, since every girl here with any interest in modeling will have been seen by the major agencies long before they will see Zola. What she needs is a girl from America."

"I have to go to America?"

"No. Milan. In two weeks when the model planes arrive. And then you have to be very lucky."

"Model planes? I don't understand."

"This business is entirely international. If a girl is going to make it big, darling, it has to be both in the States, meaning New York, and Europe, meaning Paris and Milan. How does this happen? Two weeks from now, as soon as school is out in the States, all of the agents in New York and Los Angeles will send their newest girls to Milan. There the girls will meet the Italian agents and attempt to be photographed for the fashion magazines. The girls will make little money for this work, but if they are in demand, they will return to the States with a scrapbook of clippings, and their careers will be launched. If I were in your position, young man—and I would not be entirely averse to the notion of assuming some sort of position with you—I would get my cute little rear off to Milan and try to find a girl I could bring back to Miss Zola, a girl who would otherwise be snapped up by one of the major agencies."

"Are you saying the models are traded back and forth between the agencies in Europe and the States like baseball teams swapping players?"

"Not exactly. You see, a girl signed to an agency in New York cannot properly be represented in Milan by her American agent, now can she? They must have a local agency who knows the market and the bookings, has the contacts. So the Milan agency takes the girl on, and then sends a portion of the commission to what we call the 'mother' agency, the agency that discovered the girl in the first place. There are small agencies in, say, Finland, that go out to the countryside to discover those exquisite blond girls, sign them, and immediately send them off to New York and Milan and Paris. The Finnish mother agency never actually books the girls anywhere . . . it simply collects a percentage of the money earned by the agencies around the world."

Garret soaked in every word coming out of Delph's mouth.

"It'll be easy for you to spot the model planes in Milan," he went on. "Just look for a group of Italian men, well-dressed, lurking about. They wait at the airport that time of year like sharks at the Great Barrier Reef."

"When do they start arriving?"

"Don't look so ravenous, Garret," Delph said, laughing. "There are other pleasures to be discovered in life, outside of that thing between a woman's legs."

"When . . ." Garret persisted.

Delph finally removed his hand, almost sadly, from Garret's forearm. "Second week of June. I might fly in for a day or two if I had someone to see the sights with. . . ."

"I'm sure we'll bump into each other."

The thought pleased Delph. As Garret rose to leave, Delph looked down at the table. Garret hadn't bothered to leave money for his portion of the check, but of course Delph had known that he wouldn't.

c h a p t e r
8

Once word leaked to the fashion industry that Jon Ross had assumed the role of Caddie Dean's manager, his phone rang incessantly. Not with business that Jessica routinely handled, but with offers that the callers knew would be immediately dismissed if directed to Jessica.

Jessica expected trouble, and it arrived on a Tuesday morning when she picked up a call from gossip columnist Liz Smith, who asked for confirmation of the rumor that Caddie Dean was going to do a major campaign for Heartstrings Lingerie. The silence on the phone led Smith to assume she was either entirely right or entirely wrong.

"No," Jessica said slowly, "Caddie Dean is not going to do Heartstrings Lingerie."

"Have they made an offer?"

"Liz, you know I don't discuss my clients' business. But I will tell you that they have made no offer."

Fifteen minutes later, Jon came striding into the Cartwright Agency's Manhattan offices. He walked directly into Jessica's private office, ignoring the protestations of the secretary.

He plopped down on the couch.

"I've made us a hell of a deal," he said to Jessica, looking pleased with himself.

"I don't understand," Jessica replied.

"Caddie is about to move to an entirely new level in her career."

"Is that right?"

"No more working for just paychecks. I had lunch yesterday with John Hartsook. He's president of Heartstrings—"

"I know who he is," Jessica said, feeling suddenly cold.

"He wants Caddie to do their entire catalog."

"And has for eight years. It's trash."

"It's trash that sells."

"I don't care how much it sells, it's not for Caddie."

"He offered Caddie twenty percent of the company for the term of the deal."

"Who cares?"

Jon shifted on the couch, his demeanor changed from smug to irritated.

"Did you hear what I just said?" he asked.

"Yes."

"Twenty percent of the company. They did eighty million dollars last year."

"That's what they grossed. What they earned out of that was closer to five million. Twenty percent of that is a million dollars. Caddie makes more than that from Aaron Adam, but she'll make nothing from Aaron Adam if she does Heartstrings."

"She's not exclusive to Aaron Adam for lingerie."

"That's right, but do you think Aaron Adam or any of our other top clients would be thrilled to see Caddie Dean doing crappy lingerie ads? Are you out of your mind? Caddie would end up losing money on Heartstrings because of other contracts that won't get renewed or even offered."

"You don't like it because I brought it in," Jon said, though Jessica could see that he was slowly realizing that he'd screwed up.

"Hartsook knows goddamn well I'm not going to let Caddie do their sleazy catalog, but he doesn't care, because he's about to get a million dollars' worth of free publicity."

"What the hell are you talking about?" Jon demanded.

"Wait and see," Jessica said angrily.

They didn't have to wait long.

On that night's *Entertainment Tonight* there was a major story about Caddie's being the new Heartstrings girl. They even superimposed Caddie's head on the bodies of some sexy models who were wearing skimpy lingerie. They presented various fashion editors and industry commentators expressing their disbelief. And at the very end of the broadcast they mentioned that the Cartwright Agency, Caddie's representatives, denied the story and said it was a mix-up.

Jessica's telephone rang off the wall with calls from the fashion industry press when the story broke. The one call she dreaded but knew she had to take came at the end of the day.

It was Aaron Adam.

As Jessica launched into her explanation that the Hartsook lingerie deal was all a misunderstanding, Aaron cut her off. "I know that," he said. "What I need to know is what you're going to do about Jon Ross." It was not so much a question as it was an order.

"He is married to her, after all, Aaron," she said, buying herself time while she thought.

"Yes, but what he did with Hartsook is the beginning of a very bad trend. You've built this beast called Caddie Dean. Now you have to learn how to tame it. We're shooting with Caddie in Kauai next week for spring bathing suits. Jon Ross came to a fitting, then called our stylist yesterday and said he didn't think a couple of the suits were right for Caddie. I suppose Jon now fancies himself a designer. Jessica, Caddie's marriage is her own problem, but don't let it hit your business. If her marriage begins to affect my business, I will intervene. I'm hoping you can prevent that."

And that was the end of the conversation. His tone had been pleasant but cold. His voice was a reminder that though a private breakfast with Aaron Adam was an acknowledgment that Jessica was moving into an elite circle in the fashion world, the invitation to join that circle could be quickly withdrawn.

Jessica knew what had to be said to Caddie to let her know Jon was becoming a problem. But at another level, deeper within herself, she felt uneasy about using her knowledge of Caddie's past to trigger a business move. When Caddie first came to Jessica's office, she had been a frightened, confused seventeen-year-old. Jessica signed her to the agency, even though Caddie wasn't healthy at the time. Jessica looked after her, sent her to a nutritionist and doctor, had a dentist straighten a few crooked teeth, and moved her into her apartment, where she kept her away from the city's predators.

She knew a lot about Caddie, she mused, certainly more than Jon Ross knew.

The two women met for coffee in the lounge of the Plaza Athénée Hotel, which was just around the corner from Caddie's apartment on Park Avenue. Caddie and Jon's main New York residence was a beach house at Amagansett, but they kept the apartment for when Caddie was working in the city.

When Jessica arrived, Caddie was already seated at a table near the window, prompt as always. She was staring out the window, unaware of Jessica's presence, and it struck Jessica the way it had a thousand times before how uniquely beautiful Caddie was. She was like another species altogether. Jessica took in the abundant, shiny blond hair, the creamy, poreless skin, the endless jeans-clad legs, and she had to admit to herself that whatever Jon Ross was doing to Caddie's career, his wife looked better than ever.

"How much did Jon tell you about his dealings with Hartsook lingerie?" Jessica asked Caddie once they'd settled in and ordered.

"He mentioned that they called. That's all."

"What about your shoot in Kauai for Aaron Adam?"

"What about it?"

"Jon went with you to the fitting?"

"Yes."

"Did he talk to you about the suits?"

"No. Jessica, just tell me what all this is about."

"You know me well enough to know that I don't like to interfere in my clients' personal relationships."

"What do you mean?" Caddie said with a laugh. "You've kicked plenty of men out of my life."

"That's when you were dating rock stars."

They shared a laugh. But the truth was that Jessica had stayed out of Caddie's personal life ever since Caddie had met Jon Ross. Caddie hadn't asked Jessica's opinion about marrying Jon, so Jessica had stayed out of it, though inwardly she wondered about the attraction. Caddie had said that Jon was the first man she'd ever met who hadn't tried to get her into bed right away, that he seemed just to enjoy her company away from her work as a model. He was protective of her, and didn't seem to mind the long hours in photo studios or on location. For all the men willing to date a top model for the attendant prestige, there weren't as many who wanted to fall into the role of professional coatholders, trailing their globe-trotting wives from one shoot to the next. More than one of Jessica's clients had grown weary of dating, then married the next guy to come along who seemed somewhat down-to-earth.

Jessica put her coffee cup down and looked Caddie directly in the eyes. Despite all Caddie's homes, glamorous trips, and bulging bank accounts, Jessica knew that this beautiful young woman was still not that far removed from the waifish, wounded girl who had walked into her office eleven years ago.

"This can all go away very quickly," Jessica said quietly to Caddie. "The contracts, the money, the magazine covers. Sometimes it goes as quickly as it arrives. You've worked awfully hard to get here, but it's a lot easier to have it all fall apart."

"Why are you scaring me?" Caddie said, sitting back, unused to this almost emotionless gaze coming from Jessica's eyes.

"We need to talk about what Jon's doing to your career," Jessica said evenly.

When Jon Ross returned home from shopping for some new clothes for the trip to Kauai, he paused in the hallway upon exiting the elevator on the eleventh floor. The door to the emergency stairwell was propped open with a chair, and he heard the echo of running shoes on the metal steps. He knew it was Caddie. She often used the stairwell as her personal gymnasium, running up the ten flights, then taking the elevator down to the lobby and doing it again and again. He could tell by the depth of her breathing that she had been working out particularly hard today.

He entered the apartment and dropped his packages on the couch, then went to check the message machine. But before he could reach the machine, Caddie came flying through the front door, drenched with perspiration and breathing hard from the climb, and blocked his path.

"Don't you ever call Aaron Adam's stylist and

discuss my fittings," Caddie said, spitting the words in Jon's face. "And don't talk to companies like Hartstrings Lingerie about contracts without first talking to me."

Her face was flushed red from the run and from her anger.

"We can talk about it after you've had a shower," Jon said, trying to brush past her, unused to seeing his wife this way.

Caddie shoved him backward.

His heel snagged on the oak floor and he fell back against the wall. Stunned and infuriated, he caught his balance and came at Caddie.

She didn't budge.

"Don't put one single finger on me," Caddie said.

Jon had never seen such fury in his wife's face, and he backed off.

He tried to figure out what had touched off this explosion. "This is about Jessica, isn't it?" he said.

"You said you were going to help me, Jon, not cause problems."

"Jessica is butting in, isn't she? Going behind my back."

"That lingerie company is an embarrassment," Caddie said, her voice rising. "Aaron Adam is my largest account. How *dare* you tell them you didn't like their clothes?"

"I didn't think they were right for you."

"Don't screw with my business," Caddie said, advancing on Jon, her face contorted in such anger that he almost didn't recognize her.

"What's the matter with you?" Jon said, as confused as he was surprised. "You can't be this upset over some stupid deal that's not even going to happen. Don't you understand I was just trying to stir up Jessica so that she'd be more aggressive for you?"

"Just listen to what I said," Caddie said quietly. Then

she turned and went into the bedroom, and locked the door.

Jon stood frozen in place. He had been with Caddie almost constantly for five years, and had never seen the woman who had just confronted him. Who was this? He wasn't sure. But he knew that he'd better find out.

Jon assumed that Caddie's fury would dissipate as quickly as it had arrived. But it did not. She barely spoke to him for two days after their confrontation, spending her time working out six hours a day in preparation for her bathing-suit shoot. And then the day before her departure she told Jon that she wanted to go alone, that the Aaron Adam people were so upset by his meddling at the fittings that it was best to let things cool off. His first instinct was to demand to go on the trip, insist that he was Caddie's husband and manager and no fashion house was going to tell him what to do. But the resolve in Caddie's eyes caused Jon to hold back, to remain calm. "I have some business to handle in L.A.," Jon told his wife. "This would be a good time to get it done."

Jon traveled with Caddie to Los Angeles, where she changed planes and continued on to Hawaii. He spent a few hours making the rounds of several agencies, looking for assignments as a photographer. Normally, he was on everybody's D-list as a photographer, but by naming himself Caddie's manager he managed to move up a couple of notches simply because certain smaller agencies thought they might get a chance at Caddie Dean by ingratiating themselves with Jon. After seeing the agencies, he had meetings with film financiers, trying to drum up interest in the script that he wanted to direct. The first question each financier asked him was whether or not Caddie would act in the film, but Caddie had no interest in acting, so Jon tap-danced around the issue.

The day full of meetings left Jon feeling annoyed, since he was one of those people who believed they should be doing much better in life than they actually were. Being viewed as Mr. Caddie Dean grated on him too, especially when he couldn't seem to parlay his connection to Caddie into career opportunities. But Jon was a realist and knew that without Caddie's cachet he wouldn't even have gotten into the offices he'd visited that day. Which was why the matter of Caddie's explosion of temper in New York continued to concern him, and why he hopped in his car the next morning and drove south of Los Angeles to Fullerton.

Karla Dean was only forty-seven years old but looked much older. Like her daughter, she was tall and slender, but she did not have Caddie's looks. Whereas Caddie had wide-set eyes, full lips, and the classic high cheekbones of a model, her mother's eyes were narrowly set on either side of a slightly crooked nose, and her mouth was small and surrounded by heavy smoker's lines. Despite Caddie's protests, her mother still smoked—two packs a day of Salem's—and she did it with such a heavy pull that her sunken cheeks almost seemed to touch inside when she took a drag.

Jon arrived at the house just before noon. It was a charming saltbox that looked as if it belonged in Provincetown rather than on a tree-lined street four miles from Disneyland. The yard was beautifully kept, with dozens of rosebushes lining the white picket fence and mounds of bougainvillea draped around the bay windows in front. It was the house where Caddie had grown up, though it had not always looked this charming. Jon had seen pictures of it before Caddie paid to have it restored. Caddie also paid for the gardening service and a maid who came in three times a week, and she provided a monthly stipend for her mother to live on.

Caddie's parents had been divorced ten years, and Jon had met Caddie's father only once, on the day of their wedding. Evidently he now lived in Arizona. Caddie had never said much to Jon about her family, other than that she was the only child of two normal parents who raised her in this quiet, pleasant neighborhood. It was pretty much the all-American middle-class household, Caddie always told the press, and she insisted the press respect the privacy of her parents. Caddie had been photographed with her mother in front of the storybook house on numerous occasions for magazine stories, but her father, Caddie reported, was camera-shy and would just as soon stay in the shadows when it came to his famous daughter.

Caddie usually went home for Thanksgiving and Christmas, hiring a caterer to serve a dinner for her mother and a few of her mother's friends. She always brought lovely presents for her mother, but after the holidays Caddie rarely said a word about her family.

That never mattered to Jon. He wanted Caddie's attention and didn't care to deal with the parents. He had never visited Caddie's mother alone, and knew he was taking a risk in doing so, since he hadn't discussed the visit with Caddie.

Karla Dean answered the door and looked past him, then said, "Where's Caddie?"

"Oh, she's in Hawaii working. I was in town on business and thought I'd just stop by and say hello."

He handed her the box of Sees candy he had picked along the way.

"Come on in, but I really don't have anything to offer you for lunch," Mrs. Dean said. "I was just watching the television."

Her voice was slow and deliberate.

"I didn't come for lunch," Jon said, following her into the den. "I just wanted to stop by and visit."

He noticed a tumbler filled with ice and an amber liquid on the coffee table.

"I was just having a cocktail," Karla Dean said. "Can I get you something?"

"I'll fix it," he said. "Can I freshen yours?"

"I'm fine," she said, sitting down while Jon went to the bar.

The house was immaculate. Not a speck of dust anywhere. The tumblers were crystal, a gift from Caddie.

Jon opened a cabinet, found the usual mix of bottles, and poured himself a short vodka. He paused at the bar and peeked into a cabinet below the one he'd just opened. There he saw half a dozen bottles of Southern Comfort, one of which was nearly empty.

"I guess you need a little more ice," he said, walking to the kitchen.

There had been ice in the bar, but Jon poked around the kitchen and found what he suspected he would, another almost empty bottle of Southern Comfort. He had smelled the sweet liquor on her breath the moment Mrs. Dean opened the door. Her voice had been too steady, her movements consciously deliberate. Jon knew she was stinking drunk. Whenever he had visited the house with Caddie, he'd observed that Mrs. Dean drank nothing but 7-Up or water, but he'd noticed empty liquor bottles in the trash, and suspected that Caddie's mother was a closet drinker. Again, the information had never mattered to him. Until now.

He returned to the den, toasted Mrs. Dean, and made small talk about Caddie and the weather. For several minutes, Mrs. Dean didn't touch her drink, but finally she started sipping. Jon kept talking. He finished his drink and went to fix another. At the same time he made a fresh one for her and served it without bothering to ask if she wanted it. He simply replaced her old drink with the new one and kept up his chatter. He soon realized that his assessment was correct; she had been drinking most of the day. Like many alcoholics, she had puffy, pale skin, thin legs and arms, and a slight paunch across the middle. After a third drink her words were slurred, and that was when Jon asked her about Caddie.

"Karla, Caddie's been under such pressure lately, with all the publicity of the magazine cover, I've been worried about her."

"Caddie's a strong girl," Mrs. Dean said.

"I know that, and she's usually so even-tempered. That's why I was concerned when she flared up a little bit the other day."

"Caddie keeps her temper," she answered, sipping her drink, not looking directly at Jon; her gaze fell past him, past the television, into some zone of memory trailed out in the darkness of the hallway.

"I think the pressure of the business is getting to her now and then. I'm trying to help her out. But she really snapped at me."

"Well, that girl has always been picky about business. Miss Cartwright handles her business, but Caddie has her own mind. She knows what she wants and that's the way she wants things to be."

"How does she want things to be?" Jon asked.

"The way she wants them. If that gardener doesn't do the yards here the way Caddie wants, she's on the phone to him."

"I've never heard her call the gardener."

"When she comes to visit here she'll call him. The handyman, too. She wants everything just so."

"Well, I guess that's good. She must have a lot of good memories about growing up with you in this house. I know it's very important to her to keep the house in good shape for you."

Mrs. Dean turned and focused her eyes on Jon. He looked into the watery blue eyes and saw dark thoughts churning somewhere deep behind the placid blue pools.

"She keeps the house in good shape for *herself,*" Mrs. Dean said, finishing her drink, "not for me."

Jon filled her glass.

"I don't know what you mean," Jon said.

"She likes to see it looking like the picture."

"What picture?"

Mrs. Dean stood and nearly fell over. Jon leaped over and helped her catch her balance.

"I guess I'm a little tired," Mrs. Dean said. "I didn't take my nap today. I usually take a nap."

"What picture?" Jon repeated.

She shuffled over to the bookshelf and opened a storage cabinet. She lifted out a scrapbook and handed it to Jon.

He opened it, expecting to see photographs and mementos of Caddie's youth. Instead, the book was filled with photographs of houses clipped from magazines. Forty pages with pictures of a hundred different houses. There were many styles, but they were predominantly Cape Cods, just like the house where Karla and Jon stood. He came to a page with a large photo circled in red. It was an exterior front shot identical to Mrs. Dean's house.

"That's the one," Mrs. Dean said, seeing that Jon had reached a red-marked page. "That's the one she wanted."

Jon was confused.

"She cut out pictures of houses that looked like the one where you already live?"

"Caddie used to sit in her room with magazines and look at the models and look at pictures of houses. She cut out pictures of the models and the houses and put them in different books. She wanted a house just like that one, and that's what she got. That's why she's so particular. It didn't look exactly like the picture when she bought it, but she showed the picture to the work-men and told them to make it look the same."

"Are you saying that Caddie bought this house?"

"Sure she did."

"I thought she grew up here."

"She always *wanted* to grow up in a house like this."

"Karla, now I'm very confused."

"Caddie's a good girl. She bought this house and lets me stay here. She takes care of me. She's a good girl that way."

"When did she buy this house?"

"Oh, eight, nine years ago. A few years after she started working for Mrs. Cartwright."

"She doesn't work for Jessica Cartwright. Jessica Cartwright works for her."

"I don't know about the business things."

Karla Dean took a long sip from the glass.

"Mrs. Dean, where did Caddie grow up?"

Karla Dean made her way back to the couch and sat down.

"You probably shouldn't tell Caddie I showed you the book with the houses," Mrs. Dean said. "I don't show that to anybody."

"Where did you live when Caddie was growing up?" Jon asked again, stunned and fascinated.

"I think in her mind she's always lived in this house," Caddie Dean's mother said.

"In her mind?"

"This is what she always wanted. We just couldn't give it to her. And she didn't like being around him."

"Him?"

"My husband. He . . ." Karla Dean's voice and thoughts trailed away. She just sat and stared blankly, apparently unaware that Jon was still in the room.

c h a p t e r
9

After two days of shooting on Kauai, photographer Anton Cellini moved his crew to Maui, where they camped at the Hanna Ranch, a tasteful, understated resort that featured elegant huts instead of hotel rooms. No high-rise hotels or golf courses, just the flavor of old Hawaii, but with room service.

Cellini was after sunset shots, so Caddie's mornings and early afternoons were free. She spent the time swimming and walking in the lush botanical gardens near the resort. Each morning when she took her swim, she was politely greeted by an older man who did his laps at the same time as Caddie. He looked to be a fit seventy-five years old, with silver-gray hair that he combed straight back. His skin was deeply tanned, and his lean, muscular frame bespoke a lifetime of regular exercise. He'd swim laps for half an hour, then sit by the pool for a breakfast of fresh fruit and coffee while he read the *Wall Street Journal*. Unlike most men, who when afforded the opportunity of seeing Caddie in a bathing suit stared relentlessly at her, this man made his daily salutation to Caddie, then went about his routine as if she weren't there.

One morning after she finished her swim, Caddie was approached by two girls, both armed with cameras, who asked if they could pose with her for a snapshot. Caddie complied, and noticed that the moment the girls pulled cameras from their tote bags, the gray-haired man put down his fork and left the pool area, his breakfast barely touched. When the same thing happened two days later, she asked one of the waiters about the man's identity, but the waiter replied that staff were not allowed to discuss the ranch's guests.

Finally, two days before she was to leave, Caddie performed her morning pool routine, said her perfunctory hello to the gray-haired man, then started for her bungalow.

"Miss Dean?"

She turned. The man stood and approached her.

"I wondered why you hadn't responded to my card," he said.

"Your card?"

"I sent you a note."

"I don't think I got it."

"I see." He turned and returned to his poolside table. "I'm sorry to bother you."

"What was the note?" Caddie asked him.

"Inviting you to dinner."

There were fifteen unopened pieces of mail in Caddie's bungalow. Wherever she went, she was used to receiving requests for autographs, pictures, fan letters, and the like; usually all of it went into a bag which she delivered to her assistant in New York for handling.

"I guess I haven't opened my mail," she said. "It's nice of you to ask, but I'm leaving tomorrow."

"All the more reason to join me for dinner this evening."

Dining with strangers was not something Caddie did. But she was used to traveling with Jon, and she had built up a certain curiosity about this man. Why not? she decided.

"I'm working until eight," she said, "and then I have to attend a cocktail party for my clients. Perhaps after that?"

"I thought it would be nice," the man said, "to dine at my home. I live just five minutes from here. Please bring a chaperon if you like."

"You're not staying at the hotel?"

"No. I just use the pool here."

Thinking she might still change her mind later, Caddie impulsively agreed to the invitation.

"I'll have my driver waiting out front," the man said.

"All right, then," she said. "Since I haven't read your note, I'm afraid I don't know your name."

He seemed mildly surprised that she asked.

"Davis Kellen," he said.

Caddie returned to her room, checked her phone messages, and was surprised to find one from Tommee Barkley, another Cartwright model, who, after Caddie, was the agency's second-biggest earner. Caddie was further surprised to find that the number Tommee had left was from the Kapalua Ritz-Carlton Hotel, also on Maui.

"I check into the hotel for a shoot this week," Tommee told Caddie when Caddie rang her back, "and I get an invitation from Aaron Adam's people for a party here at the Ritz tonight, and the damn party is in honor of Caddie Dean. So I thought I'd just track the damn bitch down."

"Are you coming to the party?" Caddie asked, laughing.

"Damn straight. I'm sick of you getting all the attention. I'm going to be there and shove you off the balcony into the ocean."

"Great. Jon's not with me, and I hate going to parties alone."

"I'll be looking for you."

"Oh," Caddie said, catching Tommee before she hung up. "Have you ever heard of a man named Davis Kellen?"

" 'Course I have, sugar. Haven't you?"

"No."

"Wouldn't know what he looks like, because he's one of those recluse guys."

"I'm supposed to have dinner with him tonight."

"No shit?"

"He's here at the Hanna Ranch. At least, he uses the pool."

"Honey bear, you really don't know who this dude is?"

"No."

"He's the richest man in America," Tommee said.

Aaron Adam, Inc., had taken over a ballroom in the Ritz-Carlton that opened to a terrace overlooking the Pacific Ocean. The reception was for Japanese distributors of Aaron Adam clothes, and the room was packed. Caddie did her best to smile and nod as she was introduced to a ceaseless stream of people, few of whom spoke English. She popped her million-dollar smile with practiced perfection each time the photographers snapped her picture with another guest. Honolulu press had flown in for the event, as well as hundreds of well-to-do locals who were also guests of Aaron Adam.

Suddenly a woman burst through the swarm of photographers and strode into the center of the room. Every head in the place turned. It was Tommee Barkley. While everyone else was casually attired in the tradition of the islands, Tommee wore an Aaron Adam gown, a black layered chiffon cut short into points that displayed Tommee's long, perfect legs. The bodice had laces criss-crossing the breasts, and the back plunged, exposing an elegant sweep of skin. The only jewelry she wore was a pair of silver earrings that fell sparkling to her shoulders. Her thick, black hair was mounded atop her head, a few tendrils cascading down her back. On Tommee, the look was appropriate for a night at the opera or a visit to the world's most exclusive leather bar.

Tommee had done couture ads for Aaron Adam, but her largest contracts were with Revlon and Clairol; she was also the first model to be awarded a contract with Rolex. While Caddie presented a daytime, active look, Tommee was the number-one choice for evening wear and full-on glamour. Her features were large and dramatic—wide-set green eyes, a large mouth with full lips, and hair that every woman prayed for but few got. The camera loved every inch of her, and more than one photographer had called her the world's most beautiful woman.

The flattery and accolades didn't interest Tommee much; she liked money. To her, beauty was a business, an asset to manage. In fact, she often referred to herself in the third person, saying, "Tommee Barkley should be the Chanel girl. The one they've got looks like a milk carton that's been left out in the sun too long." She felt no particular affinity for her name or look, because in her mind it was all a creation for business purposes. Tommee's real name was Eileen Bishop, a name she'd discarded the moment she left the Texas Gulf Coast town where she'd grown up.

As a child, Tommee was a skinny, oversized, gawky girl who wanted to be a singer but had a terrible voice. She had four sisters, all better-looking as teenagers than she, who married the first boys who asked them. Tommee managed to win a local beauty contest when she was seventeen—she later admitted she might have won because she walked in on one of the judges while he was having sex with an underage girl, and the guy was afraid of the consequences if Tommee lost.

Now, Tommee worked through the room, allowing the photographers to get their shots, then she spotted Caddie and beelined for her.

"Do I look like a poofy dyke in this dress?" she asked.

"I think you look spectacular," Caddie said and hugged her. "Everyone just forgot about me."

"Well, I just got through reading about you in *Time* magazine, and I realized something."

"What's that?"

"I'm finished," Tommee said matter-of-factly.

"What?"

"Finished, done, finito, end of story."

"What are you talking about? You're booked every day of the year."

The photographers went nuts photographing the two supermodels while they talked so only they could hear.

"So what? I'm not on the cover of *Time,* and I'm not going to be. I'm playing for second place from here on in, and I hate that. But you did me a favor by making me wake up and smell the coffee."

"Tommee, you've got contracts anyone in the business would kill for. Everybody still wants you. You turn down more work than you take."

"I'm thirty-one years old, Caddie. The party is almost over."

"Cheryl Tiegs is in her forties. She has huge endorsements and her own line of jewelry."

"She's one in a zillion."

"So what are you telling me?"

"That I hate getting old and I'd better damn well figure out my next move. Bank your money, babycakes. We're not vampires. We get old."

"So what's your plan?"

"Maybe I'll get into design," Tommee said. "I know

I could do better than this witch rag I'm wearing. Or maybe I'll just have to get married."

"Are you in love? Who was that you came in with?"

Tommee glanced around. "Oh, he's nobody. Prince Something-or-other from some goddamn country I never heard of. He just sat in his jet staring at my tits the whole way over here from Los Angeles. Plus, he's a drunk. And you'd need a search party to find his pecker."

Caddie laughed. "You're dating him?"

"Hell, no. I just needed a ride. I'm sending him back to wherever his palace is."

A slender, wan-looking man in his late thirties wearing a beautifully cut Armani spotted Tommee and hurried over.

"Darling, I thought I'd lost you," he said, grabbing Tommee's arm.

"Caddie," Tommee said, "this is the prince."

The prince seemed unnerved by Caddie's beauty. "Oh, I know you," he said to Caddie, trembling like a starstruck teenager. "I know you very well."

"See?" Tommee said to Caddie, ignoring the prince. "I'm finished." Then she turned to the prince. "Be a saint and get us some champagne, darling. And see if you can scare me up a pack of Marlboros."

The prince trotted off obediently.

"Jesus," Tommee said, watching him walk away. "I'd swim back to the mainland before I gave this one a tumble. So where the hell is your husband? You know, I never see you since you've been married."

"He had some work to do in Los Angeles."

"Bullshit," Tommee said, looking into Caddie's eyes.

"We had a fight," she admitted.

Tommee threw Caddie a look. "Over what? You ask him to take out the garbage or something?"

Tommee had already been a star when Caddie came on the scene eleven years ago, and of all the big-name

models Caddie had encountered during her beginnings,
Tommee was the one who had treated her most kindly
and with none of the jealousy and fear older models
usually felt toward newcomers. And she was one person from whom total directness never seemed offen-
sive, probably because she was as honest about herself
as she was about others.

"He wants to become more involved in my career.
He's my manager now."

"Manager? What the hell do you need a manager
for? You've got Jessica Cartwright."

"Jon thinks we might be missing opportunities."

"Far be it from that boy to miss an opportunity. Hell,
he married one."

"Tommee—"

"Listen, honey, I know he's your husband, but I like
you better. I could never figure out why you married
him in the first place."

"He made me laugh. He didn't talk about the business. He cared about *me*, not the model bullshit."

"Sounds like he cares about it now."

"I just want to have a family and have things settle
down."

"And what's Jon say about that?"

"He thinks we should wait."

"Hmmm," Tommee said, looking away.

Caddie checked her watch. "Oh my God, I'm supposed to meet that man for dinner. Will you come
with me?"

"This guy scary or something?"

"I just don't want to be alone with him. I don't even
know why I said yes. He seems very polite."

"Polite and rich is a good combination. Hell,
let's go."

Davis Kellen's Maui home was an island fantasy
constructed of exotic woods and walls of glass that

offered views from every room. The white-jacketed domestic staff served Caddie and Tommee an elegant meal of grilled mahimahi and greens grown on the island, and the most exquisite Montrachet they had ever tasted. During dinner Kellen asked Caddie and Tommee about their travels, and he seemed to have a detailed knowledge of every place they mentioned. His manners were Old World, his voice cultured. He asked nothing about fashion or modeling.

"No wonder you're so damned rich," Tommee finally said to Kellen, after he'd completed an intriguing explanation of the world's precious-stone markets. "You're like a wind-up computer."

"Whatever that is," Kellen said dryly. "Let's have our after-dinner drinks on the terrace."

During cocktails and dinner, Kellen had consumed only Perrier, but when the butler appeared on the terrace with a bottle of cognac and three snifters, Kellen poured, toasted his guests, and commenced drinking. Caddie noticed that he went through his snifter in two gulps, then watched while he loaded up another double shot of the Hine Triomphe. It went down warm and smooth, she thought, as it should for five hundred dollars a bottle. Kellen became very quiet. If there had been any purpose in his invitation other than acquaintance, Caddie hadn't noticed what it was, but perhaps her bringing Tommee along had changed her host's plans. In any case, she checked her watch and knew it was time for her to leave.

"I have a seven a.m. call tomorrow," she said. "Cellini has decided he wants some morning shots. So I really should get back to the hotel."

"Come on now, Caddie," Tommee said. "We've been working our little butts off, and we deserve a little kick in the ass. We're just getting started. Davis, maybe if we took the dirge off the tape deck Caddie might get her second wind."

Chamber music played from the external speakers.

"Actually, I really do have to go. I can't fake looking good in a bathing suit if I don't get my sleep."

"Well, that's why she's number one in the world and I ain't," Tommee said to Davis. They both laughed.

"If you'd like to enjoy your cognac here on the terrace with me," Kellen said to Tommee, "I'll have my driver return Miss Dean to her hotel."

"I'm gonna take you up on that, Davis," Tommee said, knocking back a slug of cognac. "It's too damn gorgeous out here to move."

As Caddie said good night, Tommee whispered in her ear, "Who knows, maybe he's got a son."

"What kind of music would you like to hear?" Kellen asked Tommee after Caddie had left.

"You wouldn't have any rock and roll on the premises, would you, Davis?" Tommee said.

He smiled his narrow lipped smile and signaled for the butler, whispered to him, then waited. Moments later the Rolling Stones pounded from the four speakers concealed around the terrace.

"Now I'm in heaven," Tommee said, leaning back in her chair, watching the tide wash over the white sand beach below the terrace, illuminated by powerful lights from the house.

Kellen and Tommee talked about the islands, and Tommee realized that Davis Kellen was downing cognacs like water.

"Aren't you supposed to sip that stuff?" Tommee said to him. He didn't answer. He continued to stare at the waiter with his enigmatic smile. "Maybe it's time for coffee," she said, walking back into the den and looking around for the butler, who had suddenly vanished.

She went to the large double doors that led from the den to the living room. The doors were closed. And locked. Tommee turned to look for Kellen. He was gone. There were no other doors in the study. She walked back to the terrace. Kellen's Baccarat cognac snifter sat upon the wooden railing.

"Jesus fucking football," she said, edging over to the railing and peering down at the sand and rocks below, wondering if he'd fallen.

"Miss Barkley," came his voice, from within the house.

Tommee turned around.

Kellen reappeared as if from nowhere. He had changed clothes. He was wearing Chinese black silk pajamas, black thongs, and a very strange, detached expression on his face.

"Where'd you go?" she said. "And where the hell did you just come from?"

Glancing around the study, she noticed a seam in the wall by the bookshelves, some kind of knobless door.

"Do you think you're Batman or something?" she answered, looking at his outfit.

"I enjoy the sensuality of silk. I'd like you to put this on," he said, and extended to her a white silk dressing gown.

She folded it open, then tossed it on a chair.

"Of all the fine things I appreciate," he continued, "what I appreciate most is beautiful women. But only the most exquisite women. Like yourself. You are extraordinary. Absolutely extraordinary."

"Thanks for the vote, but maybe it's time to call it a night. I don't like the idea of you locking those doors, Davis. And I should point out to you that I'll kick your billionaire ass if I have to."

"I don't think that will be necessary. I'd like to tell you what I appreciate most about beautiful women."

"I can't wait," Tommee said, crossing her arms across her breasts.

"Fragrance."

"Fragrance? You like the way I smell?" she said.

"Scent, fragrance. Not perfume, not something you can purchase. What you were born with, what you are."

"You put on the Chinese outfit and now you're getting all philosophical on me. How about just calling your driver for me? Better yet, I'll do it myself."

She looked around in vain for a telephone.

Kellen pulled a rolling library stepladder to the center of the room.

"I have absolutely no intention of harming you, or even touching you, Miss Barkley."

"Then what's the gig, Davis?"

"I want to smell you."

"What the hell is this smell deal with you?"

"I want you to put on that white gown, stand on these steps, and allow me to smell you. I want to smell you from top to bottom, each part of your body, savor it, the fragrance. I will never touch you, simply savor you through the gown—"

"You are one overcooked bowl of chili, my friend."

He pointed to a small side table by the seamless door. On it sat a stand of red crushed velvet. Placed upon the velvet was a pair of diamond earrings that looked like the beginnings of a chandelier.

"I can buy my own earrings, honey," Tommee said, walking over to the table to examine them. "Well, maybe not," she added, taking a closer look. Tommee knew jewels, and these were worth well over a hundred thousand dollars.

"They're a gift," he said. "Will you stand on my pedestal?"

No one's going to believe this one, she said to herself.

chapter
10

Over a period of several days in June, the customs area of Milan's airport takes on the atmosphere of a party looking for a reason to start. As the 747s from America arrive carrying a fresh crop of models, ranging in age from fifteen to nineteen, there is a large contingent of people awaiting them, some in an official capacity, others attracted by the spectacle of the annual event.

Garret Stowe arrived in Milan and made himself visible at the restaurants and bars where fashion-industry insiders gravitated. He located the top agencies in the city and drew himself a map pinpointing all of them. He wanted to know, simply by observing the movements of a model, who she was doing business with.

At the end of the week, Garret's telephone rang. It was Delph Groleau; he had just arrived from Paris. Delph took Garret around town, and Garret introduced himself as an agent from the Zola Agency in Paris. Many people seemed surprised, since they hadn't heard Zola's name in years. Was she getting busy again? "That's why I'm here," Garret told them. Delph didn't say a word. When it was time for the planes to start arriving, Delph rode with Garret to the airport.

"Now watch," he told Garret, as a 747 from Kennedy unloaded into customs.

Amid the tourists and sober-faced businessmen who wore the pallor of too much international travel were thirty stunning faces. They stood out like roses in a field of weeds. In fact, Garret found that the rest of the people not only looked plain against the models, they were annoying. "It's the disease of our business," Delph told him, sucking on a cigarette. "Average-looking people become invisible to you, and vaguely irritating." The fresh-faced models were, of course, all tall. They had prepared themselves for the landing, with hair brushed into place and faces gently made up. Compared to their fellow travelers they seemed like a separate species.

The girls arriving under the auspices of well-known American agencies were greeted by chaperons and representatives of Italian agencies, as arranged from New York by Cartwright, Ford, or Elite. Girls coming from small agencies in the states had to fend for themselves. Garret watched as groups of young Italian men scanned the girls and seemed to know exactly which girls were being met and which were on their own. And after the luggage was inspected and the models emerged from customs, it was clear to Garret that the watchers were rarely wrong. Handsome men in their late twenties and early thirties casually approached the lost-looking girls, making the encounter seem more accident than an annual ritual, and offered to help with luggage, directions, or choice of a hotel. Some of the girls kept their own counsel and ignored the interlopers, but many were delighted to have help; beautiful girls were used to men coming to their assistance. Conversations were struck up, names and numbers exchanged.

Garret sat with Delph, sipping espresso and watching the scene.

"Another plane arrives in two hours," Delph told

him, "and you will see it all over again. And so on for the next week."

"How many of these girls will make a name for themselves here?" Garret asked him.

"A few dozen will be in demand. Those that are passed over might give Hamburg a try, or Munich. Others will go on to Japan, especially the blondes. But the pictures from the fashion magazines in Japan mean nothing to the American agents. Only the ones from here and Paris. And if a girl is not successful in Milan, it is unlikely she will make it in Paris."

"The ones that just got off this plane," Garret asked, "would you sign any of them?"

"Now, Garret, this is supposed to be a bit of a holiday for me . . . will you always make me work?"

Garret sipped his espresso and waited for an answer. He knew that Delph's protests about being used would quickly evaporate; Garret had learned that Delph's life, for the past twenty-five years, had consisted of the model business and nothing else.

"No," Delph said finally. "As pretty as they are, none of them are . . . it. I don't think I'd tell you, anyway. You're not very affectionate, you know."

"I wouldn't have signed any of them either," Garret said, proud of his own judgment.

They had lunch and waited.

The next contingent was larger than the first. Four planes from different points of origin had arrived in close proximity, so customs was loaded. When the plane from the States carrying the girls disembarked, however, all heads began to turn. How could they not? Forty girls between five-nine and six feet, with swaying manes of hair and the excitement of kids going to camp.

Delph, who chatted incessantly, became suddenly quiet at one point, watching the girls through the glass. His world-weary bearing vanished for a moment, and

Garret watched him focus in on a particular face; Delph watched a tall blond girl who moved with a shyness that somehow underscored her beauty. Her hair was slicked back with gel and she wore wire-rim glasses.

"Remove the glasses," Delph whispered, suddenly unaware of Garret.

The girl reached customs, handed over her passport, then slipped her glasses into her jacket. The eyes were a translucent blue, large and sparkly.

"That is somebody," Delph said, watching the girl.

The customs official, who had done a detailed search of the luggage of the ordinary person who preceded the blond girl, simply waved her through, as if compelled by a higher force not to impede the progress of youth and beauty.

The Italian "escorts" buzzed among themselves as the girl emerged through the security doors. Passersby stopped to have a look. But none of the men approached her, which confused Garret.

Then a handsome Italian woman in her mid-fifties, followed by a uniformed driver, approached the girl.

"Signorina Gates," the woman said to the girl, "I'm Gigi Campone. Welcome to Milan."

"Oh, yes, Mrs. Campone. Please call me Wynn. Jessica Cartwright said you'd send someone to meet me. You didn't have to come yourself."

"Nonsense, my darling," Gigi Campone said, sweeping the girl out of the airport.

"Yes, I thought so," Delph Groleau said to himself, as Gigi and the girl disappeared out the door, followed by the driver, who carried the luggage.

"Who was that woman with her?"

"A very good Italian agent. The girl came from a top New York agency. She did not walk in off the street. Don't waste your time with that one. You will have too much competition. From me, among others."

Garret learned that Gigi Campone was with the Pop Agency. So first thing next morning he took a seat at a café across the street from Pop's offices. Shortly after ten, Wynn Gates arrived at Pop to meet its staff of bookers. From there, Garret picked up her trail: interviews with fashion editors, test shoots with two photographers, then dinner with Gigi Campone and editors from Italian *Vogue*. A similar schedule kept up for three days. On the fourth day of Wynn's visit, the Pop Agency took over the nightclub Tip and hosted a private party for her and other clients. Garret slipped past an overworked assistant who was unsuccessfully trying to manage the guest list.

When Wynn Gates momentarily left the table of her hosts and made her way to the bar, it was the first time in four days that she'd been unescorted. Garret watched her order a glass of white wine and take a few quick puffs on a cigarette, which she obviously was not used to smoking. Several men descended on her simultaneously, asking her to dance. She hit the dance floor and did not leave it for nearly two hours. Garret watched patiently as Wynn danced with various men, with other models, and by herself. And it seemed clear to him she did so more to avoid sitting at the table with the bookers and agents than to enjoy herself. A steady stream of male models and Italian men cruised her, but from the expressions on their faces as they were sent into retreat, Garret assumed Wynn was not interested.

He waited until she finished dancing. She sat, perspiring through her white silk blouse, with a group of other models. Men continued to press at her. Garret went into the rest room and tipped the attendant to give him a washcloth. He then went behind the bar and soaked the cloth in ice water, neatly folded it into a long strip, then boldly walked up behind Wynn and gently laid the towel around her neck.

Startled, she leaned forward and turned around.

Garret walked away. She opened the cloth, pressed it against her face, then wrapped it again around her neck.

Garret felt her eyes upon him as he took a seat at the bar, downed a glass of water, and started for the door.

Wynn Gates jumped up from her chair and caught him at the door.

"You weren't even going to say hello," she said, with a flat Chicago accent.

"I was just leaving," he said.

She stared at him, intrigued.

"But the towel," she said. "I don't understand."

"You looked rather warm."

"I was absolutely suffering," she said.

"Then I was right," he said pleasantly, then walked out the door.

He knew she was still watching him, but he did not turn around.

The next day, as Wynn Gates jogged past the newsstand outside the Galleria, Garret Stowe stood conspicuously at the end of the stand, reading a magazine. Wynn thought it to be a happy coincidence. Never would it have occurred to her that Garret had followed her for three days and learned her jogging route.

When she spotted Garret, Wynn went to a drinking fountain, soaked the towel she wore draped around her neck, and slipped up behind him. She dropped it over his head, then stood back for the reaction. Garret did not disappoint her. He spun around, angry at first, then with a look of pleasant surprise.

"You're standing in the sun," Wynn Gates said. "I thought you must be very warm."

He smiled at her, and why not? Six feet tall, slender but with beautiful curves, a face you could not look away from, and the essence of youthful exuberance that cannot be feigned or summoned.

"Every time I see you," Garret said, "you are sweating."

Wynn blushed, suddenly wanting to look pretty.

"I can look better."

"I think you look marvelous right now. Do you mean they actually give you time off to exercise?"

This was a sore spot with her, as he had anticipated.

"Last night was the first minute I've had to myself since I got here. I thought I'd get to see a little bit of Italy. No such luck."

"I'll tell you what," Garret said. "Here's my number. Call me if you have a minute and we'll see Italy."

Wynn called Garret that night at ten o'clock. He pretended to be on his way out the door. She had an hour free right then, she told him, but he declined, telling her he had a late dinner appointment. He heard the disappointment in her voice. But what about tomorrow? She had two hours in the afternoon.

Garret rented a car and took her out to the medieval village of Santa Croce, where they had an alfresco lunch of fresh bread, prosciutto, tomatoes, and mozzarella. They walked in the vineyards near the village and listened to the chimes of the church, signaling three o'clock and time to go.

For the next several days, Wynn spent all her spare time with Garret. Gigi Campone, of course, had never heard of Garret. He looked like just another of the Italian men who reveled in the model weeks of Milan. And since Wynn reported to her that Garret was an absolute gentleman with impeccable manners who refused to put his hands on her, Gigi was not alarmed. Besides, the beautiful Miss Gates was happy, and this was not a state of mind Gigi saw fit to interrupt; after all, Wynn Gates was the hit of the season in Milan.

When Wynn called Garret on the ninth day of her visit to tell him she was going to have a full day off, he told her to be ready at eight and to bring a casual change of clothes as well as something elegant. On the appointed day, Garret drove an excited Wynn directly to the airport, where they caught a plane to Paris. She was ecstatic. They had a picnic lunch on a *bateau mouche,* a walk through the Louvre, then drinks at a café with a view of the Arc de Triomphe.

"I want you to see where I work," he told her, and they walked to the offices of Marie Zola. Marie was in the lobby when Garret walked in with Wynn Gates.

"I want you to meet Miss Wynn Gates from America," Garret said to Marie Zola. "She is going to be our new star."

Marie was speechless. Before she had a chance to contradict Garret, she took a good look at Wynn and knew this was the kind of model her agency hadn't seen in years. Such a model from America would most definitely sign with Paris Models, Flip, or Fashion Faces. "Who are you with in America?" Marie asked.

"Jessica Cartwright," Wynn said, somewhat confused about what was happening.

"And in Milan she is with Pop," Garret said. "She has never been to Paris, and I thought I might help her out by bringing her to us."

From his shoulder bag Garret produced a folder with several of her photographs in it.

"We're off now," he said, leading Wynn out as quickly as they'd come in.

That night he took Wynn to La Tour d'Argent, with its spectacular view of the illuminated Notre Dame. And after dinner they boarded a plane back to Milan.

When Wynn asked about the business at the Zola Agency, Garret explained that Marie Zola would simply do some public relations on Wynn's behalf, so that if Wynn did come to Paris in the future, her name would already be established there.

"Should I ask Miss Cartwright about that?"

"She'd only get mad at me. You know how agents are. All I was doing in taking you by the office was trying to prove to Marie Zola that I've been working. You see, I was supposed to be back in Paris five days ago, but I've stayed in Milan following my heart instead of my head."

Still suspended in the love mist of Paris, Wynn looked at Garret's shy smile and thanked him for the single most wonderful day of her life.

That night when they returned to Milan, Wynn asked Garret into her apartment, and this time when he kissed her he didn't stop. The apartment's living room looked out over an older section of the city, and the tile rooftops seemed to undulate in the moonlight that shifted as clouds floated across the sky. Garret kissed Wynn very gently and for a long time, brushing his lips over her ears and down her neck. She reached to embrace him, but he held her arms away, slowly kissing her fingers and the undersides of her wrists.

Wynn's body trembled. She had been with boys before, but never a man, and the boys knew nothing of women when compared to Garret. Her experience with sex had been a few quick, awkward wrestling matches, and here was a man lacing her body with kisses so soft they made her crave more. He ran his fingers over the firm, perfect lines of her body, tracing a swirling outline inside her thighs, brushing against her panties with gentle evasion. Wynn felt as if she were going to explode, but each time she reached for him he held her off and continued to kiss and stroke her until she thought her knees were going to buckle. The clothes fell off her body and she didn't know if Garret was removing them or if she was doing it herself; they just seemed to peel away and float to the floor. It was a warm summer evening, and the soft breeze washed lightly across her skin. As he knelt to kiss her stomach, then moved lower to tug at the band of her panties, Wynn felt her breath come in gasps.

"I can't stand up any longer," she whispered, "I can't stand up."

He picked her up and took her to the bedroom.

When at last he entered her, she pulled him deeper and urged him to move faster, but he held back, working into a languid, steady rhythm. Wynn found herself rising on a wave of pleasure so intense she cried out and let it continue to rock her, over and over. When she finally calmed, Garret held her close and began to move again, slowly, sliding in and out of her, and he held her head in his hands, looked into her eyes, and said, "This is never going to stop."

And she held him as hard as she could.

The next morning, while Wynn slept, Garret telephoned Marie Zola from the living room of the apartment and asked if he had a job. "If you deliver that girl to the agency," she told him, "then yes you do."

"She's already delivered."

There was a skeptical silence from Marie's end of the line.

Marie Zola had heard of Wynn Gates prior to Garret's toting her into the office. Friends of Marie's had been back and forth to Milan in the past weeks checking out the new models, and had reported that everyone was talking about the American girl Wynn Gates. Marie Zola decided she did not want to know how Garret had orchestrated this coup, but the opportunity was not to be wasted.

"What is it that you want to do?" she finally asked him.

Garret left a note for Wynn saying that he had business to take care of but would meet her for dinner. Then he flew to Paris and took a cab to the offices of Marie Zola. The receptionist informed Garret that Miss

Zola was tied up with a conference call, so Garret walked past her and stood in the doorway of Marie's office. She put her telephone call on hold.

"Get her picture with your agency logo on it into circulation immediately," Garret said.

"I sent it to the printers, but we can't distribute it until we have a contract. I'll place a call to Jessica Cartwright." She looked at the clock. "But New York isn't open yet."

"I'm handling the contract and the Cartwright Agency," Garret said, thinking fast. "It's my deal, isn't it?"

"But is Wynn Gates even going to be available to work here in Paris? If Cartwright just sent her to Milan, they'll be booking her for the summer and fall in New York."

"Why are you creating problems?" Garret said.

"I'm discussing business," she replied.

"And I'm saving your future. Call the printer and get the pictures done. I'll be back."

And he roared out of the office before Marie could get another word in.

Garret went to a pay phone, called Delph Groleau at Paris Models, and invited him to lunch.

"I'm surprised you haven't called to congratulate me," Garret said to Delph, finding him at his usual table in Tornado.

"You've never given me your number," Delph said. "That's first. Second, for what am I to congratulate you?"

"For signing Wynn Gates, the American girl."

Delph looked slyly at Garret, waiting for the punch line.

Garret stared him down.

Finally, Delph said, "Signed Wynn Gates to what?"

"To the Zola Agency, where I am now a partner, for representation in Paris."

Delph laughed. "She's at the top of the class in Milan this year, no doubt. So much so that we've already spoken to Jessica Cartwright about her. And Miss Cartwright said nothing about Wynn Gates signing with an agent in Paris."

"It's done."

"If what you are telling me is true," Delph said to Garret, "then I should send flowers to Marie Zola. She's back in business." He took a sip of wine. "And I thought you were just . . . cute."

Garret picked up Wynn Gates's Sed card—a double-sided card of a model's photos and physical statistics—directly from the printer. The card had a full close-up of the model on one side, and smaller photos of her in bathing suit and casual wear on the flip side. At the bottom was her name and agency information; it served as a business card. Marie Zola had given Garret a list of the major advertising agencies and photographers in Paris, and by the end of business that day he had personally delivered Wynn's composite to all of them. Rather than leave the card with a secretary, Garret insisted on handing it to the person whose name was on Zola's list, introducing himself as Wynn Gates's booker and Zola's new partner.

Since there was already a buzz about Wynn Gates in Paris, the pictures set off a feeding frenzy. Seven important photographers called Zola telling her they wanted a shoot with Wynn Gates. Calls for "go sees"—personal interviews with the new model—came in to Zola at the rate of twenty an hour. Garret told them all, "We're not positive when Wynn will be back in Paris. Sometime within the next two weeks. We'll call."

Bookers at other agencies burned up phone lines trying to figure out how the hell Marie Zola had landed this season's hottest model out of Milan.

And Marie Zola, as confused as she was about the

entire matter, did not waste the opportunity to get some of her other girls out while the town's spotlight was focused on her. The flurry of phone calls went on for a week before word filtered back to America, to the Cartwright Agency, that Wynn Gates had signed in Paris with the Zola Agency.

But as soon as she heard, Jessica placed a call to Marie Zola. When she first started out as an agent, Jessica had sent some clients to Zola, though none in the last ten years. She liked Marie and couldn't believe she would sign a Cartwright model without so much as a call to New York. Garret was in the office when Jessica's call came in. He signaled Marie not to take it.

"But I have to," Marie said. "She's Wynn's agent."

"Not in Paris she isn't," Garret said. "We'll call her back."

Marie waved off the call, then turned to Garret. "We do actually have the girl, don't we?"

"Of course we have the girl. But we will not let Cartwright tell us how to market her, will we?"

"It's an industry practice to consult with the original agency. If we want to get clients from them, we have to cooperate."

"How many clients from the Cartwright Agency have you signed in the last five years?" Garret asked.

"None."

"Ten years?"

"None."

"Then we'll call her back when we are good and ready to."

"I don't do business that way," Marie said.

"You weren't doing business at all until Wynn Gates walked in the door," Garret replied.

The comment stung Marie, but then she listened to the sound she hadn't heard in years, the incessant ringing of the bookers' lines, and she knew that Garret was right.

Jessica called back the next day. This time Garret wasn't in the office, so Marie Zola took the call.

"What is this I hear about Wynn Gates?" Jessica asked.

"She's decided to sign with us—we're all very excited," Marie said. "Now we just need her availability, because we have dozens and dozens of offers."

Jessica nearly jumped through the phone, informing Marie that no one, including Wynn Gates, had spoken to her about signing with any agencies in Paris, and that Jessica intended to hold off on further European bookings because Wynn was on the verge of becoming a star in the States.

"But she signed with my booker," Marie said defensively. "She came to the office. I met her. And my booker said he spoke with you about it."

"This is ridiculous," Jessica barked into the phone.

By the time Garret arrived at the office, Marie was shaken and confused. She reported to him that Jessica insisted Garret had never spoken to her about Wynn Gates.

"She screwed up," Garret said, "and she's trying to cover her tracks."

"But do we have the contract?" Marie asked.

"What does it matter? We have the girl," Garret snapped, exhausted from his daily commute to and from Milan. He spent his nights with Wynn Gates, sweeping her away from the eyes of Gigi Campone. Since Wynn was a budding star, Gigi knew better than to order her around. Garret took her to quiet restaurants, then to private clubs and back to the apartment, where he made love to her with practiced patience, and all the skill he instinctively possessed. Wynn had no time to return Jessica's calls or Gigi's. She simply went to her bookings, then turned herself over to Garret's exciting company.

Five days into Zola's representation of Wynn Gates,

everyone in the Parisian model world knew about it, though many still doubted it was true. But in the fashion industry, appearance is 90 percent of reality. Models began showing up for open calls at the Zola office. For the past five years, Zola would see about a dozen girls a week, as opposed to the two hundred seen by the thriving agencies. And by the time Zola saw those dozen girls, they'd been turned down by every agency in town. Now a dozen models a day were turning up at Zola in search of representation. People in the model hangouts approached Garret and introduced themselves. He gave them his new Zola business cards and invited the beautiful ones to come by the agency's offices. Marie Zola had to hire a second receptionist to handle the sudden volume of phone calls and walk-ins.

Garret continued his Milan-to-Paris commute. Then one morning, as he dressed to leave Wynn's apartment, Garret listened as Wynn took a call from the concierge.

"Oh," Wynn said, checking her watch, "tell her I'll be down in ten minutes."

Garret walked back into the bedroom.

"Can you stay for breakfast?" Wynn asked.

"I have to catch a plane, my darling," Garret said. "You know that."

"But this is business, too. I forgot to tell you. I got a message from my agent in New York. She's in Milan. I'm supposed to have breakfast with her."

"Jessica Cartwright is in Milan?"

"Yes."

"Very good," Garret said, turning his back and walking slowly to the bathroom. "You didn't tell me she was coming. I would have arranged something for her."

"I didn't know she was coming until last night. I got a message. Actually, I got a lot of messages, but I've been a bad girl and haven't been returning calls." She giggled, prancing behind Garret into the bathroom, and wrapped her arms around him. "I've been too busy. But this is perfect. We can have breakfast with Jessica and talk about working in Paris. Maybe I can get a job to keep me there all summer."

"Yes," Garret said, closing his shirt. "But if I'm not on my plane there will be hell to pay in Paris. I have two dozen meetings."

"Then we'll have dinner with Jessica tonight."

"That's better," Garret said. "And now I've got to hurry." He kissed her and was out the door.

chapter
11

"Isn't he gorgeous?" Wynn Gates asked Jessica Cartwright as she stepped out of the elevator into the building's lobby, ten minutes after Garret left.

Jessica waited in the lobby with Gigi Campone, Wynn's agent in Italy.

"Who is that, Wynn?" Jessica asked.

"Garret."

Jessica's attention sharpened. That was the name that had been popping up in Jessica's New York office. She had never heard of Garret Stowe, nor had anyone in the office. Garret had instructed the new receptionist in Zola's office to give all messages for Marie from the Cartwright Agency to him, so Marie Zola had not returned any of Jessica's calls.

"I haven't met Garret," Jessica said to Wynn, "though I plan to."

Wynn was dumbfounded. "But he just left here. Didn't he mention dinner tonight?"

"He's staying here?"

She nodded coyly.

Jessica looked at Gigi Campone. The two of them

had worked with enough models over the years to make an explanation of the situation unnecessary.

"Wynn," Jessica said, "did he ask you to sign any papers?"

"No. He just introduced me to a few people in Paris. We're all having dinner tonight, I thought."

"Perhaps," Jessica said. "Right now, let's go have some breakfast."

By the time the women walked out of the building, Garret's taxi was halfway to the airport. He had taken the elevator to the basement, then navigated an emergency exit to the building's service entrance.

Once at the airport, Garret called Delph Groleau in Paris and asked him to lunch.

"I thought I might be hearing from you," Delph said.

"Why is that?"

"Because the Cartwright Agency called us to announce Jessica's arrival in Milan today, and said she'd be in Paris shortly. I assume she came over to find out what was happening with her girl Wynn Gates."

"I'll see you at lunch," Garret said.

They met at Sonne on the Left Bank. Delph languidly puffed his Gauloise and looked with amusement at Garret.

"You've been a very naughty boy, Garret," Delph said, a trace of envy in his tone. "When Jessica gets to Paris, she'll be making a deal with me to represent Wynn Gates. You never had her at all."

"It's just a misunderstanding," Garret said.

"Please," Delph said, "don't say that. Let me at least admire you for what you've done. People are talking about Zola again, which is a miracle. But she can as quickly become a laughingstock again ... and this time a dishonest laughingstock, thanks to you."

"I need to find another girl," Garret said, looking Delph directly in the eyes.

"Can't you at least spend some of your artifice

romancing me?" Delph said. "Instead of being so blunt. Why should I help you?"

"Because of him," Garret said, looking over Delph's shoulder.

There was a beautiful blond twenty-year-old boy sitting alone at a table nearby. He smoked and read the newspaper, seemingly unaware of Garret's and Delph's attention.

"He's brand-new in town," Garret said. "He came to the office looking to be a model. I might be able to find him something here and there. Not enough to make a living, though. He knows no one in Paris. I told him I might be able to find him a place to stay for a while. You have extra rooms in your townhouse, don't you, Delph?"

"Yes."

"Of course you do. Shall I give him your address?"

"I suppose that would be all right," Delph said slowly. "And what is it, exactly, that you would like me to do for you?"

"When Jessica Cartwright gets to Paris, keep her away from me and Zola. Keep her busy. Tell her to forget about the Wynn Gates incident and remind her how much money you are going to make for her with Miss Gates. I don't want her running all over Paris bad-mouthing Zola."

"I'm sure I'll have plenty of business to conduct with Miss Cartwright," Delph said.

"And I need a girl for the agency," Garret said.

"That you'll have to find for yourself. Star models are not something I give away. You won't be able to land an American girl, because agents in New York will be angry at Marie Zola. You are going to have to do some work, my friend." Delph reached into his jacket and pulled out a rolled-up copy of *Femme Nouvelle,* a fashion weekly. He opened to a column called

"Street" that had several photographs from local clubs and street scenes. "Do you read this?"

"No."

"Do. It is one of my secrets. The magazine is not too popular, but this column, this photographer, finds some excellent girls, interesting scenes. They are ahead of the curve, as the Americans say. It will sharpen your eye. Now, I show you this magazine at this particular moment for another reason." He pointed to another table. "See the girl with the dark hair and the white skirt?"

Garret spotted her, a small girl, but with perfect form and absolutely beautiful pale skin. She looked vaguely familiar to Garret; he was good with faces and rarely forgot one that potentially had significance for him.

"She writes this column," Delph said.

Garret nodded, then glanced at the byline on the column. It read simply "Nicole."

"Get to know her and you might stumble on a new girl. It's her territory."

"Can you introduce me?"

"No. I'd rather stay out of that one, my friend. Remember, I've watched you with women. Nicole has cocktails at Parrot after work. I'm sure that's all you need to know."

Jessica expected to see, and did, the disappointment on Wynn Gates's face when Garret left a message saying that he could not make it back to Milan for a few days. It was obvious to Jessica that Garret had dated Wynn only to get her into the doors of the Zola Agency. In addition to being a client, Wynn was a seventeen-year-old kid, and Jessica was determined to protect her. She arranged for Wynn to have a two-week shoot in Germany, making her not available even if Garret did happen to call.

That done, Jessica was off to Paris to make arrangements with Delph Groleau of Paris Models to handle

Wynn there. She immediately asked Delph about Garret Stowe.

"Who knows who he is?" Delph said, tossing away Jessica's concern. "Some young promoter, I suppose, who doesn't really understand our protocol."

Jessica was not that easily calmed.

"Marie Zola knows better," she said. "And she wasn't returning my calls."

"Marie can hardly dial her own phone anymore," Delph said. "We will do a wonderful job with Wynn Gates here in France. You know that. No harm has been done, has there?"

"Marie Zola tried signing my client without even discussing it with me," Jessica said. "I'm going to see her about it."

Half an hour later, Jessica climbed out of the cab that brought her to the Zola offices. Still jet-lagged from the sudden trip to Europe, and irritated by having had to make the journey at all, she paid the driver and took a moment to gather herself. Her staff in New York had been surprised when Jessica decided to fly to Italy to handle the Wynn Gates situation herself.

"Let Gigi Campone take care of it," Sascha Benning told Jessica.

"She's already supposed to be taking care of it, and she's not," Jessica replied, then left for the airport.

Twelve years of building the agency had taught her that in every company's history there were certain key moments. She had struggled to keep the business going all those years, having operated first out of her apartment, with one assistant and an answering service, then out of cramped offices in Greenwich Village. Jessica had been late with her office and apartment rent more than once in order to ensure that the models received their checks on time. And numerous times she thought she'd be closing her doors the next day, but then a check arrived, or a friend came around with a loan, or a model landed a major booking that Jessica dangled in front of her banker to buy a few more days.

During that time her marriage to a struggling actor cratered because of Jessica's long hours of work and his equally long hours of drinking. But the business survived. Now along came *Time* with Caddie on the cover and the business was flourishing. It felt good. But then Jon Ross had begun tinkering with Caddie's business decisions, and now someone was trying to manipulate her hottest new client. And the moment Jessica realized Marie Zola was not returning her calls for a reason, she flashed on every time in the past twelve years that she'd nurtured a model to the brink of stardom just to have one of the larger agencies lure the model away. If anyone in New York or Europe thought Jessica was going to go soft with success, she wanted to dispel the notion immediately.

She pushed open the Zola Agency's door and confronted a harried receptionist.

"Jessica Cartwright to see Marie."

As the receptionist buzzed Marie's office, Jessica took in the surroundings. Despite the recent flurry of business, Marie hadn't the time or money to renovate the place. The walls needed painting, the furniture was tattered and tacky; it was altogether a dreary atmosphere.

Then Marie Zola edged sheepishly toward the anteroom where Jessica stood, and when Jessica caught a glimpse of her it was all she could do to keep her jaw from dropping. It had been ten years since Jessica had actually seen Marie Zola. She had done some business with her during the first years of the Cartwright Agency's existence, but as Jessica's fortunes went on the incline during the past decade, Marie's had steadily declined, so there was no reason for contact.

Jessica had expected to see the same woman she remembered from their last meeting, but those ten years had been hard on Marie. She was nearly sixty now, her facial skin sagged, and her frame seemed stooped and more frail than Jessica remembered. It was always tough on female agents to watch themselves age, because the girls around never seemed to. New models arrived at agencies every year, fresh-faced and sixteen years old. The only constant was the agent. It took a psychological toll on most of the women in the business, but success kept them from dwelling on it. In decline, however, Jessica knew, women in the business tended to feel twice as old as other women their age. Seeing Marie stunned Jessica. When Jessica made her first trip to Paris, Marie Zola had been the top agent in Paris, lunching at the best restaurants, hosting cocktail parties at her fashionable Ile St. Louis apartment, worshiped by famous designers and advertising executives. Could this be the same woman? Jessica realized she was staring, and as she did, the anger she had built up over the Wynn Gates matter deflated within her.

"We'll be moving to new offices soon," Marie said to Jessica, "so you'll have to excuse the place."

The photos on the walls were of girls long past their success. None of them was even modeling anymore.

"Hello, Marie," Jessica said quietly, almost contritely.

"Congratulations on Caddie Dean," Marie said. "I'm sorry about this mix-up with the Gates girl. I have some new people here, and they haven't learned all the rules. But business is really picking up." She smiled sadly.

Several young would-be models breezed into the office carrying their portfolios. They brushed past Marie Zola and looked for younger faces, those of the bookers. These models had no idea who Marie Zola was; they'd only heard that this agency was suddenly a place to be.

Marie appeared to be confused by the sudden activity in the office and didn't seem bothered by the models' rude behavior.

"Business is picking right up," Marie said again.

"I'm glad for you," Jessica said, then made up an excuse to leave. "I just stopped by for a quick hello."

Garret dug out a year's worth of *Femme Nouvelle* at the Zola offices and read each of Nicole's "Street" columns. Then he parked himself at Parrot and waited for Nicole to turn up. As Delph had predicted, she did. Garret introduced himself and casually dropped references to items mentioned in Nicole's column, commenting on the striking photographs that accompanied the columns. Nicole credited the photographs to a young man called Jamm, who walked the boulevards with his camera and canvassed the club scene to capture the latest street looks.

"I've heard that Zola is back in the game," Nicole said to Garret. "Maybe you've got an item for me?"

As they chatted, Nicole spotted someone entering the bistro and signaled him to come over.

"We were just praising you," she said to the man. "Garret, meet my photographer."

Jamm was thirty, six feet four inches tall, but weighed no more than 150 pounds. He never removed his Ray-Ban Wayfarers; his thin black eyebrows shot up at odd angles from the corners of the glasses. If Jamm had been more ambitious, he would have been a top fashion photographer, since his work for Nicole's "Street" column constantly attracted the attention of advertising executives. His ability to catch new looks on the young was legendary, and more than once kids he'd photographed on the street had been tracked down by model agencies.

As Jamm ordered drinks, Nicole whispered to Garret that Jamm spent his afternoons and nights roaming the streets, clubs, and cafés with his camera; often he

didn't sleep for days on end, then would drop out of
sight for a couple of days while he recovered. He cared
little for money or fame; Jamm liked to take pictures,
to roam and party and get high when the mood struck
him. Jamm knocked back a grappa, then announced he
was on his way to the student quarter for a look-see. He
invited Garret to come along. Garret swiftly accepted,
and said his goodbyes to Nicole.

As they walked, Garret considered offering Jamm a
cash reward if he could discover a model for him. But
the more they talked, the more Garret realized that
Nicole was right, Jamm didn't give a damn about
money. Garret kept Jamm talking until he learned what
Jamm did have a passion for . . . Jimi Hendrix. Indeed,
Jamm thought Hendrix should be enshrined on Olym-
pus. As far as Jamm was concerned, all the music released in the world following the death of Jimi Hendrix
was valueless.

Next morning, Jamm found a brown package in his
letter box, a cassette of an extremely rare Hendrix
bootleg tape recorded in London's Albert Hall. Later
that day, walking through the student quarter, Jamm
spotted Garret sitting at a café reading a newspaper. He
thanked him effusively for the tape and asked him to
come along on the day's journey.

By the end of the day, Jamm had gone through ten
rolls of film. He and Garret stayed up drinking tequila
and watching the proofs of the day's work come out of
the processing equipment. It was four in the morning
and very dark in Jamm's disheveled apartment, but
Jamm sat there smoking a joint, wearing his Wayfarers, and studying the proofs, listening to the Hendrix
bootleg.

"Yeah, yeah, that's what I thought, that's exactly
what I thought," Jamm said, shaking his head, looking at one of the proof sheets through a loupe. He
pointed to a few of the frames. "That girl right there,

she's something. And this one, too, not bad, not bad at all."

The next morning Garret was waiting outside the student-quarter café where the girl in question worked. He presented his card and asked if she would come by the office. She was flattered and said she would come after lunch.

Marie Zola and her bookers thought the girl was slightly bizarre-looking for steady work, but Garret prevailed.

In a few days the newest edition of *Femme Nouvelle* hit the streets. Jamm's discovery grabbed the attention of model agents all over the city. But the girl had to tell them she'd just been signed by Marie Zola. Everyone in town by now knew Zola did not have Wynn Gates. It didn't matter. Zola had a new girl, and she was back in business.

Garret dashed off a thank-you note to Nicole for the introduction to Jamm and called the magazine to check on her last name.

Her last name was Rochas.

And upon hearing the name he finally placed Nicole's face. He had seen it in a photograph in Giselle Rochas's country home. She was Giselle's niece.

For the next several months, Garret Stowe worked seven days a week. He stayed at the agency late every night, talking to the bookkeeper, learning how the agency ran. Another placement of a girl, courtesy of Jamm, in the "Street" column meant another model signing for Garret. After that, the quality of models coming to the agency steadily improved.

Garret did not work as a booker, since he did not have the patience to listen to the models talk about broken nails and missed cabs. Nor did he apply for his agent's license. But he introduced himself as Marie Zola's partner, and though she looked stunned when this fact was reported back to her, she did not dispute it. How could she? She was making money again.

And Garret, Marie found, was not greedy. He never asked about salary, commission, or expenses. In fact, for the first month she made him nothing. He didn't ask, she didn't discuss it. Finally, she took him aside and said it was time to discuss finances. But he refused, telling Marie that he didn't know enough about the business yet, that when the business started making a significant profit again, then they would talk. When Marie casually mentioned this fact at lunch to the lawyer who handled her agency, he became nervous and advised her to immediately define her relationship with Garret. But she did not want to offend Garret by offering him too little, and in truth most of the money coming in was being used to pay off the debt incurred in the last two unproductive years.

Marie was unaware that Garret had become very friendly with her bookkeeper, a young woman who lived a quiet life in the company of five cats. That Garret had taken this bookkeeper on two weekends to Provence would never have occurred to Marie Zola.

At the end of six months, Zola was amazed to find her business turning a profit again. Her model roster had increased from seventy to 150. Still, they did not have a star, a fact that did not bother Marie; being in the black was all that mattered to her at this point in her life. With the business turned around, she planned a surprise party for Garret. He learned of it from the bookkeeper, took Marie aside, and informed her there would be no party, no surprises; surprises were something he hated more than anything else in life, he told her. What he wanted to do, he explained to her, was go to America and bring major models into the Zola Agency. That was not his job, Marie countered. Dealing with the other agencies, especially in the wake of the matter with Wynn Gates, should be left to her, the owner of the agency.

Garret patiently said that going to America was not a request. It was something he planned to do. He would pay for it out of his own pocket. Before Marie could argue further, Garret was on his way out the door.

"I'll call you from New York," he said.

part

TWO

chapter
12

The maître d' at Bilbouquet in Manhattan, approached by a young couple inquiring after a table, politely asked for their name.

"We don't have a reservation," the man said.

"We're fully booked," he said to the couple, rather shocked that the couple would even ask.

"We don't mind waiting at the bar," the man replied helpfully. "What time might a table open up?"

"June," the maître d' replied, honestly.

This being late April, the couple did not feel encouraged. They peered into the restaurant. It was packed, noisy, and vibrating with the hum of success, beauty, and the collective sense of knowing one was in the right place. The largest group in the room, a party of ten, occupied three tables that had been pushed together. There were several empty seats at their table, and the group seemed to be at the coffee phase of their meal.

"Aren't those people finishing?" the man said. "Is it possible that—"

"That's Mr. Cellini's table," the maître d' replied. "He prefers to keep it for the evening."

The couple stared at Anton Cellini and his guests.

Seated with him were four of the most beautiful women in the world, and one of the most breathtakingly handsome men the couple had ever seen. A trio of young people came breezing into Bilbouquet, floated past the couple and the maître d', and alighted at Cellini's table. A waiter was instantly there, and they ordered martinis and French fries. Cellini, a short, round man with a stringy black bread and long, thinning black hair that flew in every direction, sat at the head of the table and orchestrated the conversations. His hands never stopped moving, waving, punctuating his own words and those of others, as if he were conducting a symphony.

"He's the photographer, isn't he?" the man waiting said.

The maître d' nodded.

"I have one of his books."

The maître d' lost patience with the exchange and slipped away, leaving the couple standing in the small entryway looking as if they'd showed up at the wrong wedding.

Anton Cellini noticed them and waved them over. The man and woman glanced at each other. Cellini waved again, and the couple approached him.

"They screw up your reservation?" Cellini asked brightly.

"Well . . ." The man wasn't sure what to say.

"So sit down and join us," Cellini said, pointing to two of the empty chairs, "and order some food. But before you tell us who you are, order a martini."

Cellini seemed delighted with the addition of a new couple and began interrogating them. Tom and Barbara were antique dealers who spent their time traveling through America, Europe, and South America looking for goods. Cellini was fascinated. Pitchers of martinis were served. Other guests came and went—mostly models and people who worked behind the scenes of the fashion industry. And most everyone was young. The talk tended to be gossipy: what certain models were getting paid, what big jobs were coming up, which fashion houses were selling clothes and which weren't, which advertising agencies were gaining accounts and which were losing them. Tom and Barbara felt important when Cellini asked them about advertisements they remembered, images that stuck in their mind.

By one in the morning, everyone was fairly drunk, except for Cellini. He drank from a martini glass, with a glass pitcher kept filled and within his reach. But his pitcher contained Evian water. And when Barbara and Tom said their goodbyes, thanked Cellini profusely, and dragged themselves to a cab, Cellini was still going strong.

Barbara and Tom later learned, from a profile in the *New York Times Sunday Magazine,* that Cellini held court in Bilbouquet three or four nights a week. He had emerged from the ranks of well-known fashion photographers to become a genuine celebrity. His work was displayed in the Museum of Modern Art, and trendy New Yorkers made certain Cellini's book was found on their coffee tables. Cellini photographed all Aaron Adam collections and campaigns, and it was well known within the industry that his opinions held sway with Aaron Adam. He could launch a model toward superstardom or, if in his words he didn't "feel the magic" with a model, he could have her dropped from a major account. Lately he had directed music videos for a few of the top rock-and-roll divas, and Hollywood studios had begun sending him scripts. But he enjoyed the power of his position as the preeminent photographer in the fashion industry. He was well known in the hottest model bars and restaurants around town.

Proprietors begged for Cellini's patronage, because wherever he went, star models followed. His entourage of models, stylists, bookers, and artists constantly changed. And though to many the large entourage seemed a mere vanity on Cellini's part, to him it was business. Despite his star stature and blustery personality, he knew that prominence in the fashion world could vanish as quickly as a hairstyle. The business's craving for *new* was constant and implacable, and the perception of a photographer as old-fashioned or establishment was fatal. The entourage was a calculated strategy on Cellini's part to keep track of trends. If someone was about to get hot, Cellini wanted to know about it before anyone else. The kiss of death in the fashion industry was the whispered claim that a photographer had lost his edge. It was Cellini's biggest fear, and the task of honing his edge he considered to be a twenty-four-hour-a-day job.

It was into Cellini's floating circle that Garret Stowe, shortly after his arrival in New York, made certain he was invited. First, Garret staked out the city's model bars, made friends with the girls and boys who were struggling to gain acceptance, the kids who partied all night, spent two hours in the gym each day, and followed their pagers to whatever interviews they could get. These lower-echelon models moved him into circles where bigger fish swam: the models represented by Cartwright and Ford and Elite. He managed an invitation to one of Aaron Adam's parties, and later happened to turn up at a couple of the clubs he knew Cellini frequented.

The night that Tom and Barbara had been invited to join Cellini's salon, Garret showed up at Bilbouquet around two o'clock. Generally, as the night grew later, Cellini's crowd tended to be male and gay. Cellini's sexuality, always a subject of gossip in the industry, was part of his self-created mystery. Male models claimed to have slept with him, female models the same. But he had declared himself celibate in the age of AIDS, and in the interest of retaining his creative power. Appearing on the David Letterman show, Cellini had stirred up a flurry of press coverage when he announced that he practiced an Eastern discipline that involved semen retention. The belief was that the stored testosterone increased one's creative drive.

When Garret strolled into Bilbouquet, Cellini waved him over.

"You're the one who put Zola back in business in Paris, aren't you?" Cellini said to Garret.

Garret nodded cautiously, wondering if the Wynn Gates story had traveled all the way across the Atlantic to this table.

But there was nothing said about Wynn Gates. It seemed that the only word that had reached Cellini was that Zola was back. So Garret poured himself a martini and spent the rest of the night listening.

The party moved from Bilbouquet to Cellini's loft in SoHo, where a half-dozen of his assistants carried over a party that had started with a shoot earlier that day. Cellini sat in the room's center, a bearded Buddha, his tiny black eyes scanning the faces of his guests.

When Aaron Adam arrived, accompanied by an entourage twice the size of Cellini's, even the most jaded of the model crowd were impressed. Aaron Adam was generally known to give parties, not attend them, and for him to turn up at Cellini's loft was a sign of respect. Or something else. Garret noticed that Aaron Adam looked very serious, not as if he was out for a night of fun. Aaron and Cellini disappeared to a back room, and fifteen minutes later Aaron reappeared and quietly slipped out, leaving most of his entourage behind. To Garret, it was a curious exchange, out of rhythm with the party atmosphere of the night. Cellini emerged looking nervous and ashen. His grand gestures and ebullient chatter had gone. He sat on one of his huge leather couches and stared at the video screens, apparently deep in thought.

When the party broke up, Garret went for a walk on the quiet streets, thinking about the evening. He slipped into a dumpy saloon peopled by tough-looking serious drinkers; it was whiskey, beer, and a pall of cigarette smoke. Garret found a stool at the end of the bar, ordered a draft, and bummed a cigarette from the bartender. The fact that Aaron Adam had spoken directly to Cellini indicated to Garret that whatever was going on was significant and would be dealt with at the highest levels. Garret had no access to Aaron Adam, but access to Cellini seemed to be the next-best thing. Despite Cellini's seeming bon-vivant demeanor, Garret sensed that his every move was about business. The entourage might be having a good time, but clearly Cellini was working. So Garret knew it would be a mistake to try to become too friendly too soon. Cellini was not looking for friends, he wanted information, ideas, inspiration. Patience was required in his presence, but Garret assumed that patience would also be rewarded at some point. Cellini was a fertile patch of power in the fashion industry, and this casual access was to be handled carefully, Garret knew.

Lost in his thoughts, Garret was unaware of the man in a dark corner opposite him who had been watching him ever since he walked into the bar. The man was short and square-looking, with a massive upper body and stubby legs; his skin was pocked and shiny, and one of his front teeth was outlined in silver. He appeared to be in his early thirties, but in daylight might seem much older. The cigarettes he smoked were unfiltered, and the brown stains on his fingers and teeth meant that he'd been smoking for a long time. His name was Conley, which was the only name he used when introducing himself to somebody, and his steady

gaze usually distracted anyone from asking if Conley
was his first or last name.

With each drag on the cigarette, Conley's cheeks im-
ploded and the ash glowed. The smoke stayed in his
lungs for a long time, then came out his mouth and
nose as he reached for his drink. He smoked the cigarette with the deliberate rhythm of someone who had
spent a good chunk of his life in prison, where smoking
is a principal form of recreation. And as he smoked he
studied Garret Stowe. No one noticed him staring, because it was not the kind of bar where the patrons were
much interested in each other. But Conley was clearly
interested in Garret. He didn't take his eyes off him.
What would be obvious to anyone who happened to see
the two men was that they smoked cigarettes in a very
similar fashion.

When Garret had finished his beer and a second
cigarette, he walked out of the bar without looking left
or right.

Conley hesitated for a few seconds, then ambled outside. He caught a glimpse of Garret turning the corner
halfway down the block. Conley followed him. Garret
walked at a brisk pace, fifteen blocks back to his hotel.
Conley stopped across the street, sweating from the
pace. He lit another Camel and watched the hotel, to
make certain Garret had not just gone there for a drink.
When an hour passed, Conley was cold and out of cigarettes. So he turned and walked away, whistling.

For two more weeks, Garret patrolled the model
bars. He made no overt attempts to ingratiate himself
with Cellini, but remained visible, and gained credi-
bility by being seen with credible people, such as famous models, bookers, and stylists. Garret's vaguely
French accent, which he consciously affected, served
him well, adding a European gloss that separated him
from the usual pack of New Yorkers.

Getting the models to talk was easy for Garret. The girls liked to dish, to talk about fees and photographers and agents. They liked to talk about who had gained a few pounds, who was using drugs to keep the weight off, and who seemed to be "showing," by which they meant visibly aging. Garret paid closest attention whenever the models talked about money. The public and press focused on the glamorous side of the business, but most of the girls' interest in modeling started and finished with money. Garret discovered deep currents of jealousy about daily rates and contract bookings; some of the girls purposely inflated the rates they claimed to be paid in hopes that rumor would become reality. The agents tried to keep rates and contract amounts secret, knowing that such things could only be a source of discontent among models, but gossip was as much a part of the business as hair spray.

These nuggets of discontent he stored, while moving closer and closer to Cellini's inner circle. But not a single word was spoken about Aaron Adam, at least within earshot of Garret. A.A. was the number-one Cellini account, and despite all the gossip that the fashion industry thrived on, Cellini's employees were well schooled on that subject. When it came to A.A., people kept their mouths shut.

Garret began to observe a distinctly frenzied quality to Cellini's recent socializing. More and more people turned up at his tables: younger, street-looking kids. Many claimed to be actors, others filmmakers or writers. Cellini watched and listened to them, while retaining the manner of expansive host. Cellini's motive for this seemed transparent to Garret, but if Cellini's research was as obvious to other guests it didn't seem to matter to them—it was the price of their fun. Garret knew that it was time to learn toward what end Cellini's intense research was aimed.

c h a p t e r
13

"Goddammit, you don't get it, do you?" Jon Ross said to Caddie Dean as they sat on the deck of their Amagansett beach house. "You don't get what Jessica is trying to do."

"I'm working, and we're making lots of money," Caddie replied, "so why should I be worried about what she's doing with the rest of the models?"

"Because they're making money at your expense."

In the months that followed Caddie's trip to Hawaii and Jon's private meeting with Caddie's mother, he had stayed in the background of Caddie's career. He still functioned as her manager, but did not intrude to the point where another confrontation might occur.

"How are other models making money at my expense?" she asked him.

"Everybody calls the agency wanting Caddie Dean, and Jessica gives them some new girl she's trying to push, like Wynn Gates. You see her everywhere, don't you?"

"She's gotten popular," Caddie admitted.

"Well, how the hell do you think she's gotten popular? She's nothing compared to you, but she's got

Jessica Cartwright pushing her left, right, and center.
Who do you think an advertiser really wants, Wynn
Gates or Caddie Dean?"

"She doesn't make my rate, Jon. There are people
who don't want to pay that kind of money."

"How do you know what she makes? Have you seen
the books? I guarantee you this—her rate has doubled
twice in the last six months. And that's because
Cartwright is trying to make her a star. And how about
this? I heard from a friend that she got half a million
dollars to do Cover Girl. Half a million. Haven't you
noticed *you* don't do Cover Girl anymore?"

"That's because Aaron Adam is doing the perfume with me, Jon," Caddie said, "and I have to be
exclusive."

"And you don't think Jessica could have cut the deal
both ways? I tried to do it. I tried to get Jessica to let
me handle the Aaron Adam people, but she's so scared
of them she gave away the store."

"I thought we got a million? That sounded pretty
good when you told me about it."

"I could have gotten two million," Jon answered,
"and I told Jessica that next time I'll handle it. Period."

Jon mixed himself another gin and tonic, flicked a
glance at Caddie, and saw that he'd caught her attention. During the past months, he'd continued to have
lunches with advertising executives and representatives from various sponsors. And from these meetings
he'd become convinced that Caddie wasn't making the
money that she should be, that Jessica was cutting up
the pie to protect her agency, so that all her eggs
weren't invested in Caddie Dean.

Beginning with Caddie's mother, Jon had dug into
the parts of Caddie's background that he knew nothing
about, and what he'd learned emboldened him to nudge
her, subtly at first, and now with more confidence,
away from Jessica.

"I want you to see something," he said, setting his drink down and pulling a sheaf of papers from his briefcase. The papers displayed figures on recent deals purportedly made by Jessica on behalf of other Cartwright clients. Of course, Jon didn't tell Caddie that the figures came from a booker at another agency, who most likely had pulled them out of thin air because she knew Jon wanted ammunition to use against Jessica Cartwright.

"There are nine jobs you should have had," Jon said. "None of them are conflicts with your current contracts, and all of them are good money. Did you hear about these deals? Did I? No."

Caddie picked up the papers and looked them over, but felt a little sick to her stomach to be talking about Jessica this way. But Jon seemed to have done a good deal of homework. And as Jon continually said, business was business. Certainly, during the eleven months since the *Time* cover had pushed Caddie's prominence to a new level, she and Jessica had grown apart, primarily because both women were busier than ever.

When the call came to Jessica's office for lunch with Aaron Adam at his private dining room at his Village studios, she was concerned. She knew that Aaron usually liked the visibility of his usual luncheon locations, Le Cirque and Café des Artistes. Jessica braced for trouble.

"As I suspected," Aaron began, barely touching the lunch prepared by his chef, "there is a problem with our MaliBlues Jeans line. We had a temporary uptick in sales following Caddie's appearance on the cover of *Time,* but two months after that we experienced a decline in sales, and the decline has continued. Like all campaigns, our California approach to selling jeans has run its course. In fact, it is almost at a standstill."

Jessica knew there was no point in arguing facts with Aaron Adam.

"Our SunCoast lines are doing well, and we plan to stick with Caddie right through the term of the contract. But what I want you to do is find me a new girl. Someone as fresh and exciting as Caddie was eight years ago."

"I think Caddie Dean is still fresh and exciting," Jessica replied, forcing any disappointment out of her voice. She knew her loyalty to Caddie was overriding her better judgment.

"I've made my decision, Jessica. There's no need to fight for your client. I still believe in her for bathing suits and cosmetics. But I've got to get more dangerous with my jeans or my retailers simply won't carry them. Find me the right girl."

"What kind of campaign is it going to be?" Jessica asked.

"I don't know," Aaron Adam said flatly.

This took Jessica by surprise. Campaigns were planned, then models chosen, not vice versa.

He noted Jessica's reaction, and continued, "I haven't gone to the advertising agency because then it will be a news story that we're treading water with our jeans. I don't want that. I trust your discretion on the matter. And I don't think my inspiration for a new campaign is going to come out of committee at an advertising agency, anyway. I've discussed the matter with Cellini, and he proposed doing an upscale campaign, making the jeans rare rather than just fashionable. I hated the idea and told him so. In fact, it made me wonder if he was still as in touch with the streets as he once was. What do you think of him?"

Jessica was not in the business of disparaging other people's reputations, but she knew that Aaron Adam expected, required, her honesty.

"He is the best photographer of women working today," Jessica said, "and he finds things in models other people seem unable to. I don't particularly like the man, but I don't dispute the quality of his eye."

"I want you to find a model that inspires Cellini, and inspires me."

"What is your timetable?"

"I have business for the next two weeks in Europe. After that, the sole focus of my time will be a new jeans campaign. Cellini knows we are meeting, so feel free to discuss the matter with him."

"Caddie is doing Lipton Tea in Chicago this week. That's a major contract for her, so I'd prefer to tell her about this after that job, not before."

"I'll leave that to your judgment," Aaron Adam said.

On the same day Jessica Cartwright had lunch with Aaron Adam, Garret Stowe attended his sixth party within a two-week span at Anton Cellini's studio. During that time, Garret had detected a pattern in Cellini's behavior. In the early evenings, Cellini was friendly, even warm, as he held court at Bilbouquet. As the evening drove beyond midnight and Cellini and his entourage moved to the club scene, Cellini became hyperkinetic, talking nonstop, bursting out onto the dance floor for two minutes of waving his arms and hopping around. Then it was back to his studio, where he would sit back and watch the assembled; and, finally, as the nights skidded toward morning, Cellini's insecurity would emerge, and Garret observed him more than once dropping his king-of-the-hill veneer to complain to some companion about a magazine editor that didn't understand how to present his work, or to worry about a lack of ideas for the shoot he would be doing the next day. These outbursts were brief, and were followed by Cellini's retiring to his bedroom, sometimes with a young man, but usually alone.

At the end of one of these nights, Garret positioned

himself near Cellini's bedroom. The party was winding
down, people were either leaving or crashing on the
studio's various couches and oversized chairs, and
Garret saw Cellini starting to drink cognac. It was the
first time Garret had seen Cellini drink anything but
Evian water. He was very agitated, mumbling imper-
ceptibly beneath the blasting Pearl Jam CD. Accompanied by a twenty-year-old male model, who was
completely drunk and nodded at whatever was said,
Cellini disappeared into the bedroom. An assistant
switched the music to a classical piece—the signal for
people to head home—while another assistant began
cleaning up. Garret feigned sleep, curled up in a chair.

Soon Cellini began screaming in the bedroom,
drunken rants about Aaron Adam and Caddie Dean and
the difficulty of being an artist, of constantly having to
top himself creatively.

"He wants to meet in two weeks!" Cellini roared.
"Does he think I can solve the problems of the world in
two weeks? Nobody can. Do you find a girl like Caddie
Dean in five fucking minutes? Does he think it's my
fucking fault that his goddam blue jeans aren't selling?
I'm a goddam artist, not a marketing moron!"

The model laughed at everything Cellini said, until
finally the boy came flying out of the bedroom, tossed
by an enraged Cellini.

The main assistant hurried around the studio, waking
people up, sending them out. Apparently when Cellini
got like this, it was time to clear the decks.

Garret emerged into the cool predawn air and walked
five blocks in search of a cab. He instructed the driver
to take him to JFK Airport. There he purchased a ticket
for the next plane to Chicago, leaving in forty-five
minutes. Garret did not worry about his clothes, his appearance, or having a place to stay once he arrived in
Chicago. He had a credit card, compliments of Giselle
Rochas, and that would see him through. What he did

know for certain was that Aaron Adam had obviously instructed Cellini to come up with ideas for a new blue jeans campaign, and that Caddie Dean was not to be part of that plan. Earlier that week, Garret had met a marketing assistant from Lipton at Bilbouquet who said she was on her way to Chicago for a shoot with Caddie Dean. Garret had never been to Chicago, but he had little doubt that he could find his way around.

Upon landing it took him only a few phone calls to find out that the Lipton people were staying at the Whitehall. Garret called the hotel and asked for Jon Ross. The operator put the call through. No answer, but no matter. Garret only wanted to confirm that Jon and Caddie were at the Whitehall as well. He took a cab to Marshall Field, bought clothes and an overnight bag, then booked a room at the Whitehall and arrived at the hotel looking surprisingly fresh for someone who had not slept in two days.

Garret changed, then waited in the lobby. At seven-thirty, Caddie Dean arrived with Jon Ross. They went to the desk to pick up their mail and speak to the concierge. Garret materialized behind them. When Jon Ross turned around, he was face to face with Garret, who looked at him quizzically.

"Aren't you Jon Ross?" Garret said. "The photographer?"

Jon was surprised, not used to being recognized, and certainly not as a photographer.

"Yes," he said tentatively.

"I know your work. You photograph women beautifully."

"Well," Jon said, confused, but allowing the moment to wash over him, "thank you."

"I'm Garret Stowe. Nice to make your acquaintance."

Jon shook Garret's hand. Garret deliberately ignored Caddie, who stood next to Jon.

"This is my wife, Caddie," Jon said, finally realizing she was being left out.

Garret shook her hand briskly, but immediately turned his attention back to Jon.

"Are you here shooting?" Garret asked.

"No, no, actually. Caddie is. I'm handling some business."

"Then perhaps you'll have time for a drink. I'm arranging for some work to be done in Paris for my agency, and I'd love your input. I know it's presumptuous of me . . ."

"No, it's all right. What agency?"

"Zola. I'm the new partner. Things are quite exciting for us right now."

"So I've heard," Jon Ross said.

"Anyway, sorry to bother you," Garret said, beginning to walk away. "Pleasure to meet you," he said to Caddie, as an afterthought.

And then Garret was gone, out the front door of the hotel.

Riding the elevator up to their suite, Jon said to Caddie, "I've heard of him. He's supposed to be one of the hottest agents in Europe."

Caddie shrugged. She had not heard of Garret or the Zola Agency. But then, in truth, neither had Jon.

Garret walked around the block, allowing sufficient time for Caddie and Jon to return to their room, then he went back to the hotel and burned up the phone lines to New York. He called various contacts and uncovered everything he could about Jon Ross.

At dawn the next day, Garret was up, into a jogging suit, and waiting in the lobby. He used a newspaper to shield his face. Caddie and Jon appeared and took a cab to Lakeshore Drive, where they jogged along the breakwater. Garret followed at a discreet distance, and when he saw them hook a U-turn and head back toward their starting point, he ran hard to put a mile between himself and them. When Caddie and Jon arrived at the pickup point, Garret was there, stretching and sweating. He didn't look up until Jon said, "Garret?"

Garret's face registered surprise.

"We're catching a cab back to the hotel," Jon Ross said. "Can we give you a lift?"

Garret said little during the ride, and when Jon invited him to dinner, Garret cited a previous obligation and suggested lunch. Jon agreed; Garret wanted Jon without the presence of Caddie.

At lunch, Garret worked in references to Jon's published layouts. And Jon was dazzled. Gradually, Garret slid in an allusion to Aaron Adam and his blue jean troubles, and by the fleeting look of surprise that crossed Jon's face, it was clear he knew nothing about it. Garret then dangled a bit of information about a coming change in the campaign. When Jon became alarmed, Garret quickly changed the subject, leaving Jon with the impression that Garret was a true insider. Jon pressed him on the point of Aaron Adam and the MaliBlues campaign.

"For someone of your position not to be kept fully informed," Garret said with a touch of righteous indignation, "is obviously a deliberate omission on somebody's part. But I can't imagine why, since Caddie is the heart and soul of A.A."

"It's not A.A.," Jon said, leaning back, his eyes growing dark. "It's Cartwright."

Garret and Jon traded phone numbers, and off they went. Jon to the studio and Garret directly to the airport. Jon had wanted to meet Garret that night for drinks to discuss the matter further, but Garret insisted he must get back to New York for a dinner meeting.

After the lunch with Aaron Adam, Jessica knew that she needed to discuss the situation with Caddie, because no matter how much secrecy surrounded any impending event in the fashion industry, it was a business where secrets lasted about as long as seafood left in the sun. But with Jon Ross as Caddie's intermediary, Jessica wanted to plan her approach carefully, because she knew Jon would see a conspiracy in anything that might be perceived as a dip in Caddie's otherwise meteoric career.

Jessica decided to fly to the Caribbean and sneak in two days of sunshine and relaxation before tackling what promised to be a most challenging assignment. Besides, she had been unable to spend much time in the past few months with Phil Stein, and she missed his attention. Ever since the Caddie Dean dinner in Los Angeles and the resulting upsurge in the Cartwright Agency's bookings, Phil had displayed an increasing interest in the inner workings of the business. Rather than just handling the contracts, he began to ask Jessica questions about the growth of the agency. He became fascinated with the notion that Jessica could spot a girl, like Wynn Gates, and within months that girl could be making hundreds of thousands of dollars a year.

"Let's fly down to St. Bart's and not talk about the business," Jessica suggested. "Tell the firm your mother's sick or your aunt needs visiting or you've got a new client, but just come with me."

He did. But he didn't keep his promise not to talk about the agency, and in truth it was impossible for Jessica to put business out of her mind.

They weren't in St. Bart's for more than two hours when a bellman found Jessica on her chaise longue by the pool and told her she had an urgent call from New York.

"It can't be that urgent," Jessica told the bellman.

"The woman, Sascha, from your office said you would say that, and I was to tell you that, yes, indeed, it is that urgent." He handed her a cordless telephone.

"What?" Jessica snapped into the receiver.

"Caddie Dean wants to see you in Chicago for a face-to-face meeting," Sascha said. "Tonight."

"What?" Jessica said, incredulous.

"I tried to talk them out of it," Sascha continued. "I tried all morning. They really want to see you. They won't talk to me anymore. They won't talk to anybody. She postponed her Lipton shoot today, and it's the second time this year she's done that. Lipton is screaming because everybody is over schedule. I haven't spoken directly to Caddie," Sascha said, anticipating Jessica's next question, "because Jon won't put me through to her. This is all coming from him."

"Tell that son of a bitch he's risking a lawsuit and losing the account by canceling. What the hell does he think he's doing?"

"Whatever he's doing, he's got Caddie with him on it, because she won't take my calls."

"I don't believe this. Tonight?"

"I've booked your flights," Sascha said. "You leave in an hour and a half."

Immediately upon Jessica's arrival at Caddie and Jon's hotel suite in Chicago, Jon launched into a tirade. He accused Jessica of conspiring to replace Caddie so that the Cartwright agency could have two large Aaron Adam contracts, one for jeans and one for swimwear. And launch a second model to superstardom in the process. He further accused Jessica of using Caddie's fame to swell the ranks of the agency, to build a stable of contenders waiting in the wings to knock Caddie off her perch. Then he asked point-blank if Aaron Adam was going to sign a new girl, and when Jessica said yes, Jon screamed that Jessica's duplicitous nature caused her to sit on this information until the girl had been found, so that if Caddie quit, the backup would already be in place.

"Quit what?" Jessica said calmly. "Aaron Adam is

paying Caddie's entire jeans contract and continuing with the swimwear and the new cosmetics. That is his privilege, contractually, and he's handling this quite generously."

While the argument raged on, Caddie walked into and out of her bedroom, uncomfortable at the tone of Jon's voice, but doing nothing, as Jessica carefully noted, to stop it.

Once Jessica finally rose to leave, having managed to appease Jon to the extent that he stopped yelling, Caddie gave Jessica a stiff hug without even making eye contact.

When the door closed behind Jessica, Jon walked to the bar and fixed himself a drink, pleased that he had been able to rattle Jessica; but what pleased him the most was that Caddie had allowed him to do it. His investigations of Caddie's past had given him the upper hand when it came to controlling her business career. She knew that he could expose the secrets she and Jessica had hidden so well, and Caddie Dean's reputation and image would be ripped to shreds.

When Aaron Adam heard from Jessica about the leak to Jon Ross, his response was to arrange a large party in the Rainbow Room atop Rockefeller Center in honor of Caddie Dean, acknowledging record sales of Sun-Coast Swimwear. He did not care a whit that Jon Ross felt put out by the change in the jeans campaign, but he did care that Caddie be happy prior to shooting the layouts for next summer's swimwear line.

Jon Ross saw to it that Garret Stowe received an invitation. And for three weeks before the party, Garret did his homework and formulated a plan for the evening. He positioned himself at a bar where he had a view of the entire room. Instead of watching for the top models, of which dozens were in attendance, or the industry magnates, he scanned the room in search of Phil Stein.

Jessica Cartwright arrived with Phil, and together they worked through the room. Word was out that their business relationship was also personal, but naturally, attention flowed toward Jessica. Outstretched hands, air kisses, waves of acknowledgment. Phil Stein looked very much a decorative presence at her side. But Garret saw something else. He studied the way Phil responded coolly to the models who approached Jessica, with pleasant smiles and a deferential nod of the head. These were the most beautiful women in the world, and Phil was a study in practiced detachment. It was clear to Garret that Phil wanted to do nothing to offend Jessica. She was an attractive woman. But an attractive woman in her forties next to a supermodel could not, in Garret's mind, hold the attention of a successful man in his thirties like Phil Stein. Unless Phil was drawing something else from the occasion.

When Jessica had made the rounds of the room, Phil slipped away to one of the bars, ordered a martini, and watched the proceedings. Garret followed the direction of Phil's eyes. He took in the major players in the room—Aaron Adams, financiers, magazine publishers—people that other people liked to write and read about. Garret walked to the bar and casually introduced himself to Phil Stein. When Phil said his name, Garret responded, "Oh, yes, yes, you're the business end of the Cartwright Agency."

"I pretty much just watch the contracts," he said.

"Someone is managing those contracts well," Garret said. "I heard it was you."

The two men made a date for lunch.

Then Garret moved on to Jon Ross. He had noticed during lunch in Chicago that Jon handled liquor poorly, that it tended to make him loud and aggressive. So he worked Jon away from Caddie and over to one of the bars, got a couple of strong drinks down him. Jon brought up the sore subject of the new Aaron Adam jeans campaign.

"What surprises me," Garret said, "is that you weren't consulted. Who knows—given the chance, perhaps you and Caddie could have come up with a concept that Aaron Adam might have liked. I'm surprised your agent didn't arrange a meeting of some sort."

Garret let Jon chew on that thought and abruptly changed the subject. But he saw the flames gather in Jon's eyes as more drinks went down to fuel them.

Finally, Jon charged off in search of Aaron Adam.

Garret moved on to Sascha Benning, Jessica's ace booker. Garret had discovered that since bookers spent most of their waking hours on the telephone talking about other people, they generally developed a hearty appetite for talking about themselves. It was just that nobody ever asked. So Garret asked Sascha about her work and her legendary effectiveness. When he revealed that he was with the Zola Agency in Paris, Sascha asked about the fiasco with Wynn Gates, and Garret laid it off to Marie Zola's increasingly dotty ways. They laughed it off. By the time he was done chatting with Sascha, trading phone numbers and scheduling a lunch, he noticed that Jon Ross had collared Aaron Adam.

As always, A.A. was surrounded by a large entourage of customers, models, agents, and employees. But Jon seemed unaware that his rants were being monitored by a group of a dozen people. Jon assailed A.A. for not coming to him and discussing a new campaign with Caddie, after all that Caddie had done for MaliBlues Jeans. Aaron Adam had the steely eyes of someone who didn't care for public displays of drunkenness, and certainly not for broadcasting sensitive business matters. Finally, Jessica, who was talking

with Tommee Barkley, saw what was happening and
sent Tommee to find Caddie. Caddie, mortified, pulled
her husband away from Aaron Adam and over to a ban-
quette table, where she ordered a pot of coffee. But by
the time the coffee arrived, Jon had already passed out.

chapter
14

Until lunch with Garret Stowe, Phil Stein couldn't recall anyone asking him about the financial aspects of the model agency business. The partners in his firm only wanted to know about how the girls looked in person and if any of them fooled around.

But Garret was different. He had knowledge of the business. He had opinions. And he wanted to know what Phil thought about the entire financial basis of the model agencies, the construction of the commission and service charge structure. Phil happily explained, over lunch at the Four Seasons—and was suitably impressed by the excellent table Garret received, knowing nothing of the hundred-dollar tip that had secured it. The agency took 20 percent from the models for print work and collected an additional 20 percent from the client. If it was a ten-thousand-dollar booking, the model received eight thousand, the agency four thousand, and the "ten-thousand-dollar booking" actually cost the client twelve thousand. The agency advanced the fee to the model within a week of completion of the shoot, even though the agency might not collect the money from the client for months (and sometimes not at all, if the client went belly-up). Phil discussed cash flow and billing procedures, and all the other things no one ever expressed the least bit of interest in. And he was particularly thrilled when Garret asked him about what he saw as the financial weaknesses of the industry practices in general, and what he would do to correct them.

As the lunch neared its end, a stunning young model passed through the restaurant. Twenty-four years old, brown hair cut above her ears like a modern Audrey Hepburn, and unusually large breasts for so slender a frame. She noticed Garret and waved. He called her over and introduced Phil. Checking his watch, Garret explained that he had another appointment, but since half a bottle of Montrachet remained on the table, why didn't Felicia join Phil and finish it off? Felicia said she had a few hours before her next interview, so she took a chair, and Phil quickly filled a glass for her.

Felicia had recently completed a shoot in St. Bart's, she told Phil, and he jumped on the information and explained that he'd just been there, too; it was something to talk about. And talk they did. Felicia was a good listener and seemed interested in just about everything Phil had to say. Phil reveled in the looks that came his way from the businessmen departing the restaurant. Every man took a look first at Felicia, then at Phil—he had to be somebody to have a girl like that. In truth, he noticed all the girls around Jessica, but didn't dare make a move toward them because they were Jessica's clients. Not this one. Phil was drunk enough to ask Felicia for her phone number, which she wrote on a scrap of paper and slipped into his pocket as they walked down the stairs together; he felt her slender hand rub against his hip, and she confirmed his hopes with an inviting smile.

*   *   *

When Phil called Jessica the next day to tell her he was going out of town for the weekend—time they usually spent together—she thought nothing of it; in fact, his trip came at a convenient moment for her, because all of her waking hours were being devoted to the search for a new Aaron Adam blue jeans girl.

Jessica pulled Sascha off all daily chores other than handling Caddie Dean and focused her on the search as well. Sascha traveled to half a dozen cities in the United States, then to Paris and Milan, screening models. Cellini, as the days rolled on, became increasingly crazed, calling Jessica all hours of the day and night, wanting to know what she was finding. He wanted to see as many girls as possible, certain that one of them would serve as both model and muse.

One Saturday night during the second week of the search, Jessica fixed dinner at home for Phil Stein. Halfway through the grilled fish, the telephone rang. Cellini was calling from his beach house in the Hamptons to ask if Jessica had seen anyone promising. While she reassured Cellini that they would find the girl, Phil Stein walked over to his briefcase and pulled out a photograph.

"This is the daughter of another client," Phil said, handing the photograph to Jessica. Phil had held the world's record with Jessica for never having suggested anybody as a model. This was his first. She looked at the picture.

Attractive brunette; collagen-enhanced lips out of proportion with the nose. The breasts jutted out like safety pylons. To most people, a knockout, but to Jessica, not marketable.

"Just a thought," Phil said, returning to his dinner.

The girl in the photo was Felicia.

"I don't think that's the one," Jessica said, returning the picture to Phil.

Phil glanced again at the picture, then put it on the pile of others.

"Maybe Cellini should take a look at it, too," he said. "You never know."

"You never know," she agreed, pouring more wine. "But I do know that she isn't a girl that Cellini wants to look at."

"How can you be sure?"

"Because I've known him for twelve years," Jessica answered.

Phil took the photo off the pile of other rejects, put it back in his briefcase, and changed the subject.

The search for Aaron Adam's new model, and Cellini's inspiration, continued intensely for several more days, until Jessica brought in a bony, strangely rugged-looking girl who sent Cellini into ecstasy. He danced around his studio and sang at the top of his lungs, hugging the girl, himself, and Jessica. Then, most of all, hugging his equipment. He kissed his Hasselblad cameras and performed a war dance around the light standards, claiming that suddenly he saw the entire campaign in his head. Dozens of photographs and scenarios were now as clear to him as if he had been handed storyboards. It would be a Western-themed campaign, a sort of high-tech, multimedia Marlboro girl, revisiting the sexy Western settings of tried-and-true American movies, juxtaposed with the urban sprawl of contemporary times. Cellini spouted philosophy, concepts, colors, and angles. He described light, backgrounds, and poses.

But despite Cellini's enthusiasm, Aaron Adam would have the final say. True, Aaron treated Cellini with deference. But in the wake of her last lunch with Aaron Adam, Jessica knew that he was reexamining his relationship with Cellini, if only because sales figures of MaliBlues Jeans were not what Aaron Adam expected. Avedon and Scavullo had their day when they could make or break a model or a campaign, and now it was Cellini's turn on top. But that was just it, everybody had a turn, and the only thing permanent in the world of fashion was the need for change. That and the color black.

The morning of the test shoot, Jessica was in the limousine at six o'clock waiting in front of the new model's apartment to escort her personally to the studio, to relax her and give her the confidence needed to make the day's work go well. The plan was for Cellini to do a couple of mock layouts, present them to Aaron Adam for final approval, then start work on the campaign within a month.

The mood at Cellini's studio that morning was particularly upbeat. His staff and crew had suffered through the model search, and finally swinging into action felt like a vacation rather than work. Cellini was ebullient, cooking up a breakfast of scrambled eggs, chopped spinach, and sausage for anyone interested. Mozart played on the CD. In constant motion, Cellini supervised every aspect of the shoot, greeting Jessica and the model, keeping an eye on the makeup and hair process, checking and rechecking his lights with the stand-in model. By nine-thirty, everything and everyone was ready. Cellini cued his music, kick-ass rock and roll, and the shoot was on.

Jessica remained in the back of the studio, well out of the way, but close enough to deal with any problems that might arise from Cellini's use of the inexperienced model.

At precisely 10:00 A.M., Jessica's pager, which she kept in her purse, began beeping.

At first she didn't hear it, because of the loud music. But when she reached in her purse for a tissue, she saw the message light flashing. Irritated, she checked the tiny screen. Only Caddie, who was not speaking to her at all, and Sascha and Edie had the pager number, and the latter two were under strict instructions to use it only in the most urgent circumstances. And since this shoot was the most important of the year for the Cartwright Agency, Jessica could not imagine what could be important enough to cause this interruption.

She went into one of the private rooms and called her office. The line rang unanswered. The agency was a busy place at ten in the morning, with calls coming in every few seconds. In fact, to accommodate all of the models and clients, the agency maintained forty different lines. Sometimes the main number could ring half a dozen times before the operator grabbed it. But never more than that. And now it rang a dozen times, and kept going. Jessica redialed, thinking she had dialed wrong, or that a line had crossed. But it was the same. No answer. Jessica dialed her private extension. If that line didn't pick up, it kicked back to the switchboard after four rings. Again, no answer. She next called the telephone company to check the lines. An operator came back on after a minute and said the equipment seemed to be functioning fine. So Jessica dialed the main number a third time and let it ring. Finally, a male voice answered.

"Who's this?" Jessica asked.

"Mark," came the answer.

Jessica didn't know a Mark in her company.

"This is Jessica Cartwright. Who are you and why are you answering the telephone?"

"I'm with the messenger company," he said frantically. "Edie asked me to help. It's crazy around here."

"Get me Edie."

Moments later a frantic Edie came on the line. She was in tears. "What is going on?" Jessica asked, more confused than alarmed.

"Just get down here," Edie said. "Please. Right away."

"What is it?"

Before Edie could respond, the messenger who was helping with the switchboard accidentally cut off the call. When Jessica tried calling back, the phone rang unanswered.

The Cartwright offices were always a chaotic hive of activity, with phones ringing, messengers running in and out, models coming and going. But the chaos confronting Jessica when she rushed through the doors had a different edge. The staff looked fearful, shell-shocked. Edie ran around grabbing telephones and giving instructions. Jessica looked around for Sascha, who was nowhere in sight.

"What in God's name is happening?"

"We've lost a bunch of models," Edie said, spitting her words out, trying to organize her thoughts.

"What do you mean?"

"They've left, gone."

Models changed agents. It was part of the business. Usually, however, models left small agencies to come to Cartwright, or if they were leaving Cartwright, it was because their careers were winding down and they were going with a smaller agency in the hope of a last gasp of attention. But models did not come and go in bunches. She wondered if she was hearing Edie correctly.

"What models?"

Edie grabbed a pile of faxes. They were notices from models stating their intention to leave Cartwright's representation as of today at noon. All of the faxes had the same wording and obviously had been prepared for the models and sent by a common source. As Jessica paged through the faxes and noted the names, her confusion, and alarm, grew. These were not newcomer models. These were major girls. Big earners. She counted twelve of them, and even as she read, the fax machine spit out another letter. And then another. All of the faxes said the girls were now being represented by an agency called Vitesse.

"Who the hell is Vitesse?" Jessica asked.

"I have no idea. Nobody has heard of them. It's a new company, and I've never heard of a brand-new agency getting girls like these."

Jessica was stunned. She stared at the faxes in disbelief. If Edie had said the girls were going to Ford or Elite, this mass defection could conceivably make some sense. Those were major agencies, equipped to handle star models. But star models simply didn't sign with an unknown.

The fax machine spit out another letter.

"Where the hell is Sascha?" Jessica said, looking around the office.

Edie took a breath, knowing what she was about to say would cut Jessica to the quick. "She came in before we opened, cleared out her desk, and left a letter of resignation."

This made no sense to Jessica. Sascha was the highest-paid booker in the business. Jessica gave her whatever she wanted. And she was Jessica's right arm.

"She's gone to work for Vitesse," Edie continued. "And so has Lee." Lee was Jessica's second-in-command booker.

Gerry Bolin, one of the junior bookers, came running over. He was in his mid-twenties, gay, and, like Sascha, one of the hardest-working bookers in town. Like Sascha, he lived and breathed the business, and Jessica had earmarked him for promotion down the road. But he was still green, his circle of contacts too narrow.

"I just talked to Sharry Colt," he said, looking devastated, since Sharry had become nearly a half-million-dollar-a-year girl under Gerry's and, of course,

Jessica's wing. "She's leaving, too. She's going to Vitesse."

"Why? Who *are* they?"

"They've offered her a half million dollars a year on a two-year contract. Guaranteed."

"But that's ridiculous," Jessica said.

One of the first rules for a reputable agent was not to make guarantees. A girl might work, she might not. Even stars had dry spells when the marketplace perceived them to be overexposed.

"Vitesse is also making deals where they take no commission," Gerry said.

"How the hell are they expecting to make money?"

"They just take the service charge," Gerry said.

For a model making half a million dollars a year, not having to pay commission meant an additional one hundred thousand dollars of income. The agency would still collect a 20 percent service fee from the client, but that was not enough to cover overhead and make a profit.

Gerry knew what Jessica was thinking. He said, "From what I'm hearing, Vitesse is going to try to make money by doubling the basic daily rate for these girls."

The basic rate meant the bottom-line daily charge for work not covered by a long-term contract. The kind of girls leaving the agency were getting a basic rate of five thousand per day, which was top dollar for the tier of models below the handful of superstars.

"Sharry told me that no Vitesse model will work for less than ten thousand a day. So I guess Vitesse hopes to make up for what they're losing in commission by doubling the rate and collecting the higher service charge."

"But nobody is going to pay those rates," Jessica said. "The girls can't possibly believe this."

Another fax spit out.

"This is insanity," Jessica said, running to her office.

She placed calls to the other top agents in town. All were being hit, but none as hard as the Cartwright Agency.

One of the agents said, "And what business does Phil Stein have running an agency? I thought he was a lawyer."

Jessica didn't answer. She just hung up the phone. She felt as if she'd been gut-punched. Edie and Gerry hadn't said anything about Phil Stein only because they didn't know he was involved. Edie then called information, found a new listing for Vitesse, called, and asked for Phil Stein. A secretary said he was unavailable. When asked what Phil's position was with the agency, the secretary said, "He's president."

Numbly, Jessica took the list of models who were defecting and tried calling them one by one. None answered.

Edie picked up a call, whirled in her chair, and signaled Jessica to grab the line, mouthing the name Jon Ross.

He did not ask for Jessica, but said to Edie, "Your fax lines are all busy so we can't get through. You will be receiving a fax from us. But notify Jessica that as of noon today, Caddie Dean is no longer represented by Cartwright. She will be represented by Vitesse. I have a messenger on the way to pick up her portfolio, and I'd appreciate it if you have it waiting at the desk, because we need it for a press conference."

Jon hung up the phone, leaving Edie and Jessica staring at each other.

"Caddie?" Jessica said to Edie in a voice barely loud enough to be heard.

Jessica sat at her desk and stared out the window, while the phone lines continued to burn. Calls came in from models, other agents, clients, fashion editors, newspapers. Nobody was quite certain what was happening, only that the rules of the game in the agency business were different at noon than they had been when the day began. Guaranteed contracts from an agent to a model? No commission? Minimum daily rate of ten thousand dollars? From a business point of view, these policies seemed insane.

Yet, sitting on Jessica's desk was the pile of faxes from the models. And now the gossip-hungry fashion business had its teeth into this major story. One rumor suggested that Jessica had planned to close her business and represent only Caddie Dean and Tommee Barkley, and that the other models were now jumping ship because of it. Another rumor picked up by Gerry was that Jessica had a cash-flow problem, triggering the defections. Other rumors came and went by the second. None true. But all were damaging. Jessica tried to reach Caddie, but her service picked up. She called the head of her law firm—Phil's former boss—who arrived within the hour to assess the situation. She brought in temporary secretaries to answer telephones and take messages. And she tried without success to reach Phil Stein.

Jessica knew immediately that Phil could not have masterminded the defections, because he simply didn't know enough models or how to approach them. And what could Vitesse possibly have offered Caddie Dean? Caddie was locked into five major contracts, and the commissions from those contracts would continue to flow to Cartwright no matter what new agency Caddie signed with. Yes, the prestige of having Caddie Dean for a new agency's roster was great, but to land a model of Caddie's stature the agency must have offered something. But what?

Edie entered Jessica's office, flipped on the television, and turned to the E! channel on cable. There was Phil Stein holding a press conference. Behind him were half a dozen former Cartwright models, all drinking champagne. Jessica watched, dumbfounded and hurt, as Phil spoke enthusiastically about the agency and the signing of Caddie Dean, as well as a major coagency deal with Zola of Paris. He looked like a different person from the man Jessica knew. As reporters asked questions, he expounded on the growth of model agencies as the beginning of a new era in fashion awareness. Jessica couldn't believe what she was hearing. Before the law firm had assigned Phil to Jessica's account, he had never seen a fashion magazine. Now he was talking about the future of the business with a look of unfiltered ambition in his eyes. The reserve was gone from his face; suddenly, Phil looked like a man who had found religion.

A reporter asked who owned the agency, and Phil answered that it was a privately held company. A tall, lanky, dark-haired man stood in the background, talking with the models. Somebody asked that he be identified, since he was listed in the press release as Vitesse's chairman. Garret Stowe waved briefly to the press, then turned his back to the camera, apparently uneasy with the lights and microphones turned in his direction. Then the camera made a dizzying swing around the room to catch Caddie Dean and Jon Ross. They moved to a table in the back of the room, spoke briefly with Phil Stein, then left as quickly as they had arrived. Caddie appeared disoriented and nervous, while Jon beamed and waved. The camera turned back to Garret, who slipped out of the picture, giving his new models center stage.

"Who is that man?" Jessica asked Edie.

"I don't know."

Gerry stood in the doorway, watching as well.

"That was Garret Stowe," Gerry said.

"The guy who tried to screw us in Paris with Wynn Gates?"

"That's him," Gerry said. "He's been around New York the last few months."

"Get me Marie Zola," Jessica said.

Edie tried. The office was closed in Paris for the day.

"I need to talk to Caddie," Jessica said, looking at the nervous faces surrounding her. "I can't let this happen."

Garret Stowe sat in the living room of his suite at the Lowell Hotel. He'd moved into the three-thousand-dollar-a-day suite a week ago, when he began making formal offers to models to switch agencies. First he'd met with Giselle Rochas, who was in New York for a week for conferences with American wine importers. Garret detailed his business plan for her, including the financial statements, supplied by Phil Stein, of several top models who were planning to jump to the new agency, and capped his presentation by informing her that Caddie Dean, the world's top model, was willing to go with the new company. Giselle agreed to provide start-up financing for Vitesse, but she insisted upon total anonymity, choosing to create a corporate shell through which to make the investment.

Garret watched the late-afternoon news shows break the story of his agency, flashing up pictures of Caddie Dean and the other girls. It was, of course, a story that only a minute percentage of viewers would understand. But the fact that the news directors had taken this chance to splash the faces of several of the world's top models across their screens, teasing the story with promises to reveal the "inside story of New York's latest model wars," only reminded Garret of the power of a pretty face. His newly hired secretary arrived with copies of the *New York Post*. Predictably, there was a photograph of Caddie Dean with the headline "Billion-Dollar Beauty Jumps Ship."

"I want you to find a photographer in Paris for me,"

Garret said to the secretary. "He goes by the name Jamm. See if we can get him on the line."

Garret sat back in the leather sofa.

"And call room service and order a couple of bottles of champagne."

"What kind would you like, Mr. Stowe?" she asked.

"The most expensive," he replied.

Jessica Cartwright grabbed a rental car at the helipad in Amagansett and drove to Caddie Dean's house. A security guard was posted out front. Jessica knew him. He was with the firm that she regularly hired to watch out for the girls whenever one of them had a problem with a weirdo fan or a boyfriend who spun out of control. The guard told Jessica, with much embarrassment, that he was under strict instructions to keep the media, and everybody else, away from the house. But Jessica would not budge, and finally he relented and phoned the main house. He told Jon Ross that Miss Cartwright wished to see him.

"Tell her she can contact us through our attorney," Jon said, "or through our new agent, Garret Stowe." And then he added, "Tell her those words exactly."

Jessica stared at the gray-and-white house.

She said to the guard, "Frank, I don't want to get you in trouble. But I have to do something. I'm going around back."

The guard, who despised Jon Ross, said, "I'll go to my car to have a cup of coffee. I'll just be taking a break."

Jessica went around the dunes, walked across the beach, and approached the rear deck. The east side of the house, constructed primarily of glass, provided stunning views of the water from every room, and through the glass Jessica saw Caddie pacing back and forth in the living room, smoking a cigarette. Jessica hadn't seen Caddie pick up a cigarette since she was

seventeen years old and had just joined the agency.
Jessica had insisted that she quit, and she did.

Jon spotted Jessica walking up the beach toward the
house, and he grabbed the telephone to call security.
But Caddie stopped him.

"You can't, Jon. You just can't. We have to talk to
her."

So he put the phone down and said, "Okay, fine, let's
talk to her. I might enjoy this."

He opened the sliding doors and allowed Jessica inside. Caddie stayed across the room, drawn and thinner
than Jessica had ever seen her. Before Jessica could get
a word out, Jon threw two thick files down on the table
and said, "It's all right here, Jessica. The whole goddam story. Now, if you want trouble, I'll provide it."

"What are you talking about, Jon?" Jessica said, trying to control her anger. "What story?"

He pulled open a file and dumped the contents out.

"I've got phone logs, I've got letters, I've got a
whole truckload of offers you turned down for Caddie
that other girls ended up doing, and they all made a lot
of money from it. You've been using my wife to build
up your business, and now that game is over."

"There isn't a single offer we've ever turned down
for Caddie that wasn't either in conflict with her larger
contracts or inappropriate for a model of her stature."

"Well, now someone else will be deciding what's
fucking appropriate or not."

"Jon, a model like Caddie doesn't do advertisements
for cough syrup, no matter how much money they offer
her, because then she's no longer a star . . . she's just
another celebrity hawking a product, and she'll cool
off as fast as she got hot. We've built an image for
Caddie, and that image is valuable."

But Garret Stowe had prepared Jon with the skill of a
White House spin doctor. He had fed Jon information
garnered by Phil Stein to convince Jon that Caddie

could be making twice the money she currently earned. Garret, of course, downplayed the fact that these higher offers had come from companies whose products were almost identical to those being marketed by firms that Caddie was already under contract to, and that she was legally bound not to appear in competing advertisements. Jon had spent weeks convincing Caddie that he was simply trying to stand up for her, fighting a battle on her behalf.

The more Jon Ross tore into Jessica Cartwright, the cooler her demeanor became. Jessica sensed that the words coming out of Jon's mouth were not his own. It was clear to her that he had been primed.

"Whoever Garret Stowe is," Jessica said coolly, "he is not fit to represent Caddie, and he will never be able to live up to his wild promises of guaranteed income and no commissions. I've been in this business long enough to know that. I haven't made a mistake, Jon," she continued, "but you're making one right now. A very large one." She turned to Caddie. "You have my home number," she said. "Feel free to use it."

Jessica left.

"You do one thing to get in the way of our decision," Jon screamed, spit flying out of his mouth, "and I'll fucking—"

Jessica stopped and turned around, staring at Jon. "You're an idiot, Jon, and there was a time when I thought you were smart enough to know it."

She flashed another look at Caddie, then stalked away.

Caddie stood and started to go after Jessica. Jon grabbed her.

"We can't do this to her," Caddie said to her husband. "Maybe we are making a huge mistake."

Jon held on to her.

"The huge mistake was not doing it sooner."

"I don't know . . ." Caddie was suddenly filled with misery. Tears burned behind her eyes.

"Fine," Jon said. "Go after her. Let her run your career into the ground. Let her sign every young model in America on the strength of your name, and then when they're all stars you won't be able to get a job cleaning the floors in Jessica's office. You want to go back to living in a trailer? You want to go back to eating fucking cat food because your mother's too drunk to go to the store and there's nothing else on the goddam shelf?"

Caddie slowly looked up at her husband, her face tight with fury.

"Maybe that's what you'd like to do. Run through your money and go back and find your father and let him give you five bucks so you won't tell anybody that he used to knock the crap out of you and your mother. What else did he do, Caddie? Did he take it out and ask you to play with it? Right there in the pigsty trailer in Escondido, where the cops used to come just about every week to keep your parents from killing each other?"

Caddie's anger turned to cool detachment as she looked away from Jon's eyes. Every time she disagreed with him he threatened to expose her private past, and every time she gave in. Truly she thought she'd die of shame if her gritty secrets hit the national media.

Jon pressed his advantage. "Do you want the world to know your mother used to turn tricks in the goddam trailer where you lived, because your father would disappear for months on end, then show up just long enough to knock you both around? Do you think your adoring fans will appreciate the fact that the all-American-model bullshit you've been selling is all lies? Well, guess what, it doesn't matter. Nobody has to know if you play your cards right. It doesn't matter to me, Caddie, because I'm your husband. I love you. I won't let you go back to those days. We're going for-ward, full speed ahead. Aren't we?"

Caddie sat down on a chair and looked out at the ocean. Her eyes were a million miles away from Jon.

"Full speed ahead," Jon said quietly.

chapter
15

The Sink Bait bar was at the east end of Calle Ocho on the outskirts of Miami's Little Havana area, the neighborhood populated by expatriate Cubans. It catered to the crews of the charter boats that took tourists and sportsmen out for a day of deep-sea fishing. Most everyone there was Cuban, except for a sixty-year-old man named Luther Nevitt, who sat at one end of the bar, accompanied by the two crew members from his charter boat. His sunburned skin approached the texture of beef jerky, and it creased as Nevitt sucked in the last puff of a filterless Camel. When he finished his Miller beer, the bartender slid another in front of him and took change from the cash on the bar.

Nevitt lit up another Camel and watched the men dope out handicap sheets for that night's greyhound races. A couple of drunken men danced to the Tito Puente music coming from the jukebox. A television played soundlessly in one corner.

Suddenly, several of the men at the bar started whooping and hollering, pointing at the television.

Nevitt looked up.

They were watching a montage of Caddie Dean bikini photographs from the *Sports Illustrated* bathing suit issue. Then came pictures of several more models, wearing everything from bathing suits to formal attire. The montage cut away to the hosts of *Entertainment Tonight,* who were evidently talking about the photos, and then they rolled video from the press conference held earlier that day to announce the formation of the Vitesse model agency and its signing of Caddie Dean. There were shots of Phil Stein, Caddie Dean, and Jon Ross. As soon as they stopped showing bikini-clad models and cut to the talking heads, the patrons of the Sink Bait lost interest.

All except for Luther Nevitt.

His narrow blue eyes squinted as the smoke from his Camel curled around his cheekbones. He stared at the television. Slowly, his eyes widened. In the background of the press conference, unobtrusive but quite visible, was Garret Stowe. It was clear that Garret was keeping a careful separation between himself and the hoopla in the foreground. But once Nevitt caught sight of him, he locked in on the image. And when the show cut to a commercial, Luther continued staring, then jumped when the untended ash on his cigarette fell of its own weight onto his chin.

Nevitt's crew members got up and talked about where to go for dinner. One of them said something to Nevitt. He didn't respond.

"Are you coming with us or not?" the man asked.

When Nevitt didn't answer, just continued to stare at the screen, the two gave up and left, concluding that their captain was good and drunk. As usual.

The helicopter carrying Jessica back from Amagansett landed in Manhattan shortly before nine in the evening. Jessica returned to her office. Edie was still there, along with the one remaining junior booker.

There were two hundred messages awaiting Jessica. She spent hours tracking down models who had not defected to Vitesse, reassuring them, telling them that business would go on as usual. But already the models were complaining about the zero commissions offered by Vitesse, and why were the Vitesse models getting the highest daily rate in the world? When Jessica tried explaining to the models that Vitesse had only been in business for a few hours, that no one was actually paying those inflated daily rates, and that it was unlikely that Vitesse could survive for long without charging commission, the models promised to stick with Cartwright, but Jessica heard very little conviction in any of their voices.

She sent Edie and the others home while she took a late-night conference call from her new lawyers, Barber, Willcox & Grefe. Yes, the lawyers explained, Phil Stein's actions were an astonishingly brazen breach of ethics and fiduciary responsibility. Yes, they could bring a major cause of action against him and his firm, though he had quit the firm, without warning, a week ago. Restraining orders were a possibility, but difficult to obtain. And though the lawyers felt she might win a judgment against Phil Stein—indeed, they felt it was almost a certainty that she would—Stein obviously had anticipated legal action and would have some kind of plan and defense in place, one that would likely drag the matter out for many years. In the meantime, Jessica had a business to run. And since the model agency business was all about staying hot, Jessica could not afford to wait around while lawyers filed briefs and took depositions. She had to run her company.

Well after midnight, Jessica grabbed a taxi and sank down in the seat as it took her home. The taxi sped past several newsstands, and at each stand Jessica saw the face of Caddie Dean staring back at her, both from magazine covers and from that day's *New York Post*.

Once inside her apartment, she walked into the den. There were the usual stacks of magazines: *Elle, Vogue, Harper's, Details, Vanity Fair, Interview,* all neatly fanned out on the table by the maid. The walls were covered with framed photographs of Jessica with top models from over the years. It struck her just then that most people had photographs of family and close friends in their dens, but these were clients. Or they used to be—ten of the girls she was looking at right now had signed with Vitesse. Jessica tore around the room, pulling the photographs off the wall and hurling them into a heap of bent frames and shattered glass in a corner of the room. Finally, she opened the terrace doors and let the cool night air wash over her face. The enormity of what had happened was only now catching up with her. In one day her business had been ravaged, hundreds of thousands of dollars of future income wiped off the books.

A long time ago, after suffering through the difficult years with her husband, she had vowed to herself that she would never allow business to become too important, that she would never allow business to make her cry. Yet, standing on her terrace, that's exactly what she did.

When she awakened at five in the morning, having slept fitfully, Jessica didn't bother with makeup. She threw on a dress, raced over to her office, and began returning the dozens and dozens of calls that had come in the previous night. And in doing so, she realized that the worst wasn't over; the worst, evidently, was just beginning.

In a business in which image outweighed substance, Jessica knew the defection of her models and top bookers cast a cloud of doubt over her agency. Everyone she spoke to, from models to agents to advertising executives, responded in cautious tones, offering condolence while being careful not to fully align themselves with Jessica. Was it that Vitesse was doing something terribly new and right, or was it that Jessica and her agency were doing something wrong? Until that question could be answered, everyone in town hedged his or her bets. People who just twenty-four hours ago would have leaped to the phone knowing Jessica was on the other end now treated her calls circumspectly, as if she were under investigation for a heinous crime. The advertising executives screamed about Vitesse's doubling the basic daily rate for the top girls, claiming these girls would get no work. But by noon, Jessica learned, all of Vitesse's models were heavily booked, mostly by the same people who that very morning had told Jessica that Vitesse's scheme would never work.

"What do you expect?" one of the advertising executives said to Jessica when she asked why he had caved in to Vitesse's rates. "If I go out with a campaign that has a star in it, and the campaign fails, they can't fire me, because I can tell them I delivered a proven winner. But if I go with a brand-new girl and the ad bombs, they question my taste and out I go. So, I pay."

A friend of Jessica's at an advertising agency called Vitesse to check availability of top girls, and Vitesse claimed bookings were solid for the next two months. When told of that, Jessica said it was impossible for so many bookings to have been made in one morning. But that didn't matter. The perception of heavy action at Vitesse was being skillfully played by Garret Stowe; he ran the place like a new restaurant that had no customers, yet told callers reservations must be made two months in advance. Interest breeds interest. The fashion business thrived on gossip, and the gossip was that Vitesse, one day old, was a hit.

Gerry, Cartwright's remaining booker, did his best to keep up with the workload. But models used to speaking with Sascha or Lee were diffident with Gerry; for them, it was like having a substitute psychiatrist. And because of the turmoil, all the models called in at once, so many couldn't get through to Gerry, which made them uneasy.

After lunch, Tommee Barkley came flying into the office. She'd been up in Nantucket doing a layout and had heard the news about the model wars only this morning, at which time she told the photographer he had one hour to get the shot he wanted. He did so, and she chartered a plane to get herself to Manhattan. She walked directly into Jessica's office and said, "What the hell is going on, and how can I help?" Tommee still wore the equestrian outfit from the morning's shoot.

Suddenly, looking at Tommee's wild outfit and windblown hair, Jessica started to laugh.

After Jessica explained the events of the previous day, Tommee asked, "So who is this little asshole Garret Stowe?"

"Some agent from Paris. I'd never heard of him."

"Can he carry this thing off?"

"For the moment he's doing it."

"What the hell is the matter with Caddic?"

"It's Jon," Jessica said, breaking one of her professional rules, that of never discussing another client's business.

"Jon spends most of his time trying to reinvent the concept of being a dickhead," Tommee said. "Sounds like he's outdone himself. But what do you do now?"

"Just get back to work. Do what I always do," Jessica said with a conviction she certainly didn't feel.

"I called from my car, but the lines are always busy. It's bad for those booker lines to be tied up, Jessica."

"Bookers don't just fall out of the sky. Gerry is doing what he can. I've got temps taking messages."

"Okay," Tommee said, tossing her jacket on the couch, "then that's what I can do. I handle the girls calling in. Get me a telephone and I'll talk to these twits."

At first the idea sounded crazy to Jessica, putting a famous model on the booker lines to talk with other   But she warmed to it; after all, Tommee could charm the stripe off a skunk.

Tommee found a desk, slipped on Sascha's headset, and started taking calls.

Aaron Adam arrived alone at Cellini's studio to look at the test shots for the new jeans campaign. The pictures were spread out on a conference table, and Aaron Adam studied them for twenty minutes without saying a word, his eyes focused with the intensity of a surgeon's. The model Jessica had discovered was stunning, and the urban-Western flavor of the test shots blended the sophisticated with a sense of freedom and incivility. Cellini had stayed up all night supervising the creation of the prints and selecting which shots to show Aaron Adam. He'd been through this same procedure with A.A. many times, and he had prepared himself for the long period of nonresponse and the final, always unemotional, yes or no. Usually, the answer was yes.

Aaron Adam straightened up and said, "No, Anton. This is not it."

Cellini took a deep breath and let the awful word sink in; he wasn't used to hearing it.

"The girl or the concept?" Cellini asked.

"The girl fits the concept," Aaron said. "She's quite stunning. I just don't like the package. We're moving away from the biggest model in the world to do this campaign. If the campaign does not make news, people will assume we simply ran out of ideas."

Cellini said, "Maybe another model in the same setting would do it for you."

"I like the model just fine—for this concept. I don't like the concept."

"Well, I thought that maybe since she's a Cartwright girl you might be swayed against her."

"Why would that be?" Aaron Adam asked.

"With all the turmoil. Caddie leaving for Vitesse. With all those girls leaving for Vitesse. I thought maybe you'd lost confidence in Jessica's taste."

"I trust Jessica's taste," Aaron said.

"So do I, of course," Cellini said quickly.

"These photographs are impressive," Aaron Adam said. "But I want to be stunned, not impressed."

With that, Aaron Adam departed.

Within an hour, word hit the street that the Aaron Adam campaign was wide open again.

Cellini called Jessica and gave her the news.

Jessica sat silent for a few seconds, then said, "Was he afraid because of what's going on here?"

"No, no, not at all," Cellini said, though that was the very excuse he was circulating to prevent people from thinking that Aaron Adam was unhappy with Cellini's work. "Let's just find someone else."

She hung up the phone and absently tapped her desk with a pencil, which was Edie's signal to bring coffee and four Advil.

"Aaron Adam doesn't like the new photos," Jessica said to Edie. "We've got to find a new girl—we've *got* to keep that account. I want to see every girl who comes in on the open calls. Every one."

Even in her current mood of anxiety, Jessica knew that she could not afford to lose Caddie Dean, a dozen other top models, and the Aaron Adam account on top of it.

The French street photographer Jamm arrived in New York from Paris via Concorde, courtesy of Garret Stowe.

"What do you want me to shoot?" Jamm asked, arriving at the Vitesse offices with only a knapsack and camera bag.

"Girls in the city," Garret said. "Beyond that, anything you want."

That sounded plenty good to Jamm, who loaded up his cameras and set off into the night.

Jamm spent three days photographing New York. He caught an hour's sleep here and there, but mostly walked Manhattan from end to end, working through a hundred rolls of film, two cartons of cigarettes, and a pair of cheap shoes. He brought the proofs in for Garret, who paid him ten thousand dollars for his efforts, then told him he'd catch up with Jamm back in Paris.

Garret called in Sascha and asked her to study the proofs with him.

They spent an hour looking through magnifiers. Finally, Sascha said, "This guy is some kind of pervert."

"What do you mean?"

"All the best shots are of little girls and older guys."

She pushed half a dozen proof sheets in front of Garret; Sascha had circled a few frames on each of the sheets.

"Take a look and tell me what you see," she said.

He studied the circled frames. They were of girls between the ages of ten and fourteen. Girls walking to school, riding bikes, shopping, skating, living in the city. But in every photograph there were men, either in the foreground or background, looking at the girls. And despite their ages, all the girls selected by Jamm had a sexual component, a look, that presaged adulthood. And, clearly, all the men in the pictures were aware of that look.

"I see jailbait," Garret said.

"Right, that's the word. It's sick. Visually, though, it's interesting."

"Is it?"

"Very," Sascha said, repulsed by the context of the photographs, but compelled by it; the pictures made her uneasy, and she had been in the fashion industry long enough to know that uneasy was often good. "These girls aren't models. But the idea is there. Aaron Adam has always sold his jeans on an all-American thing. This is the opposite. It might get somebody's attention."

Garret shrugged casually and thanked Sascha for her thoughts. But the moment she left the office he placed a call to Anton Cellini.

Cellini found it unusual that Garret asked for a 2:30 P.M. lunch at an unfashionable deli on the West Side, but Garret said that he had a reason for the time and location. Just as the waiter arrived with sandwiches, a bell sounded from a building across the street. It was a private girls' school, and as soon as the students began emerging from the building, the older girls began rolling up the skirts of their uniforms, loosening top buttons on their white blouses, trying to put some "street" into their look. The girls transformed themselves from sweet-looking schoolkids into Madonna wannabes in about thirty seconds. Cellini's active eye took in the entire scene, then he looked inquisitively at Garret, who handed him a folder of Jamm's photographs.

"Taking pictures is just a hobby for me," Garret said, "and it's a bit embarrassing to be showing them to a professional of your stature, but I had a thought. . . ."

Seeing that Cellini was absorbed by the photos, Garret stopped talking. He had picked out two dozen of Jamm's "Lolita" photos and blown them up to 8×10s. Cellini glanced at the first few, then began focusing, like someone who takes a few bites of a meal and then realizes he is eating something quite special.

"What's your thought?" Cellini asked.

"Aaron Adam," Garret said simply.

Cellini looked up from the photographs.

"He's been selling his jeans with your very successful all-American Caddie Dean approach. It worked. But obviously you're looking for something else. What about this?"

Cellini's eyes flashed, and Garret could almost hear the synapses firing in the photographer's brain. He looked again at the photographs.

"What I'm thinking of," Garret said, "is something that makes Calvin Klein look like a fundamentalist preacher. Pictures that people are embarrassed to look at, but look at anyway."

Cellini masked his exuberance, leaned back in his chair, and gazed at the girls across the street.

"Listen," Garret said. "I know this is presumptuous, but I thought maybe if I threw an idea into the wind . . . It was just a thought."

"You took these?" Cellini said.

"Throw them away. Don't worry about it."

"I'd like to think about it."

"Whatever you want. They're yours."

The men finished their lunch and went their separate ways.

Cellini climbed into his chauffeured town car, grabbed the cellular phone, and called Aaron Adam's assistant.

"Where is he?" Cellini asked.

"Looking at textiles."

"I need to see him right now."

"He's backed up with five appointments. People are in from Japan and Geneva. Let's set something for tomorrow—"

"I'll be there in ten minutes."

Cellini hung up the phone.

Aaron Adam walked into the conference, curious but not irritated; Cellini had never interrupted him in the past. Cellini, in fact, had never come to the Aaron Adam offices, preferring always to meet at his studio.

"Here's my concept," Cellini said, spreading Jamm's photographs out in front of Aaron Adam. "Think of these pushed ten times further."

Aaron Adam spent his usual period of concentrated silence studying the photographs.

Finally, he said, "You're talking about starting a shit storm."

"A shit storm that rains money," Cellini said.

"This could put us out of business," Aaron Adam said, "or it could reinvent the business. I think it is brilliant."

Cellini stood up and looked again at the photographs.

"Does Jessica have a girl this young?" Aaron asked.

"I want to find this girl myself," Cellini replied. "Jessica's edge has gotten too soft, obviously."

"We have a long history with the Cartwright Agency."

"This is my concept. I have to do it the way I want."

Cellini left and immediately called Garret Stowe.

"You've got me thinking," Cellini began. "But before I can formulate my concept and discuss it with Aaron Adam, I need to know if such a young model exists. I need a girl who seen from one angle inspires you to take her to the zoo with a balloon in her hand, and seen from another angle you'd want to fuck her. And she must never have been seen in a photograph other than in her mother's wallet."

"I'll call you," Garret said.

Garret summoned Sascha and explained the nature of the search.

"I don't have to search," Sascha said. "I've already met her."

"What do you mean?"

"I've seen her. She lives in Wisconsin. She came to us with her mother last year at Cartwright."

"And you didn't sign her?"

"She was twelve years old. Jessica never went below fifteen or sixteen, no matter how good they looked. People in the business frown upon anything younger than that."

"But this girl, is she special?"

"The best girl I've ever seen. The problem is, the kinds of ads you're talking about, you'll need an eighteen-year-old girl who looks like she's twelve."

"Let me see her picture."

Sascha retrieved the Polaroid of Ginny Fischer from her desk and dropped it in front of Garret.

"This is exquisite," Garret said in a voice that chilled Sascha. She looked at him, and he seemed absorbed in the photo in a way that made Sascha's stomach turn.

"Yes," Sascha said, suddenly hesitant, "she does have the look."

There was no question that Tommee Barkley could outtalk any booker in the business, and for some weeks following the defection of models to Vitesse, Tommee arrived at Cartwright at seven in the morning and did not leave until seven at night, working the phones without even a break for lunch. The only problem was that though she had worked as a professional model for fourteen years, she had never paid much attention to the office end of the business. She had had no need to, because she was a model who arrived for work on time, did the job, and left. And that meant that Tommee was not used to dealing with the vagaries of other models' behavior. Tommee's concern for Jessica lasted for three days, then her frustration began to mount.

"You whining, ungrateful little bitch!" was the phrase Jessica heard out of Tommee's mouth that gave her the idea that Tommee might not be booker material.

"What's the problem?" Jessica asked.

"This little nineteen-year-old pain in the ass says her hotel room is on the ninth floor. She wants the fourth floor or below, and the hotel doesn't have it. She wants us to call the manager and have somebody moved."

Jessica suggested she let Gerry handle it, then dragged Tommee out for lunch and told her it was time for her to go back to work as a model.

After lunch, Jessica interviewed three prospective bookers, liked none of them, but hired one on a temporary basis.

She had the office stabilized, but the aftershocks of the raid continued to drain resources and morale. The lawyers convinced Jessica that it would be self-defeating to pursue Vitesse in the courts, because the time, energy, and money spent on such a suit would only further distract Jessica from running her company. What was needed, Jessica decided, was a positive event to offset the negative event of losing Caddie Dean and so many top models. And clearly, the event waiting to happen was the new Aaron Adam campaign.

That Aaron Adam had turned down Cellini's test campaign with Jessica's model frustrated Jessica, but there was no time to pout. She had to find another model. But Cellini was being tight-lipped about what approach he wanted to take, even though there was a rumor on the street that Cellini and Aaron Adam had privately agreed on a new concept for the campaign.

When Garret received the call from Cellini asking him to find a girl, Garret quickly checked around to see if other agencies, particularly Cartwright, had been notified that Cellini was still looking. They had. But the other agencies had been informed that Cellini was continuing to look for a girl around twenty with a fresh,

wholesome appeal, a "young Caddie Dean." Obviously
Cellini was throwing up a smoke screen. None of the
other agencies had been told to come up with a Lolita.
Only Vitesse. And since Garret had followed Cellini
after their lunch across the street from the school and
seen him go straight to the Aaron Adam studio, he
knew that Cellini had discussed the concept with
Aaron Adam and been given a green light.

Sascha found the telephone number and address for
Ginny Fischer's family, but Garret decided that rather
than calling them, he would show up in their Wisconsin town. So he flew to Chicago, rented a car, and
drove north into Wisconsin's farmland.

chapter

16

After seeing Garret's face on *Entertainment Tonight,* Luther Nevitt watched the newspapers for stories. He didn't see anything for several days, then the tabloids hit the stands. He bought all of them and went home to his small apartment just off Calle Ocho.

Nevitt didn't read well, and so he asked a neighbor to read the articles aloud to him, though he wouldn't tell her why he was interested.

Then he neatly clipped each article from the papers and underlined Garret's name and the name of the agency in New York. He sat for the rest of the evening, eating a dinner of chili and beer, looking at the photographs. The reproduction in the tabloids was not of high quality, so Garret's face in the background of the news conference wasn't vivid. But Nevitt stared at it, rolling the image over in his mind, uncertain if the face was the one he was trying to recall.

Nevitt taped the articles to the door of his refrigerator, figuring if he looked at the pictures long enough, sooner or later he'd have his answer.

* * *

Genoa City, Wisconsin, was a small town in the rolling farmland where residents were still making the transition from a rural economy to the technological age. Local clothing, dry-goods, and hardware stores had been pushed out of business by a Wal-Mart that had opened just five miles away. The single-screen movie theater no longer played first-run shows; those all went to a multiplex in a nearby town. Genoa City was a town young people got out of.

Ed Fischer owned an auto supply shop that barely broke even, but since the locals took pride in caring for their cars, he managed to keep the business afloat while many others around him had gone down. He had inherited the shop from his father, who still worked part-time, so it was a point of pride with Ed that the Fischer Auto Supply neon sign remained clean and functional. Ginny Fischer worked in her father's shop during the summer, and Nona Fischer did the books and kept track of the inventory.

On the way into Genoa City, Garret stopped at the Wal-Mart near Twin Lakes and bought some casual clothes, figuring that his Armani linens would be suspect in this territory. He found Fischer's shop and seated himself inside the Dairy Queen catty-corner across the street. A few minutes after six, the Fischers closed down the store, crossed the street to the Dairy Queen, and ordered dinner. Most of the people in the place knew each other, and all of them took a moment to peruse Garret. But he gave a friendly, disarming nod and returned to his newspaper and coffee.

Garret watched the Fischers eat. The family was popular, particularly Ed, who had once been the star quarterback of the local high school's football team. A knee injury had eliminated college ball, and Ed had settled into the life of his hometown. Since high school, he'd put on about forty pounds, and he now had the look of someone who was convinced he'd been cheated in life, but couldn't figure out exactly how, or what to do about it.

Watching Nona Fischer and her husband, Garret perceived that she did not love him, she was simply with him. Probably there had been a time when he was the high school hero and Nona the most beautiful girl in the county, but not now. Nona smiled at Ed when he asked for something, but her eyes displayed a distance that Ed didn't seem to notice. Things happen the way they happen, her face seemed to say, and that's why I'm here. But Garret sensed that somewhere deep inside Nona Fischer she felt she was young enough to dream, but she would never share those dreams with her husband, at least not anymore. Ed Fischer packed down a couple of burgers, and Ginny talked about school, but it was clear to Garret from the looks she gave her mother that they did their real talking when Ed wasn't around.

Garret focused on Ginny's look: long slim legs, the beginnings of curves, lips in a natural pout that all the collagen injections in the world couldn't sculpt. A gusher of golden hair that must weigh several pounds. She was a kid, no doubt, but Garret saw a natural sensuality in her movements and expressions. He watched her walk to the counter and back and felt a warm stirring between his legs. She was like a hot breeze that comes at you out of nowhere, then passes. Clearly, Sascha had been dead-on accurate in her appraisal.

The next morning, Garret went to the local high school, told a secretary he was trying to find an old acquaintance, and asked for a look at the yearbooks. It didn't take him long to find Ed Fischer, and his listing full of sports accomplishments; he had been voted most likely to wind up on *Monday Night Football*. Then he drove to Fischer Auto Supply and began chatting with Ed, asking him if he was the same Ed Fischer who used to play for the Tri City Wildcats, telling him that he remembered reading about Ed in the Chicago papers many years ago. Ed warmed up to the conversation, and then Garret presented his card from the agency and talked right through any negative reaction Ed might have had.

By the time Nona Fischer walked into the store, Ed was ready to close the place down for an early lunch. The three of them went back over to the Dairy Queen, and Garret told them he had happened to notice them there last night and thought Ginny had every possibility of becoming a model, a big model. Garret started talking about college money and the kind of contacts that could land a girl at Harvard or Yale. When Ed Fischer said he'd be just as happy to see his little Ginny stay near home, Nona spoke up and asked about living situations in New York and what kind of work could be guaranteed. That was when Garret took out his portfolio of Caddie Dean photographs and revealed that Aaron Adam was looking for a new model to build his blue jeans campaign around. The Fischers wanted to talk about it privately. They called Garret at his motel an hour later and expressed concern about pulling Ginny from school for several days to travel to New York for the test shots.

"That will all be taken care of," Garret said. "Tutors, accommodations, travel. I have a jet coming here tomorrow to pick me up. I want you all to be on it."

That comment brought silence. A private jet?

Garret called Cellini and asked if Aaron Adam would be willing to send a plane. Cellini immediately called Sascha Benning and asked if this Ginny Fischer was for real.

"Send the plane," Sascha said.

At 10:00 A.M. the next day, Aaron Adam's Gulfstream IV jet touched down at an airport near Lake Geneva, ten miles from Genoa City. Waiting to board it were Garret Stowe and the three Fischers.

* * *

The next morning in Manhattan, Garret took the family to breakfast, then by limo to Cellini's studio. Cellini paced the vast space of his studio, having barely slept the night before. He had an appointment booked with Aaron Adam for five o'clock that same day to show him the test shots he was about to take of Ginny Fischer. Cellini knew that if the shots were a failure, Aaron Adam could decide not only to drop Caddie Dean for the jeans campaign, but to change photographers as well. When Garret walked into the studio, followed by Ginny Fischer and her parents, Cellini paused and straightened up, like a great bear rising to take the scent of prey. He looked at Ginny Fischer for several seconds, then lurched forward, drawn to her as though by a gravitational pull. Cellini blew past Garret and ignored the parents; he hugged the startled girl and said, "God always told me you would come into my life, and now that you have, I am fulfilled!"

Nona and Ed Fischer looked stunned by Cellini's outlandish behavior and appearance—he wore one of his tentlike linen caftans and a tic-dyed baseball cap.

"Sharon!" he screamed to an assistant, not taking his eyes off the child. "Just the lightest makeup. Almost nothing or I'll rip your face off and feed it to the pigeons in the park."

Ginny giggled. The parents stared, mouths agape.

Garret steered the parents to the back of the studio as Cellini hoisted Ginny off the ground and yelled, "Look at this work of art, look at this child of God's intentions!"

"Maybe I'd better stay with Ginny," Mrs. Fischer said.

"No need," Garret said. "He's just carried away with your daughter's look. He'll calm down and get to business."

Cellini burst into an aria.

"That guy," Ed Fischer said, "seems like kind of a fag."

"He's the world's greatest fashion photographer," Garret said.

Garret signaled for coffee and kept Ginny's parents busy showing them various posters of Cellini's most famous work.

Cellini, for all his bluster, knew how to photograph women as well as anyone who had ever picked up a camera. And he spent little time with the test shots of Ginny, such was the level of his confidence and euphoria at the sight of the girl.

The film was processed immediately, and Cellini selected five simple shots of Ginny, whom he had costumed in a black leotard and an oversized leather jacket, and the prints were made.

Aaron Adam spent two minutes looking at the photos, then called in his top marketing staff. They knew they were gazing at an extraordinary new model.

"Who is she with?" Aaron Adam finally asked.

"Vitesse," Cellini said.

"What has she done?"

"Nothing. But to look in her eyes . . . *everything*." Cellini shivered.

"Sign her," Aaron said, turning to one of his assistants.

Cellini called Garret and told him that Aaron Adam's business affairs lawyers would be calling him to negotiate a contract for Ginny Fischer.

That evening, Garret took the Fischers to Le Cirque for dinner, where they saw Diane Sawyer, John Kennedy, Jr., and Tom Cruise. He told Ed and Nona that the photos had turned out well, and that the possibility of a deal with Aaron Adam was in the air.

"We'll need a couple of weeks to think about it," Ed Fischer said as dessert was served.

Garret noticed that as those words came out of her

husband's mouth, Nona Fischer hesitated with her fork, upset that he would jeopardize such an opportunity. And Garret knew that in the fashion industry, two weeks might as well be two years, with all the things that could go wrong during that time. Aaron Adam and Cellini would not take kindly to such a response, he knew, since they would interpret it as a negotiating ploy.

"I mean," Ed Fischer continued, "what kind of pictures does the guy want to take? I saw some of that stuff on the walls. . . ."

Garret nodded and said, "I think you'll be happy with Cellini's work."

"But how long would this take?" Ed Fischer asked.

"Ginny would have to live in the city for many weeks, maybe months," Garret said truthfully.

"I have a business to run," Ed said.

"Of course," Garret said. "However, this contract could make a substantial difference to your family's income. Quite substantial, as a matter of fact."

"I don't know," Ed said, shaking his head. "I don't know."

Garret said, "In any case, I want you to enjoy this visit in New York. I've arranged some things for all of you the next couple of days."

He sent the Fischers to museums, restaurants, shows, a private tour of the Aaron Adam salon. Sunday night he told them to dress nicely because he was taking them to dinner with a surprise guest.

They arrived at Bouley, and were joined for dinner by Caddie Dean and Jon Ross. Nona was stunned, Ed stared, and Ginny asked Caddie to sign her menu. Caddie told them amusing stories about working on location, and Jon boasted about some deals he had made that none of them quite understood. When Caddie invited Ginny to come to a studio in the morning and watch a photo session, it was smiles all around.

The Fischers were scheduled to leave Monday morning, and Garret knew his first call that day was supposed to be a return call to Aaron Adam's lawyer to discuss Ginny's deal, yet he hadn't even signed Ginny to Vitesse, much less convinced the parents that Ginny should do the campaign. He had, however, arranged for Caddie to make the photo shoot invitation, counting on the fact that Ed Fischer would have to return to Wisconsin and that he would allow his wife and daughter to stay an extra day. His gamble worked. Ed was unable to say no to Ginny's wide-eyed reaction to Caddie's invitation.

As soon as Ed Fischer left in the limo for JFK, Garret turned all of his attention on Nona Fischer. While they watched Caddie Dean photographed for an airline—making it look easy and fun, and surrounded by deferential assistants, makeup artist, hair stylist, and an unusually polite photographer—Garret pointed to Caddie and told Nona Fischer, "That could be Ginny."

With Ed out of town, Garret changed tactics. He took Nona and Ginny to the city's hottest clubs, surrounding them with celebrities, music, dancing, and glamour. Nona was tentative at first; it seemed to take her a few hours to realize her husband was not watching over her shoulder. But by the second night, Nona was downing champagne freely and leading them onto the dance floor.

In the meantime, Garret opened negotiations for Ginny's contract with Aaron Adam's attorney.

Vitesse had established temporary offices in the downstairs rooms of a five-floor brownstone on East 79th, just off Madison. Garret sat in the offices late one Thursday night, feeling a rush of adrenaline. Ginny Fischer had not signed, but he had no doubt that she would. Vitesse models were being booked, and though Phil Stein was nervous about meeting the guarantees they had made to top models, Garret assured him he would handle disputes that arose. Caddie Dean could not be signed to new contracts yet, but her name was now associated with Vitesse.

He opened a bottle of champagne and poured a glass for himself and one for Phil.

"This is all marvelous," Phil said, still fretting over the books, "but we'll have to land a couple of big contracts fast to cover the guarantees."

"You're boring me. You stay here and worry, and I'll celebrate alone," Garret said, leaving abruptly. He was beginning to wonder about bringing along Phil Stein. The man had invaluable information, but nerves of Jell-O. Garret refused to admit even to himself that Giselle Rochas would not finance him indefinitely, even when she saw the astronomical costs of getting Vitesse off the ground.

It was a chilly, drizzly evening, and Garret buttoned up his newly purchased Aquascutum overcoat. He turned on Madison, and suddenly sensed that he was being followed. He hadn't seen anyone or heard a sound that caught his attention, but his gut told him that something was wrong. There weren't many pedestrians on the street, and as Garret searched for an empty cab, he quickened his pace. For two blocks he walked fast enough so that anyone following would have to reveal himself; he glanced back several times and saw that he had outdistanced the few pedestrians traveling in his direction. So he stopped, deciding to wait for a cab. He stepped off the curb and finally spotted one. The cab worked down the block toward Garret and pulled over.

But as Garret reached for the rear door, he felt a hand clamp down on his forearm. Garret whirled to throw a punch, but the punch was deftly blocked. His assailant laughed. The light from the streetlamp came from the rear of the man's head, so Garret couldn't make out the face, but the man took a close look at Garret.

"Well, fuck me up the nose," the man said to Garret. "It is you, isn't it, Earl?"

"You want the ride or not?" the cab driver yelled out the window.

"Go ahead," Garret said to the cabby, who sped away.

The man had a massive upper body and stubby legs. He stared at Garret, then started whistling. He was the same man who had spotted Garret in the bar near Cellini's studio several weeks ago, then followed him to his hotel.

"Conley," Garret said quietly.

"Earl," Conley said, "you're my hero. You're in the pussy business!"

Garret stepped up to the curb and pulled his arm away from Conley's grip.

"And look at the overcoat and the shoes," Conley continued. "You got pussy and you got money. I got neither. But you were always smart. Take me some-place and buy me a drink."

"There's a bar around the corner," Garret said.

"Good. Any bar is fine with me. Don't feel like it's got to be some fancy place to impress me. Just any-place where they serve drinks. And where you pay."

Garret took him to Clooney's Pub, a dump fre-quented by serious drinkers, lonely people, and yuppies out to slum it.

"Where the fuck did you come from?" Garret said, lighting a cigarette.

"That's a hell of a greeting for a long-lost friend."

"What do you want?"

"A cigarette, for starters." Conley took Garret's pack right out of his shirt pocket, then took his good time tamping down one end and lighting the other. The smoke seemed to pour out of every orifice in Conley's face for thirty seconds. "So, how'd you happen to pick the name Garret Stowe? It sounds kinda faggy, don't it?"

"Conley, I don't owe you shit. Tell me what the fuck you want."

"I'll bet you don't talk to the models that way."

"It's a business, just like any business, and nothing I do has anything to do with you."

"I'm not so sure about that. Just because you've got all this young quiff thinking you're slick-dick Garret Stowe doesn't mean I have to kiss your goddam ring. In fact, I'll bet if I told you to kiss my ass right here in the middle of this bar, you'd do it. Wouldn't you?"

"What do you want, Conley? I'm not going to keep asking you."

"Aren't you even going to ask what I've been doing all these years? And aren't you a little curious about how I happened to find you?"

"I don't give a rat's ass," Garret said.

"Tell me this. Does model pussy taste any different than, say, normal pussy? All those long legs, short skirts. I'll bet it tastes good."

"You want to meet a fucking girl?" Garret said. "Is that it? I'll throw something better than you've ever seen your way if I don't ever have to see you again."

Conley took another cigarette from Garret's pocket.

"I'll bet you're banging all those models and they think you're some fancy-ass genius. I can't wait to meet 'em."

"I don't owe anything," Garret said again.

"I'm on you like stink on shit. And I can't think of a better way to say it."

"Five thousand dollars, and then you disappear from the face of the earth. Deal?"

"Shit, you could hire some gang-banger to kill me for half that amount. But by the time you get around to it I'll cause all kinda shit in your world, won't I? No, I don't want five thousand dollars. For now, I'll just take a job."

"A job?"

"Sure. I don't mind working for my money. You know that."

When Ed Fischer returned to New York on Friday, his wife met him at the airport and told him that she'd given Garret Stowe permission to negotiate a contract for Ginny.

Ed was stunned. As far as he was concerned, it was a family matter still under discussion. He had not given his permission for any deals to be made.

"I thought it was the right thing to do. For Ginny," Nona said, as they rode in the back of the limo provided by Vitesse.

"How could it be the right thing to do if I'm not in on the decision?"

"We've talked about it."

"Goddammit, Nona, you don't make a decision like that. I do. She's my daughter, too. Remember?"

"Listen to this. We get a hotel suite for as long as Ginny's in New York. They provide a school tutor, a food and clothes allowance, one hundred thousand dollars while they shoot the pictures, and another four hundred thousand if they go ahead with the campaign. That's half a million dollars. Half a million! How would we ever make half a million dollars?"

"We're doing just fine where we're at."

"Oh, get real, honey. Think about what this could mean."

"It means that my daughter would be in New York, away from her school and her friends."

"Her school and her friends will still be there when she's done. And I'd be here with her."

"Exactly how long would this whole thing be?"

"A couple of months."

"What?"

"It's not just for Ginny. It's for me, too. I love this city. I've never had so much fun in my life."

"Don't you get it? The only reason they're being nice to you is 'cause of Ginny. You think that Garret guy enjoys spending all his time fancy-assin' you around town?"

"He wants what's best for Ginny, and he's been very good to us."

Ed Fischer looked at his wife, and finally noticed that she'd had her hair cut short, and the color seemed to be different.

"What the hell they do to your hair?" he asked.

"Gianni Adolfo did it. Garret got me an appointment with him."

"Am I supposed to be impressed? I like your hair long. You trying to look like a boy?"

"Thanks, Ed. Thanks a whole bunch."

"I think this is a lot of bullshit. And we'll see about there being any contract. I haven't agreed to anything."

"Half a million dollars, Ed," Nona said slowly. "We'd have to sell one hell of a lot of radiator caps to make half a million dollars."

And that was all she said for the rest of the drive into the city.

When they returned to the hotel, Nona revealed that the cocktail party they were attending that evening was in honor of Ginny's becoming part of the Aaron Adam organization.

"What the hell is that supposed to mean?" Ed asked.

"That I already signed the contract."

Ed Fischer at first refused to attend the party, but finally relented when Ginny begged him.

He watched his wife at the party, parading around in a dress that he knew they couldn't afford, and a hairstyle that made her look like somebody else, and his anger mounted. When Garret arrived, Ed beelined for him, but before Ed could get a word out, Garret handed him an envelope.

"Ten round-trip first-class tickets between your home and New York," Garret said, "so that you'll never be more than a few hours from your daughter. And see these?" He handed Ed another envelope. "Aaron Adam's floor seats for the Knicks. Just in case all the sissy model stuff bores you when you're in town."

Ed behaved himself for the rest of the party, but brooded most of the weekend. On Sunday he called Garret to say he wanted more time to think about all of it, but Garret was out of town.

The Vitesse limousine was waiting to take Ed Fischer back to the airport. He kissed his daughter and his wife, then left town, still not entirely certain what had happened during the past three days.

chapter
17

Exactly eight days after her arrival in New York, Ginny was brought again to the Cellini studios for another test shoot, this time as an employee of Aaron Adam, Inc., and as a client of Vitesse.

Cellini was all business, the theatrics displayed during Ginny's initial visit tempered by the knowledge he must now deliver the most spectacular campaign of his life.

"First thing we have to do," Cellini said to Ginny, scrutinizing her as she stood before him in her leotard, "is get things in just a bit better balance. But I'm not entirely sure what I'm working with here." He turned to one of his assistants. "Do we have a bathing suit for Ginny?"

Mrs. Fischer went to the dressing room with Ginny as she changed into a string bikini.

"Don't be shy," Cellini called to her. "All of us here have seen a million girls in bathing suits."

Ginny emerged wearing a robe, walking behind her mother.

Mrs. Fischer approached Cellini.

"Do all of these people have to be here? Ginny isn't used to having—"

"Time to get used to it," Cellini said pleasantly, brushing Mrs. Fischer aside and walking up to Ginny.

"You are the most gorgeous creature walking the fact of the earth today," Cellini said to her, removing the robe. Awkwardly, Ginny folded her arms and stood in front of Cellini.

Cellini studied her figure the way a jeweler would study a promising uncut gem.

"Karen?" Cellini yelled.

A young woman with a clipboard ran forward.

"I think our Ginny needs an inch or so off the bottom, and the upper thigh could use a little tightening. Start her with the trainer, and I want a no-fat diet as of lunch today."

"A diet?" Mrs. Fischer said. "Ginny is only thirteen. She looks perfect."

"The face of the century," Cellini agreed, wrapping an arm around Mrs. Fischer's shoulders, "but every bottom can use some help. Make certain she sticks to the diet we give her. Ginny," he continued, walking away from Nona, "what's your favorite music?"

"Pearl Jam, I guess," Ginny said.

"Karen, get every Pearl Jam CD in existence and we'll play them full-blast. Ginny looks bored."

Within minutes, Pearl Jam pounded from speakers in each corner of the room.

"See that girl over there?" Cellini said to Ginny, pointing to Karen. "She is your slave. If you're hungry, she will bring you the proper food. If you want the music changed, she will change it. If you want a magazine, she's the one to find it. And if you're angry and want to yell, yell at her. That's what I pay her for."

Ginny giggled. The entire concept seemed nuts to her.

"I couldn't be more serious," Cellini said.

Beginning the next morning, a private trainer arrived at Ginny's hotel room to take her to his gym, there to be guided through a series of exercises designed to tighten and tone the butt and thighs. A menu for each day of the week had been given to Nona Fischer. The tutor accompanied Ginny to the studio and worked with her between makeup and hair tests. Cellini was not going to launch into the shoot without absolute certainty about the look he wanted to capture. They tried twenty different hairstyles on Ginny, and pumped a thousand test shots through the camera until the proper balance of makeup was found.

During all of this, Nona Fischer dutifully went to the studio, sat in the lounge or in Ginny's dressing room, worked on needlepoint, wrote letters, read magazines. She would not admit it to anyone, but at times she felt jealous of the whirlwind of attention that suddenly encased her daughter from dawn until bedtime. It struck Nona as odd that no one from Aaron Adam's design studio was coming around to measure Ginny for the sample jeans, or the other items of clothing that were going to be sold in the new line, but she refrained from asking about it. In fact, no one was saying anything to her about the nature of the advertisements. Several times Nona asked Cellini how he planned to shoot her daughter, but Cellini only shook his head and called in Karen to keep Nona at bay.

Garret sent fresh flowers regularly to Nona and Ginny and called them both two or three times a day. Everything seemed to be going well, until one day Ginny returned home from the studio rather embarrassed. The real shoot was just days away, and Cellini had asked that Ginny have her pubic hair shaved.

At first, Nona was simply confused by the request.

"Why? For what?" she asked her daughter.

"Something about the ads," Ginny said. "The way the jeans fit, I guess."

"There aren't any jeans where that would matter," Nona said, alarmed.

She called Cellini, who didn't take the call. Karen came on the line and explained that they wanted Ginny hairless except for what was on her head.

"But what in God's name for?"

"Mr. Cellini is an artist," Karen said simply. "It's better not to ask him about his vision. He doesn't like it."

"Oh, really," Nona Fischer said, slamming down the telephone.

The next morning, Ginny did not arrive on the set.

Cellini called Garret Stowe, who drove to the hotel, and managed to convince Nona Fischer that all great photographers had their quirks.

"Do you know what my husband would say if he heard about this?" Nona said to Garret.

"He shouldn't hear about it, then," Garret said. "I don't think he understands these things. This is a matter of art and design."

Then Garret drove Ginny and Nona to the studio and spent the entire day with them.

Finally, Cellini announced, it was time to do the work. He called Garret aside and suggested that things would go smoothly as long as Nona Fischer was kept off the set. First morning, fine, but after that, Cellini wanted only his model, not model and mother. Garret understood Cellini's point, and accompanied mother and daughter to the morning of the actual shoot, which, though it was not explained to Ginny or her mother, was only for publicity shots to be included in a press kit. These were portraits taken with Ginny wearing a black turtleneck sweater.

As with all layouts, Cellini first shot Polaroids to check his lighting and background. But even the Polaroids turned out stupendously, better than anyone had hoped. Every experienced eye in the studio, from Cellini to the makeup person, hair stylists, lighting di-

rector, and wardrobe person, knew this was the face of
a star. Congratulations all around, then Garret told
Nona he had a surprise for her, and whisked her out of
the studio into a limousine and to the fashion industry
ultra-insider's spa called Curves.

During the limo ride, Nona inquired about the ads,
but Garret professed to know little. Nona said Ginny
was uncomfortable with certain things she'd heard on
the set, such as having to be seminude in one of the
layouts. But Garret brushed off the concern, contend-
ing that Cellini was an artist, that he created on the fly,
and that no one, including Cellini, knew exactly what
he was going to do until the inspired moment of creation. And after all, these advertisements were for
Aaron Adam jeans, famous for taste and quality.

Besides, Garret continued, he had something else he
wanted Nona to be thinking about: her own modeling
career. Sascha had briefed Garret on Nona's secret desire to be a model, and now Garret planned to use that
unfulfilled dream to his advantage. "We're going to put
you with a trainer," he said, "one that works with you
several hours a day. We're going to resculpt your body
and change your diet, and within a month we'll ready
for test shots."

"I'm a little old for all this, aren't I?" Nona Fischer
said, her body language a bundle of hope.

"Of course not," Garret said. "Not every product is
meant to be sold to teenagers. You follow the regimen
at the spa—and I promise you it will not be an easy
one—and the reward will be yours for the taking."

"But I have to be looking after Ginny," Nona
protested, and after a pause, added, "And my husband
won't think too much of this idea."

"We have a tutor, a bodyguard, a nutritionist, a driver, and the best photographer of women in the world
looking after your daughter. Don't you think you deserve a little looking after?"

"If Ed finds out—"

"If your husband finds out that you are working hard to improve yourself, that you're doing something you deserve and have always wanted, then he should be thrilled for you. If he loves you."

Fifteen years of unspoken dreams clouded Nona Fischer's eyes as she walked into Curves, where the staff, properly prepared by Garret, treated her like visiting royalty. Ever since she graduated from high school, Nona had been looking after her husband, cooking his meals, washing his clothes, helping with his business, and the same for Ginny. And though she loved her daughter, the longing for that elusive focus she had felt so intensely in high school—when every boy on campus stared at her, when male teachers treated her with more deference than the other girls, when mothers told their daughters they should try to fix their hair and pattern their outfits after Nona's—now welled up inside her like hope reborn.

At first, when the spa assistants started with their toner baths and glycolic acid skin washes, Nona felt guilty that she was being a bad mother for not being on the set with Ginny. She slipped into the changing room, took one of the tiny bottles of vodka that were replenished daily in the minibar, and downed it in one gulp. She'd been drinking two or three of the small bottles each day ever since her husband left town, convincing herself it was the simplest way of calming her nerves. Nona returned to her workout.

Ginny's shoot continued for several weeks, and so did Nona's pampering. Garret rode in the town car each evening to pick up Ginny at the studio and Nona at the spa, and served as the co-conspirator in the women's pact not to tell Mr. Fischer about their daily routine. Everyone involved with the Aaron Adam campaign reminded Ginny not to discuss details of the shoots with anyone, and that what might seem strange or uncomfortable on the set would look quite different when assembled in an ad layout.

Ed Fischer flew in for the first few weekends, and Garret made certain the family were completely booked with theater and concert tickets, restaurants, sporting events, and any other activity that might keep them exhausted and in a crowd. He sensed the building tension between Ed and Nona, as Ed seemed to withdraw into a cocoon of silence. Nona's trendy new look met with icy disapproval from her husband. And he told Ginny that she was trying too hard to look grown-up, wearing all the stylish samples provided her by Aaron Adam.

"It's the latest stuff, Dad," Ginny protested. "You couldn't find this back home, or anywhere else."

"That doesn't make it good."

It did not go unnoticed by Ed Fischer that Aaron Adam arranged to have special tables and treatment for them at restaurants, where the staff referred to Ginny as Miss Fischer the moment she walked through the door.

"My husband's upset that the shoot is taking so long," Nona told Garret Stowe one Monday morning over breakfast, having just ridden with Ed to the airport. "He wants us home."

"Cellini is not going to be rushed," Garret said. "And neither should you be. You know, I may be able to arrange for other work for Ginny after this shoot finishes. She's exclusive here for Aaron Adam, but European companies might be interested. Of course, you'd have to stay here in Manhattan."

He watched carefully for Nona's reaction. It was not long in coming.

"I like it here," she said.

Garret prompted Ginny's tutor to call Ed Fischer and tell him how well his daughter was doing with her schoolwork.

And when Nona's trainer at Curves informed Garret that Nona had reached her target weight, down ten pounds from when they started six weeks ago, he sent Nona over a tight black minidress from the Versace boutique.

"Thank you, but I could never wear that dress," Nona said to Garret that afternoon. "I'd be embarrassed."

"Have you looked at yourself lately?" Garret asked. "The dress belongs on you."

Next time they met for an evening out, Nona was wearing the black dress.

"I told you," Garret said, looking her up and down with admiration.

"I feel silly. This is something Ginny could wear. Not me."

Garret instructed the driver to stop at Grand Central Station.

"Leave your coat in the car and come with me," he said, taking Nona's hand, leading her into the main terminal.

The station was packed with evening commuters. "Stop here," he said, leaving her near one of the doorways. "When I signal you, walk toward me."

Before she could protest, he was gone, walking across the marble floors, then he stopped and turned to face her, fifty yards away. Garret waved and Nona began walking tentatively toward him, uncertain of his point. But then the point became clear, as businessmen slowed their pace to have a look at the svelte woman in the miniskirt. The stares were obvious. Nona felt ridiculous at first, but then the attention began to feel good. Her stride lengthened and she allowed the natural motion of hips to flow. His desire for her hit her like a hot breeze, and as she recognized it he gave her a knowing smile, which she returned. She wanted this feeling to last forever; she was laughing and giddy with excitement.

"You're a bastard, Mr. Stowe," she said, her body tingling and vibrant.

"And now this bastard is going to take you to dinner," he replied, grabbing her hand and leading her to the waiting limousine.

Garret popped the cork on a bottle of Cristal and poured out two glasses. "To the dress and the woman who makes it beautiful," he toasted. As the car worked its way downtown, Garret watched Nona's eyes reflect the thoughts racing within. He saw her elation turn to anxiety.

"Is there something wrong?" he asked quietly.

"I don't want to go home," she said after a moment.

"You don't have to," he said. "We can stay out all night and finish with breakfast in the park."

"I mean, I don't want to go home to Wisconsin."

"You don't have to do that, either."

"Yes I do. This isn't my life. I have a family. Ginny has a home and a father . . . and I have a husband."

"Your life has changed, Nona. Ginny is making money, you are making money as Ginny's manager."

"Manager?"

"Of course. Aaron Adam adds ten percent to the total of Ginny's earnings, designated to the manager."

"You never told me—"

"I wanted it to be a surprise. I worked it into the deal after Cellini went nuts for the test shots."

Garret was lying, but he knew he could work out some kind of arrangement with Aaron Adam and Cellini if he told them Nona was taking her daughter home.

"My husband isn't even speaking to me right now," she admitted.

"I want you to see something," Garret said, as the limo pulled over in front of the World Trade Center.

He took her to the Windows on the World restaurant, 107 stories up in the Trade Center, but then snuck down a fire-escape stairwell and opened the door to one of the floors of business offices.

"We shouldn't be here," Nona said, giggling.

"That's your problem," Garret chided, "because that's how you think."

Garret found the first open door in the corridor and peered inside. Two janitors were emptying trash and listening to music on Walkmans.

"You can't be in here at this hour," one of the janitors said to Garret.

Garret peeled out three hundred-dollar bills and placed them in the janitor's hand.

"I want to show this lady the finest view in New York City," Garret said, "without all the noise of the restaurant."

The janitor looked at the money.

"That would be from the corner office. Number five."

He pulled out a key and unlocked it.

"You can't touch anything," the janitor said.

"We'll only be a few minutes," Garret answered.

"Hey," the janitor said, sliding the bills into his pocket, "take your time."

He closed the door and pulled Nona over to the wall of glass. She gasped at the breathtaking view of the city, harbor, and New Jersey beyond. Garret was silent for several moments, letting her take it in. Then he said, "Do you want to just be another person like one of those lights below? They are nothing, they are all the same. Don't you want to be the one up here looking down at them?"

"It's beautiful," Nona agreed.

"It's only beautiful because we are up here on top of it all," Garret said, standing close behind her. "From down there it all looks like shit. Look at all those millions of lights. And all it takes to be up here is money, Nona. Did you see the janitor take that cash from me?

That's all we needed to have this to ourselves. You're not going to see this view in Genoa City, Wisconsin."

"But this is all a dream. It's not real."

"It's real," Garret said, reaching around and lightly stroking Nona's breasts.

She pulled away, startled, but Garret drew her back and held her.

"It's real," he said again, touching her more firmly.

When her husband touched Nona's breasts, he pawed at them as if they were made of rubber, pushing and squeezing. She had never liked it. And because her breasts had developed very early in her youth, boys always had gone right for them, and always too hard. But Garret's touch was different, almost teasing, as if his fingers knew just what to do to make her want more. It was the kind of touch she imagined in her private moments, when she fantasized about a man in a movie or in one of the novels she read. It felt like the touch of a man who wanted to please, who found pleasure in pleasing her. She allowed him to keep touching her as she looked at the millions of lights below. "It's all real," Garret said to her again. "This is not a one-time thing for Ginny or for you. It is just the beginning of something much bigger. To matter in life it takes money, and you two can make more here than you'll ever be able to count. I'm going to help. All you need to do is believe that you deserve it."

"My husband—"

"—doesn't understand what you want or what you need, or what you're capable of."

Garret turned her around so that she faced him. He ran his fingers down her face, soft as mist, tracing her nose and lips and ears. She fought to keep her eyes closed, then Garret gently kissed them open. Nona felt the heat flowing from his lips and fingers right through to her core. She felt a strange weakness in her legs and arms, and she clung to Garret, afraid she might fall backward through the plate-glass window.

"I've never done this," she said.

"I'm sure you've never done a lot of things that you should have," he replied. "Don't you think you know what's right for you better than your husband does? He wants you back in that little town so he can show everyone he took the most beautiful girl in the state and made her what he wanted. But it's not what you want. You can have your own money and your own life. Ginny owes you that. You've raised her, you've done everything for her. It's your turn now."

He kissed her forehead and eyes. He kissed all over her face, except for her lips. Garret waited for her mouth to part and lift toward him, and when it did he pressed his lips softly on hers, so soft it felt like a breath of warm wind flowing over her skin. And then she searched his lips with hers and he pressed forward, began to pull back, until he felt her hand on the back of his head, pulling him into her. She kissed him deeply and with a sudden insistence, as if she were afraid that he might suddenly disappear. She wanted him to take her then and there, hard and fast, so it could overwhelm her before she had time to think about it. But he didn't. He went slowly, making her aware of every touch, drawing out each sensation. Nona felt as if she were being reshaped by his hands.

"This is you," he whispered, pulling the scoop of her dress back to kiss her shoulder, "and this is you," he said, kissing the hollow of her neck, "and this is also you," he said, sliding the black dress down the length of her body until it dropped to the floor. Light from outside reflected the sheen of perspiration on her skin. Garret held her motionless. He removed her lacy black bra and took her breasts in his hands, then leaned down to kiss one, then the other, his lips teasing her nipple, sucking the hardened peak until she heard herself moan and realized she had never made such sounds before. He was discovering parts of her body that had never been touched so subtly or so well. "My God," she whispered. "Oh my God. I've never done this." But she no longer meant she had never cheated on her husband; now she meant that she had never known that a man's touch could feel so wonderful.

And then she was completely naked, unable to remember her panties being removed. For a moment she was embarrassed, thinking of her slack hips and slight paunch of her stomach, but as his hands caressed her, she realized her training had actually transformed her body; her stomach was firm and flat and she felt the tautness of her hips and thighs. Suddenly, a sense of power coursed through her body.

"Now," she said. "Right now."

They moved to the desk and brushed away the pads and telephone on top of it. Nona pulled Garret's shirt off, and he dropped his slacks to the floor.

They sprawled on the desk, drops of perspiration falling on its polished surface.

"It's better than dreams," Garret whispered to her, somehow reading her thoughts, "because we can do this again and again. You can feel this way whenever you want." As Garret moved in and out of her, Nona gasped with pleasure and the promise of release. "Open your eyes," Garret urged. "Watch me." She did, and the intensity of pleasure increased. As he moved faster and deeper, Nona held him tighter, feeling as if she were going to explode. Then she caught her own reflection in the window, and she saw a person she did not recognize. She looked dangerous and young and powerful, and in that moment she felt she could dive through the window and soar over the city.

chapter
18

Anton Cellini's creative team and Aaron Adam's advertising agency code-named the new campaign "Fresh," and they put it on an accelerated production schedule aimed at placing the ads in magazines six weeks from the completion of the shoot. It was to be the most expensive advertising blitz in the history of the fashion industry.

Aaron Adam, after viewing the proofs of Cellini's work, decided that a test market might backfire; he anticipated a public outcry against the ads, and a bad reaction to the test market might scare off certain publications in which he wanted to run the ads. Space was reserved in *Vanity Fair, Vogue, Elle, Rolling Stone, Cosmopolitan, Allure, Time, Newsweek, Sports Illustrated*, and even regional powerhouses like *New York* magazine and *Buzz* in Los Angeles. If for any reason a publication was unwilling to run the ad, Aaron Adam had a backup plan: a white page with the phrase AARON ADAM JEANS in black block. Word of the potential controversy preceded the arrival of the ads, and everyone in the fashion industry wanted an early look. But no one got one.

The ads were hand-delivered to the publications by a representative of Aaron Adam. There were five different layouts, with a rotation selected so that each major magazine would be running a different ad. Two magazines declined to run any of them. Certain of the more extreme ads were declined by other magazines. But, in all, Aaron Adam got his launch. Once the ads were put into production, word spread that Aaron Adam and Cellini had crossed acceptable boundaries and were taking a massive gamble. In an era of family values and political correctness, the campaign blazed its own path, and a highly risky one.

Aaron Adam coolly reminded everyone that the public would be the final judge. And on November 15, the ads featuring Ginny Fischer hit the streets.

The first ad depicted a dramatically lighted Ginny Fischer standing in a drizzling rain in a potholed alley, her arms defiantly folded across her rib cage, just below her emerging breasts. She was not wearing Aaron Adam jeans—she was standing on them. Ginny was naked, shafts of light angled across her woman-child body, the expression on her face an arresting blend of defiance, innocence, and latent sexuality, her lips parted in a sullen smirk. Ginny was not alone in the ad. She was surrounded by five men, ranging in age from fifteen to fifty, ethnically diverse, with bodies that went from Venice Beach stud to rock-star sallow. All of the men were naked and on their knees, all staring at Ginny. The lighting and retouching were such that the men's genitals were in shadow, but with a little imagination the penises seemed to be visible, and some appeared to be erect. A shaft of light splashed on Ginny from behind, outlining a swale between her legs and illuminating the crumpled pair of jeans on the ground. The ad copy across the top read: YOUTH WILL BE SERVED, and at the bottom of the page: AARON ADAM JEANS.

The second ad featured a naked Ginny Fischer

clutching a pair of jeans to cover her crotch and one of her breasts. She stood at the foot of a bed. Behind her, a man reclined beneath the sheets, the outline of his body vividly depicted. Another man, a towel over his crotch, sat on the side of the bed, lighting a cigarette. A third man, wearing a robe, sat in a chair reading the *Wall Street Journal,* looking thrashed and happy. Ginny glistened with sweat, and again, the ad read: YOUTH WILL BE SERVED.

In the third ad, Ginny stood outside a school. Other female students, ranging in age from ten to fifteen, walked out of the gates, wearing uniforms, knee socks, and little-girl hairstyles. Awkward young boys shyly shadowed them. But Ginny's jeans were tight and her black T-shirt revealed the outline of her breasts. A drop-dead-handsome, tough-looking guy in leather jacket and jeans stood before her. Ginny had hold of his belt buckle.

The advertisements exploded into the print media. Aaron Adam had calculated that television spots were unnecessary because that medium would supply coverage for free. And it did. Within hours of the campaign's hitting the newsstands, religious leaders, psychologists, educators, feminists, and culture commentators were on television sounding off on the Aaron Adam jeans campaign. There were discussions of child pornography, sexual abuse, and First Amendment rights. Politicians waited to gauge the tide of public opinion before weighing in on the subject: *Prime Time Live, Hard Copy, Inside Edition, A Current Affair, 20/20, 60 Minutes, Nightline,* and dozens of other television shows signed producers and reporters to the story. Aaron Adam refused all interview requests, as did Anton Cellini, the strategy being that if the opposition had no target to attack, debates would be difficult to conduct. For fashion-industry insiders, the Aaron

Adam campaign was the number-one launch and cocktail hour topic.

And everyone waited for the sales figures to roll in.

Aaron Adam's marketing team released a limited quantity of the jeans and waited for feedback. The feedback arrived in a frenzy of orders. Telephones and fax machines in the Aaron Adam sales department operated around the clock. Bloomingdale's in New York sold every pair of Aaron Adam jeans in the store within one hour of unpacking them. Kids bought any size available, hoping to exchange them elsewhere. Even though A.A. had a supply of hundreds of thousands of pairs, he continued for the first two weeks of the campaign to ship them out on an allotment basis, giving the largest allotments to buyers who also ordered other items from the A.A. line.

Within three weeks, Aaron Adam had moved two million pairs of jeans at twenty-nine dollars wholesale, with back orders worldwide for six million more. It was a phenomenon unprecedented in the fashion industry, and analysts predicted that the jeans would pump a billion dollars into the Aaron Adam coffers within the first six months of the campaign, provided the manufacturers could supply the product. The company's stock, which had languished in the low 20s for a year and a half, rocketed to 50 in a six-week period.

Aaron Adam hit the cover of *Business Week, Forbes,* and *Fortune.* Anton Cellini received hundreds of offers to create new campaigns for other companies. *Prime Time Live* showed hidden camera tapes of teenage girls changing into the jeans at school, because their parents had forbidden them to own a pair. Four major rock stars were photographed wearing the jeans, providing the kind of publicity no company could afford. Magazines that carried the most extreme ads reported the largest press runs and newsstand sales in their histories. While certain feminist groups picketed the Aaron

Adam studios, others went on talk shows to defend a woman's right to express herself in any manner she chose. And as the tidal wave of publicity and controversy washed over the country, Ginny Fischer became the hottest face in the world.

Contractually, Ginny Fischer was not allowed to discuss the ads without Aaron Adam's permission, and for the first two months of the campaign, acting on Aaron Adam's counsel, Garrett Stowe saw to it that Ginny Fischer stayed out of the public eye. Ginny's name was not released to the media, though reporters quickly ferreted it out. But when teams of television trucks and reporters descended on Genoa City, they found only Ed Fischer and his auto supply shop. He refused to talk to anyone. They interviewed Ginny's friends, who thought the whole thing was pretty cool, while the principal of Ginny's school said she thought the girl was being exploited.

Nona and Ginny Fischer spent a month in Bermuda, staying in a beach house owned by Aaron Adam. The tutor was flown in, but there was no television, and a telephone only for emergencies. Nona and Ginny did not know the scope of the Aaron Adam campaign until they returned to New York on Aaron's private jet.

During the drive into town, Nona had the chauffeur stop at a newsstand, and they picked up half a dozen magazines. Mother and daughter thumbed through the glossy pages and showed each other the various ads. Ginny just laughed.

"It doesn't even look like me," she said.

Nona nodded, and told herself that her daughter was merely an actress playing a role in the advertisements. They had nothing to do with the real Ginny. But in the pit of her stomach Nona began feeling queasy.

"Mr. Stowe would like you to stop at the Aaron Adam offices before going home," the driver said, crossing the bridge into Manhattan.

"What for?" Nona asked.

"Don't know, ma'am, but those were his instructions."

When Nona and Ginny arrived at Aaron Adam's offices, they were greeted like royalty by the marketing and public relations staffs. Escorted directly to Aaron Adam's private office, Nona and Ginny were greeted with champagne and gift bags from Harry Winston. Then Anton Cellini and Garret Stowe appeared from another room, both bearing gifts for mother and daughter.

"We're very pleased and proud of both of you," Aaron Adam said to them, "I can already tell you that this is going to be the most successful campaign in our history. And in recognition of that, I have another gift for you." He handed Ginny an envelope, and motioned for her to open it. Inside was a bonus check in the amount of three thousand dollars. "To help get you settled in Manhattan," Aaron Adam said.

When Nona and Ginny returned to the car, Garret accompanied them.

"And now another surprise," he said, signaling the driver.

Instead of going to the Pierre, where they had been staying, Garret took them to Trump Tower. When Nona began to ask what this stop was about, Garret told her to be quiet and just follow him. He escorted them to a twentieth-floor corner-view apartment.

"This is your new home, courtesy of Vitesse," he told them.

Ginny looked at her mother, her eyes wide. "Are we staying in New York?"

"Do you want to?" Nona asked.

The look on Ginny's face supplied her answer.

"Is Daddy coming?" Ginny then asked.

"As often as he likes," Garret said. "Of course."

Ginny ran to the window and stared at the view of

Central Park. "God," she said. "Nobody is gonna believe this."

"Yet it's all true," Garrett said, looking at Nona Fischer as he did, and smiling into her eyes.

Exclusive to Aaron Adam in America, Ginny Fischer was free to work for other clients in Europe, Asia, and South America. The demand for her was staggering.

During the first ninety days of the campaign, Vitesse fielded fifteen hundred inquiries into Ginny Fischer's availability for everything from ramp work in Paris to cigarette advertisements in Japan.

Every model agency in Europe inquired about representing Ginny overseas. All were told that Ginny was exclusive to Marie Zola out of Paris and Vitesse in New York. Marie Zola flew to New York to congratulate her partner, Garret Stowe, on his stupendous success. But one afternoon, while reviewing model contracts with Phil Stein, she realized that Ginny Fischer's contract was not with Vitesse, but with Garret Stowe, Inc., an entity she did not know existed.

"I don't understand this," Marie said to Phil Stein, holding up the contract.

"Garret acts as Ginny's manager as well as her agent," Phil explained.

"But that is a conflict of interest," Marie said.

"Not as far as Ginny is concerned," Phil replied. "I know it is an unusual arrangement, but it is what the Fischers wanted."

"How could they want that? And how could Garret accept it? He and I are partners in Vitesse," Marie said.

"No, just in your Paris agency," Phil said, confused that Marie didn't understand this matter, since Garret had told him he had worked out the details with Marie some time ago.

"What you're telling me is that I don't book Ginny

Fischer for Europe? Are you mad? All of Vitesse's models go through me in Europe."

"Not Ginny Fischer," Phil said, "unless Garret deems it so."

Garret heard the raised voices and walked into Phil's office.

"Miss Zola is upset about the Ginny Fischer arrangement," Phil said.

"Marie, I put you back in business," Garret said. "Don't be annoying."

"I gave you a partnership in my agency in Paris," Marie Zola insisted, "and you told me I was your partner here."

"Sorry," Garret said. "I lied." He walked out of the office.

Wide-eyed, she looked at Phil Stein.

"You are a lawyer, are you not?" she demanded.

"It's time for you to go back to Paris," Phil said. "I'll talk to Garret. I'm sure he will be fair with you."

Fashion-industry observers who predicted, as many did, that skyrocketing sales of the jeans would be a three-week phenomenon were proved dramatically incorrect. Profits leaped 400 percent in the first three weeks following the campaign's launch, and climbed from there. The success of the campaign was so overwhelming that other companies were forced to ditch their own campaigns and slap together new concepts in hope of maintaining a foothold in the market.

Within hours of news of the campaign's success, Aaron Adam had his design and production departments expand the line of clothes sold with the jeans, and new ads, featuring Ginny Fischer, were commissioned from Anton Cellini.

Nona and Ginny readily agreed to a new set of ads.

Ed Fischer took another approach. He tried to obtain a court order granting him custody of Ginny, but failed.

Ginny chose to remain with her mother in New York, even when Nona informed her husband that she wanted a legal separation.

"Your father is jealous of both of us," Nona told Ginny.

Nona, with Garret's help, found an exclusive private school in which to enroll Ginny, and Ginny began making friends her own age. She had little time for them, however, because Aaron Adam put her on a promotional tour to several states, where he hosted cocktail parties for major retailers. To Ginny, it was all pure excitement. Jet planes, limousines, private screenings of movies, hotel suites with unlimited room service, and a credit card of her very own. She was besieged with interview requests, none of which were granted by Garret Stowe. At the height of the frenzy, acting upon advice from Aaron Adam, Garret booked several jobs for Ginny in Europe for staggering amounts of money. He had to get her away from the media, which after being refused interviews had taken to staking out Ginny's school and apartment.

Within the model business, there was also another major ripple effect from the Aaron Adam advertisements. Calls came in to bookers at all the major agencies asking for "a Ginny Fischer type." Everyone immediately knew what that meant: young, fresh, sexy, but also childlike. "Jailbait" was how advertising executives categorized this look. Bookers scrambled to find new girls, since most of the agencies, like Cartwright, weren't accustomed to signing models so young. But supply soon followed demand as kids as young as ten turned up at the agencies in carloads, open call or not.

Most of them had their hair and makeup done like Ginny's from the ads. Most were precociously dressed, wearing short leather skirts, tight jeans, and tops that all but revealed their budding breasts. Few were shy about strutting into the offices, and all knew how to turn on a sexual attitude when asked to do so by a booker. Instead of the fresh-faced, clean-cut look that advertisers were used to requesting from underage girls, now they wanted girls who looked like they could wrap a man around their finger. Even the most seasoned bookers were surprised at how many mothers were willing to trot their daughters into the agencies, even helping the girls heighten their sexuality with inappropriate clothes and cosmetics.

First stop for most of them was Vitesse, because of Ginny Fischer, but they also lined up at Ford and Cartwright, Elite, Click, and all the others.

A young woman named Ellen Cannon had been recruited by Jessica Cartwright from an agency on the West Coast and hired as lead booker. Ellen was quick and driven, and shortly after the Ginny Fischer phenomenon exploded, she informed Jessica that if Cartwright was to remain a viable agency, Jessica had better get away from the idea of not signing girls under the age of sixteen.

"It's just a bad idea," Jessica said to Ellen.

"I don't care if it's a good idea or bad idea," Ellen said. "The perception in the industry right at this moment is that Vitesse is on the cutting edge, while Cartwright and everybody else is trying to play catch-up. We either ride the bull or get stomped on."

"I just don't want to be representing thirteen-year-old kids," Jessica argued.

"What's 'want to' got to do with it?" Ellen countered. " 'Have to' is the operative term here. I know you didn't hire me to kiss your ass, and I'm not going to do it. Jessica, you made your name by launching Caddie Dean and spending a decade making her a superstar. Our friend Garret Stowe has done this with Ginny Fischer in three months. Caddie Dean was on the cover of a news magazine. Ginny Fischer *is* news."

"Let me think about it," Jessica said.

"You've got half an hour," Ellen said, "and then I'm out of here, because I've got to make a living. If not here, someplace else."

There was a time when one of her bookers wouldn't have dared to speak to her that way, Jessica knew, as she returned to her office and slammed the door. But bookings at Cartwright were down 60 percent since Vitesse opened its doors. Reporters who used to call Jessica whenever they wanted an authoritative quote on the model business now called Garret Stowe. It galled Jessica, after years of hard work, to have people in the business look at her agency and assume her success must have been due solely to Caddie Dean, because without Caddie business plummeted. Before she became an agent, Jessica had tried to be an actress and a model. The model agents at the time had told her she should consider another line of work. So she had started a damn agency. And now her own booker was telling her she should think about dumping the agency if she didn't want to move with the times. As much as she was against the signing of children, Jessica did not want the agency to collapse. So she walked down to Ellen's desk and said simply, "Go ahead."

Within days, Ellen had found two girls, one twelve, the other fourteen, who clearly were model material, at least by the new standards. Jessica signed them without personally seeing them; she told Ellen to use her judgment and handle it.

Jon Ross, like Jessica, was unnerved by the trend toward younger models. With Caddie's jump to Vitesse, Jon planned to use the increased income to pursue his own dream of becoming a filmmaker. Since no film studio would consider hiring a third-rate fashion photographer to direct a film, Jon convinced Caddie that they should finance the project themselves.

"We only need to put up seed money of our own," he explained to her, "to lock up the script and give a guarantee to the star. Then I can package the rest with financiers."

Jon invested nearly a million dollars, then beat a path to agents, managers, film financiers, and just about anyone connected to the film industry who would grant a meeting with him. But when he reached the part of his pitch where he told industry professionals that he planned to direct the film himself, the meetings rapidly deteriorated.

Jon took his idea to Garret Stowe, who deftly sidestepped the matter until Jon casually mentioned that Caddie had met billionaire Davis Kellen in Maui, along with Tommee Barkley, and that if he could just get his project a bit further along he might ask Caddie to approach Kellen, who owned, among other things, an entertainment conglomerate.

"I could go to him for distribution," Jon said. "If I go to him for financing I'll appear weak, and a guy like that spits out weakness for breakfast."

"Davis Kellen," Garret said, his agile mind shifting into high gear as he remembered a recent *New York Times Sunday Magazine* piece about Kellen's vast empire. "What did he want with Caddie?"

"What else? He saw her out by the pool at the Hanna Ranch and thought he might get some. Caddie brought Tommee along, and I guess he chased her all around the house. Old coot has got a thing for models."

"Let's have lunch with him," Garret said. "But it's too demeaning for you to have to sit there and ask the guy for anything. You're the filmmaker, you're the artist. You should talk about the script and how you plan to direct the film. Let me talk to him about the money. We play good cop, bad cop. You never know, it might work."

The lunch was arranged.

"Dress sexy," Garret told Caddie the morning of the lunch, "and it might help Jon land a film."

Caddie wore a short black leather skirt and a white silk blouse. The play of the fine silk against her breasts gave Kellen something to look at during lunch, while Jon rattled on about the concept of his film.

Garret never mentioned the need for financing during lunch. "I'll do that in a follow-up phone call," Garret explained to Jon. And Jon had been too enraptured by his own words in the presence of the famous billionaire to note that Garret, as Kellen walked them to the door of his private dining room, had made a quiet, direct suggestion to Kellen, meant for his ears only. The suggestion had to do with models, not movies.

"I'll have someone get in touch with you, Mr. Stowe," Kellen said. "I'm very interested in your notion."

When Jon Ross called Garret to inquire about the follow-up with Davis Kellen, Garret told him that Kellen had decided Jon's film wasn't for him, though he'd been very impressed by him at lunch.

Despite striking out with Davis Kellen, Jon announced that he had raised two million dollars and would commence filming the low-budget thriller within sixty days.

He made good on his word, but two weeks into filming his lead actress walked off the picture, announcing to the press that Jon Ross was a total amateur and that the dailies were a disaster. Production halted, at considerable expense. To start again, it would be necessary to reshoot the first two weeks of film, since all of it featured the departed star. Jon announced to anyone who would listen that the film was going to resume within the next couple of months—and he resumed scrambling for money.

He began by calling Caddie's largest clients, Aaron

Adam and Lipton Tea, and asking for advances on future earnings. Word of this got quickly back to Garret, who, despite the fact that the commissions on those contracts still flowed to the Cartwright Agency, called Jon and told him to cease his actions.

Jon stormed into Garret's office.

"Listen, you son of a bitch, you don't tell me what to do. That's first," Jon screamed. "Second, if you didn't spend all your time promoting that little thirteen-year-old piece of ass, we might be making some more money. In fact, I'm thinking of yanking Caddie from Vitesse."

The angrier Jon became, the calmer Garret appeared, lounging behind his desk with the demeanor of someone passing the time of day with an old pal.

"Caddie has longterm clients," Garret said. "Some of her other contracts are coming up for renewal, and when they do I will negotiate excellent contracts for her."

"In the meantime your fucking agency got famous on her name. Aaron Adam wouldn't have even listened to you about that Fischer kid if it wasn't for the fact you represented Caddie. I *gave* you Caddie. Now what are you going to give me?"

"I don't understand."

"Money, Garret. I want cash, and a lot of it, for Caddie to stay with your agency."

Just beneath all of Jon's bluster, Garret detected a simmering fear, like a virus ready to explode and consume Jon.

"Are you having money problems, Jon?" Garret said. "How is that possible?"

Jon backed off, and Garret immediately knew that he had struck a nerve. He guessed that Jon's story about raising two million dollars from investors to begin his film was a lie.

"I'll tell you what," Garret said, suddenly brightening,

walking around the desk and putting a hand on Jon's shoulder. "I'll talk to Phil Stein and see what we can do about raising the financing for your film. How about that? Give me a few days, though."

Jon couldn't believe his good luck, and realized he'd finally learned how to play Garret Stowe. Just threaten the man.

After the meeting with Jon, Garret called Phil Stein.

"Who is handling Caddie Dean's money these days?"

"Jon Ross," Phil said. "He fired Lever & Kaplan six months ago and hired some accountant instead."

"I see," Garret said. He hung up his phone and yelled for Sascha to come down to his office.

"Where's Caddie?" he asked her.

"Chicago, shooting a Lipton."

"You can reach me there if you need me, but no one else is to know where I am, understood?"

"Sure. Problem?"

"No. But I realize we are not paying enough attention to our star client."

chapter
19

"I hesitated calling you," Garret said to Caddie, sitting on the couch of her twelfth-floor suite in Chicago's Whitehall Hotel.

"Why?" she asked, looking spectacular in sweatpants and a big T-shirt, her bare feet tucked up under her legs. Spectacular but not happy, Garret thought, studying her face.

"It is my policy never to get involved in the personal lives of my clients."

"What are you saying, Garret?"

"How are things with you and Jon?" he asked, appearing to be very uncomfortable with having to ask the question.

"You flew here from Manhattan to ask me that?"

"Frankly, yes."

"Why?"

"We've had you heavily booked, and I know that Jon has been under great strain with his film. You two haven't spent much time together lately, have you?"

"No, we haven't."

"Caddie, I'm going to come to the point. Jon is your manager, and you are the model. But at the end of the

day, that means you are my client, and my concerns
have to begin and end with you. And what I'm concerned about are rumors I've been hearing around New
York."

"I find it hard to believe you came here to tell me
some rumors about Jon," she said nervously. "Is he
having an affair with some actress?"

"No, of course not. It's about money."

He watched as Caddie's face registered surprise.

"No model in the history of the business has worked
harder than you."

"What's wrong?" she asked.

He noticed a glimmer of deeply seeded fear behind
her famous blue eyes.

"I've been hearing that there are problems with your
money. I may lose you as a client for telling you this,
but I have to take that risk. I'd rather you fire me than
find out a year from now that you're broke."

"If you know something, tell me. What do you mean,
broke?"

"There are stories circulating around the office that
Jon is spending an awful lot of your money."

"I see the statements every month from the accountant. He watches every penny."

"But who watches him?"

"Jon." Even as she said it, the color drained from
Caddie's face.

"I'm not one hundred percent certain," Garret said,
"but I think more money has gone into Jon's film project than you know. And I don't want to see my best
client blindsided."

Caddie rose and walked over to the window.

Garret watched her intently. It was a calculated
gamble on his part. What if he was wrong? Then he
would surely lose Caddie as a client. But something in
Jon's demeanor during their recent meeting had caught
Garret's attention: the faint sheen of perspiration on

Jon's upper lip, the clammy hands. Garret had been in poker games where he was down two thousand dollars, with fifty bucks in his pocket, and the winners carried guns. He knew what fear felt like. He smelled it the way an animal senses the presence of wounded prey.

After a long silence, Caddie said, "What do I do? I have to be sure."

"He's your husband. Ask him."

"I don't want to accuse him of anything. I mean, after all . . ."

Garret noticed something he'd never seen before in Caddie. Fury. Bottled but under high pressure, threatening to blow as she contemplated being ripped off by her own husband. But Garret perceived something else, too: a lack of righteous innocence. She was hiding something. She was afraid of Jon.

"Will you help me?" she asked.

"Of course."

"It's just that I need to be certain."

He nodded.

"Let me work on it. Finish your shoot here. By the time you get back to New York, we'll be ready to talk."

Garret returned to New York and called Conley. Garret knew the phone number, because he paid the phone bill every month. He knew where Conley lived, because he paid Conley's rent. Garret also provided Conley with a small office near the supply room at Vitesse's headquarters, and used him to drive a few of the girls around town.

"Find out where Caddie's money is going," Garret said to Conley, as they sat in McDougal's Tavern on 23rd Street. He scratched down the address of Jon and Caddie's accountant.

"What the hell do I know about accounting? Everything I know about money is what I got in my pocket."

"You don't have to know a damn thing. Just find out

how much Jon Ross is spending of Caddie's money on his fucking movie."

Conley stuffed the piece of paper in his pocket.

Two days later, Conley wandered into Garret's office, looking smug and sucking on a cigarette.

"He's hacking Caddie's money all right," Conley said.

"How much?"

"About three and a half million so far."

"Jesus."

"I told the accountant I was a private investigator. The guy is just a fucking bookkeeper who is painting the books for Ross. I sit in the guy's office and blow smoke in his face and stare him down. He was shitting. He told me he just does what Jon Ross tells him. Phonies up monthly statements that the wife sees. But he's in deep. Ross has sold off her investments, taken loans, all kind of shit. She's about tap city, man."

Conley was clearly very pleased with himself. "That little bookkeeper is gonna shit for a month," he added, smiling.

Garret leaned back in his chair, thinking.

Jon Ross knew it was uncharacteristic of his wife to stay at a location after a job was done, yet following the Lipton shoot in Chicago she called and told him that she was exhausted and wanted to rest up before returning home. Caddie was never exhausted. In fact, her stamina and energy were legendary in the fashion business. His agitation grew when he called Garret Stowe to check on the film fund-raising efforts and Garret refused to take his call and never bothered to call back. Then Jon's agitation turned to panic when his bookkeeper called and said he was quitting, and before Jon could jump through the phone at him, the man hung up.

Jon hopped into a cab and raced to the bookkeeper's office. The office was closed, the door locked.

He dug around in his briefcase and pulled out a notebook, tore through the pages until he found a telephone number, and called it on his pocket phone.

A woman's voice came on the line.

"Sally, this is Jon Ross. I need to speak with you again. Right away."

"Man, I really don't have anything else to say."

"No, this is important."

"I don't give a shit," Sally Kane said.

"Don't hang up," Jon said quickly. "Just listen to me. There's money in this for you."

"Money for what?"

"Just meet me for coffee. We'll talk."

"I'm going out."

"No! This has to be now. And I promise you, the money will be good."

"Fuck, man . . . like how good?"

The jet bringing Caddie Dean back from Chicago touched down at seven in the evening. She'd spent most of the last two days in her hotel suite in Chicago with her lawyer. The bookkeeper had flown in as well. Conley had promised him that nobody would prosecute him if he'd just explain the books to the lawyer. He did so. Jon had gone through $3,145,000 in cash during the past four months. He'd signed promissory notes totaling $2 million, using brokerage accounts as collateral. He'd taken out second mortgages on the Amagansett and Los Angeles houses, effectively wiping out any equity in them. Jon had run through $7 million, $3 million of which remained to be paid.

"You have contracts that will guarantee you money for the next two years," the lawyer explained to Caddie, "but that money will go to pay off debts that Jon has incurred in your name."

"My name?"

"You signed the notes," the lawyer said.

Jon had given her things to sign in the past, but she didn't recall signing promissory notes.

"He may have attached the signature pages to other documents," the lawyer said. "That's a common technique. In any case, you did sign them."

Garret sent a limousine to meet Caddie at La Guardia and asked if she wanted someone standing by when she confronted Jon.

"I'll talk to him myself," she said.

Jon was home, waiting for her.

He gave her a hug and instantly felt her stiffen. She walked past him into the living room and stood at the window, facing Central Park.

"You spent all our money," Caddie said simply.

"What do you mean?"

"I've seen the books, Jon. You spent all our money on your movie. You had the bookkeeper send me false reports. You lied and stole. How could you do that?"

"That money isn't gone, Caddie. It's invested, it's—"

"Please don't say that. Don't lie any more."

"Who put you up to this?"

"No one."

"Bullshit. Fucking Garret Stowe put you up to this because he wants me out of the way so he can screw up your career some more."

She turned around and looked at her husband.

It unnerved Jon that Caddie didn't seem angry, not like the times she'd screamed at him when he committed her to things without telling her or behaved rudely to her friends and colleagues. Now her eyes were cold and her face looked deadly calm. He felt chilled.

"What do you mean, screw up my career?" she asked him.

"Just what I said. Has he been promoting you? Have you signed all sorts of fabulous new deals? No. In case you haven't noticed, Ginny Fischer is the hottest damn model in the world, and the little bitch is *thirteen years old*! That's who he's promoting. He's going to make money off her for the next fifteen years. What have you got, two, maybe three good years left? He doesn't give a shit about you. He used you to get famous."

"That's what you said about Jessica . . . all the same things."

"And I was right."

"Were you? What happened to those deals that were supposedly offered to me that Jessica steered to somebody else? Was that bullshit, too, Jon? You're the one who lied to me about money, not Jessica."

"Just remember something. We're married. It's *our* money, not your money."

"I earned it."

"You had your fucking picture taken!"

"It was my damn money, Jon."

"It was our fucking money!"

He closed on her as if he intended to strike her. But Caddie didn't move. She squared her shoulders, and the look in her eyes told him she was willing to kill him if he touched her.

"You came to me when you needed seed money to start your film. Did I complain? No. I told you to spend it, that we were a team, that my life was your life. That's how goddam stupid I was. It's all been a lie, hasn't it? Every single goddam word out of your mouth."

"That money is going to come back to us, Caddie. I promise you."

"Oh, please."

"You just have to goddam stand there and let someone take your picture and the money comes in. I'm working my ass off trying to do something, and I have to *earn* it. Do you understand? Earn it. You've never had a real job in your life. You don't know what it is to

really work. Okay, I screwed up. But I screwed up trying to do something with my life."

"Stealing isn't what I'd call screwing up. It's more
like committing a crime."

Jon realized it was time to hit the bottom line.

"What are you going to do, Caddie? Go to the police? Tell them you've spent all your money? You
signed the checks, you signed the notes. If a crooked
bookkeeper sent us false statements then they can arrest him. I never looked at the statements. I trusted the
man. He told me he raised the money for the film. How
was I supposed to know he was taking the money from
us and giving it right back to me?"

"No, Jon," she said, "I'm not going to call the
police."

"Then give me a chance to make it back."

"I don't want to ever see you again. As of this moment. Get out."

"Don't tell me to get out of my own house."

"Please don't play that game with me."

"You think you're just going to kick me out and
I'm going bye-bye? Sorry, honey, then you don't
understand."

She looked at him. Her detachment made him angrier, made him want to hurt her.

"You think I've spent all these years being called
Mr. Caddie Dean so that I can walk out of here broke?"
he said. "No, no. It's not going to be that way, sweetie.
I'm not going anywhere. I'm staying right here."

"Do you really think I'm going to allow that?"

"I know you will, Caddie, because you grew up in
that dogshit trailer park with that fucking pig drunk of
a mother and ex-con of a father and you hated being
the little shitcan-poor kid. You hated every damn second of it. You swore you were going to make money,
so much money you could erase everything you don't
want to remember. But I'm remembering for you.

You'd crawl through a lake of rat shit before you'd go back to that life. Why else would you prop your old lady up in that house in Orange County and tell everybody your life was American Pie? You hated who you were, and you like who you are now, and you don't want that to change."

"Is this some kind of stupid threat?"

"No, this is what's called good advice. You're not going to be a star model forever. You need to make your money now. Because you know if you don't, you'll keep waking up in the middle of the night, shaking with that nightmare you have. What is it, two, three times a month you wake up in a cold sweat, shaking and sobbing and asking me to hold you? And you'd never tell me what that dream is all about. But I know what it is now. It's a nightmare about being back in that shit-ass trailer. Broke, sick, and despised. That's what you don't want, that's what scares you more than anything else in life."

She was still staring at Jon, but he knew that behind her stare was a seed of fear, and that seed was growing. He knew he had touched the deepest nerve within Caddie Dean.

"No, I'm not going anywhere," Jon said. "I'll just go right on living my life, right here in my home with my wife, because she needs to bank all the money she can the next few years. And in order to do that, she's got to be America's pretty little girl next door, so lovable, so fuckable, and so much in demand. But nobody is going to want to pay the all-American girl all that money if they know she isn't really the all-American girl."

Jon picked up the phone and punched in a number. When the person at the other end answered, Jon said, "Come on up now."

Moments later the buzzer sounded and the doorman announced a Miss Sally Kane.

"Send her right up," Jon said, then turned and smiled at Caddie.

"I'm sure Garret Stowe thinks he's so goddam smart. He's sitting somewhere drinking champagne, celebrating the fact that he's got me out of his life and he'll be able to do whatever he wants with you. Let's see about that."

"Who's Sally Kane?" Caddie asked.

"Oh, she had a different name when you knew her. Some street name like Catsy or something stupid like that. But you'll recognize her. She hasn't aged as well as you, but then you've taken better care of yourself, while she's gone on and off the shit. But she sure remembers hanging out with you down in the Village. What were you—sixteen, seventeen? Fresh in New York and a little hophead. Running away from that trailer park. Don't blame you for that. But America's sweetheart shooting smack? People are going to be crushed. You and Catsy used to fuck guys if they'd buy you a bag. Wow. What a story. A few months later you stumble into Jessica Cartwright. She cleans you up. Doctors, dentists. A year later you're a working model. All this sound familiar?

"Jessica doesn't ask any questions, she's riding a winner. But I ask the questions, I ask a lot of questions and do a lot of homework, and I find out just who the girl next door really is. And man, wouldn't that make a great story in the *Enquirer*? Wouldn't the Coca-Cola Company love to hear their star model was a smack addict who turned tricks, then lied to the world about who she is? This girl Sally, she was hard to find. Very hard. But I found her. And if you try and make any trouble for me, I'll make trouble for you like you can't believe. So let's just be a happy little man and wife, and we'll all live happily ever after."

Sally Kane knocked at the apartment door.

"Or," Jon said, walking toward the door, "our friend

Sally is going to become real famous, with her face at every checkout counter in America. Can't wait for the television movie."

Jon opened the door and Sally walked in. She was about five feet six, with stringy brown hair, her face pockmarked. She'd obviously cleaned up for this occasion.

Caddie recognized her right away.

"Hello, Caddie," Sally said. "Everybody calls me Sally now."

Caddie couldn't speak.

"So," Jon said, "shall the three of us have dinner and talk over old times?"

Sally walked toward Caddie. She was hard-looking, but clearly uncomfortable in these surroundings. Looking at her, Caddie saw everything she might have become. And the old nightmare flashed again through Caddie's head. Indeed, she had never told Jon the content of that recurring dream, but somehow he had put it all together, right down to the details.

"Caddie," Sally said, her expression suddenly softening. "I don't know what this is all about, but your husband over there offered me fifty thousand dollars to make up a lot of bullshit about you. All I remember is us rooming together awhile, and you being very kind to me at the time. You never touched the shit I was doing. I hated you for it then, but admire you now. Nice to see you again."

Jon Ross went white. He was so astonished by Sally's change of heart that his throat constricted and he couldn't get a sound out.

"Sally," Caddie said, "can I help you with things?"

"I'm doing okay."

Caddie wrote her phone number on a pad and gave it to Sally. "Call me if you change your mind."

Sally Kane left, flashing Jon a look of disgust.

"I'm going to stay at the Plaza for a few days,"

Caddie said to her husband. "That should give you time to get your things out of here and the Amagansett house. You can have the house in Los Angeles. I'm sure you'll do well there."

She went into the bathroom, closed the door, and turned on the faucets to fill the tub.

Jon walked to the window and looked down in time to see Sally Kane leave the building and walk briskly around the corner and out of sight. What he did not see was Sally Kane stepping into a limousine.

Inside the limo, Sally looked at Garret.

"How did it go?" Garret asked.

"Like you said it would," she answered. "Exactly."

He handed her an envelope and said, "You come around the office once a month and keep in touch."

True to her word, Caddie left her apartment after the confrontation with Jon and checked into the Plaza for several days, days spent meeting with lawyers regarding divorce proceedings from Jon Ross, and with a new business manager in an attempt to restructure her finances. In the quieter moments she sank into a depression when she contemplated Jon's betrayal, and her own foolishness in not responding to the changes in his behavior that followed the surge of fame unleashed by the *Time* article.

Jon's threat was a reminder to Caddie that the image of Caddie Dean, Supermodel, was one she had created herself. Deep down there was no happy-go-lucky girl next door who happened to hit it big as a model. In fact, she realized, much of what Jon had said to her in the apartment that night was true. She wanted to erase anything to do with a childhood that caused nothing but pain. She'd tried as a teenager to escape from it through drugs. Then along came Jessica Cartwright, who showed her a different avenue. She'd learned that her look was a valuable commodity, something to be managed and nurtured. Somehow, others didn't see the truth of Caddie's past when they looked at her. The blond hair and blue eyes and ready smile triggered some all-American fantasy in the minds of the public, and when Caddie realized that, her life changed.

Jon wanted to reach into that past and rub Caddie's face in it, take away her present by exposing the girl she'd left behind. As she sat in her hotel suite it infuriated Caddie to think that Jon might have the power to reconnect her to that world. And she felt grateful to Garret Stowe for intervening on her behalf.

She never asked Garret how he had found Sally Kane so quickly after Jon had done so. Of course he didn't tell Caddie that he'd put Conley on Jon's tail, and Jon had led them directly to Sally Kane.

And in the days that followed, she never asked why Jon so readily accepted the divorce settlement put forth by her lawyers, an agreement that denied Jon any future earnings from contracts that were negotiated during the marriage, money that he was under the law entitled to. Jon's own lawyers were, in fact, stunned when Jon agreed to a paltry settlement, and told him so. He simply signed the papers and disappeared. And, of course, Jon did not tell the lawyers or anyone else about the visit he'd had from a man who made it clear that if Jon in any way gave Caddie Dean a difficult time he would not live much longer. At first, Jon laughed at the stocky, rough-looking man who had stopped him on the street. But anyone who looked into Conley's eyes for more than half a second knew he would make good on any manner of threat.

"Go to the police, go to your lawyers, go to anybody you want," Conley said to Jon. "I'm sure they can make all kinds of trouble. But when it's all said and done, you'll be dead, and dead in a way that will hurt. So you think about it, hotshot."

He did think about it. And he did what he was told.

Caddie gave him the house in California and two hundred thousand dollars. He took the deal and ran.

Caddie didn't ask any questions, and Garret offered no explanations. But she knew that Garret had facilitated the agreement with Jon, and she was glad to be rid of the man.

When she moved back into her apartment, stripped it of any signs of her life with Jon, and completely redecorated it, she felt her life slowly starting to repair itself. She tossed every photograph of Jon and her into the trash. She wouldn't discuss him with friends or answer any questions about what had happened. She wanted to erase Jon, as she had tried to erase other painful memories.

And when some measure of quiet returned to her life, she did realize that, given all of Garret's involvement in the matter with Jon, he, too, was in a position to exploit her past, to burst the image she had so carefully created. But she did not raise the subject with Garret. He went out of his way to be solicitous of her. He sent flowers wherever she went on location. He sent gifts and notes of encouragement. He became a friend.

chapter
20

Luther Nevitt did not earn much money as a charter-boat captain in Miami. His was not one of the fancy tourist boats with the amenities wealthy customers demanded. Mostly, his customers were college students who showed up with coolers full of beer for a day of drinking and occasionally catching a fish. The hours were long, and he only took Mondays off, and not even Mondays if business was good. Most of the money went to pay off the loan on the boat. What was left had to cover the crew, his apartment, food, and the beers at the end of the day. So the idea of saving for a trip to New York galled him, but he had no choice. Luther Nevitt knew that until he found out if the man who went by the name Garret Stowe was the same person that he'd been trying to find, he would not get a decent night's sleep.

It required several months, but Nevitt saved up a thousand dollars for the trip. He couldn't take more than a few days away from work, so he splurged on an airline ticket rather than travel by bus.

Once in Manhattan, he found a seedy hotel near Times Square where he could stay for under a hundred bucks a night. He didn't have a plan of what he would do once he found Garret Stowe. But he just had to look him in the eyes. He had to know.

Nevitt walked thirty blocks from his hotel to the Vitesse office and sat on the bus-stop bench catty-corner to the offices for most of the day, watching the coming and going. A lot of beautiful young women and handsome young men came and went. A few normal-looking people. But no Garret Stowe.

The next morning, Nevitt arrived at seven, perched himself on the same bench, and watched. Same thing. About four in the afternoon he walked across the street toward the office. He caught his own reflection in a window. Faded dungarees, work boots, a tattered plaid shirt, coffee-stained pale blue windbreaker, and a weather-worn cap. Not only did he not look like any of the people who came and went from the Vitesse offices, he realized, he didn't look much better than some of the bums who slowly worked their way down the street toward the park.

He decided to buy better clothes, and spent what was left of the afternoon finding a discount store and purchasing a sport jacket, a pair of double-knit slacks, stiff leather loafers, and a white shirt with thick plastic stays in its collar.

Vitesse opened at nine in the morning, and Nevitt was there at nine sharp the next day, wearing his new outfit. *If I can just look into his eyes,* Nevitt told himself, *I'll know for certain.*

"I'd like to see Garret Stowe," Nevitt said to the receptionist.

"Do you have an appointment?"

"No. He told me to stop by if I got into the city. So I'm here."

The receptionist looked at him as if he had just walked out of a spaceship.

"I can give your name to Mr. Stowe's assistant."

"Connors," Nevitt said, making up the name on the spot.

The receptionist called Garret's assistant, there was a brief exchange, then she told him, "If you can leave your name and number with me, they'll call you."

"I'm only here for today."

"Those were my instructions."

"Where's he from?" Nevitt asked the receptionist.

"Excuse me?"

"Stowe from around here?"

The receptionist looked back into the main floor of the agency, where the bookers were already lighting up the phone lines and assistants prepared books to be delivered to clients.

"Is this sort of like . . . a joke?" she asked him.

Many years of running a charter boat had not enhanced any social or perceptive skills Nevitt might have possessed. "Honey," he said, "tell me where Garret Stowe is from."

"Sir, I really don't know."

"He here?"

"As a matter of fact, no. He's in Europe. I really think it's better if you just leave your name and number."

"I think it's better if you stop smart-mouthing me and answer my damn questions."

"Will you excuse me a moment?" she said, disappearing into a back office.

She returned with Conley, who dragged on a cigarette and motioned Nevitt to walk over to the office's front door.

Nevitt actually liked the look of Conley. He seemed like a man he could talk to.

"What's the problem, bub?" Conley said, his eyes boring into Nevitt.

"Got no problem, just trying to find something out."

"About what?"

"Garret Stowe."

Conley thought for a moment. He looked at Nevitt's calloused and leathery hands, noticed the yellowish tinge to the fingertips on the right hand, and the yellowed teeth. He reached into his jacket, pulled out a pack of Camels, and said, "Smoke?"

part

THREE

chapter
21

Anton Cellini effectively spread the word around the industry that the failure of his initial attempts at presenting a new concept to Aaron Adam had resulted directly from Jessica Cartwright's inability to find a model suitable for the job. And the proof was there for all to see; for the first time in many years, Aaron Adam had gone with a model outside the Cartwright stable. Following Ginny's success, Cellini used other Vitesse models for Aaron Adam shoots, and that fanned whispers about Jessica's losing her edge.

In fact, Ellen Cannon, Jessica's newly hired booker, did a decent job of signing and promoting new models, but only after those same girls had been passed on by Sascha Benning at Vitesse. Jessica allowed Ellen to sign thirteen- and fourteen-year-olds, if only to let the industry know that Cartwright was moving with the trend, and only with a promise to herself not to allow them to be exploited by her agency or the advertisers. Yet, without Caddie and its former stable of stars, Cartwright's revenues plummeted. Office overhead became a burden, but Jessica knew that scaling back operations would fuel more rumors of her troubles. So she took the losses, worked overtime, and searched for a spark to ignite a turnaround.

One evening Tommee Barkley strolled into Jessica's office, took one look at her slumped at her desk, and closed the door behind her.

Jessica looked up.

"You're getting old right in front of my eyes," Tommee said.

"Thanks for the encouragement."

"Will you get your butt out of that chair? We're going to dinner."

"Tommee, I've still got work to do here."

"Whatever you're doing, you're wasting your time."

Tommee grabbed a phone and punched in a number, fast-talked a maître d' at one of the hottest restaurants in the city, and made a reservation.

"I can't go there looking like this," Jessica said, peeking into the wall mirror.

"Honey, you can't go anywhere looking like that, but I'll shake my tits and wiggle my hips and give you plenty of cover to get to the table."

Watching Tommee Barkley stride through a restaurant was like watching a great baseball player trot the bases after a home run. She floated through the room, taking in the silent accolades great beauty commands, and seated herself. Jessica had no choice but to follow.

"So what's your problem?" Tommee asked Jessica, after ordering a bottle of champagne.

"My problem is that business is lousy and I don't see the prospect of its improving in the near future."

"Business isn't lousy," Tommee replied. "*Your* business is lousy. I hear they're printing money over at Vitesse. And you're not doing a damned thing about it."

"What do you mean? We're signing the best models we can. We're all working seven days a week."

"And it ain't working. Look, I'm thirty-two years

old. I made a million dollars last year, but that's because I can still fool 'em with my hair. That won't last.
I can drop ten pounds, I can date the CEO of Revlon, I
can do a lot of things, but sooner or later it's a losing
game for me, because I'm selling my looks. You're
selling your brains, but not lately."

"What am I supposed—"

"Get over Phil Stein, for one thing."

"Phil Stein?"

"Goddammit, Jessica, do you think it was any big secret that you were taking a piece off that little pony?"

"I thought we had a halfway decent—"

"I guarantee you dated him because he was the only
guy who didn't hit you up for models, right?"

"No, he didn't hit on my models. He just stole most
of them."

"Well, I hope the fucking you got was worth the
fucking you took, but so what? The guy is thirty years
old or so, he's ambitious as hell, and this Garret Stowe
must have waved a pile of money in his face. So he
screws you over. You weren't going to marry the guy,
were you?"

"No."

"Never let a guy that close to your business if you're
not going to marry him. That's rule number one. My
problem is that my body is my business, so I'm in
trouble from the get-go. But we're talking about you."

"I was hurt, Tommee."

"Right, you had your heart broken and pocket
picked. Your heart is going to get better, but you are
letting those schmucks go on picking your pocket by
not doing anything."

"I'm signing little girls just as they are, and I
hate it."

"All you're doing is what they do. You got famous
because you took me and you took Caddie Dean and
made us into stars. You didn't copy what some other

agency was doing. Nobody was buying my look when you signed me, and nobody was buying Caddie's look when you signed her. I don't know how to run a business, but I do know that I've changed my look every couple of years, and I'm still here. So what are you doing?"

"I don't know."

"I do. You're sitting in that office every day not believing that a guy who was sleeping in your bed would sell you down the river. Well, he did. Get over it."

Tommee had struck the bull's-eye. Jessica had dealt with Phil Stein's personal and professional betrayal by burying herself in work. She had not admitted to herself the depth of pain she felt, and continued to feel, every time she thought of her relationship with Phil.

"It's been almost a year, hon," Tommee said more gently, signaling a waiter to refill their glasses. "Word around town is that the Cartwright Agency is sinking, and I don't want to sink with it. But I'll be God damned to hell if I'll sign with Garret Stowe. So you've got to turn the ship around, sister, and you ain't gonna do it sitting in your office going cross-eyed looking at your balance sheet. You've got to make some moves."

Tommee waved the waiter over and asked for a telephone.

He brought one.

"You ever been to La Valle?" Tommee asked, finding a number in a tiny red book that she pulled out of her handbag.

"No. Where's that?"

"It's the best spa in Italy. I go there every time I dump a guy so he can't find me. It's sort of magical there. All the high society of Europe, and occasionally someone like me."

Tommee located the number, dialed it, and managed to get the spa's owner on the line.

"Gianni, Tommee Barkley. I'm sending my friend Jessica Cartwright to you next week and I want the best room in the place for her."

Jessica signaled frantically that she couldn't go any-where next week, but Tommee just waved her away. The fact that Tommee had to practically shout to be heard on the international call also mortified Jessica, but she knew Tommee, and when Tommee was siz-zling, she listened to no one, nor did she care what any-one else thought.

"I know you're booked two years in advance," Tommee yelled into the phone, "but if you ever want to see my ass out by your swimming pool again you'll take care of Jessica Cartwright. Now, I mean it, Gianni, so help me, you silver-haired son of a—"

And then he agreed.

Tommee, delighted with herself, hung up the phone.

"Done deal," she said. "And stop looking at me like that. I'm paying for it and you *are* going."

"Tommee, it's the busiest time of year for me."

"It's not busy enough. You've got to get away and get your head cleared, and I know you'll think of something."

"It's impossible."

"Listen to me. When a man gets his heart busted, he goes out and shoots an elephant or builds a skyscraper or something like that. What do you do? Put on fifteen pounds and never leave your office. Bullshit on that."

Sitting on the Alitalia flight to Florence, Jessica could not quite believe she was leaving New York dur-ing the busy September season, nor could she believe she was leaving her office in the hands of Ellen Can-non, a booker who had worked only eight months for the Cartwright Agency.

But Tommee Barkley had been right. Things had to

change. And sitting in the agency's offices fretting
over the future was changing nothing.

La Valle was located in the foothills outside of Florence, with views of the rolling Tuscan terrain from
every room. The main building was an eighteenth-
century villa originally built by a Florentine banking
clan. When Gianni Bello acquired the estate twenty
years ago it had been in severe disrepair. He spent two
years, and many billions of lire, restoring and convert-
ing the villa into twenty guest rooms, with an attached
spa, gardens, walking paths, and modern amenities.
The food, service, attention to detail, and serenity of
the atmosphere attracted a devoted clientele from Europe's moneyed cognoscenti.

Jessica's room was heaven, with 350-count Porthault
linen, a pile of bath towels thick enough to cushion a
leap from a building, and a terrace view so beautiful
she could not possibly look at it and think of business
problems at the same time. A gorgeous flower arrangement and a note fo welcome from Gianni greeted Jessica in the suite, as well as an invitation to join him for
dinner.

He gave Jessica a tour of the spa and grounds and let
the staff know that any want or whim of Jessica's was
to be immediately met.

"I feel guilty that Tommee strong-armed you into
making room for me," Jessica said to him.

"Nonsense," he answered. "She has added such
sparkle to La Valle over the years. She is a treasured
guest, and so shall you be."

From the look on Gianni Bello's face, Jessica con-
cluded that Tommee provided more than just sparkle to
Gianni's life.

For two days Jessica indulged herself with late
mornings, breakfast in bed, massages, whirlpools,
walks in the countryside, and champagne every
evening. At first, she felt self-conscious about being

alone. But the Europeans were very accommodating to a woman on her own, unlike most Americans. Taking the sun by La Valle's lovely pool, Jessica was reminded that Europeans were also less self-conscious about their bodies than were Americans. And much to her pleasure, Jessica noticed men noticing her, a rarity for a woman accustomed to traveling in the company of models. Apparently the European men truly liked women, and did not expect them all to look like magazine covers.

Jessica's stay at La Valle was so pleasant and relaxing, she spent little time thinking of business. The Saturday night before she was to leave, she asked Gianni Bello if she could extend her visit another two days, and he made the necessary arrangements.

On Sunday, most guests had checked out and the incoming guests had not yet arrived, so Jessica had the pool area to herself for most of the afternoon. So when another guest walked out of the spa and crossed the sundeck, Jessica took notice of her. But then again, Jessica would have noticed her immediately, even in a crowd. The woman paused near the center of the sundeck, waiting for an attendant to unfurl a mat atop one of the lounges. She was unusually tall and slender. Squinting into the afternoon sunlight, Jessica focused on the woman's face. And when the moment of recognition set in, Jessica realized the other woman was looking back at her.

The new guest was Caddie Dean.

They had not spoken in nearly a year, yet here they were, thousands of miles from home, tucked away in this golden retreat, with nowhere to turn because there was nobody else out there, other than pool attendants.

"So," Jessica said, unable to bear the silent tension, "how do I look in this bathing suit?"

"Like a million bucks," Caddie answered, visibly grateful for Jessica's light tone.

"I'm the one who's supposed to say that to you."

"Except you don't have to anymore," Caddie said with a small smile. "You can tell me how I really look."

"Like a million bucks."

They embraced and worked through a few minutes of awkward small talk, then Jessica said, "I heard about your divorce. I'm sorry."

"It was pretty ugly at the end. But then you never did like Jon, did you?"

"No."

"I was pretty stupid, I guess."

"We've all taken our turn being stupid with men. In fact, I'm way ahead of you on that score."

Caddie exhaled a deep breath. "I guess I'd feel better right now if you said something awful to me. You must hate me for what I did to you, Jessica."

"I wish you had discussed it with me, is all."

"I was letting Jon make the decisions. Which, I know, is a pretty poor excuse."

She nodded.

During the past year, Jessica had thought of writing Caddie a letter, or calling her, just to express her feelings of betrayal. But that would have been an emotional response, and she wanted to run her business like a business. And now that she had the opportunity to say whatever she wanted, Jessica couldn't muster much anger at Caddie, who stood a few feet away, tall and lean and, somehow, sad.

"Are you here with someone?" Jessica asked.

"No, I just wanted to get away. I've worked for almost a month straight. What about you?"

"I've been shacked up here with an Italian lover for six weeks. I can't get the guy to leave me alone."

"You're kidding?" Caddie said, suddenly sounding girlishly excited.

"I am, but I loved saying it. Actually, I just need to

take a little time off. Tommee told me I was looking like hell."

"You look good, Jessica."

"I don't care if it's true or not, but thank you."

An hour later, Jessica and Caddie were into their second bottle of Pinot Grigio, sitting at one of the umbrella tables on the terrace.

"Sooner or later we're going to have to order food," Jessica said.

"Later," Caddie said, emptying the bottle into their two glasses.

Jessica detected a sadness and vulnerability in Caddie, sitting across from her in the Tuscan hills, that she had not seen since the first day Caddie had set foot in her office. On that day, Caddie was gaunt and pale and appeared to be just a few beats away from serious illness. Still, Jessica had spotted an extraordinary beauty in the girl, a look, that jumped out even when masked by a debilitating lifestyle. At the time, Jessica didn't ask Caddie what was wrong, she simply said, "If you want to work as a model, you need to get healthy. I'll help you do that."

Caddie had complied, saying nothing about the two lost years of her life spent traveling the youth underground in Paris and New York, a time of drugs and self-abuse, and abuse by others. She had stumbled into Jessica Cartwright's office because it was the closest model agency to where she was living in the Village. Jessica put Caddie up in her apartment, fed her, and sent her to doctors and dentists, and Caddie demonstrated a fierce survival instinct. And when success arrived, Caddie did not discuss those early days or anything that came before them. In all the years since then, Caddie had pretended that she had burst onto the scene a star, and Jessica said nothing to alter that story, and it became her accepted biography for the press and the public.

* * *

The two women carried their conversation over to dinner, and over coffee Caddie admitted that at thirty she was feeling the pressures of the youth trend that raged in the fashion business.

"Everyone asks me what I think of Ginny Fischer," Caddie said. "Suddenly I'm in competition with a kid. Six months ago I thought *I* was a kid."

"You can thank Mr. Stowe for that particular turn of events."

"Actually, Garret's been good to me, especially during the troubles I was having with Jon."

"Well, I'm glad to hear it."

"But I know he's not sitting up nights thinking about how to make my career last longer. He's always on the phone talking about taking over this and taking over that."

"Taking over what?" Jessica asked, a note of sobriety entering her voice.

"Expanding," Caddie said.

"The only way to expand," Jessica said, "is for an agent to open up all over the world. What else is there to offer your models? This is a global business, so if you can represent your models in every country in the world, you have a lot to offer them."

The comment came off the top of Jessica's head, but as the words came out of her mouth, she realized that she'd been doing more than getting massages and taking the sun the past week. Though she had purposely *not* been thinking about the model business, her mind had been percolating. She knew full well that sitting in New York and simply trying to sign better models than did Vitesse or Ford wasn't the answer to rebuilding her company. Ever since the near debacle with Wynn Gates in Milan and Paris, when the name Garret Stowe first entered Jessica's awareness, she'd been thinking about how obsolete the current system of sharing models with agencies around the world had become. The business had gone that way because local agencies had the parochial knowledge of the business in their area. But the world was shrinking. Careers had to be watched and nurtured from start to finish. Global marketing of a model, from a single source, seemed to Jessica to be the future.

"I think," Caddie said, "that Garret is going to go after Paris Models and Pop in Milan. I hear him talking. Who knows?"

"Those would be first on my list, too. But how is it that you hear Garret talking so much?" Jessica asked, fixing Caddie with a look.

"Guess." Caddie actually blushed, unable to hide her secret.

"No. Him?"

"He's been so good to me from the moment he found out what Jon was doing. He really has. He's built up my finances, pulled in a lot of foreign bookings. He likes to sit down and talk about whatever is on my mind. I like that."

"How well do you know him, Caddie? Nobody seems to know anything about this guy."

"After it went bad with Jon, I just wanted to disappear and hide. Garret didn't let me. He let me use his apartment in Paris. We started going out for dinner and things. Just friends. It's sort of evolved from there."

Thinking about Caddie with Garret gave Jessica a sick feeling in the pit of her stomach. But Caddie wasn't asking for Jessica's opinion of the man.

"Go slow, Caddie."

"I know. You always told me models pick the wrong men."

c h a p t e r
22

Shortly after Caddie returned to Paris from La Valle, she accompanied Garret to a dinner party at the fashionable estate of the French entertainer Liné Rinaud. Dressing for the party, Garret had seemed uncharacteristically edgy, as if he was anticipating a confrontation, but he fluffed off Caddie when she asked about his mood.

It was a sumptuous party, peopled by the social elite of Paris, and Garret seemed truly dazzled to mingle in such company. He searched the crowd until he found Giselle Rochas, who was surprised to see him at this gathering but managed to mask her reaction with social skill. Garret introduced Caddie to Giselle, then Madame Rinaud swooped in and scooped Caddie away to parade her among her more impressionable guests.

Taking Giselle aside, Garret slipped an envelope from his jacket and into her hands.

"What's this?" she asked.

"Two hundred fifty thousand dollars," he replied.

"For?"

"It's your initial investment in Vitesse. Everything from here on will be profit to you."

"You're in profit already?" she asked.

"Have you heard of Ginny Fischer?"

"I don't know the models."

"Vitesse is a huge success," Garret said.

"I'm impressed."

"You don't look it."

"How do I look?"

"Like someone trying not to act impressed," he said. "I think I've proved what I can do," Garret continued, "and I think it is time to expand our business relationship."

She eyed him warily.

"Garret, I lent you money. Now you've repaid it. That is the extent of our business relationship." She pulled her eyes away from his.

"I am at this party," he said, "because the hostess knew I would bring Caddie Dean. People are impressed by Caddie. As for me, they know I must be successful, but the people here think of the model business as a silly one. These people own banks, they own shipping companies, they manufacture things. They own the companies that own the companies that hire the models. These are the people I want to do business with. I want them to call me and ask me to come to their homes for dinner because they want to hear what I have to say, not because they know I will be bringing Caddie Dean."

"That's got nothing to do with me," Giselle said firmly.

"Of course it does. These are your friends. You do business with them, and they respect you. Now it's time for us to take our business partnership out of the shadows. You can open these doors for me."

"You've turned your business into quite a success, and you have this beautiful woman on your arm. Why don't you just count your blessings? I've nothing to offer you."

"Your château is famous around the world, so these people seek you out for other business opportunities. Let's invest together. Perhaps start a company, build a new business."

"We're not friends, Garret. Let's not pretend to be. You've paid me. Our past does not exist."

"Do you see the way these people look at me?" he said to her, not turning his head. "The men are jealous of me because of Caddie. The women are curious. But it is all about my being with a famous model. Well, models come and go, while the people in this room stay the same. This is the room I want to be in, and you can give it to me. I've earned that chance."

Giselle glanced around, searching for a familiar face to come to her rescue.

"I've earned the chance to do with other businesses what I've done with Vitesse. Already, I am going to expand Vitesse dramatically. But it is still all about models. I want more. I need you to arrange dinners, to introduce me, to make calls for me. And, as with Vitesse, you will profit also."

"Garret, I have my own life to live."

"What are you afraid of?"

"Can you accept the fact that we had a mutual interest that has now been satisfied? I have moved on. You've moved on. And now we are finished. Let's let this evening be our goodbye. There is no need to send me any of the profits. I was not expecting to see even this back. I commend you."

Giselle walked away and joined a group of her friends.

Garret was left standing alone by the bookcase. Without a drink or a cigarette, he felt awkward standing there. Foolish. As if he had just arrived at a party wearing a costume, but the party was not a costume ball at all.

That night Garret didn't sleep. He paced the balcony

of his apartment, smoking and looking out at the lights
of Paris. Caddie Dean, on anyone's short list of the
most beautiful women in the world, lay sleeping a few
yards away, her blond hair cascading across the jade
silk sheets. But Garret did not want to get into bed. All
he could think about was Giselle Rochas's cool dis-
missal of him at the party.

When the sun came up, he showered and shaved and
walked to a café for breakfast and the papers. He didn't
even know what he was reading, and kept checking his
watch every few minutes. Shortly after ten, he went to
a phone and called the offices of *Femme Nouvelle,* the
fashion weekly, and asked for the editor of the "Street"
page, Nicole Rochas.

"It's been much too long since we've had lunch,"
Garret said to her. "Better yet, let's make it dinner."

Two weeks later, Garret flew to New York to meet
with Davis Kellen. He arrived for dinner at Kellen's
Carlyle Hotel apartment with two stunning twenty-
year-old models. Garret took Kellen aside for a few
moments to discuss Kellen's investment in the expansion of Vitesse and then suggested another investment
to him.

"Not a significant amount of money, in your terms,"
Garret said deferentially, "and it has nothing to do with
the model business. But it would be very meaningful
to me."

As Garret explained the new investment, the purchase of blocks of stock in the closely held shares of
Château Rochas, he positioned himself so that Kellen
was facing toward the two models, who stood on the
balcony and drank champagne.

"They're very beautiful, aren't they?" Garret said,
following Kellen's gaze.

"They're charming."

"They're dogs compared to my top models."

Kellen nodded and quickly took Garret's point.

"Mr. Stowe," Davis Kellen said, "there is nothing complicated about doing business with you. I like that."

Dinner was then served, and before it was time for more champagne and dessert, Garret excused himself from the table and quietly slipped out of the apartment.

He called Ginny Fischer.

Before becoming involved with Caddie Dean, Garret had introduced Nona to a male model who was a favorite in the Ralph Lauren ads. The model understood that it would be appreciated if he took care of Nona's social life in New York. Since Garret was spending most of his time now in Paris, he did not want an unhappy mother of his star model. And since he knew that Nona and the model had gone to Martha's Vineyard for a weekend, he decided to look in on Ginny. Ginny's nanny was a young woman who served as a maid for Nona and saw to Ginny's needs the rest of the time; the nanny was also on Garret's payroll.

"Get dressed up," Garret said to Ginny on the car phone. "It's only nine o'clock, and I'm taking you out on the town." Ginny jumped at the chance.

First stop was Windows on the World, where he had taken Ginny's mother the night he persuaded her to allow Ginny to do the Aaron Adam campaign. With dinner, Garret ordered a bottle of Cristal champagne, and though Ginny was barely fourteen years old, she was a celebrity, so waiters and management looked the other way when Garret kept her glass filled.

From there they went to a private dance club on the Upper East Side, where Garret ordered more champagne and danced with Ginny until one in the morning. Next he took her to an all-night record store and bought her a hundred CDs. He instructed the limousine driver to tour the city streets, while Ginny played her favorite music. There was a chilled bottle of champagne in the limousine; Garret slid open the moon roof and shot the champagne cork into the night sky. He drank from the bottle and handed it to Ginny, who was already reeling from alcohol but took a sip anyway.

"Are you having fun, Ginny?" he asked.

"Yes."

"It's a good night, isn't it?"

"It's the best night."

"Do you get to have enough fun, between work and school?"

"Not like this," she said.

"You call me whenever you are not having enough fun. Wherever I am, I'll see that you're happy. Concert tickets, parties, whatever you want. You call me. You are too young and beautiful not to enjoy life."

"I like this best of all," Ginny said, "because my mom doesn't let me stay up too late."

"She's just trying to do what's right. Do you have a boyfriend?"

She laughed. "No."

"Have you ever?"

"Yes. It wasn't any big deal."

He guzzled champagne and closed the opaque privacy window that separated them from the driver.

"Does it bother you," Garret said, "the way men look at you?"

"It's all right."

"You like living in the city, don't you?"

"Yes."

"It's fun being grown-up."

"I guess so."

He leaned over and kissed her on the cheek.

"You're so beautiful," he said. "I'm going to put you on every magazine cover in the world and tell everyone that I've kissed that beautiful girl."

She laughed and grooved to the music.

"Was that okay?" he asked.

"What?"

"To kiss you."

She laughed. "Yes. I guess so. Don't tell my mom."

"We have a special friendship. I would never do that."

"Don't tell her you gave me champagne," Ginny said.

"I wouldn't tell her. Would you?"

"No."

Garret kissed her again, this time on the mouth. She began to draw away, but he pulled her in and continued to kiss her. She felt dizzy from the champagne, but it was exciting to do something bad that felt grown-up and secretive. And in this dizzy, disoriented condition, there was a part of her that wanted to be dangerous; she wondered what Garret did that made her mother act so crazy.

Garret kissed Ginny and ran a hand down her narrow back to the firm, small hips and squeezed her close to him.

He swung her around and sat her across his lap, facing him.

"We're not going to do anything," Garret said to Ginny. "I don't want you to be worried. We're just having fun. You see, you are so gorgeous to look at, you're such a fantastic-looking woman, that sometimes I forget you are a little girl. I want to touch you and I know that I shouldn't. I'm terrible. But you will forgive me, won't you? It's the champagne."

"I saw you doing it to my mother one night," Ginny blurted out.

"Doing what?"

"Doing it to her."

"We were probably just hugging."

"No you weren't. I saw you put your thing in her mouth and then I saw you put it inside her."

Garret smoothly covered his surprise.

"How long did you watch?"

"I'm not telling."

"You're a bad girl."

"No I'm not."

"You shouldn't be spying on your mother," Garret said, spanking her lightly. "Very bad girl."

"I think it's yuck to put it in your mouth."

"How do you know?"

"Yuck."

"Do you want to try?"

"No. Yuck."

"Someday you might like it. There are good surprises about growing up. You'll see."

She laughed. "I've *seen* a lot of things. I saw two of the guys who did that ad with me in their dressing room. I saw them doing things to each other."

"Yuck," Garret said.

That made Ginny laugh.

"Kiss me right there," he said, pointing to his crotch.

"No way."

"Go ahead. I want you to know something."

"No way."

"Do it."

She swilled some champagne, giggled, then leaned down and kissed Garret's crotch. She jerked back, because when she kissed him she felt the firmness of his erection.

"You see," he said, "that is your power. That is why these companies pay money to take your picture. Because you are a very powerful girl, an extraordinary girl. And now it's time for you to go home and go to bed."

"No! I like driving like this."

"Do you?"

"It's the most fun."

"Of course it is," Garret said. "That's what I wanted you to know."

Then he lifted her off his lap and set her on the seat next to him. A few moments later she passed out.

When Garret's seven-o'clock wake-up call kicked in, he debated canceling his reservation on the ten-o'clock Concorde to Paris and just sleeping in. But he remembered that he had another dinner date scheduled in Paris with Nicole Rochas that night, and that was not something he wanted to cancel, so he dragged himself out of bed.

He was supposed to have breakfast with Conley, who had been after Garret for a meeting for three weeks. However, the thought of staring at Conley, with his pocked face and revolting table habits, turned Garret's stomach. So he instructed his secretary to cancel the meeting with Conley and decided to head to the airport early.

Garret downed half a pot of coffee, checked out, and stumbled into his limousine just after eight. Before the car could pull away, a rear door opened and Conley slid in. Half asleep and heavily hungover, Garret nearly bounced off the ceiling with fright, at first not recognizing Conley.

"Expecting someone else?" Conley asked.

"What the fuck are you doing? I canceled our meeting."

"I know," Conley said. "You shouldn't have."

"Why not?"

"We need to talk."

"I don't feel like talking."

"Sure you do."

Conley signaled the driver to head out. The driver waited for Garret's confirmation. Garret studied Conley a moment, then nodded to the driver to go ahead.

"Smells like champagne and Aaron Adam perfume in this limo," Conley said, looking around. "Somebody had some fun last night."

"Don't ever surprise me like that," Garret said angrily. "Ever."

"You're on the jumpy side, no doubt about that."

"Just get to the point."

Conley raised the privacy panel.

"I made a new friend the other day," Conley said. "Guy named Luther Nevitt."

The name snapped Garret into sobriety. Conley enjoyed the reaction. "Mean something to you?"

"Who the hell is Luther Nevitt?" Garret said, settling back in the seat. But he knew his reflexes were too slow this morning; he had already given himself away.

"He came to the office a few days ago. He was sorry he missed you. You were in Paris."

"What did he want?"

"He says he's looking for a girl."

Conley waited for Garret's reaction. This time there wasn't much of one. He simply leaned forward with a curious expression.

"Really? A girl? What girl?" Suddenly, Garret seemed to relax a little.

"Judy something. But he said she probably didn't go by that name anymore. He hasn't seen the girl in thirteen years. His daughter. Said she ran away. Said he got calls and cards from her for a while. But not in the last few years. Never told him where she was or what she was doing. So then this Nevitt guy says he saw you on the news last year when you started this company. They showed pictures of all these models, he said, and one of the girls looked like his daughter, all grown up. He didn't catch the name she was going by. Just saw the picture in the paper or on TV."

"So what does he need me for? He could talk to one of the bookers."

"Exactly what I said to myself," Conley replied. "Exactly. If he's just looking for this girl, why does he want to talk to Garret Stowe? There are plenty of people in the office. But then I start thinking to myself, this guy is anxious to see Garret Stowe, so maybe that means Garret Stowe knows the guy. And I'm thinking, Garret must have known the girl, too. Must have been dicking her at some time when she wasn't quite legal. But then he dumps her and moves on. But she runs away from home because she doesn't like the old buzzard of a father. Garret gets himself in the model business . . . the girl looks him up, and they're both happy. She's a model, he's an agent. Only problem is, the old man turns up, and he's still got a mad-on about Garret dicking his daughter, blames Garret for the girl running away. Now, the old man Nevitt, he isn't sure the girl he saw on TV was even his daughter, and he ain't sure Garret Stowe is the guy he thinks he is. He wants to ID Garret, and he wants to find out if his daughter is now a model living in New York City. It all adds up in my head."

"What's in the envelope?" Garret asked, referring to a legal-size manila envelope that Conley had taken from his briefcase during his speech.

"That's the girl," Conley said, handing the envelope to Garret. "The guy left a picture of his daughter. I showed it to the bookers. They never seen her or heard of her. 'Course, she's a lot younger in the picture than she would be now. But it looks like Nevitt was just barking up the wrong tree. End of story, right?"

Conley watched Garret carefully. Garret stared at him.

"Not exactly," Conley continued. "I say to the Nevitt guy, 'Can I take your picture?' He thinks it over and says no. He gets a hotfoot and decides he wants out of there. The guy is kind of rattled by now, like it took all he had to tell me this bullshit story about his daughter, like it took him months to think it all up and spit it out. This guy Nevitt is kind of dumb-ass jack, see. So he's all rattled by now, but on the way out the door he says to me, 'Tell Earl I'll be around to see him.' And I shrug and walk away, and then I realize he'd been calling you Garret Stowe the whole time, then he gets nervous and spits out the name Earl. I don't even think he knew what he'd said. It just popped out. So I realize his whole story about the girl was bullshit. There has to be another story, though, for this guy to turn up in the office. I have to wonder if that girl's picture means something else to him, and to you. Why don't you look at the picture and tell me . . . Earl?"

Garret slipped the envelope, unopened, into his briefcase. "I've made your life quite good here in New York," he said quietly. "And now you're pushing me a little too hard, Conley."

"Nobody ever said I knew when to quit. But I've got copies of that picture, too. And guess what? You don't think I let old Nevitt just slip away, do you? I followed him to his ratty hotel, and I followed him to the damn airport, and I watched him get on the plane. And from the looks of the guy I wouldn't be at all surprised if I could find him in a couple of hours. And my guess is that this guy could make a hell of a lot more trouble for you than I could. I just wonder what he knows, and what it's worth to you to keep him away."

"Find out where he lives."

"I might. But you're rich, Earl. I've got a few bucks and a few broads now. But I ain't rich. Nowhere near it."

"We'll make an arrangement."

"I'll be anxious to hear all about it," Conley said, as the limousine pulled up to the Air France terminal at JFK.

"Conley, I don't want you to use the name Earl in reference to me again. Ever. Am I clear?"

Conley said, "You can buy three-thousand-dollar suits and change your name to Elvis Presley if you want. But that still don't make you Elvis Presley, now, does it?"

c h a p t e r

23

Instead of returning to New York following her stay at La Valle, Jessica flew to Milan, where Tommee Barkley was doing a layout for Italian *Vogue*.

"Was I right or was I right?" Tommee asked Jessica, of La Valle.

"You were right."

The two of them jogged along a quiet road on the outskirts of the city. The sun had barely risen, and the air was still fresh with the dawn.

"But you didn't fly here to tell me that."

"No. I didn't."

Ever since the lunch with Caddie, Jessica had been thinking about the notion of expanding, rather than consolidating, her business. The idea would not let her rest.

"I want to open in Paris, London, and Milan, for starters," Jessica said to Tommee. "And shortly thereafter in Madrid, and perhaps Tokyo."

"Did you get laid at La Valle?" Tommee asked Jessica, surprised at this sudden burst of enthusiasm.

"No, I didn't. But I was able to think, and I know what needs to happen. I want to be able to represent my models all over the world. And if I sign a great girl,

like Tommee Barkley or Caddie Dean, I don't want to
have to share my commission with every agency in
every country she does business in. If I was good at being an agent in New York, which is the toughest
town in the business, why shouldn't I be good at it
elsewhere?"

"But it's about the bookers," Tommee said. "How
are you going—"

"Buy the best agencies in each city, or the second-
best and then make them the best."

"If they are successful, why should they sell?"

"For the same reason you got on an airplane and flew
to Milan, when you'd rather be at your beach house in
Nantucket. The right price."

Tommee stopped in her tracks, breathing hard. "Jesus Mary priest, honey," she said. "You really do have
a bug up your ass."

Jessica faced her squarely. The sun was fully up
now, illuminating their faces. "I need your help," she
said at last.

"What the hell am I going to do?"

"Find me the money."

"Give me that again?"

"If I go to my bankers in New York, they're going to
look at my current books and tell me I'm nuts. Maybe I
am nuts, but I think I can make this work. But I have to
move fast, and I have to have substantial capital. Who
do I know who has a better Rolodex than the chairman
of Goldman Sachs? Tommee B."

"I'm listening, hon, keep talking." A big grin spread
across Tommee's face.

"I don't know how you do it, but you've dated more
rich men than anybody in America, right?"

Tommee shrugged. "Rich men can be as good-
lookin' as poor men. They're just usually older."

"And somehow you've remained friends with most
of them."

"More or less."

"Well, you've told me a thousand times they all want to set you up in some business."

"Yeah, they love the idea of me working for them."

"I want you to raise the money and be my partner."

"What the flying fuck do I know about business?"

"More than most people. I'm working on a business plan right now. We'll put together a syndicate of investors."

"Those guys would shoot their wads just sitting around the club with the boys telling them they own a piece of Miss Fancy Ass on the cover of *Vogue*."

"Exactly. We give up no control. We'll invite them to the Christmas party. And we'll make money for them." Jessica looked at Tommee seriously. "You keep telling me you're worried about your life after modeling. Well, here it is."

"Jesus, girl, you ought to take more vacations. It's hard to get me excited this time of the morning, but you're doing it."

"I'll have a business plan ready in two weeks. What do you say?"

"You got laid at La Valle, admit it."

"I did meet a nice polo player from Brazil. I think he said he played polo. Or maybe that was his name. Paulo."

The women laughed and ran back toward the hotel.

Nona Fischer returned from a long day's shoot in Connecticut, part of a two-week gig Vitesse had booked for her. The job was for a regional department store, and Nona played the role of a working mother in a series of advertisements. The job paid little, but Nona was thrilled to do it. To have makeup artists and costumers fussing over her, to see the dozens of eyes around the set focused on her when the photographer began to shoot, felt like the fulfillment of a long-ago promise.

Yet she also felt guilty, because the shoot coincided with a two-week booking for Ginny in Greece. Nona had begun to allow Ginny to go to local New York shoots accompanied only by her tutor and the Vitesse bodyguard. But when the location shoots were booked in Florida, California, Italy, and Paris, Nona had always been at Ginny's side. Not this time. The lure of her own booking, plus the fact that she had enrolled in an acting class with an instructor who became irate if any of the students missed a session, motivated her to allow Ginny to make the trip without her. Garrett had arranged for the tutor and one of Ginny's friends from New York to make the trip with her.

Besides, Nona told herself, the brief separation might do them both some good. Ginny had become quite assertive lately, objecting to curfews and house rules laid down by Nona. She wanted to go to clubs and concerts with some of the other models, and when Nona pointed out that Ginny was only fourteen years old, Ginny replied that all the clubs let her in because she was famous. It had become a running battle between them. On nights when Nona returned late from one of her classes, she often found Ginny still up, music blasting, dancing in the apartment with friends; twice she had smelled alcohol on Ginny's breath.

Nona thought about Ginny all the way back from Connecticut, so when she reached the apartment about midnight, she called Ginny's hotel in Athens. Ginny answered in a foul mood. It was seven in the morning in Greece. This was a day off for her, so she'd stayed out late the night before, and now wanted to sleep in. She did not want to speak to her mother. Ginny's voice sounded strangely detached and jumbled, and Nona became alarmed. Finally, Ginny just stopped answering her mother's questions and slammed the phone down.

Nona called the tutor's room. No answer.

Next, she called Sascha Benning at home, but her machine picked up. Then she called Garret in Paris, but he was out of town on business.

Nona lit a cigarette and paced around the apartment. *Goddammit,* she told herself, *it's my turn, it's my turn to have some fun in life, to do things I've wanted to do.* She'd been waiting on Ed and Ginny hand and foot for fourteen years. She was sick of it.

She decided to call Ginny back and give her a piece of her mind. How dare her own daughter hang up on her?

But when Nona got through to the hotel switchboard and asked for Ginny Fischer, she was told that Miss Fischer had left instructions not to be disturbed.

"I'm her mother," Nona said. "Put me through."

"We'll call the room. Hold on, please."

The operator went off the line for several minutes. When she returned, she said, "Miss Fischer does not wish to be disturbed at this time. May I take a message?"

The plane carrying Nona Fischer to Greece, after what seemed like an interminable delay in London, touched down in Athens shortly before midnight. Customs was backed up because of a terrorist alert, so by the time Nona got out of the airport and reached the hotel it was past three. She was nearly asleep on her feet, and given the hour, she decided not to call Ginny until morning.

Nona had calmed somewhat in the two days since her daughter had hung up on her. But Nona felt it was time to remind Ginny that she still had a mother who insisted on respect.

The bellman brought Nona to her room and opened the sliding doors to allow the Aegean breeze to flow in. She kicked off her shoes and walked out on the terrace.

The hotel, in a fishing village fifteen miles outside Athens, overlooked a beautiful cove. Moonlight reflected off water as smooth as glass. Nona's head throbbed from the plane travel and the vodka she'd knocked back in an attempt to sleep. But the sea air was warm and fresh, and some night-blooming vine imbued the soft breeze with a citrus scent. The headache began to recede.

And then Nona heard her daughter's voice.

Ginny was giggling and mumbling unintelligible words.

The voice came from the beach below.

Then Nona heard a man's voice. Ginny giggled and muttered a reply.

Nona whirled and left her room, found a stairway, and asked the desk clerk how to reach the beach. He pointed without looking away from the television he was watching. She crossed a terrace, then went down a dozen steps to the sand, where she stopped and listened. Nothing for several seconds. Then the distinct sound of Ginny's voice. Nona walked across the beach, which was dotted with lounge chairs, to a cabana that was open toward the water. She quietly edged around to the shoreline until she could see inside the cabana. Two lounges were pushed together, and Nona could make out the lines of various limbs. She waited until her eyes adjusted to the moonlight, then cautiously moved in for a closer look. After so many hours of traveling, Nona reminded herself, she could be hearing anything; the voice that sounded like Ginny's might belong to anyone.

The unmistakable scent of marijuana hovered around the cabana, and Nona saw moonlight glinting off glasses, and heard ice cubes clinking. She realized there were three people draped on the lounges. A boombox played a Pearl Jam CD, and Nona used the cover of a screaming guitar solo to move within a few yards of the cabana.

She caught sight of Ginny's face. Ginny was on her back, head propped up by a pillow; she took occasional pulls on a joint. There was another pillow under her hips. Ginny, Nona realized to her horror, was naked. And a man knelt on the lounge, his face buried in Ginny's crotch. There was a third person there. A woman. She was on her back underneath the man, sucking him. The woman underneath pulled away for a moment, and as she did a shaft of moonlight flashed across her face. Nona recognized her, too. She was Ginny's tutor.

Frozen, Nona stared, her throat constricted and her stomach heaving. She wanted to believe she was hallucinating, that the girl wasn't Ginny. For a moment, she considered running back to her room, grabbing her suitcase, and heading straight to the airport. She could go back to New York without being certain of what she'd seen; pretend it was the ugliest invention of jet lag. But as the light shimmered off the water, she saw Ginny's eyes open, dazed and distant-looking; then she giggled as the man tickled her stomach. Nona's face burned with anger, embarrassment, and guilt as she stood wondering what to do.

She ran back to the terrace steps, tried to calm herself, and then called out Ginny's name.

The music stopped, and there was a rustling of clothing and flurry of whispers.

"Mother?" Ginny said, in a tentative, spacey voice.

"Where are you?" Nona called.

"Over here."

Nona steeled herself and walked over to the cabana, where Ginny sat alone. She wore her bathing suit and a large sweatshirt.

"I felt I should be here," Nona said, her voice quivering, waiting to see how Ginny would react.

"God," Ginny said, giving her mother a hug. "You're such a nutcase."

"I was home worrying about you, so I thought I'd just get on a plane and come here. Why are you up so late?"

"I was sleeping."

Nona looked around. Not a sign of the others.

"Are you all right?" Nona asked, hugging her daughter, who felt limp in her arms.

"Yeah."

"I smell something."

"I was smoking a cigarette."

"That's not what I smell. I smell pot, or something."

"You smoke pot," Ginny said, giggling.

Nona realized her daughter was completely stoned.

"I'm going to help you to your room."

"Sure."

She got Ginny upstairs and put her to bed.

Nona trudged up to her own room and fell onto the bed. She cried. And kept crying until, sometime just before dawn, she fell asleep.

Her sleep was fitful and laden with dark dreams—a jumble of herself, Ginny, New York, her husband, and what she had seen on the beach. Nona awoke disoriented and exhausted, dressed quickly, and rushed to Ginny's room. She knocked on the door. No answer. A maid in the hallway refused Nona's request to unlock the door until Nona made such a scene that the maid finally relented.

Ginny was sound asleep.

Nona sat on the bed and spoke softly to her daughter until she stirred awake.

Ginny seemed completely surprised to see her mother. She had no recollection of their encounter in the cabana.

"Mother," Ginny said, "you're crazy."

That was enough for Nona.

She dragged Ginny into the shower and turned it on cold. Ginny screamed, but Nona held her firmly under the cold stream, soaking herself in the process.

"Who were you with last night?" Nona demanded.

"What are you talking about?"

"Who was the man?"

"Nobody."

"Don't tell me nobody, because I was standing there and he had his head between your legs, so I assume you have some idea who he was."

"You're so sick."

"No, I'm just stupid for having let you come over here by yourself."

"I wasn't doing anything."

There was a knock at the door. A male voice identified himself as hotel security.

Nona opened the door. Standing with the security man was Ginny's tutor, who looked pale and nervous.

The tutor began to say something, but before the words could come out, Nona slapped her across the face.

"You're fired," Nona said. "If you ever come near my daughter again, I'll have you arrested. I may have you arrested anyway."

Ginny stayed in the bathroom until the security man and tutor left.

"I want to know what's been going on, Ginny," Nona said. "I want to know what you've been doing. Do you know how much trouble you can get into here? Doing drugs in a foreign country? Do you have any idea what you're doing?"

"Mother," Ginny said in a suddenly assertive voice, "don't tell me what to do."

"Don't give me orders," Nona said.

"Then stop telling me what to do."

"You're fourteen years old. That doesn't mean it's

time for you to be ... sleeping with men. You're not ready."

"I wasn't sleeping with him. And I don't think you should talk. I saw you giving head to Garret while Daddy was in a cab on the way in from the airport. So what makes you so great?"

The words were a body blow. To hear her daughter say "giving head" made Nona want to throw up.

"We're leaving here today," Nona said. "We're flying to New York and then we're flying back to Wisconsin and in the fall you're going back to school where you belong."

"Yeah, right—"

"Don't turn your back on me, young lady," Nona said, following her daughter over to the terrace.

"How can I go back to school?" Ginny said. "I'm booked for the next six months, and you know it. I have contracts. And you know what? I like modeling and I don't like school. And the money I'm making is paying for everything you're doing in New York, too. So don't tell me what to do."

Nona had never struck Ginny in her life. She stood there squeezing her own arms so she wouldn't do it now. Ginny was old enough, and Nona young enough, for them to be sisters, and that was how they'd lived for the past year, talking about modeling, New York, traveling, money, and all the amazing things that were happening to their lives. Nona knew that what Ginny had seen and done in the past year was more than most kids would do in a lifetime. But suddenly she was looking at a fourteen-year-old girl she didn't recognize.

"Pack your suitcase," Nona said.

"Go talk to Garrett," Ginny said. "He always calms you down."

"What do you mean?"

"You do whatever he says."

"No," Nona replied, "I don't do whatever he says, and I can't talk to him because he's in Paris and we're getting out of here."

"You *can* talk to him. He's in the hotel."

Nona felt the temperature of her blood drop.

"What?" she asked, almost in a whisper.

"He's been here all week."

Ginny picked up the phone and asked for Garret Stowe's room. When he came on the line, Ginny said, "Will you talk to my mother? She's going ballistic."

Ginny listened for a moment, then turned to her mother.

"He wants you to meet him in the restaurant."

Nona stood trembling on the terrace, looking at the water, as scenes from the cabana flashed through her mind. And the longer she stood there, the clearer the one thing she had tried to block from her mind became: that the man who had been with her daughter was Garret Stowe.

Nona belted down three slugs of vodka from the convenience bar, then went downstairs. Garret sat at a corner table in the terrace restaurant, casually eating a late breakfast of eggs and fruit, sipping coffee, and reading the Paris *Herald-Tribune*.

He surreptitiously studied Nona's face as she paused at the maître d's station.

The moment she sat down—rigid, with an icy rage in her eyes—he said, "Nona, you really should have called and saved yourself a lot of worry for nothing." He shoveled a forkful of fruit into his mouth and took his time chewing. "As much as you'd like to think so," he continued, "Ginny is no longer a child. She is very grown-up for her age. It's simply a fact you have to face."

"I'm going to have you arrested and sent to jail."

"Are you?"

Garret signaled for the waiter to bring more coffee. He offered some to Nona, who refused.

"Before you decide to wade into waters that are above your head," Garret said, "let me make a few things clear. If you try anything, Ginny's career and future will be ruined. Your husband will file suit against you for custody of Ginny, and he will win. Ginny will be humiliated throughout the world, and she will never forgive you for it. And when you take the witness stand and have to explain to the judge why you seduced me in the first place, and offered me your daughter in exchange for obtaining modeling jobs for you, I think your own future will be slightly . . . damaged, shall we say? So be a good girl. Ginny has a shoot to finish, then I'm sending you both on vacation to a private villa in Fiji, where mother and daughter will have ample time to repair their relationship. After that, we get on with business."

"Garret, this is my daughter. Don't you see what you're doing?" Nona hated the desperation that had crept into her voice, but she didn't know what else to do except plead.

"What I've been doing is making your dreams come true by pulling you out of that shithole town in Wisconsin and getting you away from your brain-dead life with that husband of yours. You like your new life, Nona. And you like the fact that your daughter is a star, that everyone in the world knows who she is and bows and scrapes to her. You wish you were her. But you'll take what's left, won't you?"

Nona set frozen, disgusted with herself for even listening to Garret, yet silenced by the truth of his words.

He pushed a plate of rolls toward Nona.

"Eat something," he said. "You're pale."

c h a p t e r
24

Jessica flew to New York and practically moved herself into the law offices of Barber, Willcox & Grefe, which assigned a team of top lawyers, led by senior partner Harbert Raines, to draft Jessica's business plan. Tommee Barkley lined up a dozen potential investors, all of whom had balance sheets that soared north of a hundred million dollars. One of Tommee's friends, heir to a vast real estate fortune, immediately took the lead investment position in the proposed company and provided the use of his Gulfstream IV jet for Jessica, Tommee, and Harbert Raines to travel to their meetings.

Ten million dollars was raised within two weeks. And then Jessica was back on the Concorde, flying to Paris for a meeting with Delph Groleau of Paris Models.

"I'm forming a company that is going to consolidate several of the world's leading model agencies," Jessica explained to Delph, whom she'd known for a decade, as they sipped tea in Jessica's suite at the Crillon. "We're going to control the top models in every territory worth having. I want Paris Models to be the French component of this new company."

"And I thought your company was reeling over there in New York," he said, only mildly surprised that Jessica Cartwright had bounced back so quickly.

"Business has been lousy," Jessica admitted. "At least, mine has."

"Yes, Vitesse has put quite a dent in New York, hasn't it?"

"But Vitesse models haven't done particularly well here in Paris or in Milan, have they?"

"Well, Garret has been using that silly Marie Zola. She's back in business but simply can't match our clout."

Jessica didn't bother to hide her satisfaction. She knew she'd found weakness in Garret Stowe's plans.

"Jessica," Delph said, "Paris Models is doing well. Merging or selling control would not necessarily be in our interest."

"Except to keep a top model these days you have to be more than the best agency in one city. Think of the revenue you lose when Claudia Schiffer is booked out of New York, or even in Los Angeles. The model business is behind every other industry in the consolidation of its worldwide resources. It's time for that to change."

"You're not the only person thinking this way, Jessica. And you're not the only person who has approached us about taking over Paris Models."

"Garret Stowe wants to buy you and make you part of Vitesse. So what? Then he still can only offer models in New York and Paris. Our company is going to have New York, Paris, Milan, London, and Los Angeles in the first year. Other cities will follow six months later."

"Did you win the lottery, Jessica?"

"No, but I have substantial backers."

"I shouldn't tell you this, but I will, because we've known each other for so long. Not only has Garret

Stowe expressed interest, he's made an offer. Things are dragging a bit, since he's always off on some secret adventure. He's turned the negotiations over to his subordinate, a Mr. Philip Stein."

"Here's my proposal," Jessica said, blocking out Phil's name and refusing to acknowledge Vitesse as a viable competitor. She handed Delph a file folder. "In it you will see certain assumptions we've made about your revenues. If our assumptions are correct, then the buyout figure you'll see on page six can be considered money on the table. However, the offer is only good for seventy-two hours."

"I don't know that we are prepared to move that quickly," Delph said, thumbing to page six to have a look at the number. "And I don't know that your offer could—"

He saw the number and shut up.

Delph looked at Jessica.

"Who in London and Milan?" he asked.

"Cathews in London and Pop in Milan."

She was playing high-stakes poker now, since she had conducted only preliminary conversations with those other agencies. She was flying to London in an hour, and tomorrow to Milan, where she would repeat the strategy she'd used with Delph.

"Where will I reach you?" Delph said.

"Call my office in New York, and they will patch you through to me."

Delph, seeming almost shaken, closed the folder and went to the door.

"I must say," he observed, turning, "that in all the years we've done business and exchanged pleasantries, I didn't really have you figured for someone quite as ambitious as this."

"Neither did I," Jessica said, "but I don't take kindly to being systematically destroyed."

"It's a shame, really, what happened with you and

Caddie," Delph said. "She's one of the better ones. And I can't say I approve of what Garret is doing. I really wonder what it is he has that women find so appealing. I'll admit to having been interested in him myself, for a time. But I've always liked Caddie, and she's going to be embarrassed by him."

"How so?"

"He's living with Caddie Dean, but he's running around with that little society girl who writes for *Femme Nouvelle*. Nicole Rochas. It's supposed to be a big secret, but I see it as plain as day. That's why he's turned over his negotiations to Stein. He's too busy being romantic."

"I've seen the column. I don't know Nicole Rochas."

"Worth more money than God. Her aunt owns Château Rochas, and the niece has a nice stake in it herself. Nicole works to amuse herself. I happen to know that every time Garret goes away on business, Nicole has been going with him. For months. It must be a little ego trip for her, you know? The guy who has Caddie Dean in his bed would actually rather be with *her*. I suppose she's loving every second of it. Fool. And I don't think Caddie actually knows about it, because she doesn't have all that many friends in Paris. You know me—usually I think these models get what they deserve. But Caddie has been a class act. Garret is such a bitch to act this way. I don't like it."

The venerable Château Rochas, after hundreds of years in the same family, was now owned primarily by Giselle Rochas, who, with the block of stock owned by her niece, Nicole, controlled the direction of the business. There were also dozens of small blocks of stock, control of which had been diluted by marriages, deaths, and the vagaries of trusts and wills. Thus, ownership and control of the family business had never been a concern of Giselle's, until she received a telephone call at the close of business one day from the château's financial manager, Bernard Decroix.

"I have very strange and distressing news," he said. "Twenty of the minority holders of our stock have today tendered their holdings to a single buyer, creating a rather significant block of stock."

"None of the sellers called to ask if we were interested in buying their holdings?" Giselle asked, irritated.

"No. Clearly this was a well-orchestrated financial maneuver. Someone has been working on it for a while."

"Who is the buyer?"

"A holding company, which I've investigated. It is funded by an investment banking concern owned by an American named Davis Kellen. Doubtless you know who he is."

"Of course."

"I placed a call to Mr. Kellen and was referred to the law firm representing the holding company. So we are not going to get any immediate answers."

"What I don't understand," Giselle said, with growing alarm, "is why someone like Kellen would have any interest in our château. The profits would be insignificant to him. Unless it was a pure vanity purchase. But then, why us? Why not an even more famous château?"

"It's a mystery to me," Decroix said. "I hope to know more tomorrow when I find out who is on the board of this holding company. There must be an answer in there someplace."

Giselle replaced the phone on its base. She felt queasy. Château Rochas was hers; her blood and family and past were imbedded in it. No matter how many of the minority holders sold their stock, no one could amass a block larger than that controlled by Giselle and Nicole. Still, the matter unsettled her.

Her concern turned to astonishment and rage the

next morning when Bernard called to inform Giselle of the results of his investigation. Among the names on the board of the holding company that was buying all the stock was Garret Stowe.

"These other people are legal and financial advisers to Davis Kellen. But this Mr. Stowe, he runs the holding company. He, in effect, controls the stock. And I've never heard of him. I've called bankers and people in the wine business. No one has heard of him."

"I've heard of him," Giselle said.

"Then perhaps you would have some idea how to contact him. I'd like to speak with him regarding his intentions."

"I'll speak with him," Giselle said.

She hung up the phone and walked to the window of her office, thinking it best to cool off before calling Garret.

But she did not have time. Her assistant buzzed through and said that Mr. Stowe was on the line.

She snatched up the phone, but before she could get a word out, Garret said, "I thought you might want to have lunch with me today."

"What is this insanity you're involved in?" Giselle hissed into the phone.

"Just business," he said coolly. "*Our* business, as it appears."

"But what's the point, Garret? There is nothing you can do with this stock other than watch the company from a distance."

"I think we should have lunch."

"I don't want to have lunch. I want you to meet me right now at my office and we will settle this matter."

"No, I'm actually very busy, and I'm only in Paris for the day. I've blocked out lunch. That's all the time I have."

"Nonsense. I already have an important lunch scheduled with my American importer. It would be embarrassing to cancel it."

"Cancel it."

"There is—"

"Cancel it," Garret said again, in a voice that Giselle had not heard before. A dark, flat tone that chilled her.

"Will you explain to me, then, what is the point of all this effort?"

"La Tour d'Argent. One o'clock. Your favorite table," Garret said to her.

Phil Stein screamed at his secretary in the New York offices of Vitesse.

"He's got to be somewhere, goddammit. He didn't just fall off the face of the earth."

"I've left messages for Mr. Stowe everywhere. Here, Paris, his country house there. I've called Caddie. Everyone."

"Call the other one . . . Nicole Rochas."

"I've called her as well. I've left urgent messages."

"But this is three days!"

The secretary was nearly in tears.

"I've sent faxes. Everything I can think of. Mr. Stowe said he would be in Paris. I don't know where else to look."

"Get me on the next Concorde to Paris," he said, leaping up from his desk.

Garret, in fact, had been on a yacht near Monte Carlo for a week. The yacht had been chartered by Nicole Rochas as a surprise for Garret. "It's the only way I can keep you away from the telephones, and away from your beautiful models," she told him. "And since you won't be seen with me . . . "

"That's going to end. I simply didn't want people to think my models were in your magazine as some kind of favor. It would be bad for both of us. But I don't care anymore," Garret told her, looking into her eyes. "I don't care at all."

Much of the week had been spent in the yacht's stateroom. Nicole had never met a man who seemed so attuned to her desires. He kept her in a state of fulfillment, and she had never felt so alive in her life.

"But what about Caddie Dean?" Nicole said to Garret, for the umpteenth time during the three-month romance.

"If I loved her, I would have married her," he said simply.

"She's living in your apartment."

"Not for long," he said. "But I didn't want to just throw her out on the street. She needed a place to live, she's been through this awful divorce. As her agent, I felt a responsibility to help."

"And sleep with her at the same time?"

"It was nothing, and it's over," he answered. "And now I have to fly to Paris for a business lunch, but I'll be back tonight."

"Can't get enough of that view," Garret said, seeming to materialize from nowhere, "can you?"

He sat down at the prime table and looked at Giselle Rochas.

"You wore that dress for me," he said. "A simple black dress with white pearls. Sensible. But sexy. I like that in a partner."

"Don't you think this has gone far enough? You've recruited Davis Kellen to provide money to buy Château Rochas stock. Heaven knows what you're giving him in return. But to what end? Is this stock purchase supposed to irritate me? I've lent you money countless times. I've been a friend to you."

"And I gave you everything you wanted from me, as well," Garret said. "Didn't I? And I gave you a lot of things you didn't know you wanted until you had them.

I'm a success, Giselle. And I simply wanted you to participate in that in your world, not just in mine."

"We have our own lives to lead. Why don't we leave it at that?"

"But we can't, now that we're going to be partners."

He nodded at the waiter, who brought a bottle of champagne on the prearranged signal.

"I don't want champagne," Giselle said.

"But I do. You see, I'm getting married. Finally, after all these years. And to the most wonderful young woman. Quite special. An aristocrat, actually, though she doesn't act like one."

"Who's the lucky woman?" Giselle asked sarcastically.

"Your niece, Nicole."

Giselle didn't react at first. She thought it just another of his sick jokes. But he kept staring at her, his eyes darkening, the humor leaving the mask of his face.

"You could welcome me to the family," Garret said, "though I suppose we are already closer than most in-laws ever get."

"If you ever put a hand on Nicole, I'll see that—"

"Stop," he said. "Don't say anything you'll regret. And I don't want to hear anything that might displease my future bride."

"You're being serious," she said, after a long pause.

"Nothing seems all that serious when champagne is on the table. But, yes, Nicole and I are going to be man and wife."

Only then did the terrible realization hit Giselle. The combination of stock owned by Nicole and the block recently purchased by Kellen and controlled by Garret would give Garret a share in Château Rochas equal to hers.

She stared at him for a long time, then said, "If in fact you've been seeing Nicole, I'm sure she will listen to reason. But before we get involved with all that, just tell me how much you want."

"I don't understand."

"You do understand."

"Then I'm offended," Garret said, sipping his champagne.

"No you're not," she said. "Just tell me how much you want to leave my family and Château Rochas alone."

"Your family? You've never been that close to Nicole. At least, according to her."

"By her choice. She's very independent. Obviously. Now, just tell me how much money it is going to take to end this nonsense."

"You don't understand," Garret said, leaning forward. "I'm not looking for money. Is the idea of my being your partner, your equal, so disturbing to you?"

"I've come here prepared to offer you a million dollars, taxes paid, simply to vanish from my life," she said. "In return, you will arrange for us to repurchase the stock your holding company has acquired."

He laughed. "You still don't understand," he said.

"Two million."

"No."

"Here it is, and it is final. Three million dollars, Garret. Do you know how much money that is? Think about it."

"No."

"Don't be stupid."

"I haven't been so far," he said lightly.

"You are going to force me to speak frankly with Nicole," Giselle said.

"And do you think she'll listen? Don't you think that what you have to tell her about us would sound so bizarre as to be ridiculous? I would consider that carefully."

A waiter approached the table.

Garret tried to wave him away, but he handed Garret a message.

Garret glanced at the message, then abruptly rose to leave.

"I have other business," he said to Giselle. "However, I've taken care of the lunch bill, so you're welcome to stay as long as you like. Order another bottle of champagne."

Garret climbed into his waiting limousine and dialed Marie Zola.

"What is it that's so urgent that you would interrupt my lunch?" he said when Marie came on the line.

"Your New York office has been frantic to reach you," Marie said, "and I thought you should know. Mr. Stein is arriving in a couple of hours and left explicit instructions that he needs to meet with you immediately."

"Stein is flying to Paris?" Garret said, confused.

"Yes. I suppose it has something to do with the rumor about Paris Models."

Garret had not told Marie of his negotiations to buy Paris Models. "The Paris Models negotiations have been very delicate," Garret said. "I'm sorry I could not discuss them with you, but of course I plan to fold you into the new company. With more money and better terms."

"What new company?" Marie Zola asked.

"Didn't you hear what I just said? The rumors you've heard are true. I'm buying Paris Models and it is going to become Vitesse Europe."

"How strange," Marie Zola said. "The rumor I heard is that Jessica Cartwright has started a new international company and as part of that company she has purchased Paris Models."

Garret went silent for several seconds. The model

business was constantly awash with rumors, but this one was absurd.

"*I* am buying Paris Models," he said again. "Why do you think Phil Stein is flying in? The deal, I'm sure, is ready to be signed."

"I'm just telling you what I heard."

Garret clicked off, then dialed Delph Groleau.

"I thought you'd dropped off the face of the earth," Delph said. "I thought you'd stopped loving me since you haven't called in, what, a month?"

"Delph, Phil Stein is arriving tonight. Did you schedule a meeting?"

"Why?"

"Do we have a deal or don't we?"

"Garret, darling, don't tell me that for the first time in your mysterious little life you are the last to know something! Haven't you talked to Stein? We've been negotiating with him for three days, or, at least, attempting to. I'm sorry we couldn't work things out. But the Cartwright deal was far superior to yours. You can't fault us for that. We held off as long as we could."

"What the fuck are you talking about?"

"We gave you the opportunity to counter her. But Jessica's offer was of a much broader scope, though I can't discuss the details. Besides, Mr. Stein did not respond with a solid new proposal. He said he couldn't without your approval. Do you mean you've gotten caught with your pants down and I'm not there to see it?"

"You stupid fucking faggot son of a bitch, what have you done?"

"Now, wait a minute, dear, I haven't done anything. You were the one who was supposed to do something. I've been a big help to you in the past, Garret, so don't get bitchy with me."

Delph hung up.

Garret threw his cellular phone against the wind-shield, startling his driver, who nearly crashed the car.

Delph Groleau stared at his telephone, furious that Garret Stowe had spoken to him in that sneering tone, as if Delph were nothing more than an errand boy who had misdelivered a package.

Now that the Vitesse deal had fallen through and Cartwright had filled the void, Delph knew he wouldn't ever be working with Garret. Still steaming from Garret's scorn, Delph called Caddie Dean.

"I need to talk to you, Caddie," he said, "and I'd like to do it in person. A quick espresso."

"Are you all right?" she asked, noting the agitation in his voice.

"I'm fine, I'm fine," he said, "and this will only take a moment, but it's important. And I'd rather you not mention it to *anyone*." He emphasized the word.

"Sure, Delph," she said. "When?"

"Sooner is better."

"Okay. Café Sass. Half an hour."

"You imbecile," Garret growled at Phil Stein, the moment Phil stepped into his suite at the Ritz. Garret had been there waiting for him.

Phil was discomposed by his hasty trip, and the sight of an enraged Garret unsettled him further.

"How could you let this happen? I thought we had a deal with Paris Models. Where the fuck did Jessica Cartwright come from? And why wasn't I called?"

"You *were* called. For days. I've been frantic trying to call you. Your own secretary can't reach you—how am I supposed to? I'm your damn partner and I can't reach you. The Cartwright thing came out of nowhere. Suddenly I have Delph Groleau calling to say he has another offer. I thought it was bullshit. He wouldn't tell me who it was. I thought it was all a bluff. It wasn't. They've *sold* to Jessica Cartwright. But what can I do about it when nobody knows where you go and what you do, Garret? And I for one think it has all gotten out of control."

"Out of control? What is out of control?" Garret screamed.

"Our damn company. Take a look at these, in case you haven't been reading my memos." Phil pulled a sheaf of papers from his briefcase and handed them to Garret.

Garret skimmed through them.

"Models' earnings," he said. "Yes, I've seen them."

"Then you'll know we owe a lot of money to a lot of girls who aren't making money for us. It was your brilliant idea to offer them guarantees. Two *years* of guarantees, while you were at it."

"Yes, what's your point? I'm talking about buying Paris Models and you're showing me fucking memos."

"The point is obvious," Phil said, pointing to the numbers. "Guaranteed contracts, Garret. We'd be doing just peachy if we only had our ten top girls. But we don't. You gave guaranteed contracts to fifty of them. We're looking at a shortfall of almost a million dollars in two months when we have to make good on those contracts. And I've been trying to talk to you about it for three months. But do you want to talk about it? No, evidently you're too busy trying to spend more money."

"If the girls aren't earning what they should be earning, then we don't pay them," Garret said.

Phil laughed. "That's your plan?"

"It's not a plan, it is an order. We don't pay them."

"Then we'll be in breach of contract."

"So what?"

"We'll be bankrupted."

"Bullshit."

"You think those models are just going to smile and

not complain when I tell them they are not going to get their guarantees? I can't just *not pay* them," Phil said.

"Then you don't have to worry about it. You're fired."

Phil's face went florid, first in confusion, then in anger.

"You can't fire me, Garret, because I don't work for you. We're partners, remember?"

"No we're not."

Phil had to stop and think for a moment. Had Garret gone completely mad? Of course they were partners. They had agreed on all the terms of the partnership over a year ago. Papers had been drawn and signed.

"Do you think I want someone running Vitesse who is willing to steal company books and hand them over to a competitor? Which is what you did to your old friend Jessica Cartwright."

"You asked for that information. It was your idea."

"But I didn't work for her, you fucking idiot. I can ask for whatever I want."

"I'll have you in court and I'll close Vitesse down," Phil said, his mind racing to understand why Garret seemed unconcerned by his threats.

"I'd think about that rather carefully, Phil." Garret reached into his pocket, pulled out a cassette tape, and tossed it at Phil. "When you have some spare time, pop that into a machine. You were so thrilled about getting your puny little dick sucked by Felicia that your mouth just never stopped flapping. You wanted to impress that girl with what a genius you are, so you explained to her how you were going to get those models away from Jessica. You explained how you had the facts and figures and were setting everything up. You explained the whole thing to Felicia, who recorded it for me. Now, I don't give a fuck if you call this legal evidence or not, Phil. But if you think you'll ever work in this industry again after I'm finished with you, you're wrong. And if you think you'll ever get another job as a lawyer, you're wrong there, too. No, you're fucked, Phil. I'm going to give you a small amount of money and you're going to get the fuck out of my life and never bother me again. Isn't that right?"

Phil felt his throat closing up and sweat rolling down the inside of his newly tailored shirt and suit.

"I've only helped you," Phil said finally.

"You want to help somebody? Go put on a monk's robe and ring a bell somewhere. But if I ever see you again I'll rip your fucking face off and piss on what's left of you."

chapter

25

"I hope you don't think I'm a fool for this," Delph Groleau said to Caddie, after telling her about Garret's involvement with Nicole Rochas. "I know one is supposed to mind one's business. Normally, I hate models. But I don't hate you, and would be much happier if you were never hurt."

They sat in a quiet corner booth at Café Sass. Caddie had not touched her expresso from the moment Delph began his story.

"Does the entire city know this?" Caddie asked.

"A lot of people do. But you know how they are in this industry. They won't tell a star model anything for fear of being the messenger who gets killed."

"Wow," she said, looking out the window. "Am I just a complete idiot, or is Garret pretty good at pretending to be something he's not?"

"He's very good at it, Caddie."

"I think I'll go home now," she said.

She kissed Delph on the cheek and let him hold her for a moment.

She walked briskly down the boulevard, hoping the exertion would distract her from her own thoughts.

Finally, she slowed. And she felt the eyes of passersby upon her. That was a familiar feeling. People recognized her, and even those who didn't know she was Caddie Dean knew she was a beautiful woman. They looked at her, envied her. But right now, to her, it felt as if they were laughing at her. If Garret could fool her so completely with his attentions and kindness, she wondered, what else had he fooled her about? Jon Ross had quietly looted her life savings, while slipping into bed with her each night. Garret had provided emotional support. He listened, tended to the little details that made her feel womanly—the special gift, a meal prepared at home, the tape of a movie she had mentioned in passing. All things meant to please *her,* not Caddie Dean, Supermodel. And, yet, with all that, he was completely involved with somebody else.

Caddie slipped into a brasserie and ordered a cognac, then another. She had a third and fourth before walking home. The cognac buzzed in her brain, and that's what she wanted, to shut off thoughts and feelings. When she entered the apartment, she went straight to the den and poured herself another large cognac. She thought of telling the maid to pack her things so she could be gone before Garret returned from wherever he was. But she couldn't muster the energy to do it. She sat, and she drank.

Following his meeting with Phil Stein, Garret had the chauffeur drive him around the city for almost two hours, so that he could calm down and think. And when he finally returned to his apartment, he found Caddie sitting in the living room with the lights off, staring out the window at the fountain in the courtyard. Garret smelled the cognac as soon as he entered the room.

"We have some things to talk about," Garret said.

"No," Caddie said.

"Fine, then I'll do the talking," Garret replied.

She sat yoga-style in a chair in the darkened room.

"I'm going to tell you something so that you are not surprised when you read it in the newspapers," Garret said. "I've met someone and I'll be marrying her in a couple of months. I'm sorry, but that's the way things are."

"Congratulations," Caddie said flatly.

It puzzled him that she did not have more of a reaction.

"I hope we'll remain friends. This is just something that happened. I can't explain it."

"I haven't been earning enough for your agency, I suppose," Caddie said.

"Actually, I'm in love."

"Oh."

"And I plan on working very hard to push your career forward."

"Gee."

"Don't make light of that, Caddie. You can always use a boost in this business, and you know I can still provide that."

"From what I hear, the person who is going to be boosting models from now on is Jessica Cartwright. I understand her business has just crossed the waters."

"I don't understand," he said, suddenly alarmed that Caddie seemed to know something about Jessica's buyout of Paris Models. "How would you know that?"

"She told me that she was going to buy Paris Models."

"When?"

"A couple of months ago."

He walked slowly toward Caddie. She felt his approach and stood up to face him, her back to the picture window.

"You knew Jessica Cartwright was planning on buying Paris Models and you said nothing to me?"

"Why should I have?" Caddie answered. "You never talk to me about business."

"You never told me you even spoke to her anymore."

"I ran into her at La Valle."

"Caddie, you should have told me that."

"Oh," she said. "I guess I forgot."

"Caddie," he said quietly, taking her gently by the arms, "I'm going to ask you something, and I want you to tell me the truth."

"You can take your hands off me, Garret."

He didn't.

"Tell me what you said to Jessica Cartwright about my business," Garret said. His mind raced, thinking of telephone conversations he'd had from this apartment with Delph Groleau and Phil Stein, conversations about buying Paris Models.

Caddie pushed his hands away and stared into Garret's dark eyes.

"You cunt," he whispered.

She said nothing.

"You told her what I was going to do. You listened to me talk on the telephone, and then you told Jessica Cartwright exactly what I was doing. That was a mistake."

"I don't answer to you, Garret," Caddie said. "So take your fucking hands off me and get out of my way."

"Of course I will," he said, raising his hands and backing up.

Garret took a couple of steps toward the hallway. Stopped. Turned and looked at Caddie for several seconds. Then a primal, guttural growl rolled up and out of him as he raised his right hand, stepped forward, and hit her so hard that she spun around and was knocked face first through the picture window and, amid a shower of glass, into the courtyard.

He picked up her snifter of cognac and tossed it through the broken window. It hit the ground near her.

"Finish it," he said to the unconscious figure of Caddie Dean.

Jessica was in London with Tommee Barkley, meeting the owners of the Cathews Agency to finalize the buyout of their business, when she heard the news about Caddie. The call came from Sascha Benning, Jessica's former booker. Jessica picked up the message at the Dorchester Hotel that Sascha had called from New York. She assumed it had something to do with the purchase of Paris Models—that Sascha was calling to inquire about a job at the new "superagency" Jessica was building.

"Caddie had an accident," Sascha told Jessica. "I thought you'd want to know."

"Is she all right? What happened?" Fear surged through Jessica. No matter what they'd been through, Caddie was still like a daughter to her.

"She's in intensive care at the hospital in Paris. Evidently she'd fallen through a plate-glass window."

"My God."

"I don't know many details," Sascha said.

"Was he there?" Jessica asked. Sascha knew without asking who Jessica was talking about.

"He came home and found her. He called the ambulance."

There was a silence on the line; neither of them believed that story.

During the flight to Paris, Jessica had time to think about the fact that she had not spoken to Sascha since she had jumped to Vitesse. And Jessica knew Sascha's call meant more than just the transmission of news. After all, Sascha had to assume that many people would be calling Jessica with the news. For some reason, Jessica thought, Sascha had wanted Jessica to hear the anger and concern in her voice when discussing what had happened to Caddie. Sascha was giving Jessica a message with the call, and Jessica reflected on the meaning of that message.

When she arrived at the hospital, Jessica was stunned by the size of the press group that crowded the lobby. There were at least fifty reporters and news crews chasing the story, hoping for a picture of the great model in distress. Beautiful models were usually confined to the fashion pages, but beautiful models in accidents moved up to the front page, since the only story more compelling than the realization of great beauty was the destruction of it.

Gendarmes kept the press in check, while extra security guards hired by Garret stood outside Caddie's room. No visitors were allowed.

The next morning, Jessica called the hospital, and was told that the hospital would update the press once a day on Miss Dean's condition. All other calls from friends, family, or business associates were being referred to Garret Stowe's secretary.

The media reported that Caddie Dean, a client of Garret Stowe's, had been using his apartment while in Paris. Mr. Stowe, who had been away on business, arrived home to find Miss Dean unconscious in his courtyard. A police spokesman said the accident was being investigated, and rumors swirled that Caddie Dean had been extremely intoxicated and, in fact, had been seen drinking heavily in a local bar just hours before the incident occurred. The press speculated that Caddie Dean, completely drunk, had stumbled in the living room and fallen through the window; had Garret Stowe not returned home to find her, she might have bled to death. Two world-class cosmetic surgeons were seen arriving at the hospital within hours of Caddie's being admitted, so wild rumors about the nature and extent of her injuries were also rampant.

Jessica tried for three days to get in to see Caddie, but was told that Caddie was conscious, resting, and would see no visitors until further notice.

Tommee Barkley flew in to Paris as well, but had no better luck trying to see Caddie than had Jessica.

"Fell through the fucking window my ass," was Tommee's comment to Garret's secretary.

Garret knew that Nicole Rochas would be uneasy about going public with their relationship on the heels of Caddie Dean's accident. So he rented a home in the country, two hours from Paris, and brought her there as a surprise. He did not want her in Paris, where he knew Giselle Rochas would hound her.

A butler opened the door of the country estate when Garret and Nicole arrived, and a maid stood by with a tray of caviar and glasses of chilled champagne.

"Have a look around," Garret said to Nicole.

Nicole walked into the living room. There were silver-framed photographs on the piano, and as Nicole approached them, she realized they were pictures of herself with Garret. Pictures from their private engagement dinner, pictures from picnics and outings they'd taken together. As she walked from room to room she found pictures everywhere, even pictures of her as a child and a teenager.

"I don't understand," she marveled. "Where did you—"

"I like being surrounded by pictures of my bride," he said.

"But—"

"I wanted this to feel like home."

He'd had an assistant go into her apartment, take dozens of photos out for duplicating, then return them to the exact locations from which they had been borrowed; she'd never known they'd been touched.

She opened the closet in the master bedroom and

was further surprised to find it filled with women's clothes. They were all brand-new. All by her favorite designers. And all in her sizes. Right down to the matching shoes.

She turned to Garret, amazed.

He smiled. "As I said, I wanted you to feel at home."

The cook Garret had brought in from Paris prepared a lavish dinner and presented it on the rear terrace, which overlooked gardens and the rolling terrain of the countryside.

As cognac and coffee were served, Nicole Rochas tilted her head back and looked at the stars.

Her upbringing had been in the rarefied circles of upper Parisian society. Private schools, socially acceptable friends, a moneyed future. Her secret affair with Garret was the first thing she'd done totally on her own, without the approval of family, friends, or coworkers. It made her feel alive and independent. And now that they were going to be married, Nicole felt that she had taken control of her own future, that her life was going to be her own, not set out for her by the constraints of her pedigree.

"My aunt finally got hold of me in Paris yesterday," Nicole said.

"Did she?" Garret said, almost absently, as if the mention of Giselle Rochas did not concern him at all.

"I haven't been returning her calls, so she showed up at my apartment."

"Presumptuous of her," Garret said.

"And she said all the things you told me she would. It was really embarrassing. For her."

Giselle had clearly fretted over revealing to Nicole what she knew about Garret, and her own connection to him. Giselle and Nicole had never been close, but Giselle always included Nicole in any social events she hosted, and Giselle's management of the château had increased Nicole's inherited wealth tenfold. She knew that Nicole thought of her as older, conservative, establishment. So when she swallowed her pride, drove to Nicole's apartment, and told her niece that marrying Garret Stowe would be a lifelong mistake, she had not expected a warm response. But what she got was laughter. "Garret predicted all of this," Nicole had said to Giselle. "He predicted you would say anything to protect your power at the château. Why don't we forget this conversation ever happened, and that way we can be civil to each other in the future. Let's just forget what you said, and you can wish me well in my new life." Giselle tried again, describing the *fracasser* and her later sexual involvement with Garret, but there was no getting through to Nicole; she had been thoroughly prepared by Garret for this eventuality.

Now, as they lingered over their coffee, Garret could see that Nicole had not been unnerved by Giselle, and he was relieved, and pleased with himself for smoothly manipulating such a complex situation.

"It's probably very hard for her to accept the fact that you have your own life," Garret said. "After all, I know that she lost her daughter many years ago, and I'm sure somewhere in her mind she'd like you to replace her. But she can't control you. And that's difficult for her."

"I'll just be happy when we're married and we don't have to think of anything but our future."

"And I'll drink to that," Garret said.

They drained their glasses of cognac, and Garret poured another splash for each of them.

"Is Caddie going to be all right?" Nicole asked.

"I hope so. When she's well, I'm going to see that she gets help. She should never touch a drop of alcohol for the rest of her life."

The butler came out to the terrace and whispered something to Garret.

"Nothing is important to me right now," Garret

replied, loud enough for Nicole to hear him, "other than my fiancée and this evening."

Undaunted, the butler leaned down again and spoke quietly into Garret's ear, almost urgently.

"Tell Sascha I will call her in the morning."

He waved the butler away.

But the butler didn't leave. He insisted Garret listen to him, and this time Garret excused himself and went to the library to take the call.

Garret was gone for half an hour. From her chair on the terrace, Nicole watched him walk past the library window, the telephone to his ear. He paced and spoke in quick bursts.

When he returned to the terrace, Garret looked angry.

He stared in the direction of the hills, which were wrapped in darkness.

"I came here for the quiet," he said.

"What's wrong?"

"In thirty minutes it is going to be noisy here."

"I don't understand."

"A helicopter is coming to pick me up and take me to Orly. Then I have to catch the next Concorde to New York."

"Tonight? Right now?"

"Yes. Right now," he said.

Anton Cellini was unhappy. He was shooting a layout for Aaron Adam's blue jeans line and, in his words, no magic was happening. After the spectacular success of the first Ginny Fischer launch, the industry, the media, and the public eagerly anticipated the new campaign. How do you top the most outrageous campaign to come down the road in years?

The Ginny Fischer campaign had pushed the envelope of sexual permissiveness about as far as mainstream magazines would allow. Cellini and Aaron

Adam agreed that now a different approach was called for. People would be expecting something more outrageous than last time, so why not, Cellini decided, make them search for it. Offer them an ad that at first viewing would seem minimalist . . . ethereal . . . even spiritual. An ad that would cause people to wonder if Cellini and Aaron Adam had gone mad, made a mistake, sent in the wrong negative. But the idea was that as you looked at the ad, you would slowly realize there was more going on than first met the eye. An ad that revealed itself in stages, in layers.

For the ad Cellini photographed a model in Aaron Adam jeans; actually, he shot her voluptuously shaped rear end. Then he scanned the photo, put it into a computer design graphics program, and worked on the image so that you had to look at it for a while before you realized it was a young woman's butt filling out a pair of A.A. jeans. Next, he decided to shoot Ginny Fischer in various naked poses, which he then planned to superimpose on the jeans photo in ghostlike layers. He wanted the advertisement to become a sort of Rorschach test; some people would claim to see a naked Ginny Fischer in the ad, others would say the image was a shapely cloud, or just a pattern in the fabric. He wanted an ad that would cause people to gather around it and argue about what they were really seeing. Cellini even photographed a model with her legs spread wide open and superimposed the image of her genitals on the jeans transparency, just to see how far he could push the conceal/reveal process. He became so excited with the artistic possibilities of this new concept that he created thirty versions of the ad, and Aaron Adam's team worked on arranging a special exhibit at the Museum of Modern Art, the idea being both to ignite a controversy and to establish the ads as "art." Though the original Ginny Fischer campaign had not been Cellini's idea, this follow-up was his alone, and Aaron

Adam declared it the final achievement of Cellini's true genius.

But the night he was to shoot the Ginny Fischer nudes, Cellini wasn't getting what he wanted. He spent four hours lighting one shot, using a double because Ginny refused to sit while Cellini fussed with the lights. But once the shoot started, Cellini still wasn't pleased with the results. He sent Ginny back to her dressing room while the lighting team returned for more work.

At midnight they sent for Ginny. Cellini cleared the studio except for the makeup person and one assistant. Ginny dropped her robe and Cellini went to work. The photo involved complex lighting, special-effects fog, and electronically programmed camera moves and focus changes. Still, Cellini wasn't happy. He realized that the problem was Ginny. There was no vibrancy to her form; she wasn't putting out; she wasn't focused.

"I'm looking at you and I don't want to fuck you, Ginny, and that means something is wrong."

"I thought you liked boys," Ginny said.

"Ah, but the right look from you will make anybody with a Noel get itchy. I want that look."

"I'm tired."

"Let's change the music. What do you want to hear?"

"Nine Inch Nails."

"No, no, all wrong."

"That's what I want."

"That's not fucking music. It's head-banging."

"Put on Nine Inch Nails," Ginny demanded.

"Do we have it?" Cellini called to an assistant.

"Yes."

"Put the bloody CD on and let's see what happens."

The CD was slipped into the machine, and the grinding, pounding music blasted from the speakers.

"How about it, Ginny? How does it feel?"

She grabbed the plastic bottle of Evian water she'd brought with her to the set, took a long swig, then started dancing. She kept moving off the mark that Cellini had set for her, which rendered his elaborate lighting setup useless; he motioned for her to move back toward the mark, but her eyes rolled around and she danced harder.

"Turn it up!" she screamed.

Well, why not, Cellini decided. Maybe she'd dance some energy back into her body. He signaled the assistant to pump up the sound.

The blasting music rattled the lights.

Ginny danced around the set and found her mark, then Cellini fired off a hundred motor-driven shots.

Just when Cellini was beginning to get something he liked, two lights blew, a circuit breaker popped, and the music died.

Ginny slumped to the floor.

Cellini cursed and kicked his own water bottle across the room.

"Reset!" he yelled.

The makeup girl threw a robe around Ginny and brought her back to the dressing room to wait for the repairs.

"I can't do this anymore," she complained. "I want to go to a club."

Cellini followed her down the hall.

"We're just getting there, angel. We're just about to get something wonderful."

"I'm meeting my friends, and it's late. You said we were going to be done by midnight."

"It's not me," Cellini said, "it's the fucking lights."

"I'm supposed to be meeting my friends," Ginny whined.

Cellini collared an assistant and told her to go to the club where Ginny's friends were waiting and bring them all back to the studio.

Half an hour later the entourage arrived and crowded into Ginny's dressing room. They raided Cellini's well-stocked bar, piped some music into the room, and started their own party.

The lighting repairs took an hour and a half. Ginny was exhausted, but Cellini insisted on continuing the shoot. He was in what he called his "artist's zone" and didn't want to break the moment. An assistant gave Ginny a fifteen-minute call to the set, and the makeup and hair people worked feverishly to get her ready. She grabbed one of her friends and disappeared into a bathroom. When she emerged, her eyes were rolling around in her head, and the assistant dragged her to the studio, where Cellini was ready to shoot.

"Nine Inch Nails!" Ginny screamed.

The music started. Cellini signaled to pump it up to ear-shattering levels.

Ginny lolled around for a while on the mark, while Cellini took his rapid-fire shots. Then the combination of speed, cocaine, and heroin that Ginny had popped in the bathroom kicked in. Like an express train.

She jumped to her feet, ran naked to the CD player, and turned it full-blast. She danced around the studio like a demented ballerina, whirling, jumping, diving, rolling.

"What the fuck is the matter with her?" Cellini screamed at an assistant. "Get her back to the set."

The more they chased her, the more wildly she danced.

Ginny climbed up a ladder to one of the huge windows fifteen feet from the floor. The large drape was closed to shield city lights, but Ginny ripped the drape away and danced naked on the ledge, looking down three stories to the street below.

Cellini raced to the CD player to pull the plug.

But just before he reached it, Ginny's eyes rolled up and her body shook convulsively. Her arms fell, like a marionette with its strings snapped, and she wobbled on her legs for a moment, then dropped toward the floor, where the assistant and the makeup girl waited to catch her. Her small body shook again, then she went limp.

chapter
26

Because of the swelling and discoloration, the damage to Caddie Dean's face revealed itself in stages, over a period of several weeks. She had been moved to a Paris apartment in the middle of the night, to avoid the press, and was provided with around-the-clock nursing care. But as the swelling diminished, and despite the intricate work of the cosmetic surgeons, there was no escaping the fact that Caddie's face was permanently damaged. One scar ran from her left cheekbone, jagged as it passed the corner of her mouth, then deepened and dropped to her chin. A second scar, perhaps three inches long, cross her forehead at a forty-five-degree angle. And a third scar angled from beneath her right ear across her cheekbone. The scars were thin, looking as if they'd been drawn in with a fine pink pencil, but they were there.

Police interviewed Caddie about the accident. She said nothing about Garret's striking her; in fact, the entire evening was a blur in her mind, a fact not surprising to the police, since her blood-alcohol count had been quadruple the legal driving limit.

As soon as the press discovered where Caddie was

living, they set up watch stations, hoping for a picture, knowing that the first photographer who caught a shot of her might end up making hundreds of thousands of dollars in worldwide sales. For the benefit of the press, Garret besieged Caddie with flowers, none of which ended up in Caddie's room. She had them all sent to various charities.

Other than the nurses and a maid, Caddie wanted no visitors.

Jessica Cartwright and Tommee Barkley called daily. The conversations were brief. Caddie thanked them for caring, said she was recuperating and would see them when she felt up to it.

Most days she sat in the darkened bedroom, aimlessly surfing the cable channels. When she went into the bathroom, she did not look at herself in the mirror. She felt the lines on her face and was not ready to look at them.

And when she finally did, three weeks after leaving the hospital, she looked into the mirror and saw her mother's eyes. She recalled coming home to visit when she was seventeen. She wanted to apologize for running away and let her mother know that she was working and off drugs. Her mother, already into her fourth or fifth scotch by four in the afternoon, stared at a check that Caddie showed her. It was from the Cartwright Agency; six hundred dollars for one day's work. Mrs. Dean had looked at the check in disbelief. And then looked at Caddie, not with appreciation or pride, but with hatred, a look that Caddie would see again from certain other women who despised her simply because of her looks. "You don't deserve this," Mrs. Dean said to Caddie. "You should be ashamed."

"I brought it to give to you," Caddie said.

Her father came by the trailer the next day to find Mrs. Dean hoarding the check. He ripped the check from his wife's hands.

"What did you do to get this?" he asked Caddie.

"They took my picture," Caddie said. "I'm a model."

He backhanded her halfway across the trailer and called her a dirty little whore.

Mrs. Dean threw her drink at her husband, who then hit her so hard she blacked out for several minutes.

Caddie hid beneath the pillows in her tiny bedroom and trembled when she heard her father's heavy footsteps stop outside her door. She smelled the gin on him from across the room.

"That's what I make in two weeks of working my goddam ass off," he said. "And they pay a little whore like you six hundred dollars to take your fuckin' picture?"

Caddie froze.

"Fuckin' little bitch—think you're something special because you're a looker?"

"No, Daddy," she'd whispered through the pillow, terrified that she was going to be struck again and wondering what on earth had made her think that her success would change her parents.

A neighbor yelled that the police were on the way. Mr. Dean got out of there and took the check with him. Caddie was too embarrassed to tell Jessica about the incident and never mentioned the check again.

And now, in the bathroom of her Paris apartment, Caddie peered into the mirror, thinking that her beauty had given her everything and given her nothing. She thought of her mother's hateful eyes. Every man in the world worshiped her beauty, except for Garret Stowe and Jon Ross, and those were the two men she had allowed into her life.

For the first time since leaving the hospital she looked in the mirror and saw the scars. Caddie had to look at them for a long time before she really saw them, before she could believe they were a part of her face.

She looked at the woman in the mirror and had no idea who she was. But that had nothing to do with the scars.

Cellini locked himself in his office and did not come out until the paramedics had taken Ginny from the studio to the hospital.

Ginny's friends got the hell out of there, too.

The makeup girl phoned Sascha Benning, who rushed to the studio. By then, police were taking statements from the studio crew and tracking down the kids who had split.

News crews assembled outside the studio and at the hospital.

Sascha phoned Garret at his country house in France and implored him to get to Paris and fly to New York, which, finally, he agreed to do.

While awaiting the Concorde in Paris, Garret called Aaron Adam and persuaded him to charter a jet to return Nona Fischer from Miami, where Garret had arranged for her to do a photo shoot for Burdines. He also dispatched Sascha to Nona and Ginny's apartment to remove any sign of illegal drugs.

Caddie awoke the following morning and clicked on the television. She was startled to see Sascha Benning being interviewed on CNN. The reporter asked Sascha about unconfirmed reports that Ginny Fischer had suffered a drug overdose.

Caddie turned up the volume.

"We believe she was simply exhausted from overwork, and passed out," Sascha said.

"People don't end up in intensive care because they're tired," the reporter said.

"I have nothing else to say at this time," Sascha replied.

The picture cut to video of Garret Stowe arriving at

the hospital. The voice-over announced, "Vitesse founder Garret Stowe arrived in New York just hours ago and had this to say."

A solemn-looking Garret said, "I don't know what happened, but I can promise you that I will not be leaving this hospital until I know this child is well."

Then they cut to a black-and-white photograph of Ginny Fischer, oxygen mask on her face and IV in her arm, being taken from the ambulance into the hospital—a lucky shot by a freelance photographer.

Caddie looked at the photograph of Ginny, yet in her mind the image of Garret remained superimposed on the television screen. It was the first time since the night of her fall that Caddie had seen him. Her memory of that night was hazy, dreamlike. An image of Garret's hand coming at her in slow motion had recurred in her mind at odd moments. She didn't know if it was a real memory or drawn from a dream. But looking at the frail figure of Ginny Fischer roll by on the stretcher, Caddie saw herself beneath that oxygen mask.

She picked up the phone and booked a flight to New York.

Caddie Dean often traveled under the name Katherine Donald in order to ward off unwanted attention. Despite the false name, whenever Caddie boarded an airplane or checked into a hotel she was usually recognized. However, when she boarded the Concorde from Paris bound for New York, she noticed something unusual. When the flight attendant reached Caddie's seat to take a dinner order, she did the usual double take, but this time it did not produce a smile of recognition. Instead, the attendant forced herself to look into Caddie's eyes, trying not to stare at the scars on Caddie's face. "And what would you like for your dinner, Miss Donald?" the attendant asked politely.

Moving through customs in New York, Caddie attracted some stares, but they were not accompanied with whispers of "Isn't that Caddie Dean?" She was just a young blond woman with a damaged face.

She checked into the Plaza Athénée, where the bellman who delivered Caddie's bags to the room clearly did not recognize her and made considerably less fuss over her than she had grown accustomed to.

Caddie ordered dinner from room service.

"Will there be anything else, Miss Donald?" the waiter asked politely, averting his eyes from Caddie's scarred face.

"Thank you. No," she replied, scribbling her name on the check.

After dinner she went out. Wearing jeans, a light sweater, and a Bogner country coat, Caddie walked out of the Plaza Athénée, turned west on 64th, and walked north on Madison Avenue.

At 84th and Second she buzzed the apartment of Sissy Siegel, a makeup artist who did most of Caddie's New York shoots. Sissy opened the door, looked at Caddie, and said, "Yes?" Caddie's hair was pulled up under a baseball cap, and her baggy clothing gave her an almost boyish form; without the distinctive purity of her face, she simply didn't register with Sissy. And when she did, Sissy's right hand went involuntarily to her mouth to stifle a gasp.

Hugely embarrassed, Sissy begged Caddie to come in. Caddie accepted with a smile and thanked her for the flowers she had sent to the hospital in Paris.

After all, Caddie was not here about her face. Sissy was one of the most successful makeup artists in the business, and Caddie was sure she had worked with Ginny Fischer many times. She must know something. Makeup people always did.

"I don't want anyone to know that I'm in town," Caddie said on the telephone to Sascha Benning.

"Especially Garret. But I'd like to arrange for me to see Nona Fischer. Alone."

The meeting was arranged two days after Ginny's collapse, when she was out of intensive care. Caddie went to Nona's Trump Tower apartment. She walked into the apartment and gave Nona a hug. Caddie had only met the woman twice in her life, but Nona held on as if Caddie were a cherished sister.

"I only have half an hour," Nona said. "I need to be back at the hospital."

Nona looked haggard. She hadn't slept in days. Since the incident in Greece, Nona had made fumbling attempts to retake control of Ginny's life. But Garret managed to get Nona enough bookings of her own to keep mother and daughter from spending too much time together. Nona had retreated into a haze of alcohol and denial that was shattered by the phone call about Ginny's overdose.

Caddie saw that she was dealing with a woman who was dangling on a slippery precipice.

"It's my fault," Nona said, looking out at the lights of New York City below. "It's my fault. I've hurt my little girl. I've let my daughter get hurt."

"How is she?" Caddie asked.

"The doctor said they'll know more tonight," Nona said, then broke down in convulsive sobs.

"I think she'll be all right," Caddie said, knowing something about drug abuse. "She's young and healthy. But now her life has got to change."

"My little girl," Nona wailed. "I did this."

"Mrs. Fischer," Caddie said, "you have to get Ginny away from Garret Stowe, and away from this business."

Nona's head snapped up, and she looked at Caddie. It horrified her to think that anyone knew about what had happened between Garret and Ginny. In fact, Caddie did not know what had happened. But she knew

Garret, and that he was not the person to supervise Ginny Fischer's recovery.

"I don't know what to do," Nona said. "I just don't. You don't know what's happened."

"I'm going to tell you some things about my life," Caddie said, guiding Mrs. Fischer over to a couch and sitting her down. "And then I want you to allow me to help your daughter."

chapter
27

Though Nicole Rochas was disappointed that Garret had to leave for New York, the situation causing his departure was obviously an emergency. Still, it was lonely sleeping by herself in the large country house, so she sat awake in bed, deep into the night, occupying herself by making a list of guests for her wedding. She had with her a copy of Garret's own handwritten list, which, she had already commented to him, contained many business associates but no family at all. He explained to Nicole that he'd never known his father, and that his mother had long since died. "You will be my family," he told her. "We will have children and create our own family, and our own past."

When the telephone rang around three in the morning in Garret's study, it sounded like a fire alarm shattering the quiet of the country night.

Nicole nearly jumped out of her skin at the sound. She hadn't known that Garret maintained a separate telephone line in the upstairs study. She tried to ignore the ringing, but realized that it might have to do with the urgent circumstances surrounding Garret's sudden trip to New York. Someone was probably desperately trying to reach him. So Nicole hopped out of bed and hurried down the hall to the study, just as the phone stopped ringing. She turned to leave, then heard a machine click. The telephone was connected to a fax machine, and paper was scrolling out onto the desk.

She went and had a look.

It was from a man named Conley in Miami, Florida. Evidently it was a report about a man named Luther Nevitt that Conley had been tracking. Even though Nicole Rochas was fluent in English, she found Conley's prose difficult to follow; the man was barely literate. However, she was able to deduce that Conley had spent a couple of weeks following Luther Nevitt, recording his activities. The wording of the fax indicated to Nicole that there had been previous reports.

If her aunt, Giselle, had said nothing to her about Garret, Nicole would have ignored the fax. But the tiny seed of doubt about Garret had been planted by Giselle, and after all, marriage was a lifetime decision. She poked around in the desk.

Nicole found a 9mm Beretta, which did not alarm her, since Garret had told her he kept guns in both his Paris apartment and the country house. There was a box of ammunition and a couple of file folders. Nicole opened the first folder. It was stuffed with faxes. She glanced through them. All dated within the last couple of months. All from Conley, and all in reference to this Luther Nevitt. Nevitt was referred to by name in only a couple of the faxes, but because the locations and activities were all very similar, it seemed obvious to Nicole that these were all about the same man.

She wrote the name on a piece of paper, stuffed it in her pocket, then replaced the files and closed the drawers.

*   *   *

Jessica Cartwright was staying at the Dorchester Hotel in London when she got a call from her booker relaying the news about Ginny Fischer.

She flicked on the television to CNN, and there was Ginny Fischer on the gurney. Garret Stowe and Sascha Benning were interviewed, followed by comments from famous models about drug use in the fashion business. Aaron Adam and Anton Cellini had refused comment on the matter altogether. The reporter also mentioned that supermodel Caddie Dean, thought to be in Paris in seclusion since her devastating accident, was rumored to be in New York and to have paid a visit to Nona Fischer, Ginny's mother. Could that be possible? Jessica wondered. She had spoken by telephone several times with Caddie since the accident, but Caddie had been adamant about not seeing visitors and not being ready to face the world. Why would Caddie fly to New York? And did she actually know Nona Fischer so well that she would pay her a visit during this crisis?

Jessica's speculations were cut short by a knock at the door. It was her attorney, Harbert Raines, back from a meeting with representatives of the Cathews Agency, the current target in Jessica's expansion plan. Flush with her victory in the buyout of Paris Models, Jessica pressed Cathews to close the deal as quickly as possible. And all indications were that a deal was imminent.

But now Raines seemed distressed and confused.

"They seem to be backing away," the lawyer said to Jessica, taking a seat on the couch.

"Why?"

"They have another suitor, for one thing."

"Stowe."

"Possibly. I hear he's livid over what happened with Paris Models. But I don't think it's just money. Suddenly they're asking for all kinds of financial documents from the last couple of years of your agency."

"What's that got to do with our buying them? Aren't we the ones who examine *their* documents?"

"It's all very strange. I had one of our London associates speak off the record to somebody in the firm representing Cathews. Evidently, they claim to have come across some documents supposedly belonging to us, that have the taint of fiduciary irresponsibility to certain of your clients."

"That's impossible."

"So I've told them. Jessica, I've only been on your account for a year and a half. Phil Stein was the lawyer prior to that, and these documents were executed under his watch."

"What kind of documents are you talking about?"

"Contracts that would indicate you were extracting a managerial fee from some of your models on top of commissions and service fees."

"That's ridiculous. I have no idea what you're talking about."

"Here's the problem. We're offering to compensate the principals of Cathews for the purchase of their agency via employment contracts and consulting fees that will be paid out over five years. If you are sued by some of these models who signed the tainted contracts, the Cathews people are worried that they might not see the money due them."

"Harbert, this is insane. There are no tainted contracts." She looked at some of the contracts the lawyer slid in front of her. "These are forged. Somebody has invented this."

"Possibly. And we'll look into that. But in the meantime it's thrown a monkey wrench into our negotiations while at the same time they are being pursued by another suitor. Somebody is casting a shadow over you at a very crucial time. We're trying to buy Pop in Milan, and I'm hearing rumblings that these same documents have surfaced in the vicinity of Pop's lawyers as well."

"This is Garret Stowe," Jessica said. "It has to be. He may have had Phil Stein phony up some documents, because never in my life did I extract extra fees from models. Never. And Stein knows that, and so does anybody that ever worked for me."

Harbert said, "Stein no longer works for Vitesse. We heard that he was fired over his handling of the Paris Models deal, so I don't see how he would have any incentive to provide documents to Mr. Stowe harmful to us."

"Unless he created them to kiss Stowe's ass. Buy his way back in, so to speak."

Jessica paced the suite. She had made plenty of mistakes during her career in the model industry, and she'd done a lot of things right, as well, but she knew that none of her mistakes involved ethics. It just wasn't possible.

"I'm going to get that man," she said to Harbert Raines.

He wasn't certain if she was referring to Phil Stein or Garret Stowe. But from the look on Jessica's face, Harbert Raines had no doubt that she was indeed going to get somebody.

Garret returned to France and operated out of the country house, communicating with staff and lawyers by phone and fax. He was absorbed by the battle with Jessica for control of Cathews in London and Pop in Milan, and was determined not to lose them to her, as he had Paris Models.

The phone in his upstairs office rang incessantly, while in the downstairs study Nicole Rochas proceeded with her plans for the wedding. She waited until late one evening, as she and Garret walked on a tree-lined lane near the house, to bring up the matter of Luther Nevitt.

She mentioned having inadvertently come across the fax while he was in New York.

Garret maintained his poker face at the mention of Nevitt's name and took his time forming a reply.

"I would be just as happy if you hadn't seen the Nevitt business," he said to Nicole. "He's somebody I'd just as soon forget about."

"Why is that?"

Garret thought back on the fax in question, berating himself silently for not taking more care; and though she hadn't mentioned other faxes, he assumed she might have found them in the desk. He chose his words carefully, while his mind raced. "Nevitt is someone who aims to take advantage of the fact that I've worked hard, pulled myself up."

"What does he want to do?"

"It's really nothing to worry about. I have the situation in hand," Garret said casually, hoping to end the conversation.

"I gathered he was stalking you, something of that nature. It worried me."

"He's no threat, just an annoyance."

"All I'm afraid of is secrets," Nicole said, "because they are rarely good. They destroy relationships, and they destroy people. Giselle said so many things. I know she was just trying to poison our relationship. But I don't want secrets, Garret."

Was she testing him, he wondered, talking that way about secrets? Was she giving him a chance to explain himself, or to hang himself? What if she had already done some investigation? Certainly she had the resources. Garret had hardly slept in the past week, and he knew his mind was not working efficiently. He was close to marrying Nicole, close to controlling the stock of Château Rochas.

"When I became somewhat known, Nevitt tracked me down," Garret said carefully. "He wasn't there when I was born, or when my mother died. Or when I was working to put myself through school. Never then. Just when my name got into the paper as someone who was rich and famous."

"I don't understand . . . He's your father?"

Garret released a deep breath, as if letting go of a terrible burden.

"Biologically. Nothing else, of course. My mother never talked about him, though I did ask and did look for a while. She had warned me. So I gave up on it. But he found me. And what he wanted was money. Still does. I met with him, and I did have hopes of some reconciliation. But that didn't happen. He played me along for a bit, but in the end it was about money. I sent him checks on a regular basis, for a while. He asked for more. He became a problem. So I ended it."

"Why the investigation? Did he threaten you?"

"He began telling people he worked for me, using my name. It caused trouble. I could go to the police, but I don't. I made it clear to him that if he continued his activities, I would have to go to the authorities. I've kept an eye on him."

"It's sad," she said. "I'm so sorry."

"No need to be. I grew up without him—I expect I can continue. And that's one of the reasons I love you so much. I think about the good things to come in my life, not the bad things that have already happened."

"But maybe things don't have to end like this between you."

He saw the compassion in her eyes, then took her hands in his, and said quietly but firmly, "It's done. Believe me."

"He did it, didn't he?" Jessica Cartwright said to Caddie Dean. They were sitting in Jessica's suite at the Dorchester Hotel in London.

Jessica looked into Caddie's eyes and saw her answer.

"Why didn't you go to the police?" Jessica asked.

"I hardly remember what happened," Caddie said. "I was drunk, I was angry. I can't go through a trial."

"But—"

"I didn't fly to London to complain about my face," Caddie said.

She had called Jessica from New York and asked to see her. When Jessica opened the door and saw Caddie's damaged face, rather than stare, she had reached out and embraced her, and simply said, "Caddie."

The women held each other and did not say anything for a while. In the same way that Caddie instinctively knew that Garret Stowe was intimately involved in the near destruction of Ginny Fischer, Jessica knew that Garret was the cause of Caddie's disfigurement. She knew it by the anger and fear she felt emanate from Caddie when she mentioned Garret's name.

"He's poison," Caddie said, "and it's cost me a lot to figure that out. But I want him stopped. He should never be near another model."

"What is it that you propose we do?"

"I don't know. But I do know that he was around Ginny Fischer a lot more than just as an agent."

"What?"

"I spoke to a makeup girl who was in Greece on a shoot with Ginny not long ago. The mother wasn't on the set, but Garret was, playing more than footsie with Ginny. My friend said the whole scene was sick. Ginny was using drugs, and Garret seemed to think that was amusing." Caddie moved to the window and looked out at the street. "I want to bring this man down, but I don't know how to do it. I want your help."

"How do I help?"

"Nobody I talk to seems to know anything about the guy. It's as if he's got no past. As if he just dropped out of the sky. There's got to be something there. I thought you could help me find out."

Jessica nodded. "How is Ginny Fischer doing?"

"She'll live," Caddie said. "I went to see her mother in New York. She'll do anything she can to help us."

"I'm leaving for New York tomorrow," Jessica said. "I'll give Mrs. Fischer a call. From what I've heard, she might know Garret Stowe better than most."

Jessica didn't have to wait for Nona Fischer to return her call, because Nona showed up at Jessica's office.

"You're probably disgusted by me," Nona Fischer said to Jessica, standing like a supplicant in front of her.

"I don't really know you, Mrs. Fischer," Jessica replied, "but I am very sorry about what happened to your daughter, and I hope she's on her way to getting well."

"It's going to take a while."

"I understand."

"I was so happy that you called. I don't really know who to talk to. Caddie Dean came to see me."

"She told me."

"She asked me about Ginny, and about Garret. She wanted to know what he'd done to her."

"Yes."

"I'm afraid of Garret, Mrs. Cartwright. He's very dangerous. I've allowed my daughter to get into tremendous trouble. And I don't know where to turn to pull us out of it."

"What about your husband?"

Mrs. Fischer looked away. "We're divorced. He's filing for custody of Ginny."

"I'm sorry."

"I've done some terrible things, but I don't want Garret to get away with what he's done. Tell me what I can do."

Jessica thought for a moment in silence, then said, "I

have to be careful about what I say, Mrs. Fischer, because I'm involved in business negotiations that his company is also involved in. But I would like to help. Nobody seems to know him, though. Who are his friends? Who is he close to?"

"I couldn't tell you that," she answered. "But I've spent a lot of time with Garret, and what I can tell you is that there's only one person he ever seems uneasy around. Maybe even a little scared. And what's strange is that he's a man who works for Garret, for Vitesse. His name is Conley."

Jessica learned from Sascha Benning that Conley currently worked as a test photographer for Vitesse.

"It's a joke," she whispered over the phone line to Jessica. "The guy is no more a photographer than I am. I won't send anybody to him. But a couple of people here send girls who don't have a snowflake's chance in hell of becoming models to the guy. He's Garret's buddy, and I guess this is Garret's way of saying thank you for something."

It made no business sense to have an amateur photographer of Conley's embarrassing caliber connected to an agency of Vitesse's stature. There were scores of sleazy test photographers in the city who preyed on hopeful models, encouraging them to sit for roll after roll of film, at considerable expense, telling them that the right shot just might get them signed. Scam artists like those, however, never got near the big agencies or the working models.

Jessica found the address of the studio used by Conley and parked herself in a coffee shop across the street. She watched the girls come and go. Four over a six-hour period. One was inside the studio for only twenty minutes, then came rushing out in tears. Another girl, a tough-looking brunette with no hope of becoming a model, emerged from the studio two hours

later, angry and disheveled. Conley's game was obvious to Jessica, but it still confused her that Vitesse
would allow itself to be a source of girls for this man.

Jessica called Frank Pesci, a New York City detective who over the years had helped the Cartwright
Agency whenever a loony stalked one of the models.
Pesci, a tall, solidly built man in his mid-forties who
wore his brown hair just a bit longer than most of his
colleagues and liked to listen to rock and roll while he
studied case files, ran a local check on Conley. He reported to Jessica that the check came up dry, but added,
"I don't want you to do anything silly, but I could dig a
little deeper if you had the guy's fingerprint."

Jessica mentioned the problem to Tommee Barkley,
who said she had a niece named Lane in town who was
dying to become a model. "Girl used to rope steers
down in Laredo, so I expect she can handle herself with
Conley."

Lane Barkley brought an old glossy contact sheet
with her to show Conley and discuss new shots. She
made certain that Conley handled the sheet.

"You might be a little old to get started with the
agency," Conley told Lane. "Most of the girls starting
out now are fifteen or so."

Lane feigned disappointment, but sat through the
twenty-minute session anyway.

Afterward, Conley said, "I might be able to help you
out with the Vitesse people. You know, have them send
you on a few jobs, even if they don't sign you. Plus, I
hear of things now and then. I could set you up with
work."

"Really?"

"Sure. My girls go out to dinner with some of our big
accounts when they're in town. That kind of thing.
Limos, nice restaurants. You just have to dress up and
look good. You don't have to fuck 'em if you don't
want to. That part is up to you."

"Well . . . I'll think about it," Lane said.

" 'Course, you'd want to throw some stuff my way now and then. Just to stay on my good side."

"Which side is that?" she asked him.

"The side that decides who makes the good money and who don't. Know what I mean?"

"I guess so."

"Tell you what. I know a man that likes girls who look just like you: blond, nice tits, firm ass. I know he'd like you fine. And with this guy, if he likes you, you can write your own ticket."

Conley scribbled a telephone number on a piece of paper and handed it to Lane.

"Call this number and ask for Janis, then tell Janis that I recommended you call. She'll set you up with her boss. First-class guy, great deal all the way. Worst that comes out of it you have a nice dinner."

"Who's the man?"

"Just call Janis, but you have to give her my name or she'll pretend she don't know what the hell you're talking about. Got it?"

"Okay."

Lane collected her contact sheet, held it by the edges, slipped it into an envelope, and left.

She met Jessica down at the coffee shop and turned over the sheet to her.

"He doesn't know which end of the camera to use," Lane told Jessica. "He's some kind of half-assed pimp. He gave me a number to call if I wanted to have a date with a rich guy who was going to make all my dreams come true."

Lane handed Jessica the envelope containing the contact sheet with Conley's prints all over it.

chapter
28

It took three days for Detective Pesci to run the prints through regional and national data banks. Then he found a match. Conley had a criminal record in Florida.

"Grand theft auto twice, arrested for fencing stolen merchandise three times, did three years on an assault and attempted rape charge. Not to mention a shitload of minors. He's the kind of perp that's probably done five hundred things he hasn't been collared for."

"Just the kind of man you'd want around models," Jessica said.

"Yeah, class guy."

Jessica told the detective about Conley's giving a phone number to Lane and offering to set up dates.

"No doubt it's a bullshit deal, but it's not the kind of thing we've got the manpower or the money to chase down. If a couple of these girls come in and swear out a complaint against the guy, then I might be able to do something about it. But this kind of guy isn't somebody you want to start pushing too hard, either. I'm dead certain that he wouldn't lose any sleep over knocking somebody around if he thought they were about to make his life difficult."

Jessica knew that most aspiring models didn't want to make negative waves in the business, and if a photographer like Conley was perceived to be a direct link to Vitesse, the hottest agency in town, the girls were likely to look the other way when he made his moves.

She called Lane and asked how far she wanted to play out what could be a dangerous game. Lane said, "I'll call this Janis and we'll see what's up."

Janis's voice-mail message asked the caller to leave a phone number and reason for calling. Lane left her pager number. Two hours later she was beeped and another number popped up on the pager. She dialed the number and a man with an English accent answered. Lane made up a name and told the man she had been referred by Conley; she was then given an address and invited to lunch the following day. Jessica drove by the address. It was an office brownstone in the fashionable Turtle Bay area of Manhattan. There was only a brass number plate on the front, no sign.

The man with the English accent had a small office off the lobby of the brownstone. He explained to Lane that these were the offices of Kellen Enterprises, and that Kellen owned many other companies around the world and was always on the lookout for hostesses for corporate events—well-paid, reputable work. However, Mr. Kellen enjoyed selecting the girls for this enviable and elite division of the company himself.

Mr. Kellen was waiting in his private dining room if Lane cared to join him.

"I've heard of Kellen, of course," Lane said to Jessica, back at Jessica's office after the lunch. "At least, I've seen his picture in the paper."

"It was Davis Kellen, you're certain?"

"Yeah. He didn't say much at lunch. He checked my

body out and talked about fiber optics and Malaysia. Smooth, huh?" She laughed. "There was talk about corporate hostesses, but it was a lot of bullshit. He was looking for a piece."

Jessica called Caddie Dean in Paris and asked if Garret had ever mentioned Kellen around her.

"Tommee and I had dinner with him once in Hawaii, and when I was married to Jon we had cocktails with him one time in New York. Then Jon and Garret met with him again to talk about financing Jon's movie. Jon complained about Garret's having used him to get to Kellen."

"Very interesting," Jessica said.

"It's sort of strange that you ask me about Kellen," Caddie then said, "because a woman called me this afternoon to ask about Garret, and she mentioned Kellen. She's Nicole Rochas's aunt. Her name is Giselle. She owns Château Rochas, and evidently Garret knows her and has been buying stock in her company. She said Garret is marrying her niece just to get control of that business, and that Davis Kellen was the money behind it all."

"What did this Giselle Rochas want from you?"

"She was fishing for information on Garret."

Jessica said, "Kellen seems to be Garret Stowe's private financier. And in return, Garret has this pimp Conley send girls his way. What a lovely arrangement."

Jessica sat back in her chair, looked out the window, and thought for a few seconds.

"Have you met this guy Conley?" she asked Caddie.

"Yeah, a real sleazebag. He used to hang around the Vitesse office, and he'd call Garret here in Paris now and then."

"Not exactly somebody Garret would want front and center in his life. . . . Unless he had no choice?"

"What do you mean?" Caddie asked.

"Conley's got a prison record. Birds of a feather," Jessica said. "Did Garret seem scared of him at all?"

Caddie thought a moment.

"Edgy," she said. "He definitely seemed edgy around him."

While the Ginny Fischer story swirled through the tabloids, Garret remained in France, paying as much attention as possible to Nicole Rochas, while still directing the negotiations for an attempted buyout of the Cathews Agency in London and the Pop Agency in Milan. Garret was bidding in a stratosphere where the deal began to make no economic sense.

And Jessica's lawyer confirmed that fact, as well as the fact that the documents floating around that allegedly exposed financial mismanagement on the part of the Cartwright Agency had, indeed, been provided to Cathews and Pop by Phil Stein. When told this news, Jessica correctly assumed that Stein was doing this on behalf of Garret in an attempt to repair his relationship with him after losing the Paris Models deal.

In the midst of all this, Nicole told Garret that she needed to make a trip to New York on behalf of her magazine.

"I'd love it if you came along," she said to Garret, "since we haven't done New York together."

"I can't leave right now," he told her.

She had secretly counted on that being his answer, because though she did have business to attend to in New York, the true purpose of her trip would have to be achieved out of Garret's sight.

Nicole had a notion about what kind of wedding present she wanted to give Garret. Materially, there was nothing the two of them couldn't buy for themselves, so she conceived of a very special personal gift.

Nicole had consulted a psychologist in Paris about the fact that Garret seemed wounded when speaking of his birth father, Luther Nevitt. Nicole wondered if there might be a way to clear a path between the two men, so that Garret wouldn't go through life haunted by the pain of a parent who didn't want him. Besides, she was planning to have children with Garret, and prior to doing so she wanted to shake loose any demons from the family trees.

Following her session with the psychologist, Nicole hired a private detective in Miami and, using information from the faxes, located Luther Nevitt.

She flew from New York to Miami and approached Nevitt one afternoon when he was walking away from the docks.

"I'm Nicole Rochas," she said, "and I want to talk to you about your son."

"Wrong guy, lady," Nevitt said. "Ain't got a son."

"I'm going to marry him," Nicole told Nevitt.

"You're looking for somebody else."

"I'm looking for Luther Nevitt," Nicole said.

The eyes in Nevitt's weather-beaten face narrowed, and he took a careful look at Nicole. He smelled of fish, salt water, and cigarettes.

She was casually dressed, but he had seen enough rich folk on charter boats to know there was money in this girl's life.

"I'm Luther Nevitt right enough," he said to her, still walking, "but if I've got a son it's news to me."

"I'm not going to cause you any trouble. In fact, I only want to help. I know very well who your son is, and I'm engaged to him. Garret Stowe."

Nevitt kept walking, but at the mention of Garret's name, his chin jutted forward and his lips pursed.

"Garret Stowe," he said finally.

"I mean no trouble at all, honestly, and neither does Garret. I know there've been problems between you, but I'm starting a life with him and I'd like to get rid of any cobwebs between us. I'm very much hoping that the two of you might make peace."

Nevitt chewed on what she'd said and kept moving along the docks.

"You drink, lady?"

"Now and then."

"I like a beer at the end of the day," Luther Nevitt declared.

"Then maybe you'll let me buy you one," Nicole said.

"I was thinking of buying *you* one," he replied.

"Even better," Nicole said, brightening.

They went to El Cubano Pesce, where Nevitt ordered a pitcher of draft.

"I'm listening," he said, pouring out two glasses.

"I grew up without my parents," Nicole began, "so I know how family things can just go awry. In my new life I want a clean slate. And a family that's intact. I know it's a tremendous intrusion to barge in on you, but I've come all the way from Paris to talk to you."

"That where Garret lives? Paris?"

"Some of the time, yes."

Nevitt nodded.

"Never been there myself."

"Perhaps one day you'll come."

"You never know," he said.

Nevitt finished his beer and poured out another one.

"Tell me about him," he said. "I hear he's done pretty well for himself."

"Your son is a tremendous success. But frankly, he's still haunted by his early life."

"What's he say about it?"

"That when he was younger he made an effort to find you. However, you didn't want to be found. At least, not until Garret became well known. He says you only found him once he had money." She said it as gently as she could.

Nevitt's expression changed little. Years of working outdoors had burned his skin to a creased, dark brown sheen. When he talked, the skin of his cheeks seemed to implode and his teeth barely opened, causing the words to come out in short, guttural bursts.

"We both seen bad days in our time," Nevitt said to her. "That's all."

"I understand."

"So what is it you want?"

She thought for a moment. "I want you to come to our wedding in Paris. I will arrange the transportation and accommodations. If it's a problem for you to be away from work, I'll see to it that you're compensated. Garret doesn't have to know about any of the arrangements. In fact, I'd like it to be my surprise wedding gift to him. Of course, I can only do it if there's some common ground between the two of you, a basis for reconciliation."

"What's that mean?"

"If there's bad blood between you, then obviously I don't want to do something that's going to upset my husband."

"Wouldn't want that," Nevitt agreed.

A flicker of something she couldn't quite read came and vanished from his eyes.

"I've talked to a counselor about it. Someone who specializes in these kinds of situations and relationships. And she thought you two could build up a trust. Or at least make a new start. She suggested you break the ice by writing a letter. Just tell Garret how you feel, father to son. If you're sorry about the way things went in your lives, then tell him. I'm sure you had your reasons, and I think Garret needs to hear those reasons. I'm not saying that the two of you will be best friends. But if just for that day there could be a happy reunion, I think it would be the best gift I could give my husband."

Nevitt frowned. "I'm not much for writing letters."

"Maybe I could help you. If it's something you feel in your heart you want to do. If it's not, let's just drop it here and now."

"He know you're here?"

"No, no. Of course not. I promise you, this is all my idea."

"Maybe you could help me," he said. "But I don't think Garret Stowe would like it too much if he knew you were here."

"He's not going to know. Not unless we can work this out, and then at the appropriate time."

"Need some time to think about it," Nevitt said, pouring out the last of the beer.

"I'm going back to New York for a few days, then to Paris. I'll give you numbers where I can be reached privately. Collect, of course. Would you willing to talk to my counselor about the letter? Just on the telephone, you don't have to go anywhere—"

"Yeah, I'll think about it."

The waitress came over and asked if they wanted another pitcher.

"Nope," Nevitt said, paying the tab and putting down a tip.

From the look on the waitress's face when she picked up the tip, this was much more than he usually left.

She slipped it into her apron and winked at Nicole.

Nona Fischer returned to her apartment late one night after spending the entire day, as was now her routine, at the hospital. Ginny was gradually recovering, and Nona was doing what she could to begin repairing her relationship with her daughter.

Frightened by what had happened, and completely drug- and alcohol-free for the first time in months, Ginny clung to her mother. They didn't have a lot to say to each other—the past year had built barriers they weren't yet sure how to scale—but they spent the long hours of the days in the hospital in each other's company, remembering different times.

To see her daughter, hour upon hour, in a hospital bed, with IV tubes running into her arms like synthetic spiders, left Nona sobered and exhausted. Each night she staggered home and hoped for a peaceful sleep.

Tired and distracted, she slipped into her apartment and went straight for the bedroom.

The hands that grabbed her seemed to materialize from nowhere. The scream never reached her lips as a large, callused hand locked over her mouth.

"Why don't you let me talk first," the man holding her said, "and then you'll have plenty of time to get your two cents' worth in."

He pulled her into the living room, pushed her down on a couch, and let her have a look at him.

It was Conley.

Then he slowly removed his hand.

"So," he said, "what's new?"

"I don't like the idea of you becoming a cop," Detective Pesci said to Jessica as they worked their way on foot through the crowds in Columbus Circle, "because then you'll have to start smoking and drinking and eating a lot of lousy meals. You'll have to get divorced and forget all your friends' birthdays. Of course, you're not married, so you're ahead of the game right there."

"I'm not becoming a cop," Jessica said, stopping at the hot dog stand that was their goal. "I just want to know more about this guy, and I think I'm going to have to make a trip to Florida to do it."

"Maybe, but here's what I'll do first. There's a guy used to work vice here, then his wife got a good job down in Miami and he got his ass into the sunshine with the Dade County P.D. I'll see if he can pull records. What I'm guessing is that this guy Stowe has more than one name, because he's squeaky-clean under this one. We'll sniff around Conley's prison records. That's where most of these guys make their friends. Lots of big promises about what they're going to do on the outside. Obviously, Conley's got something on Stowe."

Two days later, Pesci turned up at Jessica's office with a sheaf of photocopies. He slid a couple of faxed photos in front of her. "Either of these boys look much like Stowe?"

The mug shots were grainy, but one of them resembled a younger Garret Stowe, though with a beard and long hair, and the man was thirty or forty pounds heavier than Garret Stowe was now. But Jessica saw a resemblance. Something in the eyes. She pointed to it. "That could be him."

"That's Earl Lee Baley," Pesci said, reading from the sheet. "One count of larceny with intent to commit fraud, one count grand theft auto. He wrote a few bad checks and stole a car. Nothing too impressive there. What gets interesting is that he couldn't make twenty-five thousand dollars bail, so he sat in county for a while, shared a cell with your friend Conley. Then he finally made bail, and jumped it. Never turned up again. Kind of interesting that it was cash bail, not from a bondsman. Meaning somebody put up the dough for Mr. Baley, then ate it."

"They never found him again?"

"Not according to his record. What we have to do now is get Garret Stowe's fingerprints and see if they match Mr. Baley's. All in all, though, if it's the same guy, he's not much of a criminal. Piddling kind of stuff, really. He would have done no more than a year if convicted, but he chose to run. Maybe spending time in the cell with Conley put him over the edge." Pesci laughed at his own mild wit, a deep, easy laugh that made Jessica look up at him and smile.

"It's hard to believe that the man who owns Vitesse and is partners with Davis Kellen is a car thief," Jessica said.

"Anything's possible, but from his sheet he looks small-time to be involved in the kind of business you're talking," Pesci agreed. " 'Course, the fact that Baley jumped bail tells you something right there. Usually means there's more to the story and a guy doesn't want to wait around for the cops to dig it up."

"Did anything else come in on Conley?" Jessica asked.

"Oh, a whole pile on Conley. He's a real aristocrat. Been in and out of jail fifteen times. He's out legit at the moment, though. 'Course, he's not supposed to be out of Florida. He could get nailed on parole violation."

"If Garret Stowe really is this Earl Baley, why would he be so afraid of Conley? They only shared a cell for three weeks."

"But take a look at these," the detective said. "My buddy went to Miami-Dade and pulled another file. It gets more interesting." He dumped more documents on Jessica's desk. "Conley was in prison three weeks with Earl Baley, then Conley makes bail and is off to do whatever."

"Right."

"Two days after Conley gets out is when Earl Baley's twenty-five-thousand-dollar bail turns up. Bang, Baley is out and riding the wind. Now, look at this," he continued, sliding a document out of the pile. "A month later, your friend Conley deposits thirty-five thousand dollars in a Florida bank. This is a guy with no job and no friends. Where does he suddenly get thirty-five thousand bucks?"

Jessica sat back, confused. "You're saying he got it from Earl Baley?"

"No proof, but not a bad guess," Pesci said. "Here's

what it looks like to me. Earl Baley tells Conley that he's got to get out of jail right away. So when Conley gets bailed out, he in turn posts bail for Earl Baley. Now, Earl Baley didn't stick around for trial, but he did pay off Conley's twenty-five thousand, plus ten thousand profit to Conley for raising the bail. Or, more likely, for stealing it. They couldn't have been great buddies—they didn't know each other long enough. But Conley found a way to make a quick ten grand, and Baley got himself out and gone."

"If Baley paid this Conley guy back the bail money plus ten thousand, then why would Conley still be on his neck?"

"Earl Baley made the mistake of becoming successful. Publicly so. Conley sees his picture, recognizes him, and starts blackmailing him. If Baley wanted out of jail real bad, then he had a reason. Even though he was just arrested for a stupid fraud charge and car theft, he might have been scared something else was going to pop up. He wouldn't have jumped bail except for something a hell of a lot worse than facing up to a few bad checks. Remember, back when this went on, computers weren't what they are now. Everybody thinks there's one big database with all the bad guys in it. Doesn't work that way, unless somebody went to the FBI, and they wouldn't have done that for a two-bit criminal like this Earl Baley guy. But he wasn't taking any chances. He wanted out of there before anybody got too curious about him."

Jessica nodded. She was disturbed by the findings but certainly impressed with Pesci's work.

"I'll send Earl Baley's prints to the FBI and see what bubbles up. In the meantime, you get me Garret Stowe's prints," Pesci said.

"Okay," Jessica said. She looked at her watch. "Now can I at least buy you dinner? I know you'd probably rather have one of these models you see on the wall, but I can't do that."

"Actually, dinner with you sounds great," Detective Pesci said.

"I just don't think we can or should compete with the kind of offers Garret Stowe is making," the lawyer Harbert Raines said to Jessica, speaking to her from London. "The numbers don't make sense. At these levels, he's just trying to buy Cathews and Pop so that you can't, because the economics aren't there. He's trying to get even with us for pulling Paris Models out from under him, and he's willing to pay an astronomical price in order to do so."

"But I need Cathews and Pop," Jessica said, looking out the kitchen window of her apartment, watching the Manhattan morning traffic creep along far below. "I've promised my investors the largest presence in Europe and can't do that if I have to go with start-ups. I want the top agencies."

"You won't make your money back for ten years if you overbid Stowe. And I don't care how deep the pockets are that Tommee Barkley has rounded up, Davis Kellen's pockets are deeper. Period."

Dejected, she hung up the phone. Buying Paris Models had turned the industry take on the Cartwright Agency from sinking ship to innovative gambler. The industry was waiting to see if Jessica could pull off her bold plan. If she didn't do it well and quickly, then it would look like a last desperate attempt to unseat Vitesse from its throne of power.

These thoughts clouded her head as she exited her apartment into the hallway. When the elevator arrived, she quickly stepped inside. Its door closed before she realized there was another person in with her.

It was Conley.

Jessica reached for the control panel, but Conley's hand stopped her.

"You'll be late for work this morning," he said, stopping the elevator.

Her heart pounded. "What do you want?"

"What everybody wants in this world. Money."

"For what?"

"I'll get to that. First, I understand you been checking up on me."

"I don't know what you're talking about."

"Lady, don't bullshit me. Nona Fischer came to your office and you wanted to know all about Stowe, and all about me. Then you send some half-assed model to see me, check out what's going down in my studio."

"If you've done anything to Nona Fischer—"

"Oh, she's fine, just a little shook up."

"Then tell me what you want."

"You want something on Garret Stowe. Maybe I can help you. I might know a little more about him that anybody else in this city. But it's gonna cost you."

"I already know that his name is Earl Baley, and that he was in jail with you down in Florida. So release the elevator and we'll forget about this conversation."

"I'll decide when this conversation is over."

He stared at her until finally she said, "All right."

"Good. Now, how about we help each other? You see, I don't give a shit about Garret Stowe any more than you do. But he pays my bills and keeps the lights turned on. If you can improve upon that situation, I'm listening. You want shit on this guy, I'll give it to you. But it's gonna cost, say, couple hundred thousand."

"What can you tell me that's worth that much?"

He released the elevator, and it started for the lobby.

"I'm all talked out," he said. "If you want me to keep talking, it's gonna require cash. Lots of it. In advance. You think about it."

*   *   *

"I doubt he knows a damn thing that we don't already know," Frank Pesci said, having rushed to Jessica's office following her call about the encounter with Conley. "If he had something good, he would have been smarter in how he tried to sell it to you."

"He threatened Nona Fischer," Jessica said, "and Nona told him she'd been to see me."

"I'll check in on her," Pesci said.

"Conley might be watching her," Jessica replied, "and if he thinks she went to the police, he might go after her."

"Well . . ."

"I think she has to get out of that apartment, and get her daughter out of the city, before you see Conley."

"Okay. But I can only push Conley so far. He won't be scared of a little parole violation, so I won't get too far with that. He doesn't have any outstanding warrants. And a lifer like him usually knows the law, knows what I can and can't do."

Jessica thought a moment, then said, "I've got an idea that might pry a little more information out of him."

Pesci smiled. "Now just how do you plan to scare this guy?"

chapter
29

Detective Pesci strolled into Conley's studio, flashed the badge, and locked eyes with him.

"I ain't done a fucking thing," Conley said, staring right back, "and you know it. I got an honest job. I'm clean as a nun's pussy."

"What makes me think if I call Florida I'm going to find a parole violation? Who knows what I'll scare up down there?"

"You'll scare up jack shit."

"Yeah, I guess you're right. You're probably clean by now. So I guess I'll just have to take you in for statutory rape. Four counts." Detective Pesci dropped a sealed manila envelope on the desktop.

He let Conley have a long look at it.

Then the detective continued, "You just haven't been asking to see proper ID from some of these girls, Conley. Because if you had, I know you wouldn't have had sex with them, as I'm sure you're aware that in the state of New York it is illegal to have sex with a minor."

Conley stared at Pesci, trying to give him a good poker face, but Pesci had seen enough cons to notice and interpret Conley's twitching cheek muscle.

"These girls," Pesci said, tapping the envelope, "were scared to come forward. Thought their chances of becoming models might be hurt if they turned you in. But we've been watching you for a couple of months. We took our time. Talked to a lot of girls. And now we've got four real good witnesses. You're in a lot of trouble, chump."

"I ain't done nothing," he said.

"You're not saying that with the same conviction you were a minute ago," Pesci replied. "Whoops. I shouldn't use the word 'conviction'—I know it probably upsets you."

"What do you want, asshole?"

The detective took one of Conley's cigarettes, and took plenty of time lighting it. He coughed.

"Jesus, now I know why I quit these things." He stubbed out the cigarette on the desktop. "Why are you bothering nice people like Jessica Cartwright?"

"I done nothing to her. I just told her to stop spying on our business. She's breaking the law."

"And you had a lot of time to study the law when you were in prison. Well, then you'll be delighted, because by the time you get out of the bucket for these rapes, you'll know enough about the law to be a Supreme Court Justice."

Conley walked over to the window and looked across the street, toward the coffee shop where he'd seen Jessica Cartwright take an envelope from the model who had been in his studio. He'd thought he'd been smart to watch Lane Barkley leave, because she'd been too cool, almost like a cop. And when he saw Lane turn over the envelope of contact sheets to Jessica Cartwright, he knew he was being set up for something, but he'd assumed it had to do with Garret's and her fight over the European agencies. Now that he looked at the café where Jessica had been, he realized that a cop on surveillance could have been quite happy there for two months, what with all the pastries and free coffee. Maybe they did have four models ready to testify against him.

"You don't want me," Conley said.

"I don't?"

"You're more interested in Stowe."

"Why should I be interested in him?"

"You tell me," Conley said.

"I really don't have to tell you a fucking thing. Do I? I'll just Miranda you to save myself the trouble of having to look at you much longer."

"Stowe's the one who fucks kids, not me."

"Excuse me?"

"Just tell me what you fucking want," Conley said. Small drops of sweat trickled down the sides of his pockmarked face as he stared out the window and thought about returning to a jail cell. And rape meant hard time.

"I want you to tell me something I don't know about Stowe," Pesci said, "because I already know he fucks kids, and I know he did time for piece-of-shit crimes down in Florida, and I know you boys were bunk buddies. And I know you bailed his ass out, and then he paid you off, and he jumped bail. But here you are up in New York, messing with his new respectable life."

"That's all I know about him, what you said."

"Yeah?"

"Yeah. There ain't nothin' else to know. You got it all. You're way ahead of me."

"There must be something, all that time in the cell. And Stowe being so anxious to get out. I mean, what was he worried about? All he had was bad checks and a bullshit car theft. Six months and gone. But he jumps bail like he's nervous somebody is going to find out who he really is and what he really did. He got out of here before they had the chance. Right?"

"He wanted out. I helped. No law against that."

"Right. But why did he want out?"

"Never told me," Conley claimed.

"Not a thing? Not even a little pillow talk during some romantic evening in your jail cell?"

"Fuck you, asshole."

"Is that what you liked, for you to talk dirty to him? Is that how you got off?"

"Look, man, he just shows up in jail down there slick and scared. He figured how I could get him out, and I did it. Then I happen to find him up here in New York with his fancy-ass business and his fancy-ass pussy, and I find a way to take a slice. Straight-ahead, legit work."

"Banging fifteen-year-olds isn't legit work, Conley."

"I'm telling you, I don't have anything else on the guy. I'll get something, though. I'll make a deal with you. I'll get something else out of that fucker, but you've got to let me skip, because I ain't going back in. No fucking way."

"I don't have time for that. Tell me what you know right now," Pesci said impatiently.

"I fucking *told* you. You know it all. He comes into that cell like a man with his dick about to catch fire. And now I see him eight years later with this bullshit French accent and two-thousand-dollar suits. Back then he was a pure shit-scared workin' man. His hands were fucked up and he said he worked the boats down in the Gulf. That's as much as he ever said. Nothing else."

"Well, you better do some thinking, Conley, because you're not being too helpful." Pesci dropped his business card on the table. "Give your mind a real workou and see what you can come up with." With that, Pesc picked up the manila envelope and waved it in Con ley's face. "I'll hold on to this until I hear from you say, within twenty-four hours."

Pesci left. On the way down the stairs, he smiled

thinking that Jessica's idea to bluff with a threat about underage girls had really rocked Conley. He knew Conley was upstairs wiping sweat off his face. Still, Pesci didn't think there was much more information to glean from Conley. The tip about Stowe's working the boats in the Gulf was probably the end of the line.

When he got around the corner from the studio, Pesci dumped the manila envelope in the trash, since all that it contained was junk mail.

While Pesci went to see Conley, Jessica called Nona Fischer, who answered in a tentative, shaken voice. She told Jessica that Ginny was being released from the hospital that afternoon.

"I'm going to have a car pick you up. Have a suitcase packed for the two of you. You need to get out of the city, and I know where you can stay."

"Conley told me to stay put. If he knew I was talking to you—"

"Don't worry about him. Just do what I tell you."

Next, Jessica called Caddie Dean, who had returned from Paris and rented a country house near New Canaan, Connecticut.

"I need to get Ginny Fischer and her mother out of the city for a while," Jessica said to Caddie. "I'd feel better if I knew they were with you. And I think maybe you can help Ginny." Caddie immediately agreed.

Frank Pesci returned to his office and pulled out his file on Earl Lee Baley, a.k.a. Garret Stowe. The police record started and finished in Florida, but based on what Conley had said, Pesci initiated a criminal-data-bank search of the states bordering the Gulf. "Run the uvies, too," Pesci told the assisting officer, "just for good measure."

After a two-day scan of the Gulf states, the record came up clean. But on the third day a fax came in from the state police office in Texas.

There was a file on an Earl Lee Baley going back twenty-three years. The prints matched those from the Florida Earl Baley file. Bingo.

"For a kid," Pesci told Jessica, "your friend Earl Baley had one hell of a record. Listen to this. Kid was born a John Doe, bounced around the foster system, then got lucky and was adopted at age seven. Lived with these people until he was twelve, then—and here is where his charm started coming out—he beat the hell out of both adoptive parents. Nearly killed them. After that, he did a few years in the Texas juvenile system, then was back in and out of foster care. Evidently he's got a juvenile file down there thicker than the phone book."

"Where does it end up?"

"He dropped out of their books at eighteen. No Texas records after that. The trail ends until he showed up in Florida when he was twenty-six. I'd like to do some firsthand checking down in Texas, but there're bad guys right in New York that I'm supposed to be chasing down."

"I'll go to Texas," Jessica said. "You just tell me what to do."

One evening, while he sat in the upstairs study of his country home and reviewed his final offer for the Pop Agency of Milan, Garret Stowe flicked a curious eye toward the fax machine. The machine had been humming all evening with spreadsheets sent by the peniten Phil Stein. But the fax that was scrolling out now appeared to be a handwritten letter. Garret glanced at the signature at the bottom of the page.

It was from Luther Nevitt.

He pulled the letter out of the paper tray and read it disbelief.

Nicole entered the room, bringing Garret a glass of wine, and saw the ashen color of his skin.

She had known very well that the fax was going to be sent, having exchanged several calls with Nevitt in the past few days. Nevitt had sent her a preliminary copy of the letter and made changes based on Nicole's suggestions.

"Are you all right?" she asked, handing Garret the glass of wine.

He nodded, not looking up. He took the glass of wine, and waited for her to leave, then continued reading.

Dear Garret,

The past is something we cannot change, though God knows there are many things about it that I would like to change. The future is what we've got, so I think it's time we forget the things in the past. I'm willing to do that if you are. We both have our own lives now, and I'm happy that yours has become a success. Evidently, you've worked real hard, and that's a good thing. I have no complaints. I have my health and I get by just fine. I'm sorry if I've made you uncomfortable, and, who knows, in the future maybe we'll even be friends. Life is too short for people not to get along, and it's taken me a long time to learn that. Hopefully, you won't make the same mistakes I did.

I saw in the papers that you're getting married, and I hope this is a happy thing for you. Kind regards.

Luther Nevitt

Garret closed his door, grabbed the phone, and called Conley in New York.

"Nevitt sent me a fax at my goddamn *home*," Garret screamed. "Now where the fuck did he get this fax number if he didn't get it from you?"

Conley hadn't mentioned anything to Garret about the visit from Detective Pesci, and was in no mood to take any guff from Garret.

"I didn't give the damn fax number to anybody. He must've got it from somebody in your office."

"Find out."

"Yeah, yeah, when I get time."

"I mean now. Has Nevitt been back to New York?"

"Hell no. We're paying a PI down in Miami to let us know if he doesn't show up at the dock, remember? And he ain't been anywhere but on that boat in months."

"Get your ass down to Florida and stay on Nevitt full-time until I tell you differently. I want to know everything the fucking bum is doing."

"I'm telling you," Conley said, "Nevitt is a goddamn old drunk who works all day, drinks at night, and sleeps it off the rest of the time."

"Do what I say."

"I want more money then," Conley said.

"You're getting more money than you ever dreamed about, you piece of shit."

"So are you, ace. Remember?"

Jessica told her attorney to conjure whatever magic was necessary to delay Cathews or Pop from making a deal with Garret while she went to Texas to follow up on Earl Baley.

Her first stop was Galveston's Hall of Records, where she obtained the portions of Earl Baley's adoption records that weren't legally sealed. At the age of seven, he'd been adopted by Rita and Jason Baley, who had long since moved from Galveston. It required nearly an entire day of telephone calls, but she traced the Baleys to Amarillo, and Jessica was on their doorstep the next morning.

Mrs. Baley stared at Jessica through the locked screened door. Her hair was brown with streaks of gray through it, her face lined and gaunt, as though she' spent most of her life in pain. Her arms were locked across her chest.

"That was twenty-three years ago that Earl left us," Mrs. Baley said to Jessica. "Once we turned him over to the authorities, we didn't see him anymore. We were scared to. I got nothing else to say about it." She refused to look at a photograph of Garret Stowe.

"It's very important that I find out—"

"Ma'am," Mrs. Baley said, "you need to leave. I don't know anything about Earl. You talk to Gus Laden if you want. That's the man come to get him."

Gus Laden turned out to be Earl Baley's first counselor at the youth detention center. Laden was now a salesman at a Ford dealership in Houston.

Jessica showed him a photograph of Garret Stowe.

"If you tell me that's Earl, I might believe you," Laden said. He was a rail-thin man who somehow spoke with a toothpick sticking out one side of his mouth and a cigarette out the other. "What you're saying, basically, is that one of our boys actually made a success out of himself. He changed his name and owns a big company?"

"I'm not sure if it's the same man. That's what I'm trying to find out. He attacked the daughter of a friend of mine," Jessica said.

"Why you talking to me? I ain't the police. I sell cars now."

"Can you tell me anything else about him?"

"If Earl Baley did some things that were wrong, I'd be the last person surprised. We had to move him to a couple of different facilities, because you put him in a situation and within a couple of months he's running the place. Had all kinds of schemes to get whatever he wanted, you know? Thing is, he always had a bad temper. Smart kid in his own way—not that he ever spent time in school. Just gut-smart. I used to tell him if he ever learned to control his temper he could make something out of himself. Maybe he did. Earl was always talking about that, too. How he had rich friends who were going to help him when he got out of juvenile. He said he had friends with yachts and beautiful girls and jet planes. He talked a lot about that stuff. But that's not unusual. Lot of kids do. Difference with Earl, I think he really believed it."

"After he got out of juvenile, you never saw him again?"

"He had all kinds of probation and parole, but he learned how to play that real smart. Earl figured out after a while he didn't want to do one more day in the bucket than he had to. So he learned to play the game. The boy did his time and got out. Who knows after that?"

"He was arrested in Florida," Jessica said.

"For what?"

"Some kind of stolen car thing. Then he jumped bail. And that was the last anybody saw of him."

"He wouldn't have done much time for that, first offense. He took a pretty good risk in running," Laden said, thinking something over. "There was nothing on his juvenile record that would get him hauled back to Texas. And you say he has no arrest record in Texas as an adult?"

"None."

"Who knows, then? Probably was running from something. But you won't get him now. If he's as rich as you say he is, he'll have the kind of lawyers that make cops want to quit their jobs and sell cars."

Conley faced the agent at the American Airlines ticket office on Park Avenue and started to ask for a round-trip fare to Miami. But he stopped. "I got a different idea," he said to the man behind the counter. "How about a ticket to New Orleans?"

"We can get you there," the agent said, tapping data into his computer.

"Yeah," Conley said to himself, "that's a better idea." After all, he told himself, what did he need any more of this shit for? He had this cop up his ass, and he was probably going to bust Stowe for something. Why should he go down and chase that fucking Nevitt around Miami? Bullshit. He had twenty grand in cash. He had everything he needed to get out of this gig. Why wait around and end up in jail with Stowe, like a dumb shit? The cop was giving him a chance to run. So he'd run.

He paid for the ticket, then went to his bank and closed out his account. It took him fifteen minutes to pack what he wanted out of his apartment, then he hopped a cab to JFK.

"What airline?" the cabby asked as they approached the airport.

"The one gets you to New Orleans," Conley said.

"Going home, are you?"

Conley shrugged and sat back. "Yeah," he said.

c h a p t e r
30

Jessica spent a few more days in Texas trying to turn up something else on Earl Baley, but came up dry. As she packed to leave, she got a call at her hotel from Gus Laden, Earl Baley's former juvenile probation officer.

"You seemed so concerned about Earl that I did a little asking around. Last night I had drinks with a buddy from the department. He's a private counselor now. So I asked him about Earl, and he didn't really know what happened to him either, but he did know one thing. He ran into Earl thirteen or fourteen years ago in Matlan. Walked into a liquor store to buy a six-pack on the way to a hunting trip, and Earl was stocking the shelves."

"Where's Matlan?" Jessica asked.

"Not that far from Galveston. Kind of godforsaken. Near the Gulf. Town full of shrimpers."

"How do I find Matlan?"

"Miss Cartwright, to find Matlan you've got to want to get there real bad."

"I want to get there."

* * *

The owner of Starlite Liquors in Matlan was Pedro Bedilliano, a native of Mexico City who had lived in the United States for twenty-five years and was now a citizen. His dark face was heavily creased from too many days spent fishing in the searing Gulf sun.

"I remember Fancy Earl," Bedilliano said at the mention of Baley's name. "I called him Fancy because he was too good for the work, know what I mean? Boy worked hard, but he was always talking about what he was going to do when he was rich."

"Do you know what happened to him?"

"No, I don't," Bedilliano said, "but Johnny Banks, he might know something. He'd like to know something, anyway. He spent enough time looking for the boy."

"Why was he looking for him?"

"Banks had it in for Earl. He had his reasons."

"Where should I look for Mr. Banks?"

"Police station. He's the police chief."

When Jessica entered the police station and asked the deputy on duty about seeing Chief Banks, she was told that she'd have to come back when she had an appointment. But Jessica talked the deputy into giving the chief a note, then had to wait only five minutes for Banks to stride into the front lobby.

Johnny Banks was sixty-four years old, six feet six inches tall, with a head that belonged on a smaller man. He smoked a meerschaum pipe that appeared to be affixed to his mouth. His brow was raised in a look of surprise, and he had a habit of making all his sentences sound like questions. He peered down the end of his pipe at Jessica, politely introduced himself, thought for a few moments, then said, "I'd be awfully surprised if we're talking about the same Earl Baley."

She handed the chief Earl Baley's mug shot from the Florida police file.

Banks stared at the copy of the photograph for what seemed like forever to Jessica.

A look of sadness came over his face.

"When you're police chief of a small community like this," he said to Jessica, apparently pleased to have an outsider to talk to, as if he'd been waiting for the opportunity to share his philosophy, "people don't look upon you so much as a law enforcement officer as they do somebody who hands out speeding tickets and keeps the boys from having too much fun."

Jessica wasn't certain if she was meant to respond. So she waited.

Banks continued, "I did my time studying law enforcement, but generally what's served me best in this job has been this." He pointed to his stomach. "Can't make an arrest or go to court on a gut reaction, but it's always there and it's usually right. What I'm winding up about, ma'am, is that I've been looking for that boy for a long time. Yes, ma'am, Earl Baley."

"May I ask why?"

"I believe he killed a girl."

The chief noted Jessica's startled reaction.

"More than you wanted to hear?" he asked her.

"No. No, actually. I'm just a little stunned."

"I understand. Killing is a real thing."

"Was he charged?"

"No. I never arrested him. But I sure wanted to talk to him. Talked to him plenty when he lived here. Never saw him after he left."

"I think Earl Baley may have changed his name to Garret Stowe," Jessica said. "But I'm not certain."

"Where is he?"

"Paris."

The chief nodded, as if he expected as much.

"He owns a model agency," Jessica said. "A very successful one. You may have heard of a girl he represents—Ginny Fischer? She was the model for Aaron Adam jeans."

"I saw some ads. Trashy."

"Recently, Ginny nearly died of an overdose."

"Baley have something to do with that?"

"He was intimate with both Ginny and her mother."

"How old is the girl?"

"Fourteen," Jessica said.

Banks nodded and pursed his lips. "That sounds like something Earl would be interested in. Fourteen-year-old. Thing about Earl," Banks continued, "is most people around here liked him. Even the ones didn't like him liked him, if you know what I mean."

"I think so."

"He worked at Starlite Liquors, then down the auto parts store for a while, Fran's Coffee Shop, even did some boat work and ranch-hand stuff."

"Sounds like you knew him pretty well."

"Feel like taking a walk out back?"

Curious, but also filled with a sense of dark foreboding, Jessica followed the chief out of the station, through the parking lot, to an impound lot at the far end of the property. There were several stripped-down cars in the lot and a couple of newer ones. Under a sun shed in the far corner was a vehicle covered with a tarp. The sheriff pulled the tarp back to reveal the rusted out, patched-up shell of a Pontiac Trans Am.

"Been sitting here a long time," Banks said. "It was Earl's car. I'd been looking for it for about six months when the Mexican federales turned it up down near Oaxaca. Of course, Earl wasn't driving it by then. Couple of kids had gotten hold of it. They were drinking and speeding around. One of the cops who pulled them over took a look in the car and saw bloodstains. Old ones, but stains. Smart cop, the Mexican guy. One thing leads to another and I get a call. Sure enough, the blood matched the blood of the girl who was missing from my town. People thought maybe she'd just plain run off with Earl. But she was awful young. Not even fourteen at the time. Well, somebody found her out in the desert, or what was left of her, about a year after she was reported missing. Can't say for sure if she went down there with Earl. Might have gone on her own. Don't have the hard proof. Just the gut. And the blood. But Earl was long gone before I ever got a chance to talk to him about it. Always wanted to, though. Me and some others."

Chief Banks walked Jessica back through the parking lot, but stopped at his patrol car. "Hop in. I'm going to show you something else."

He drove her to a small cemetery on a hill near the outer edge of town.

"Folks in town thought I was a crazy cop," Banks said, getting out of the car and walking through the old gravestones, "the way I kept my eye on Earl. They all liked him. He had a way of getting people to do things. After working at the liquor store, he got himself a job on the boats. That's where he met the girl. Nobody ever saw them together in any bad way. But I had a feeling about it, the way you do sometimes. When she went missing same time as Earl, I pretty much knew it had gone bad and wished I'd done something about it beforehand. I'd seen her grow up. I don't have my own family, so I took some pleasure in watching her get along in life. Her father grew up around here, and nobody liked him much. Kind of a sour guy. Worked the boats, kept to himself. But I liked him well enough. Knew him most of my life. The girl's mother took off, so he did the best he could to raise his daughter. Kids don't do real well without a mother, in my experience.

"Anyway, when she disappeared, her old man realized Magdalena was pretty much all he had in the world and all he would ever have. When she turned up dead, he drifted around Mexico for a year or two looking for Earl. Lots of stories went around that Earl got the girl pregnant, then took her to Mexico to do something about it. They found Earl's car, but nobody ever did find Earl. So if they picked Earl up in Florida and he jumped bail, the reason was he figured sooner or later they'd find out we were looking for him. The old man came back here but couldn't stand being around town any more. Memories and such. So he took off, and I haven't seen him in seven, eight years."

Chief Banks stopped at a grave. He pointed to it.

"That girl buried down there would be a twenty-seven-year-old woman today if it wasn't for Earl Baley. This kind of town you don't see too many kids disappear or die, or that sort of thing. So when one does, and it's your job to make the town safe, it just stays with you. And when you know that the guy who did it is going to do something like this again sooner or later, and you can't do anything to stop him, it just bothers you every night. It's such a shame about little Magdalena. Thirteen years old and she really had a look. Would have grown up to be a beauty."

Jessica looked at the grave.

The inscription on the headstone read: *Magdalena Nevitt—God bless her.*

"If there's anything I can do about Earl Baley, you can bet I'm going to do it," Sheriff Banks said. "But he covered his tracks pretty good. I suppose that's what ate away at Luther Nevitt. He knew Earl was responsible for his girl's death, and he couldn't do anything about it either. It's a bad feeling. Don't know what happened to Luther Nevitt. He dropped off the map, just like Earl."

The wedding of Nicole Rochas and Garret Stowe, remarkably, began only five minutes late, reflecting Nicole's determination not to be thought of as the typical scatterbrained bride who fussed with her hair while friends and families wilted inside a church.

The hundred formally attired guests were treated to the soothing sounds of a renowned string quartet prior to the ceremony. All marveled at the beautiful timing of the service, because just as it commenced, the evening sun struck the west wall of the church, illuminating its stained-glass windows and casting rich columns of color within.

Nicole's gown was a Givenchy original that drew appreciative gasps from the guests when the bride made her entrance. After the ceremony, guests were transported by carriage to the stately grounds of Madame Brassard de Sonneville's estate a quarter mile away. The estate was in its seventh century of family ownership. Its château served as a private museum for a priceless collection of art and furniture that was open to the public two days a week; it was used for French cultural events and by private corporations for receptions and special dinners. Though the château did have living quarters upstairs, they were rarely used by the family.

The landscaping of the gardens, the presentation of food and wine, the musical selections, and the table gifts had all been planned by Nicole in meticulous detail. She'd had tablecloths and place settings especially made to match the floral patterns of the gardens. Well-known classical musicians played pieces that left no one unmoved. Somehow, Nicole managed to create a reception that was elegant, but harmonious to the setting, so that it seemed formal yet almost impromptu. It promised to be the talk of Parisian society for weeks, and even people not in attendance would make certain they knew all the details.

For his part, Garret remained quiet for most of the evening, greeting the guests in French, exchanging pleasantries, but initiating little conversation. He seemed in awe of the occasion, as though he had stepped into somebody else's fantasy and if he made too much of a show of enjoying it, it would evaporate right in front of him.

But by the time he and Nicole bade the guests good

night, Garret felt he belonged at the magnificent estate; the thought even crossed his mind that it, too, might soon be within his reach.

Nicole and Garret ascended the stairs to the château's master suite, where they would spend their wedding night. A chilled bottle of Cristal awaited them. Garret eagerly opened it, having drunk very little at the reception for fear of not responding properly to his guests' greetings and conversation. He took a long drink, then poured another glass.

He gave his wife a dazzling smile. "The wedding was beyond what I could have imagined. Are you happy?"

"Yes, very. Very happy. Everyone I care about was there, and it all felt wonderful."

"Yes, it did. Because you're wonderful."

They toasted.

Then Nicole said, "I was disappointed that I could not make peace with Aunt Giselle, but I guess I've never really known her that well. I didn't know that business matters would obsess her to such a degree. I extended invitations to her right up until the end, you know."

"She is the loser for not responding to your kindness."

Garret opened a dresser drawer and took out a gift that he had instructed a maid to place there for him.

He handed it to Nicole.

"The wedding ring was about our marriage," he said, "but I wanted you to have something that was just for fun, something special."

She opened the box. It contained a magnificent Bulgari diamond-and-ruby necklace. Nicole began to cry.

Garret said, "No tears. It was not meant to make you cry. You see, what I truly want is for you to wear the ring and the necklace . . . and nothing else."

She smiled.

"And I have something special for you," she said. "Can we go out on the terrace?"

"Do we have to stay dressed?"

"Just for a few moments. For a special toast."

"Whatever you wish," he said, taking her arm and escorting her through the sitting room toward the terrace. The terrace doors were closed, and Nicole stopped Garret as he was about to open them.

"We are going to start our family soon," she said, "and that's something I've always wanted. Since we both come from broken-up backgrounds, you understand what a family will mean to me. I'm sure even Giselle will come around sooner or later. And I want the same for you."

Garret looked at her quizzically. Some instinctive misgiving gave him a sudden *frisson,* but he did not betray it to his bride.

"What do you mean?" he asked.

"There is someone who very much wants to wish us well on our wedding day," she said, opening the doors to the terrace.

Nicole looked surprised to find the terrace empty. For the first time in a perfect day, something she had carefully choreographed had finally gone wrong. She walked outside, and Garret followed. When Garret was a few feet out onto the terrace, the doors closed, and a man blocked them.

He was dressed in a dark suit, hair neatly combed. The man looked uncomfortable in the suit, and he rocked back and forth in his hard-soled shoes.

Nicole was relieved and clearly delighted to see him.

But the man did not return her smile. He looked only at Garret Stowe.

"Hello, Earl," Luther Nevitt said.

Garret had been staring at the man, who was partly hidden in shadows. But when Garret heard Luther Nevitt's voice, a look of disbelief branded his face.

Garret glanced at the three-story drop to the ground, then decided he'd have to charge at Nevitt rather than jump.

But Nevitt had expected that. When Nicole and he had discussed the scenario for the surprise, she had at first wanted it to occur at the reception, but Nevitt had dissuaded her from that, convincing her that a more private situation would be easier for all concerned. And when they agreed on this terrace, Nevitt had paced it out and made his plan.

As soon as Garret moved toward him, Nevitt raised his right hand and aimed a small-caliber gun. And then he fired. The first bullet struck Garret in the right knee. He hit the ground in agony. The next bullet hit the other knee. Then in rapid succession Nevitt pumped rounds into each of Garret's arms as he writhed on the terrace. It was a .22 caliber pistol, so the wounds were small. But they were disabling, and horribly painful.

Nicole stood frozen in shock. She didn't scream. She didn't move. She was absolutely paralyzed.

Nevitt approached her.

"Go inside now," he said.

She stared at him.

"You have to go inside," he said, "because you don't want to see this." He pushed her toward the door, opened it, and edged her inside.

"The gun!" Garret called to her in an agonized voice. "Get a gun!"

Nevitt closed the door and wedged a piece of wood through the handles so that it couldn't be opened.

Then he walked calmly toward Garret, who tried to drag himself toward the railing. Nevitt reached inside his jacket and pulled out something that glinted in the moonlight. It was a seven-inch fisherman's fillet knife.

"I have a wedding present for you, too," he said.

He brushed the blade across Garret's throat without cutting the skin. Garret tried lifting his arms to fight back, but the pain and damage from the bullets was too much. He was helpless. He could only stare back into Nevitt's eyes as Nevitt raised the blade. But when the blade came down, it didn't touch Garret's throat. Instead, it slashed open Garret's pants, ripping a gaping flap across the crotch. Garret's mouth opened in agony and fear. He stared at Nevitt, and Nevitt stared back at him.

Nicole had run to the upstairs den, found Garret's 9mm Beretta, and charged back to the bedroom, pointing the gun through the glass doors.

She fired a shot that sent shattered glass across the terrace, but the bullet never came close to Nevitt.

Nicole aimed again.

"Yep," Nevitt said, looking into Garret's eyes, seemingly oblivious of Nicole. "It's you all right, Earl. And this is for my daughter."

Then he grabbed hold of Garret's testicles. Garret's eyes rolled back in his head. The last thing he saw was Nevitt's blade plunging down into his body.

Nevitt stood and looked at Nicole, who was frozen by what she'd just witnessed, her eyes wide with horror.

"You're very young and very pretty," Nevitt said, lifting his gun.

He pulled the trigger. Nicole screamed as the bullet exploded from the barrel.

But she felt no pain. She opened her eyes.

Nevitt's body collapsed on the terrace, blood draining from the hole he'd just blown in his head.

chapter
31

Nicole Rochas remained in seclusion for several days following the murder of her husband, in contact only with her lawyer and the police, and then only because they insisted upon it.

The European media first reported the story as a blood feud between a birth father and his estranged son. However, when Garret's fingerprints were forwarded to Florida police, a match was made with those of Earl Baley. Luther Nevitt was also traced back to Florida and Texas, but he had no criminal record, and there was certainly no record of his being Garret's birth father. That information was relayed to Nicole, but she expressed no interest in learning any more about Garret Stowe or Luther Nevitt; at least, not for now.

Only Jessica Cartwright and Chief Banks in Matlan knew the correct link between Stowe and Nevitt, and Banks made no effort to get in touch with French authorities. "What's done is done," Banks told Jessica on the telephone. "If somebody wants to know more about Earl, he can call me." Nobody did.

Jessica explained the link between Garret and Nevitt's daughter to Detective Pesci in New York, and he told her, "Maybe that guy Conley knew something about that, but I doubt it. Anyway, he's skipped town. I don't think we'll be hearing from him."

When the coroner released the body, Nicole's attorney explained to her that funeral arrangements needed to be made, and since there was no next of kin, it fell to her to make the decisions. But Nicole refused to speak about it. After four days of this, the attorney turned to Giselle Rochas for help.

Giselle arranged for Garret to be buried in a small cemetery outside Paris. There was no ceremony or service, and Giselle was the only person present at the time of interment; she watched from behind the tinted windows of her limousine as Garret's body was lowered into the ground.

A month after Garret's death, Nicole met with her attorney to discuss Garret's estate. Garret had died without a will. Given the success of Vitesse, it was widely believed that Garret was a vastly wealthy man. Certainly his move on the outstanding stock of Château Rochas had required enormous personal resources. However, Nicole's attorney explained to her that quite the opposite was true.

At the time of his death, Garret was effectively broke. He had shielded the books of Vitesse from its employees, but once the attorney accessed them, he found that tremendous amounts of money had been channeled by Garret to pay for his lavish homes, as well as for his private jet and astronomical hotel bills; he had cash flow but no cash.

When the fifty-million-dollar block of stock in Château Rochas, purchased by Davis Kellen's holding company that Garret fronted, was untangled, the attorney learned that the complex agreement in effect made Garret nothing more than the titular owner of the stock—Kellen controlled all of it. And within weeks of

Garret's death, the investment bankers representing
Kellen asked Giselle Rochas if she would be interested
in acquiring Kellen's stock. The transaction was completed within forty-eight hours of the call. Giselle Rochas was once again in complete control of the château.

Nicole retained her own stock, and inherited Garret's
wardrobe, his debts, and his interest in Vitesse.

The Vitesse proposal to purchase Cathews in London
and Pop in Milan evaporated with Garret's demise. Jessica Cartwright quickly consummated the purchase of
both agencies on behalf of her new partnership. At the
same time, Jessica announced that Caddie Dean was
joining the Cartwright Agency, not as a model but as an
executive, a liaison with the dozens of advertising
agencies and companies that Cartwright did business
with. The appointment was at first viewed by the industry as a courtesy move on the part of Jessica toward her
most successful former client, but the value of Caddie's
appointment soon revealed itself. The amount of good-
will Caddie Dean had generated by being the most
hardworking, disciplined, and professional model the
ad agencies had ever known over the years paid off in
her ability to garner business for Cartwright; clients
loved meeting with Caddie, and she steered their interest directly to Cartwright's bottom line.

Anton Cellini approached Aaron Adam with the idea
of cashing in on Caddie's damaged face by relaunching
the blue jeans line with Caddie again as its centerpiece;
he proposed a campaign in which she wore no makeup, flaunting her scars rather than trying to hide
them. Aaron loved the idea, but Caddie turned it down.
She was finished with modeling.

Tommee Barkely was still Cartwright's top model,
but she too was being groomed to join Jessica and Caddie in managing the agency. Tommee was about the
smartest and brashest person Jessica knew, and though
she knew Tommee would never be a go-to-the-office

executive, Jessica wanted her always on Cartwright's team.

Vitesse's dozen top models left the agency soon after Garret's death. Others followed. Suddenly, Vitesse was awash in red ink, with a stack of guaranteed contracts that would never be paid out. A class-action lawsuit against Phil Stein was filed on behalf of two dozen Vitesse models. Sascha Benning left for the Elite Agency, causing what was a steady bleeding of business at Vitesse to become a complete hemorrhage. The lawsuits smoked out a tangled web of ownership that Garret Stowe had created for Vitesse. When it was revealed to Nicole Rochas that Giselle Rochas was one of the original backers and silent owners of Vitesse, she was shocked, but the revelation also made it apparent to Nicole that Giselle's admonitions about Garret probably had been founded on truth. The lawyers for Nicole and Vitesse worked out an arrangement with the bankruptcy courts in New York that isolated Phil Stein's liability from the agency's remaining assets, since the guaranteed contracts Stein had created were drawn upon a shell corporation outside of Vitesse.

In her attempt to sort out the affairs of the agency, Nicole turned to her aunt Giselle for counsel. Since Giselle's warnings about Garret had turned out to be more than a ploy to protect ownership in Château Rochas, Nicole was repentant, and in return Giselle was generous with emotional support and business guidance. In time, they contacted Jessica Cartwright's lawyers and inquired as to whether the Cartwright Agency would be interested in acquiring Vitesse's male model division, which was small but relatively profitable. A meeting was scheduled.

It was held in a conference room at Barber, Willcox & Grefe, the Manhattan law firm that represented the Cartwright Agency. Nicole and Giselle arrived with their lawyer, and Jessica arrived, to the surprise of the others, with Caddie Dean. Caddie's success as an ambassador-at-large for the global enterprises of Jessica's new company had been tremendous, and had emboldened Caddie to learn more about the actual mechanics of the business; Caddie knew that as a businesswoman she was starting from ground zero, but Jessica had provided the access, and the rest was up to Caddie.

As the meeting progressed and the lawyers for both sides discussed the involved finances and the complexities of the lawsuits against Vitesse, Jessica let her eyes move to the faces of the other women in the room.

She had heard from Caddie that Giselle Rochas had arranged for Garret Stowe's burial, and there had been talk that Giselle had had a secret relationship with Garret. Clearly, Giselle was a strong, resilient woman, and she seemed pleased to have her niece folded back into her life. Nicole had suffered a loss and a humiliation, but she was very young; she would go on. And she seemed strengthened by the presence of her aunt.

And then there was Caddie. Jessica had accompanied her to her first public dinner since the accident. They went to the Four Seasons. Stunned silence trailed Caddie's entrance through the restaurant. Her accident had been worldwide news, and her subsequent seclusion had only deepened the public's interest in the story. But she strode into the Four Seasons, wearing slim black slacks and a white silk blouse, her hair cut short for the first time in her life. Heads turned and whispered throughout the restaurant as Caddie and Jessica made their way to the table; and as they did, Jessica recalled that night in Los Angeles when they had celebrated Caddie's appearance on the cover of *Time*, when every head in L'Orangerie craned to witness the beauty of the world's top model. Her entrance now was different; the patrons looked at Caddie as if she were a Fabergé egg that had been dropped. Yet Caddie was fit, and radiant. She knew she was being stared at, and she was testing herself. And whatever private standards she applied to this test pleased her—she smiled.

Now, sitting in this conference room, Jessica thought Caddie appeared happier than she'd ever seen her, more focused and confident. She couldn't pinpoint what it was. Just something in her look. No longer being dependent on the camera, on its ruling on how she should feel about herself, had liberated Caddie, and Jessica knew her well enough to see it in her eyes.

One of the lawyers interrupted Jessica's thoughts with a question. It was time for the women to get down to business.

EPILOGUE

Publication of Caddie Dean's memoir, *Cover Girl,* caused an avalanche of media attention. In the year and a half since her accident, she had given no print interviews, turned down hundreds of requests for talk-show appearances, and devoted her time to working behind the scenes for the Cartwright Agency and to completing her book. For the book's jacket, she posed without makeup and gelled her hair back so that her scarred face filled the photo.

The book told the true story of Caddie's childhood, from her mobile home, to life as a runaway and drug abuser, to meeting Jessica Cartwright and working her way to the cover of *Time* magazine. She described the attack by Jon Ross, and her affair with Garret; she revealed that the "accident" that had scarred her face was the result of a punch thrown by Garret, and she recounted in detail the emotional changes she had gone through since losing her look as one of the world's great beauties. Caddie became one of the most in-demand speakers on college campuses, and her talk-show appearances sent the book to the top of the best-seller lists in twenty-five countries.

Nicole Rochas, after a six-month hiatus, returned to *Femme Nouvelle* magazine; she was promoted to managing editor, and the changes she instituted promptly revitalized the publication's sagging circulation. She ran a feature story about Caddie Dean's book, and hosted a reception for Caddie when she arrived in Paris on her promotional tour.

Giselle Rochas attended the reception, but said only a brief hello to Caddie, then departed. Giselle had read the book only because Nicole had sent it to her. Actually, she scanned it, then she came to the portion where Caddie wrote about the two years of her midteens that she spent drugged out. In this section Caddie described a six-month period in Paris when she lived with an older French woman who had met her at a nightclub, provided her with a place to live, and one night took her to a bizarre, ritualistic sex scene called a *fracasser*. Caddie wrote that she had been stoned on hash and downers at the time and remembered little of the evening, other than that there was a man there who had been chained and teased and then turned loose on the women. She remembered no faces, nor even what she had or had not done that night. Giselle Rochas read the passage in complete shock and amazement. It was the first time in the eight years since she had attended the *fracasser* that she had heard anyone, other than Garret, even mention the cultist event.

When the book sold its millionth hardcover copy, the publisher threw a huge party at the Rainbow Room in Rockefeller Center. Caddie moved through the crush of guests, greeting friends and shaking the hands of strangers. Among the guests were Nona and Ginny Fischer. Caddie had spent a good deal of time with Ginny during the past year, helping her through her drug rehabilitation and generally taking on the role of an interested big sister.

Ginny had done no modeling since her brush with

death. Instead, she had enrolled in a Manhattan private school and continued to live with her mother in a new, modest apartment on the West Side. Nona had enrolled at City College and promised herself that she would not leave without a degree.

Jessica was late arriving to Caddie's party at the Rainbow Room, having just returned from Paris, where she had held meetings with the heads of her European offices. The Cartwright Agency now had branches in Paris, London, Milan, Madrid, Tokyo, Hamburg, Miami, Los Angeles, and Rio de Janeiro. Much of Jessica's time was now spent on airplanes, but this past year of hard work had propelled the agency to its preeminent position in the industry.

She was wedging her way through the crowd inside the Rainbow Room, anxiously looking for someone, when she felt a strong hand take her forearm and pull her into a dark hallway.

It happened so fast she at first didn't see the face of the man, who now had her pinned against a wall, out of sight of the partygoers.

"You can run but you can't hide," the man said.

It took Jessica's eyes a moment to adjust to the dim light of the hallway.

"Sorry I'm late," Jessica said.

"You know how I hate these things," he replied.

"There are a hundred beautiful models for you to look at in there."

"Yeah, and you have to fight them to get near the bar. I want you to promise me something," Detective Frank Pesci said to Jessica.

"What's that?" she asked.

He'd called her about a month after the Garret Stowe murder dropped out of the papers and invited her for coffee. Three months later they were dating. She found him to be smart and funny, and best of all, he hated the fashion business.

"When we get married, two things have to happen," he said. "First, I don't have to go to these damn parties. Second, you don't travel so much."

"Okay," she said.

Then she thought a moment.

"Frank," Jessica said, "we haven't talked about getting married, have we?"

"We're talking about it right now."

"That's what I thought."

"Is that okay?"

"Yes," she said, "it's very okay."

He leaned forward and kissed her.

"Why don't we get out of here?" Frank said.

"I have to say hello to Caddie. It's her party."

Frank stepped back.

"I don't really have to say hello to her," Jessica then added. "I'll just give her a look."

"And then we're out of here?" Frank asked impatiently.

Jessica gazed out the sixty-fourth-floor window and looked over the glittering island of Manhattan. For the first time in her life, Jessica was truly happy to be where she was. She felt a sense of promise rather than a need to prove herself.

"Yes," she said. "Then we're out of here."